CHINA
WHITE

CHINA WHITE

A NOVEL BY
TONY KENRICK

LITTLE, BROWN AND COMPANY
BOSTON   TORONTO

FIRST EDITION

Library of Congress Cataloging-in-Publication Data

Kenrick, Tony, 1935–
China white.

I. Title.
PR9619.K49C44 1986   823   86-4713
ISBN 0-316-48917-4

RRD VA

Published simultaneously in Canada
by Little, Brown & Company (Canada) Limited

PRINTED IN THE UNITED STATES OF AMERICA

For Joan. Still the world's champion person.

ACKNOWLEDGMENTS

As this is a work of fiction, the characters that appear in it are entirely imaginary. However, the milieu they inhabit is a real one, and for help in describing it, or inside information, or generous assistance in other areas, I would like to thank the following kind people in Australia, England, Holland, Italy, Spain, Switzerland, and the United States:

Captain Bruce Allen; Diana, Lady Avebury; David Belsham; Captain Rod Brown; Bunny Carlson; Ina Chadwick; Derek Cook; John Crosby; John Davis; Bill Dowling; Betsey Drake; Karl Eckhardt; Ron Edgley; Louise Fordham; Fredrica Friedman; Captain John Giles; Jeff Hackney; Chris Humberstone; Ray Johnson; Melanie Kenrick; Captain Mike Laws; Captain Greg Madden; Dr. Vincenzo Mancuso; Helen Morningstar; Jean Naggar; Bob Prior; George Rike; Richard Snailham; Captain Ronald Verhoef; Professor Barry Zeller.

CHINA
WHITE

PROLOGUE

$50,000,000.

Five times a million dollars, then ten times that.

The thought that it would soon be his engulfed Charles Bendroit as he inched forward in the endless line of traffic mired on the Expressway. He was just one of thousands of drivers Manhattan-bound after a weekend on Long Island, most of whom found nothing to do but sit uncomfortably in their automobiles, and fume and curse at the creeping progress. But Bendroit hardly noticed the delay. For one thing, the prospect of such a fabulous amount of money kept him in excellent humor. For another, none of the other motorists had such a wonderfully comfortable automobile to sit in.

It had been custom-made for Bendroit by the Cartel Company in Woking, England, a firm that built cars for Arab princes and the more successful Hollywood producers.

It was an automotive miracle, years ahead of its time.

The suspension, controlled by an on-board microcomputer, "read" the road and ironed out bumps and filled in depressions, while the aircraft-type hydraulic system allowed the car to corner without a hint of dip or sway.

The interior was like a model apartment set up for a glossy magazine feature: virgin wool Wilton carpeting underfoot, white Draylon overhead, soft leathers and suedes everywhere else except the seats, which were pigskin: two-tone brown and cream. The dash, the tape tray, and the door trim were fashioned from Italian black walnut veneers and African *makore.*

The Richter people had installed a stereo with twenty-four speakers, each individually baffled and insulated.

The Rockwell Group had put in a radio phone that automatically called any of ten preselected numbers in Europe or the Far East.

On a sunny day the roof, made of tinted polycarbonate (the body was part Kelvar and part hand-laid, glass-reinforced plastic) folded into the trunk at the touch of a button.

There was only one other car like it in the world, and Bendroit owned that one, too. In London.

The pair of them had set him back seven hundred thousand dollars.

Expensive, he felt, but then the best always did cost a little more. Coddled and cosseted, surrounded by luxury, Bendroit let his glance fall on the radio phone, and button A.

Button A was Hong Kong.

In the harbor of that lovely city was the little island of Po Toi, an island riddled with dark sea caves.

And in the deep recesses of one of those caves, protected night and day by fighters from the Sap Sei K Triad society, were several drums, the contents of which were worth fifty million dollars.

His fifty million dollars.

Once again the thought of that amount of money sent a delicious little shiver trembling through him.

Charles Bendroit was about to be something he'd always wanted to be.

A rich man.

1

WHEN THE WHITE THUNDERBIRD with the National Car Rental decal on the windshield came around into Ponce de Leon for the third time, George Chaska said, "Some poor slob's lost. Let's give him a break," and got out of the car.

Marcus got out, too.

Nothing was happening anyway. The tip they'd got about the possible hit on the Georgia Federal Savings was turning out to be yet another example of the public's idea of humor.

The T-bird had stopped outside the Fox Theater, and the driver was on the sidewalk looking around him. At four o'clock, on a hot and heavy morning, there wasn't a hell of a lot to see. The theater had a funereal appearance, as if the actors whose names were spelled out on the dark marquee had died during the evening performance. The sidewalk beneath it was like an underground cave, the street lighting missing the recess of the theater's doors, the blackness collecting there in thick, deep pools.

George Chaska, coming around the back of the Thunderbird, said, "Where you going, buddy?"

George was always abrupt and businesslike, so his words sounded more like a demand than a question.

The man on the sidewalk looked at Chaska, looked beyond him at the car George and Marcus had been sitting in, a blue Ford: four doors, no whitewalls, a bottom-of-the-line model.

Salesmen drove cars like that.

So did cops if the car had a radio antenna.

And the Ford had a radio antenna.

The man was just an outline against the dark, a big guy with a long neck, his sport jacket hugging shoulders that sloped like a fighter's. He said something — it sounded to Marcus like "Al" or "Mal" — and swung away.

Marcus, stepping up level with the T-bird now, heard the passenger door open. So did George Chaska, who turned to look.

Then the guy with the neck was pulling something from his armpit, beginning to swivel.

Marcus knew there was a gun out — twelve years in the business gave you a feel — and he went in under his jacket for his own piece, took forever to clear it, staring at the guy, trying to freeze the moment. He yelled "George!" and fired the instant he'd freed his weapon, heard the blast of two answering shots, saw the muzzle flash and felt the hit, not in his stomach or his chest, but in his back. His legs jellied on him, and he collapsed against the trunk of the car, clutching at its shiny metal with both hands, which meant he'd dropped his revolver.

Doors banged, an engine turned over, and Marcus's platform went from underneath him as the T-bird got out of there.

He hit the pavement, momentum rolling him so that he finished on his left side facing the gutter.

George Chaska was lying on the sidewalk; the two of them were facing each other like a couple curled up on the far extremities of a king-sized bed.

The expression on his partner's face was a mixture of surprise and I-told-you-so, Marcus thought, as he lay there

[6]

trying hard to doubt the fact that the last thirty seconds had actually happened.

George panted wetly a couple of times, then seemed to take a deep breath as if he were holding himself in for a photograph.

The breath didn't come out again.

With agony beginning to boil up through his body, chasing the shock from his brain, Marcus started wondering about things.

He wondered if there'd been three shots besides his own; decided there'd been only two: what had entered his back hadn't been a slug but a blade.

He wondered how far it had got, and what it had got.

And he wondered about George Chaska.

George had been a practicing Catholic.

Marcus wondered, lying there in the gutter outside the Fox Theater with blood pumping from him, where George was now, and whether, in spite of being born a Protestant himself, he'd be seeing him again shortly.

2

HINKLER AND BOYLE.

Marcus found out their names three weeks later, about an hour after a doctor at Piedmont Hospital had signed a release form.

He went home, got into his car, drove out to the airport, and checked with the National people. The rental firm had a dozen T-birds, only two of them white. One had been taken by a woman, for a week, on the ninth, three days before the incident outside the Fox Theater. The other had been rented on the tenth on a two-day basis. Roy Hinkler was the principal on the rental agreement. Alvin Boyle was down as Other Driver.

Both were from New York City.

In the statement Marcus had made to his division commander, and the looey from Homicide, he hadn't mentioned being able to identify the car. It had been two days before he'd been able to talk, so it was too late for a nitrate test on anybody. As for a visual ID, he would've been guessing at the guy who'd shot George, and he hadn't seen hide nor hair of the knifer who'd blindsided him.

There were good striations on the .44 slugs they'd dug out of his ex-partner, and the gun that had fired the bullets was right there in the computer run by the GBI, the detective division of the State Police: an S&W Model 29, stolen six months back from the factory in Springfield, Massachusetts.

No gun, no gun hand, no positive ID, no prints on the body.

Just one more for the Line of Duty file, Persons Unknown.

The rental car had been returned at ten in the morning on the twelfth, round about the time Marcus had been coming out of the anesthetic minus a couple of pints of blood, which had been replaced, and a spleen, which had not been replaced.

He'd spent two days in Intensive Care, then the rest of the time in a semiprivate room reliving the moment on the hour, every hour, seeing his clumsy, fumbling draw, wondering how he could have missed the guy from such short range. Okay, to drill him through the head or the heart would've been pure luck, but to not even get a single piece of him, just enough to make him miss that second shot. . . . George would have got him then.

George had been one shit-hot shootist.

George had also been a popular guy in the division, which was why Marcus's commander transferred Marcus to another section for a while; kept him riding a desk, chasing down leads for people until he was all better and had his strength back.

It was a wise move.

On the morning Marcus returned to the Robbery squad, on the third floor of the Main Police Station on Decatur Street, Frank Henning moved toward him in the locker room with a mean and flat look on his face. Henning had been a drinking buddy of George Chaska's, and knew all about Marcus's lack of prowess with a gun. Everybody did. Marcus had been suspended once when he'd flunked his half-yearly range qualification. Seventy was the pass mark, two points for every shot placed in the kill area; thirty-five shots out of fifty had to hit within the outline or you failed. Marcus had hit on only twenty-nine.

Marcus just wasn't crazy about guns; there were cops in every police force in the country who felt the same way: that to have to use a gun, to resort to the criminal's weapon, was a degradation of standards. It was a position that made no sense at all to the vast majority of cops; certainly Marcus's fellow officers didn't understand it. All they understood was that Marcus's dislike of guns had led to a man with twenty-one years in, and a wife and two kids, getting wasted because his partner was too incompetent to do anything about it.

Frank Henning, a big, thick-muscled type, came over to Marcus and said, "Welcome back, you sorry sonofabitch," and knocked Marcus down. Thinking that was that, Henning turned and walked away.

Marcus caught up with him at the door, spun him, and hit him twice while the man was standing there, and once while he was on the way to the floor.

Marcus got back to his regular duties with a new partner, and things smoothed over to some extent, although the names Hinkler and Boyle burned constantly at the back of his mind.

He'd run the names through the National Crime computer, and there were no surprises. Both men had served time, Boyle in Leavenworth, the military prison. Aggravated assault with a dangerous weapon. Boyle the knifer.

Hinkler had done time in Ohio on a shooting charge: attempted murder reduced to grievous bodily harm.

The printout sheets listed all kinds of information about them except what Marcus wanted most to know: what two guys from New York had been doing waiting outside a theater in Atlanta at four in the morning.

For the answer to that he had to wait until a man named John Safranski came back to town.

John Safranski — Johnny Safran, as he liked to be

[10]

known — was what was officially known as a cooperating citizen. Marcus had met him not when he'd been in Vice, which was where most street cops made their best contacts, but when he'd been in Burglary. He'd caught the guy cold, with two sapphire rings and a diamond bracelet lifted from a suite at the Westin Plaza. Safranski had been to prison once and didn't want to go again. He had a cherubic face, fair hair, and was plump enough to have pronounced breasts, so he'd been a jail wife for his entire stretch and had never grown to like it much. So Marcus had "found" the jewelry, returned it to the hotel, and kept Johnny forever in his debt, which was always a productive arrangement between cop and informer.

"Roy Hinkler," Safranski said, biting into a double-dip cherry ice cream in Gorin's parking lot on Eleventh Street, "is quality muscle. Works for a guy named Bendroit. Charles Bendroit. The other guy, Boyle, he works for Hinkler. Boyle's your garden variety lean-till-you-scream guy, although very good with a blade."

"I know about his talent," Marcus said.

Johnny Safran put two and two together.

"It was him, huh? Stuck you? Sorry about that, Sarge."

"Who's this guy Bendroit?"

"He's a limey. Very la-de-da. Lives in London, got a house in Manhattan. He's a shipping guy, a lot of it legit, although he makes his big bucks in cargo scams, hull scams, stuff like that."

"What's a hull scam?"

"Like he'll buy a rust bucket for a hundred grand, some dogged-out freighter that's been around since Columbus was a boy. He pays off an appraiser, insures the hull for twice what it's worth, pays off the captain who pays off the crew who pull the plug out there in the Atlantic, and bingo, the cruel sea claims another ship."

Marcus shifted position behind the wheel of his car, lowered the visor against the sun bounce from the other automobiles. Some people said the weather was the best thing about Atlanta, and maybe when the dogwoods were doing their thing, and the little green parks looked like a biblical artist's rendition of Eden, maybe it did have the best weather in the country. But there were also the Hades-hot days that came out of nowhere and exacted payment for the rest of the year.

"Okay. But he wasn't planning to scuttle the Fox Theater. So what were his men doing down there?"

"Ah, well, you see," Safranski said, going in at the other side of his ice cream, "because Bendroit's a shipping man, he's got the connections to dabble in the importation of controlled substances. He sells seats on the vein train express."

Marcus brought his head around gradually, his words keeping pace with the slow movement.

"Those guys were down here on a drug deal?"

"So I hear."

Marcus closed his eyes for a long moment. George Chaska had pegged them for a couple of lost motorists, but Hinkler and Boyle had been circling the block looking for their contact. They'd recognized a cop car and assumed they'd been set up.

A mistake.

His partner was dead because of a simple fucking mistake.

Although he knew only too well his partner wouldn't be dead if Sergeant William B. Marcus of the Atlanta Bureau of Police Services, Robbery Division, had been a little more accomplished with a side arm.

"Okay. Go to work on Bendroit. Anything you hear I want to hear. Listen up big, all right?"

"Whatever you say, Sarge."

George Chaska had scolded him often enough; George the old-line cop who had a sticker on the inside of his locker door: "I'm for Law EnFORCEment."

"Billy, you got to get to know your piece a little better. Your badge gets you into trouble, your gun gets you out of it."

"I'm a detective, not an executioner," Marcus had once replied.

"Yeah, well, you see," George had answered, his tongue worrying something on his lip, "with some of the crap you meet on the street, it's just the reverse."

The irony was he'd never been thinking about his own hide, that it'd be nice if he had a partner he could rely on in a tight one.

He'd been thinking about his partner's safety.

After his shift was through that first day back, Marcus drove out to Key Road, to the Police Academy.

That's where the pistol range was, in an area of Atlanta that was still waiting for the magic wand which had transformed the business section. The view of the city, anywhere outside of the downtown part, never failed to remind Marcus just how new and fast-growing his adopted city was. It looked to him sometimes like an instant town, as if an immense alien spaceship had lowered those pencil-thin buildings into the middle of a flat, green plain.

"Hi, Teddy," Marcus said.

Teddy was Teddy Hepplewhite, the range instructor, a man with a face like a brown paper bag that had been scrunched up and smoothed flat again.

"I got my test coming up soon. Thought I'd get a jump on it this time."

"Good idea," was all Teddy said, knowing full well why Marcus was there. He'd seen the same kind of thing once or twice before.

Marcus went out to the range every chance he got after that; all his free time, even lunch breaks, he spent there learning from Teddy. Daytimes he plugged away at the outline targets with the four-inch .38 Special that was standard issue for Atlanta detectives. Nighttimes

[13]

he worked with a laser gun on the good guy/bad guy simulator.

It was no surprise to his instructor that his student got so good so fast.

"Guns is like anything else," Teddy would tell anybody who'd listen. "You need a itty-bitty dose of talent, and a whole pisspot full of application."

A couple of weeks into it Teddy took the .38 away from Marcus and had him request a Government Model .45 auto, which he smithed for him. Teddy did a beautiful job. He lowered the ejection port, reprofiled the slide, beveled the magazine well, replaced the original sights with a set of Millets, took the trigger pressure down to two and a half pounds, and throated the barrel so that the lightweight loads Marcus was using wouldn't hang up on the feed ramp.

He had Marcus making the rounds himself now; taught him handloading. Marcus went the whole nine yards and bought everything: a reloading press, a powder measure, a bullet mold, a sprue cutter, a case trimmer, a full set of swaging and resizing dies.

He also learned how to get a pistol into his hand in a hurry.

Teddy started him off at home using a flashlight in a holster. Marcus began by putting a strip of reflective tape on his bedroom mirror. Then he'd switch off the lights, whip out the flashlight, and point it and freeze in one fast action. He got so that nine times out of ten the flashlight beam would wink on the strip of tape.

On the range he'd practice a quick-draw-and-fire for real, with a bullet deflector in the shank of his holster so that he didn't shoot off a toe.

It didn't take long for word of all this to get back to Decatur Street.

"I hear you got Wyatt Earp out there these days," somebody said to Teddy when he dropped by the local bar for a drink.

"You mean Billy Marcus? Yeah, he's out there all the time."

"Hittin' anything?"

"Shot a ninety-four yesterday."

"Sheezus! Marcus did that?"

"They say he's pullin' pretty good, too," somebody else said.

Teddy dumped a shot of rye into his second Coors.

"I seen a greased snake once was quicker."

"Little late to become a shootist, ain't it?" another voice suggested.

"I'll bet you Jack Harmon don't agree with that," Teddy answered.

Jack Harmon was Marcus's new partner. Asked if it wasn't a little boring to be forever picking up and dropping off his partner at the Police Academy, Harmon said that at least he always knew where his partner was, unlike some.

Hinkler.

Boyle.

Bendroit.

The weeks of instruction and practice stretched into a couple of months and Marcus was no closer to doing anything about the men who'd killed George Chaska. There were some cops he knew who would've simply pulled a handgun pass, faked their commander's signature, cleared it with Delta's security people, flown to New York heavy, blown the three of them away, then flown back to Atlanta and slept like babies.

Trash removal, they called it; collecting street garbage.

One-man death squads was another way of looking at it.

Marcus didn't regard police work as a war between "us and them," as many of his fellow officers did; he felt that his job brought him into contact with as many good people as bad. He'd originally gone into the work as a stepping-stone to studying law. Marcus had been born up near the

Finger Lakes into a family that had had to work hard to stay out of debt. He'd done well scholastically at high school, and had shown a talent for football which had attracted the attention of Syracuse U. Once there he'd been big enough but not quite fast enough to make the varsity, had switched to rugby and broken all kinds of records. After graduation he'd thumb-tripped south, stopped over in Atlanta, liked the people and the air of future growth about the place, and had joined the police department intending only to get a little experience on the ground. But he'd been too good at his job; promotion had come quickly into the detective division, and somehow the idea of getting on to the legal side of law enforcement had faded. He'd never regretted it: he wasn't sure how good a lawyer he would have made, while he knew that, as a cop, he was a good one, and he was a guy who liked to excel if he could.

Marcus had spoken to Johnny Safran several times, but the man had heard nothing from his contacts in New York. However, about twelve weeks after Marcus had been back on the job, all that changed.

Safranski called and claimed he had something.

"I got some good gossip," he said, getting into Marcus's car. They were in the lot at Lennox Mall, halfway between McDonald's and Neiman's. Johnny liked to bomb the department store for countertop trinkets, then eat his head off next door.

"How good?" Marcus asked.

Safranski grinned and rubbed his stomach like a cannibal.

"Worth a couple of Big Macs and a double side of fries."

Marcus took a bill from his wallet.

"And your continued freedom."

"Your pal Bendroit's got something coming out of the oven. Probably definitely gonna move some weight."

Marcus let the plump man have a long sigh.

"You already told me he's Captain Narcotics. Naturally he's gonna move weight. Thing is, do you know where and when?"

Safranski looked a little hurt.

"You never been a narc, right, Sarge? Believe me, only them with a piece of the proceeds get a map and a calendar."

"So that's it? I spend twenty minutes battling the Buicks on Seventy-five to hear that a drug smuggler's probably gonna smuggle drugs someday soon?"

Defensively, Safranski said, "You told me you wanted to hear anything I heard about him. That's what I heard. Plus one other thing I heard."

"What other thing?"

"He's looking to hire a good man."

"What kind of good man? What for?"

"To run the shipment maybe. I dunno. I'm guessing now."

"I thought Hinkler was his main help. Why wouldn't he run it?"

"Maybe he's sprained his ankle. Maybe he's gone to Jamaica for two weeks. How the fuck would I know?"

"Ask somebody."

Johnny Safran raised a pudgy hand in appeal.

"Hey, Sarge, c'mon. I'm around guys, they say things, I listen. But once I start in quizzing 'em, I could end up in the Chattahoochee trying to breathe through my neck."

Marcus couldn't argue with that, so he handed over the ten-dollar bill. "Keep up the good work, Agent Seven."

Johnny said he'd see him, got out of the car, and waddled off to buy his lunch.

Marcus got out, too, after a minute, and walked through the heat into Rich's for a little free air-conditioning.

A salesgirl arranging perfumes saw him, straightened up, and stuck out her chest. She liked men who looked like this: tall guys with builds, athletes. This one had the wide stringy shoulders of a ball player, an outfield slugger, maybe. Quick strength in the arms to get around on a fastball, power it out of the park, then lope gracefully around the bases. No Robert Redford, but a handsome face all the same; a face that had seen a lot of weather, the features made doubly interesting by the firm nose swollen slightly up near the bridge, and the scar splitting one eyebrow, perhaps the legacy of a bad hop. The slight disfigurations went nicely with the strong jawline and the short dark hair, finger-combed into place.

"May I help you, sir? Something for your wife, or your girlfriend?" She'd found that a good opener; a man could come back at that any way he chose if he liked what he saw.

"No thanks."

The girl cocked her head provocatively to one side, dark hair falling.

"Just browsing, are we?"

Marcus was staring at a bottle of perfume. The make was Yves Saint Laurent. The brand name was Opium.

"No," Marcus answered. "Just thinking."

3

THAT WAS TUESDAY.

Wednesday was a normal day, as was Thursday.

Friday wasn't.

Marcus and his new partner, Jack Harmon, had driven to a large residence on Pace's Ferry Road. The day before somebody had backed up a van to the owner's basement and cleaned out the freezer. People were stealing anything now.

They were getting out of their car when the radio squawked an Officer Down Signal 63, a signal that was never ever ignored. The location was a package store on Peachtree and Collier, not that far away. It took them less than three minutes to burn the roller-coaster dip and rise to Habersham, shoot up the slope and along the flat, and howl through the light at Peachtree.

It was a sight Marcus had seen many times: Red-and-Whites slewed in at crazy angles, dome lights circling in blue panic, patrolmen with riot guns out and working, pedestrians down behind parked vehicles, scared, fascinated, and surprised that the guns sounded different from the way they did on TV.

The package store was shaped like a T, all big glass windows in back of a parking lot, an Amoco gas station next door. Some of the windows on the long side of the T were shattered, and another one blew in as a patrolman bobbed up and got off a couple of quick ones.

A handgun replied from inside the liquor store, the boom of a heavy round, the shot spanging into a squad-car door.

In the middle of the parking lot, lying awkwardly on the asphalt, a patrolman was clutching his thigh.

Jack Harmon took the Ford belting into the far side of the lot, where both of them jumped out, Marcus going into the store through a side door, his partner going around the back.

The smell hit Marcus immediately: booze and gun smoke, like a Western saloon. The crash of window glass came from the next room, gunshots melding into the higher, more brittle sound of breaking bottles, the noise echoing away replaced by the splash of liquid falling onto carpet.

Marcus ducked in behind a counter, went by a huddled, angry-looking clerk, crept along to where the room opened into a bigger one, and called out.

"Hey, champ!"

A shot smashed bottles over his head, and wine poured down on him. Marcus swore, moved smartly away from the stream, stayed down.

"Listen, you got five guns against you already, and there are ten or twenty more on the way. Throw out your piece before they take your ears off."

A gun banged, and a few feet above Marcus's head a bottle splintered and shards of glass and a fifth of Scotch showered onto him.

"What do you say, fella? You spill any more booze, the locals are liable to get up a necktie party."

A piece of the front window blew in.

The gunman replied, sending two shots blasting out through the new exit.

Marcus took a fast peek around the corner of a shelf.

The man, screaming obscenities, was on his feet rapid-firing a big revolver at his tormentors. In a withering answer, sheet glass burst and flew apart, and the man was slammed back against a shelf of shattered bottles. He went into a quick, head-nodding frenzy as if he were agreeing emphatically with somebody, then disappeared. Behind him, where he'd been standing, the champagne pouring from busted bottles turned red.

Marcus crawled into the other room, put his back against one corner of the counter, held his gun flat against his chest, then took a look. The man was lying on a mess of green broken glass like an Indian fakir, his revolver no longer in his hand.

Keeping below the counter, Marcus duck-walked underneath a clear fountain of gin and vodka, keeping his gun trained on the figure until he was close enough to see the guy wouldn't be giving him any trouble.

From somewhere in the rear came the thump of a door being forced.

"Billy!"

Marcus raised his voice.

"Call 'em off. It's all over."

He reached into the dead man's jacket and removed a wallet, flipped it open, checked a driver's license.

Boyd A. Dubin. A Baltimore address.

Glass crunched: somebody coming.

Marcus slipped the wallet into his own jacket, surprised by his action even while he was doing it.

Two patrolmen leaned over the counter to take a look at their handiwork. Then Jack Harmon appeared.

"You okay?"

"Yeah."

Harmon wrinkled his nose as Marcus rose and peeled off his soaking jacket.

"You smell like Saturday night." He looked down at the body. "Who's the reindeer?"

"He's keeping it a secret," Marcus heard himself say.

Somebody brought in the counter clerk, who was blinking and breathing fast.

"He come in here, he was knee-walkin', latrine-huggin' drunk. Wants a fifth of Dad. I wouldn't take his personal check. We got a sign up there says that. I tell him, no personal paper. Sonofabitch calls me a cocksucker. Stomps off outside, turns around, starts back this way holdin' a gun, so I call the cops right smart. The fucker dead?"

"Nah. Fainted from all the excitement," Jack Harmon said.

"Shit. Lookit this mess I gotta clean up," the clerk moaned.

Getting into the car later, Harmon was carrying something under his jacket.

"What you got?" Marcus asked.

His partner brought out a bottle of Jim Beam.

"Important evidence."

As Marcus drove away, Harmon said, "If the guy didn't have a wallet, how was he gonna give the clerk a check for the bottle of booze?"

Marcus kept his eyes on the road.

"The clerk said he was sloshed. When you're sloshed you think the whole world's free."

Harmon broke the seal on the bottle and said happily, "Well, this little piece of it was."

To make it look good, Marcus put three names on the TX 500 he sent off to the Baltimore Police Department, two of which he made up. He asked for a rap sheet on all three, requested an urgent callback on his Atlanta ID number, then tried not to think about what was in his mind for the next twelve hours.

The information was waiting on the pegboard the following morning: two negatives on the fictitious names, but a full rundown on the gunman in the package store.

Dubin, Boyd Arthur, had flitted between Baltimore and

points south. There'd been numerous misdemeanors, a couple of suspended felony charges, then he'd graduated to the big time. He'd been hauled in for a bank job but had walked on a technicality. He'd been lucky again six months later when he'd been fingered for a Brink's truck robbery and had slid away from that one, too. But he'd been nailed finally in 1980 for masterminding an armed robbery on a courier service. He'd been bound over in Fulton County Jail, been tried and convicted, gone through five weeks of quarantine in Jackson Distribution Center to make sure he had no communicable diseases and was therefore fit to associate with the crème de la crème of Reedsville State Prison, where he'd served two-thirds of a six-year sentence. Clean since coming out, apart from a couple of Drunk and Disorderlies. He'd been thirty-eight years old when he died; three years older than Marcus, who tore up the sheet, tossed it in a wastepaper basket, and thought about a friend of his named Dan Mead.

If he could get Mead to play along, he could swing it.

When the wagon had come for Boyd Dubin's body, it had first taken it to Henry Grady Hospital so a doctor could officially pronounce a dead man dead. From there it had gone to the morgue, on Coca-Cola Place, above which were the offices of the County Medical Examiner.

Danny Mead was his chief assistant.

Mead, six-five, 230, had succeeded in spending six years at the University of Michigan without once being inveigled onto the football field. He claimed he'd gone there to become a doctor, not to have to employ the services of one.

"Why, it's Billy Marcus," he said, coming out of his chair. "Brilliant young robbery detective and mediocre tenpin bowler."

"Me mediocre?" Marcus shook his hand, winced, sat down. "Last time we bowled you missed an eight-and-ten split in lane five."

"So? An eight-and-ten ain't exactly candy."

"Yeah, but we were bowling lane four."

Mead smiled. He liked Marcus. Most everybody in the department did except the hard-nosed, button-lip types who didn't think style had any place in law enforcement.

Mead's chair squeaked as he returned to it and picked up a phone.

"You want coffee or formaldehyde?"

"What's the difference?"

"One's hot, one's cold."

Marcus said, "You get a thirty-eight-year-old male DOA in here yesterday? Multiple gunshot wounds upper body?"

Mead asked somebody for coffee, put down the phone.

"I'm doing the post after lunch. You didn't bag him, did you?"

"No, but I was in the bleachers."

"He's just a toe with a tag right now. I won't have a name for you till tomorrow, the day after."

Marcus fingered the fine scar in his eyebrow, a five-year-old cut that should have been stitched but hadn't. A thief had done that; Marcus had caught him cleaning out an office supply store, and the guy had snatched up a steel ruler and got in a pretty good whack before Marcus had kicked his legs from underneath him.

He said, watching Dan Mead from beneath his hand, "When you send off his prints for identification, will you do me a favor?"

The big man made a face.

"I can mark it rush, urgent, now, but you know how those —"

"Danny, I want you to hold onto his prints for a while. I want you to pull a set from the JD file and send them off."

Mead blinked at him and said, "You want what?"

Marcus began a reply but the other man spoke through him.

"I send out John Doe's so I get back John Doe's?"

[24]

"Right."

"I can't do that. Besides, this isn't even your case."

"I didn't say it was. I just responded to a Sixty-three."

"Is this switcheroo temporary or permanent?"

"Temporary."

"How long's that?"

When Marcus shrugged, Mead began shaking his head. "How do I explain it? I'd have to say I made a mistake. I'm not gonna have that on my record."

Marcus said slowly, examining a roughened nail, "Not all our mistakes show up on records."

Mead didn't answer for a moment; he knew what Marcus was referring to. At a Department party a year back Dan Mead had got pretty high on some confiscated Colombian one of the Narcotics boys had brought along. On the way home he'd been stopped by a patrol car. Georgia was death on driving under the influence of anything but common sense, and the tickets were unfixable. So Marcus, sitting in the passenger seat, had done an outrageous thing: he'd pulled his gun on the patrolman, backed him off, changed seats with Mead, and got them the hell out of there, just barely beating a hail of bullets. He'd taken quite a risk, but he'd saved Dan Mead from becoming a pedestrian.

The pathologist compressed his lips, let out air through his nose. It sometimes seemed to him that police work was totally built on obligations made and called in.

"Okay. You got it."

Marcus got up.

"Thank you, Danny."

"Just don't say I owe you one. The next guy says that to me gets a free esophagotomy."

"I think I already had one of those. Rain check on the coffee, okay?" Marcus had his hand on the door when Mead said seriously, "Billy. You run into some kind of trouble?"

"I wouldn't say run into it," Marcus said, on his way out. "It's more like I'm backing into it."

4

OPENING HIS EYES, coming back past the edge of consciousness, Charles Bendroit wondered, as he had for the past week, if the new batik print on the canopy over his head had been the right choice. It was a jarring sight first thing in the morning, and Bendroit liked to accomplish his return to the world smoothly and easily, and without upset. It was like dying, going to sleep, a temporary demise with no guarantee that you'd awaken.

A risky business when you thought about it.

Perhaps that was why he felt so virile in the mornings; perhaps he liked to celebrate his successful return from the dark night, to affirm life and his reestablishment in it.

He reached for the woman curled in a fetal position on the far side of the enormous bed.

Sugar Watts. Ridiculous name. Bendroit refused to call her Sugar; he didn't call her anything when he spoke to her. It saved confusion that way because he brought home so many girls; brought them home from parties like prizes he'd won. If they pleased him, and they came up to his standards — if they were athletic in bed, and had clean personal habits around the house — he'd invite them to move in for a trial period.

He was beginning to tire of this new one, although he

had to admit she was a fetching little thing: petite and curvy with excellent breasts and a plump little bum. And quite skilled for an American; it was Bendroit's candid opinion that American women couldn't fuck their way out of a paper bag.

When he moved back the silk comforter, her bottom curved a smooth invitation to him, her hippy outline pressing against her thin nightdress. It had ridden up, revealing a juicy scallop of white flesh behind her knee. He began to lift her nightdress, causing her to groan into semiwakefulness.

"Charlie . . . I'm still asleep. Not now . . . tonight."

Bendroit gave an impatient little tug, got her bottom revealed.

"C'mon, Charlie. I'm gonna leak all over Bergdorf's."

He rolled her toward him, slid down his pajama pants, and straddled her. The woman moved her head on the pillow, the wings of her mussed hair covering her closed eyes.

"Gimme a minute . . . I'll blow you."

Bendroit got a knee between her legs. "I think I'd prefer a gentle screw, if it's all the same to you."

"I'm not up to any acrobatics."

"None required, dear girl. Just the" — Bendroit slipped easily into her moist morning warmth — "quiet violation of your alabaster-like body will suffice."

The girl pantomimed a snore, but she brought her legs up and hooked her feet behind Bendroit's calves, rising to him as he pumped on her. One of the things Bendroit liked about this one was her instant readiness. There'd been one woman who'd shared his bed and board for a while who'd needed tubes and jars of messy things, a lube job, as a ribald friend of his called it. But not this girl; she had an educated little box that knew what was good for it.

Bendroit moved faster, thrust harder, his voice tightening.

"Close."

Which was her signal.

She sighed and said blandly, "Fuck me. Screw me. Lay me."

"More," Bendroit gasped.

"More. I want more," Miss Watts said through a yawn, then flexed her legs as Bendroit gasped again, shook, jerked, and flopped on top of her.

It wasn't what Bendroit wanted; he wanted what she used to do: moan and thrash and buck-thrust into a saucer-eyed orgasm, driven to the edge of hysteria by his knowledgeable technique and Olympian exertions. He was definitely going to have to bring in somebody else.

Bendroit withdrew, toweled himself, pulled up his pajama bottoms, and got out of bed. The woman turned over and went back to sleep. She hadn't opened her eyes anyway.

He crossed thirty feet of swollen white broadloom, went into a bathroom, sat on the toilet, and perused that morning's *Wall Street Journal* and the airmail edition of the *Financial Times* from London. He paid particular attention to the shipping news, noting, with some surprise, that a freighter named the *Northern Star* had docked in Rio. Bendroit had once owned the ship along with his ex-partner Nicky Kazadoupolos. They'd bought the ship to make money for them on the bottom of the ocean, but before their plans had come to fruition Bendroit had severed his relationship with Kazadoupolos. Kazadoupolos, the grimy Greek who boasted that he'd sunk more tonnage than a crack German U-boat in 1942 . . . how pathetic his half-million-dollar hull frauds were now alongside what he, Charles Bendroit, had waiting for him in a cave in Hong Kong. If Kazadoupolos knew about that he'd have a heart attack, he'd be so envious.

Bendroit dismissed the man from his mind, finished his newspapers, and his transaction, and went upstairs to a room where, laid out on a table like a store display, he found pressed white shorts, a lime-colored polo shirt, a pair of briefs, a pair of white socks, and a pair of just-cleaned

[28]

sneakers. He dressed and chose a squash racket from a selection of eight hanging on the wall. When Bendroit had finished using it this morning Mathews, his valet/butler, would send it to Foran's, who would strip the sweat-soaked green gauze off the grip, rebind it, and return the racket by five.

Swishing the racket of his choice, Bendroit crossed the room, rapped on the safety glass of a small window, and went through the door onto a squash court. As far as Bendroit knew, it was the only squash court in Manhattan built on an upper floor of a private residence. He had a court in his London home, too. Even though there were several fine clubs he could have belonged to in both cities, Bendroit disliked mixing with the hoi polloi that inevitably crept into even the best establishments.

"Good morning, Singh."

A dark man in a red track suit immediately stopped hitting a ball against the front wall, and nodded a little bow.

"Good morning, sir."

Singh was fifty-five or so, built like a fireplug, with white hair and a splendid matching mustache. He was a pro at one of the better downtown clubs and came every morning of every weekday to rally with Bendroit. Bendroit had the same arrangement with a Pakistani pro at his London town house. Singh always took it easy on his employer, which gave Bendroit a false sense of his abilities. One morning Bendroit, feeling extremely fit and confident — the morning sex only stimulated him — invited Singh to play all out, expecting to lose perhaps 9–3, 9–2, 9–1, which he felt would be an honorable defeat against a man of the Indian's caliber. He'd been incensed when he hadn't scored one single point. But he'd gotten even. Three mornings later, with Singh at the front of the court during a warm-up, Bendroit had dumped a short one, which the pro had lobbed back, fat and high. Bendroit had sighted the ball quickly, leaned back, and put all his considerable weight behind an overhead smash directed, not at the front wall, but at his teaching pro, raising a huge red welt on the back of the man's thigh.

"So sorry," Bendroit had called.

"Quite all right, sir," Singh had answered.

Now the Indian smiled at his student, held up the ball, and asked if he was ready. They set out to play three games as they usually did and, as usually happened each morning, early into the third game Bendroit pounced on an easy shot, slammed it for a winner, and said, with his chest heaving, "I think we'll stop there for today, Singh." He quit the court, showered in an adjoining room, threw on a terry robe, and went back downstairs annoyed at his squash pro and his cunning, unplayable shots. Perhaps he should get rid of the man, although he'd need some kind of excuse.

By the time Bendroit had reached the bedroom he'd thought of an excellent one: the Indian sweated like a pig on the court, and used a towel quite frequently. He'd simply tell the man that the laundry had complained — they were unable to get the smell of curry out of the towels.

Feeling better, Bendroit went by the sleeping girl, who had recurled herself into a ball, entered a dressing room, and blow-dried his thinning hair. He smoothed it into place using two bone-backed military brushes he'd stolen when he'd been a weekend guest at a house in Greenwich.

He threw open the doors of a built-in closet. Mathews had chosen a selection of clothes from the main wardrobe, every stitch London-made. As he liked to dress according to mood, Bendroit assessed his state of mind and concluded that he felt confident, extremely so. This new man that was coming, Dubin — was that his name? — had checked out rather well. It often seemed to Bendroit that of all the different grapevines that were used to spread and gather information, be it social, financial, or political, the one that worked the fastest was the one which served the more nefarious types, the denizens of the underworld. Bendroit had been given the name of a man down in Grand Street who could supply either equipment or manpower. This person had put the word out about the vacant position, and Dubin was one of the men who'd applied. The Grand Street supplier had run a thorough check on him, and Dubin's credentials sounded excellent. Of course, Bendroit reminded himself, the man still had to pass the personal interview.

Metal squeaked as Bendroit slid hangers apart and mulled over his options. He vacillated between a midgray worsted from John Lester and a light pinstripe from Huntsman, decided finally on the Lester. He'd wear the Huntsman when he flew back to London. It would be slightly crumpled after the flight, and the Huntsman people would clean and press it properly themselves.

He selected a cream silk shirt from Deborah and Clare, and an appropriate tie, then turned his attention to footwear. The Poulson, Skone brogues, or the dark brown suedes from Wildsmith? Yes, the Wildsmith for today.

Suit, shirt, tie, shoes, and a pair of blue full-length socks from W. Bill Ltd. He strapped on the watch he'd bought at Turler in Bern, a skeleton version of the 1932 Olympic chronograph in yellow gold, which had cost him fifty-five thousand Swiss francs. Bendroit had since learned that an Englishman named Roy King made the best watch in the world for almost three times as much. He'd put in an order.

There was a slim, flat wallet on the dressing table containing several crisp ten-dollar bills for cab fare and incidentals. Bendroit never carried coins; they spoilt the hang of a suit jacket. Whenever he was handed change by a cabdriver, Bendroit would tip him exactly the correct amount, then throw whatever coins were left into the nearest litter basket.

He turned side-on to the mirror to check his profile. The suit had been cleverly cut to shave ten pounds off him, which still left him five pounds overweight. But his height saved him from appearing dumpy, and he looked impressive rather than plump. He had a handsome face with strong bones in it, and soft gray eyes which more than one person

[31]

had mistaken for a benign approach to life. Women were attracted to the veneer he presented: the Englishman in his early fifties with the commanding presence, the airline-captain look of worldliness and sure knowledge. They saw strength in him, solidity, assuredness.

Bendroit walked through the bedroom, ignored the slumbering girl, and walked down a long corridor whose walls were bright with oils — Walter Sickert, Harold Gilman, a glowing Louis Valtat, a luscious Arthur Hughes — thinking again about the new applicant, this Dubin chap. If he was acceptable it meant the final operation could begin, and that possibility set his mind and body tingling. If everything went smoothly, and there was no reason why it shouldn't the way he'd set it up, it meant a whole new life for him.

Fifty million dollars.

Charles Bendroit dwelled on the thought, savored it, as he went by a glass case containing what had once been half the Mahboubian Gallery's collection of Mesopotamian vases. No more making do with just a few million or so; very soon now, a matter of months, he'd be joining the ranks of the rich.

The very rich.

Marcus arrived at the house on the dot of nine-thirty and considered giving it a few minutes. No, it would be in character to arrive on time, a guy looking for a job. He began to wonder about something that, curiously, he hadn't given much thought to: how to appear to be a man he'd only ever seen dead. He wouldn't have to try to sound like a cracker, thank God; Dubin, according to his sheet, had spent most of his time in Baltimore and Cleveland. Marcus figured he could be more or less himself, an easy impersonation.

He mounted the steps, rang the bell; Eighty-fourth just off Fifth, right across the road from the Metropolitan. He had to be impressed; these were the kind of town houses that countries bought for their embassies. Marcus was no stranger to the city; during his college years he'd spent a lot of time driving up and down the Thruway from Syracuse to the Big Apple for blowout weekends, as well as to use the city's unparalleled museums and libraries.

He gave his name to the house man, stepped through the door out of the heat, and was asked to wait in a cool black-and-white foyer. There was plenty to look at: an Italian coffered ceiling, a black-and-gold embossed suit of armor, busts in niches scooped out of high pilastered walls.

A minute later there was something else to look at.

Roy Hinkler.

It had to be him walking in; there were the sloping fighter's shoulders, the long neck, the muscular frame Marcus remembered coming out of the dark in front of the Fox Theater.

"About three months back," Marcus said in his head, "did you kill a cop in Atlanta?"

Hearing the guy say, "What of it?" in a surly voice that went with his expression.

"Just making sure, that's all." Then take out the Airweight he had on his left hip and blow him away. Boy, that would have been satisfying.

Hinkler moved his head in a kind of reverse nod. He had long arms, knuckly hands, a plain and unkind face.

"You Dubin?"

"That's me."

"You carrying?"

"Funny you should ask."

Hinkler's frown got a touch deeper.

"The fuck that's supposed to mean?"

Marcus just looked back at him until the other man said, "Bendroit don't like guns in the house. You wanna check it?"

He indicated a low table, a small silver tray on it that, in years gone by, might have been a receptacle for calling cards.

Marcus slipped the revolver out of the Baker Pancake holster slotted onto his belt, and placed it on the tray.

"How times change," he murmured, which was the second thing he'd said so far that Hinkler didn't understand. Hinkler didn't like things he didn't understand. He didn't like this guy.

He put the gun into a drawer in the table and said, "He's waiting," and turned and walked away. Marcus followed the man down a hall, walking on a carpet that looked as if it belonged in the museum across the street. It led to a sitting room, and somebody waiting in there.

If Marcus had been certain he'd recognized Hinkler, he was positive that this was Bendroit: a thousand dollars on his back, a goddamn fortune glinting on his wrist, he was the kind of tight-suited, barber-pampered millionaire you only ever saw in New York. The Southern rich wore blazers over polo shirts or tailored jeans held up by leather and silver. And most of them spoke and swore like good ol' boys, a couple of planets away from the toffee accent Bendroit employed — even on the phone it had sounded like he had a plum caught under his tongue.

"Good morning. I'm Charles Bendroit."

"Hi."

"Will you take coffee, or shall we get straight to business?"

It was in no way an invitation to refreshment.

"Straight to it."

"Very well."

They hadn't sat down; the three of them stood in a circle in the middle of an expanse of polished parquet floor: Hinkler with his sullen, watchful look, Bendroit with one hand half in the pocket of his beautifully cut suit jacket, standing ramrod straight, getting every centimeter out of his six feet one, clearly pleased that he was an inch taller than the man he was interviewing.

"I am in the shipping business, both here and in Europe," Bendroit began. "I'm about to import into this country a very valuable cargo from Asia. However, this cargo won't

[34]

be shipped from point of origin in the usual manner. It will have to be fetched, and there'll be a danger attached to this endeavor. But none, I might add, from any law enforcement agency."

"From your competitors, right?"

"I have no competitors. Only partners. We'll get to specifics in a moment." Bendroit paused to cough behind his hand, a little affectation he had that also served to show off his white platinum Charles de Temple cuff links. "I have hired men to safeguard the transportation of this cargo. However, I need someone to oversee these men, to be in charge of things in Asia, and to handle the sale of the goods here in New York." Again the little cough. "I am prepared to pay the right man fifty thousand dollars. Are you interested so far?"

"For fifty grand? Hell, yes."

"I take it you like money, Dubin."

"I've got nothing against it," Marcus said.

Bendroit's remark seemed to be Hinkler's cue. The big man took a twenty-dollar bill from his pocket, tore the bill across the middle, and tucked one half of it into the top pocket of Marcus's jacket.

"You like it so much," Hinkler said, "let's see you eat some." He pulled a small, fat revolver from somewhere near his armpit. "Go ahead. Eat it. Right now."

Marcus checked with Bendroit, but the man was busy brushing something from his lapel as if his henchman's little foibles were no concern of his.

Marcus switched his gaze back to Hinkler. This was the second time he'd seen Hinkler holding a gun — this was a guy who liked to shoot people.

He took the torn piece of bill from his pocket, and put it into his mouth.

"Now chew on it," Hinkler growled. "Do it!"

With the revolver eyeing his gut, Marcus began to chew.

"Now swallow it. Go ahead."

[35]

Marcus gulped, spluttered, and began coughing violently. He bent over, a man in trouble, took a couple of lurching steps forward, struggling for breath.

A beat later he grabbed hold of Hinkler's wrist, forced the gun off line, and belted Hinkler in the mouth with the back of his left hand as he stripped away the gun with his right.

Hinkler, shocked back a step, came forward again, rage boiling up in him, shouting through teeth that were beginning to turn bloody. "I'll fuckin' *kill* ya!"

He would've kept coming but for the gun swinging on him. Marcus spat out the green paper ball, which bounced off Hinkler's shirtfront.

"Hinkler!" It was Bendroit speaking sharply, cutting off a second furious reaction. "I suggest you go and attend to that cut."

Hinkler hated it but he took the directive without argument. He backed away, dabbing at his lip and looking murderously at Marcus. Then he nodded at him, in some kind of silent promise, and left the room.

Bendroit motioned to two Bergère chairs, unbuttoned his jacket, hitched at his trouser knees, and sat down carefully. Marcus took the allotted chair opposite him.

"I think you knew you were being tested, Dubin. Am I correct?"

"I wondered about it. It's hard to be deep when you've got a gun in your face."

Marcus checked the weapon: a three-inch Charter Arms Bulldog with a set of Pachmayr Signature rubber stocks. It was a powerhouse, a .44, but it wasn't the gun that had killed George Chaska. He hit the cylinder release, shook the bullets out: Peters 240 SJHPs, the same kind of slugs they'd dug out of George. Hinkler had changed guns but had stayed faithful to his loads.

"You are the fourth applicant for this job, Dubin. The other three all did what Hinkler told them to do. Ate the money. I can't use a man who'll let another man order him around. The man I need for this job will have to tell others what to do. You've just demonstrated that quality."

It was merely an observation, Marcus noted, not a compliment; Bendroit wasn't the type that went in for praise. He put the gun into his pocket, picked up a round, and tossed it into the air a couple of times.

"Just what kind of job is this?"

"I've arranged to buy one hundred kilos of heroin in Burma."

Bendroit said it as if he were talking about potatoes.

"A hundred?" Marcus caught the bullet and held onto it, then told Bendroit the truth. "I don't know much about the drug business. I've never been into that side of things. But a hundred kilos sounds like one hell of a shipment."

"I have an agreement with a supplier at source," Bendroit said with a touch of pride. "I've been acquiring it steadily for the past twelve months. I already have five hundred kilos. With this lot, it will be six hundred kilos."

Marcus was genuinely floored. Six hundred kilos! It was an absurd amount, but then this guy Bendroit was absurd, so it was probably true.

"How many times has it been cut?"

"It hasn't been cut. It's ninety percent pure."

Joe Remsen; that was Marcus's first thought, a pal of his in Narcotics. Several months back Joe had bought drinks for everybody when his team had pulled over a truck and come up with twenty-five pounds of pure. It made the front page of the *Journal*. And here was a man talking about over half a ton of the stuff.

"That's got to be worth a fortune. Zillions."

"It will mean a fortune for my buyers," Bendroit conceded. "They have the connections necessary to market the product. But for me, the exporter, it will merely bring a tidy sum."

Oh, sure, Marcus thought, but what he said was, "You certain there'll be no problem with the law?"

"There seldom is with the really big shipments. The

[37]

danger, if there is any, will come from some of the natives in Burma."

Bendroit took a moment before explaining. He was enjoying this, Marcus could see that; there couldn't be many people he could brag to about his colossal deal, a major drawback for a guy as vain as Bendroit.

"The five hundred kilos came down from Burma to Thailand in one-hundred-kilo lots. However, since the last shipment, the Thai Army has suddenly become diligent again about policing the border areas. So this last caravan will have to travel a different route." Bendroit held up a restraining hand as Marcus inched forward in his chair. "Before you jump to any conclusions, it's not the army you have to elude. It's a group of bandits."

"Bandits," Marcus said, not giving the word any particular emphasis.

"The idea is to move the shipment through their territory because the Thai Army doesn't bother to patrol it. They feel, quite correctly, that the regular caravans wouldn't risk a brush with these chaps."

"What makes this caravan any different?"

"The guards. They're nothing like the usual ones. They're ex-military men with modern weapons. Experienced in jungle warfare."

"Mercenaries."

"Exactly. A man in London hired them. They're standing by ready to go."

"They're English?"

"The leader is," Bendroit said, as if the leader would naturally have to be. "Ex–British Army officer. Knows the country well. Used to lead tour groups through the area apparently. The rest are a mixture. London, it appears, is a good place for hiring soldiers of fortune. There are any number of skirmishes going on at the moment in Africa and the Middle East, and many of these men go to London for," Bendroit frowned at the Americanism, "rest and recuperation, I believe you call it."

[38]

"I better tell you now. I don't have any military experience," Marcus said, pretty sure that none would be required.

"That isn't important. I need a man who'll be responsible for the shipment from point of purchase to point of sale. Hinkler would suffice but he'll be engaged in another area."

"Okay. Break it down for me so I know what I'm getting into."

"Specifically," Bendroit said, crossing his legs and admiring his handmade shoes, "your job will be to fly to northern Thailand, where the drugs will be paid for, cross into Burma, pick up the drugs, accompany them back into Thailand, then fly to Hong Kong and see them safely loaded on board a ship. When that ship gets here, you'll oversee the sale to the buyers. The buyers will then send the payment to me in London."

"You're trusting them to do that?"

"In this case, yes."

Marcus put on a little show, mimicking some of his street people when they tried to raise the ante.

"I don't know. I have to cover all that territory, plus I have to get past a bunch of bandits —"

"You'll be amply protected, I can assure you of that."

"Plus I have to deal with the Mob, who are probably the only people that could handle six hundred kilos of anything, am I right?"

"The man who represents the buyers, the man you'll be dealing with dockside, does, in fact, have an Italian name. But his associates need not concern you."

"If I'm gonna be dealing with the Maf," Marcus said, "I have to be concerned. I hear they don't hit from the ladies' tee." He went in for a little teeth sucking and head shaking. "Fifty grand. I have to tell you, Mr. Bendroit, for all you want me to do I'd be seriously underpaid."

"I don't intend to haggle, I can assure you," Bendroit said, frost on his words. "Fifty thousand is the price, and that's that."

"Your price, maybe, not mine. You say there's no risk from the law. Maybe you're right. If you're wrong, and I fall, I can't see my lawyer claiming that six hundred kilos of smack was only for my own personal use."

Bendroit made an annoyed sound in his mouth; flippant Americans and their warped sense of humor.

Marcus bore down, nicely into the part now.

"And the bit with the Mob. It's gonna be C.O.D., right?"

The question brought a grudging affirmative.

"Then there's another hernia. Maybe *the* hernia. The arrangement is I give them the junk, they let me count the money. Only maybe after I hand it over all I get is a ride out to Coney and some air in my head."

"No!" Bendroit thumped the arm of his chair, annoyed by the suggestion. "There'll be no duplicity on their part. I've insured against it by guaranteeing them a similar shipment next year. They won't do anything to jeopardize that because I'm giving them what they want, a colossal amount in one shipment, and of such high quality they can cut it till the cows come home."

Marcus allowed some time to edge in, giving Bendroit a chance to simmer down. It was obviously a point that was bothering him, the chance of a double cross. But he'd done the right thing in making himself into a repeat customer; always the best way to ensure a straight deal the first time around.

"What about Hong Kong? What happens there?"

"I've already explained that. You'll put the consignment on a ship. You and Hinkler. The ship is all arranged, and Hinkler will look after the delivery from Thailand."

"We'll be working together, Hinkler and me?"

"You'll be together here, too. At the sale."

"I don't know if that'll work out. I don't think he likes me."

Bendroit rose from his chair. He was relieved to be back on his feet, Marcus saw; probably happier now that his suit was hanging properly.

"Hinkler has an unfortunate temper. We are none of us perfect. You, for example, according to our inquiries, have a penchant for getting drunk and disorderly."

"Not when I'm working," Marcus said, giving Boyd Dubin a quality he'd probably never had. "I drink after a job. Never before or during." He got to his feet, too, taking away Bendroit's commanding position. "Anybody say anything good about me?"

"Several things. Mainly that you're honest in your dealings with your business associates."

Marcus tried a modest little shrug.

"I figure I got enough to contend with taking on the law. I don't see any sense in getting my partners mad at me, too."

"A wise philosophy," Bendroit said, very much the university dean with an errant student on the mat. "Because I can assure you I will come down extremely hard on anyone who tries to cheat me."

"You had any practice in that kind of thing?"

Marcus knew he shouldn't have asked the question, but the cop in him hadn't been able to let the opening go by.

Bendroit had been looking down the room, perhaps at his reflection in a rococo gilt mirror framed on the end wall. Now he swiveled his gray eyes on Marcus; little life in them, looking only to make contact.

"I once bought a small freighter and arranged for its demise fifty miles off Bermuda. However, the first officer threatened to expose my little plan unless his fee was increased. The ship went down on schedule with the loss of only one life."

"Okay, I've been warned. But I'll be honest with you, fifty grand on a deal where everybody else's making a fortune, I'd be tempted to cut myself in for a little more, even with what you just told me. But you give me fifty grand up front, and fifty when the job's over, I'd be willing to settle for that."

"I should think so, too," Bendroit snorted. He pursed

his lips, scowled over it for a moment, decided that what he'd just heard was the truth, and that fifty thousand dollars was therefore cheap insurance. "Very well. But in return I expect absolute loyalty, and a first-rate job. No slipups."

"You got it." Marcus gave it a beat. "So. When does all this happen?"

"In two weeks. Be here at noon tomorrow. You can pick up your preliminary payment and a written list of details."

"You bet," Marcus said, and started for the door. It opened before he reached it as Bendroit's man came in.

"Excuse me, sir, but Miss Tanner is here."

Bendroit dismissed him and called to Marcus. "One second, Dubin. This is somebody you should meet."

"Who's Miss Tanner?"

"A lawyer. She'll be going with you to Thailand."

"A lawyer? I'm gonna have to ask why on that one."

"To handle the payment for the shipment. I'm not about to hand over three hundred thousand dollars to a perfect stranger like yourself, so I've given her power of attorney. She'll withdraw the money from a bank in Chiang Rai, and pay for the shipment up on the border. She knows nothing about the true nature of the deal, of course."

"What does she think she's buying?"

"Rubies. They're an important export of Burma, and there's a brisk trade into Thailand. Legitimate but unofficial. Much of the country's too wild for an air service so the stones are brought in overland. Naturally this attracts marauders, which is why you're taking an armed guard. It's close to the truth, and therefore that much more believable."

"Okay. But seeing we're not going to Burma for stones, she can't bring 'em back to you. So who's supposed to do that?"

"A man named Agosta. He's been running things for me in Thailand. As far as Miss Tanner is concerned, Agosta is a bonded courier. I'll go over names and places with you tomorrow," Bendroit said with an edge of impatience. "Do you have everything straight?"

[42]

"Sure."

They left the room together, crossed the lobby, and went through double doors into a galleried library that smelled like a saddle shop. The walls were solid, floor to ceiling, with leather-bound books, the chairs and sofas all dark studded suede. The person who was standing there, a girl with yellow hair, put down a volume and glanced up.

Bendroit spoke first.

"Good morning, Miss Tanner."

"Good morning."

"Miss Tanner, may I present Mr. Dubin."

The woman nodded and said, "Mr. Dubin."

"Hello," Marcus said.

"I've just engaged Mr. Dubin," Bendroit told her. "It will be his responsibility to see that everything goes smoothly in Southeast Asia, so you'll be seeing something of each other."

It seemed to Marcus that the unintentional second meaning had occurred to the woman just as it had occurred to him. For his part Marcus wouldn't have minded seeing something of Miss Tanner. She was no centerfold but yummy in a mildly severe, straight-laced kind of way. He'd seen quite a few woman lawyers in the time he'd spent testifying against criminals in court. Some were as dull-voiced and unimaginative as most of the male lawyers. But others, like one assistant DA he knew, were super bright, impaling the opposition on fine points of the law, and never tried to either disguise or parade their femininity. Marcus was pretty sure that Miss Tanner was one of these, which meant he'd have to watch himself; if anybody was going to recognize a cop, it would be a smart lawyer who was around them all the time.

Bendroit excused himself saying he had to get some papers, and left behind several moments of silence, which lasted until the girl asked Marcus if he'd been to Thailand before.

"No. You?"

"No."

"I haven't been outside the country much," Marcus said, which was true. "But I'll bet you have."

"Why do you say that?"

Her eyes were brown, very steady, the yellow hair breaking in a wave from left to right over her forehead, then allowed to fall softly down to her shoulders. Her upper lip was as full as the lower one, a mouth made for kissing.

"I don't know. I just get the impression you've been to Europe quite a bit."

"Three times. That's all."

"That's three times more than me."

She sat down, engulfed in one of the big leather chairs; a petite woman, five-three maybe, small-boned. She crossed her legs, her skirt high on her knee but not worried about it. Marcus remained standing.

"I don't wish to appear impertinent, Mr. Dubin, but may I ask about your background?"

Impertinent. Good word.

"Law."

With no change in her expression she said, "The upholding of?"

"The dodging of."

She nodded at that, something confirmed.

"I wasn't sure."

"I think you mean," Marcus said, taking a frontal approach, "that you've seen guys like me in courtrooms, you being a lawyer, and you weren't sure which side of the handcuffs to put me on."

"Something like that, yes."

She didn't drop her eyes or look away, yet Marcus knew his answer must have caused her some embarrassment.

"Cops and robbers, Miss Tanner. Different sides of the street but a lot of them are from the same block."

"You'll have to excuse me asking questions I probably have no business asking, but this kind of undertaking is

[44]

pretty new to me and I want to get into it as soon as I can."

"It's new to me, too. I've never been hired to guard anything before. Usually the other way around."

Marcus wondered if he wasn't piling it on too thick, but then she'd been half convinced he was a cop. It was important to disabuse her of that notion.

"Are you bragging, Mr. Dubin?"

"Just being honest."

She said, "I was in criminal law before switching to the corporate side, so I've defended quite a few thieves. I had sympathy for some of them, but I never admired any of them."

"And now? You never meet any crooks in the boardrooms?"

"None that are my clients."

Marcus had had a lot of practice at a blank expression. He just gave that a nod and wondered how a guy like Bendroit, an admitted fraudster and murderer, had been able to keep his image so spotless.

The man he was thinking about appeared at the door then, and remained there holding it open.

"Nice meeting you, Miss Tanner," Marcus said. "Or do you prefer Miz Tanner?"

"Whatever you're comfortable with, Mr. Dubin."

Marcus left the room, said good-bye to Bendroit, and came out in the foyer to find Hinkler waiting for him. Through a busted lip the big man said, "You got something belongs to me, putzo." The temper had gone but the anger had dug in deep.

Marcus opened the drawer in the table. It was empty.

"You got something belongs to me, too."

Both men reached into pockets and traded revolvers. Marcus mocked the other man.

"Now you're gonna say don't ever try to take it away from me again."

"You already done that."

[45]

"Too late, huh? Well, don't hate me too much, Hinkler. I hear we have to work together."

"We'll work together. Then we'll have a little chat."

"Fine. I got something to say to you, too." Marcus held Hinkler's flat gaze for a moment, then opened the door, ready to leave.

"Dubin." Hinkler brought his clenched fighter's body closer. "You got any thought of rippin' yourself off a piece of that caravan, you can forget it. I got a man going along works for me. He's a weapons expert. Ex-army."

Marcus didn't know how many men Hinkler had on his payroll; he only knew of one for sure, and that man had served time in Leavenworth, the military prison.

"What's this hotshot's name?" A kind of tingling started up inside him as he saw Hinkler's swollen mouth shape a *B*.

"Boyle. He's a friend of mine. Mess with him and he'll hand you your liver."

Boyle was going on the trip.

The tingling sensation increased, and Marcus felt a sharp twinge above his hip where the knife had gone in.

"He in London?"

"This town."

"Maybe I should meet him before I go."

"Why?"

"Well, if he's as big a badass as you say he is, maybe I won't want to go."

Hinkler tried to curl his busted lip.

"Mister fucking cool." He glared at Marcus for a moment, then moved his head on his long neck as he thought of something. "Sure. Why not meet him. I'll set it up."

A psych job, Marcus figured. A little intimidation by Boyle to soften him up for Hinkler later on.

"Try for tomorrow night," Marcus said, going out of the door. "If he's a friend of yours I can't wait to meet him."

*   *   *

[46]

Half of the bar looked like what used to be standard Sixth Avenue: a steam table immediately inside the door, red wedding-cake stools with yellowing Scotch tape over the tears in the vinyl, neon signs spelling out "Miller" and "Ballantine" buzzing and crackling in the window. The other half of the bar was done in the newer Upper East Side look: tables and chairs instead of booths, sawdust on the floor, Tiffany repro lamps on exposed brick walls, and the stamped-tin ceiling painted a chocolate brown.

Marcus bought a bottle of beer and took it to a far corner but didn't get a chance to drink much of it. As he sat down, a man detached himself from the bar and came over. Stitched in white on his green satin bowling jacket was the name "Al."

"Your name Dubin?"

"That's right."

"I'm Boyle. What're you drinking?"

"I already got one going."

Boyle eyed the bottle of Heineken, not liking what he saw.

"Me, I buy American. Drink American, too. That imported crap tastes like shit anyway."

"I wouldn't know," Marcus said.

"You mean you never tried it?"

"I mean I've never tasted shit."

Boyle's face turned in on itself. It wasn't a nice face; everything seemed too small in relation to the size of the head. The mouth, the nose, the eyes were of a mean proportion, and he had small pointy ears like a garden elf. Above his pencil-thin eyebrows his forehead enlarged, bulbous and wide, moving up into a scalp that had lost a lot of hair and would lose more. He was a round-looking man with tiny feet like a dancer, the belt of his pants worn low to accommodate a hanging gut. But he didn't move clumsily, as might have been expected; the very reverse: he sat down at the table with a light, fluid action. Marcus had

[47]

seen his type before: the fat man with the quick, good moves.

And it had been a very quick and good move that had laid him low that early morning outside the Fox Theater.

Marcus took a gulp of beer, not surprised to find himself a little afraid of a man who'd almost killed him.

"Hinkler said you were a wiseass," Boyle said, settling into a chair. "I'm surprised they didn't kick that outa you down there in Reedsville."

"Hinkler told you about that too, huh?"

"He's mad at you, buddy. You don't belt a guy like Hinkler around like he was some jerk botherin' you in a bar. He's gonna want a piece of you for that."

"He may have trouble getting it."

"Don't kid yourself. That guy's good with a gun. Fuckin' deadeye dick. If it was me on his shitlist, I'd find myself a bazooka."

Boyle took off his jacket displaying solid, dead-white arms, the sleeves of his T-shirt finishing high above his tattooed biceps. The left bicep showed a rampant eagle and, underneath it, the letter I, then a red-white-and-blue striped heart, then the word "America." On his other arm was an illustration of a skull with a green snake crawling through the eye sockets and the words "Mess With The Best, Die Like The Rest." The legend printed on his T-shirt read "Napalm. Only We Can Prevent Forests." Boyle seemed to like messages.

"You know Reedsville?" Marcus asked.

"Heard about it. Atlanta, right?"

"Yeah, that one," Marcus answered. Then, with his mouth going into his beer glass, he said, "You ever been there?" Just a casual question; not much interest.

"Down there a few months back, matter of fact. A real shit hole, that town."

"Didn't appeal, huh?"

"I tell you one thing. That's where I'd go I wanted to

[48]

clean up. Christ, the cops they got. Fuckin' patsies. They roll over like cocker spaniels."

"No kidding."

Getting close now. Boyle was about to start bragging.

"We were down there on a job, Hinkler and me, and these two rinky-dinks walk up and brace us. Shit, we turned them crackers around so fast they didn't have time to say hi y'all."

So there it was, if Marcus had had any doubts. Which he hadn't. Hinkler and Boyle.

"Zip 'em both, did you?"

"Nah." Boyle slugged some of his drink, niggardly disappointed. "One of 'em must've been wearing a Second Chance, although it didn't say nothin' about it in the Atlanta paper I bought. Bastard's name was Marks, Markum, something like that, the cunt. That stuff they got in those vests, that plastic nylon stuff, it can't make up its fuckin' mind. It'll stop a thirty-eight, a forty-five. Stop a fifty-seven. But it won't stop a nine-mill or a twenty-two. Won't stop an ice pick, neither. But with a blade it's iffy. Sometimes yes, sometimes no."

Marcus had to bear down to look the same, sound the same.

"Yeah, well, the big A's the kind of town where things work good one day, bad the next."

"A shit hole," Boyle insisted.

"Good place to put a joint, though. You don't freeze your ass off in the yard like you do up here," Marcus said. He sipped his beer and asked a question. "Where'd you do your time?"

"Who said I did time?"

"You got the look."

Boyle didn't like that, being pegged as an ex-con.

"I never did a single fuckin' day in my life. Only dumb asses go to jail. Get themselves caught. Dumb bunnies." With a dirty look at Marcus, Boyle finished his drink. His right hand, gripping his glass, had very thin white scars on the knuckles and first joints of the fingers and thumb. It was something Marcus had seen now and then: knife fighter's pox, it was called.

Still annoyed, Boyle said, "What'd you want to meet for, anyway? I got better things to do than drink with jailbird assholes."

"I like to know something about the guys I'm gonna be traveling with. Hinkler said you were ex-army. What department? I figure it wasn't Intelligence."

Boyle reacted to that, his almost hairless eyebrows shunting together. "That mouth of yours, sport. It could use a little hem stitching."

"Tell me about the army."

After a long moment Boyle said, "I was a grunt. MOS. Eleven B. A one-one bullet stopper."

Marcus nodded at Boyle's napalm-message T-shirt.

"You serve in Vietnam?"

"Nah. I got a DD down there at Dix before I got to make the trip."

"DD?"

"Dishonorable Discharge. I went round and round with a striper and left my initials in his navel."

"What about your training? What are you expert in besides being obnoxious?"

Marcus couldn't stop baiting him. He was mad because Boyle scared him. This was the man who'd caused him agonies; a fat piece of street crap, that's all he was, yet he feared him. And for that Marcus was quietly furious at himself.

Boyle moved his oversized head, looked to one side, looked back at Marcus again.

"You're a real fuckin' card, Dubin, you know that? We gotta get you on Johnny Carson."

"Hinkler said you were a weapons expert."

"You bet your balls I'm a weapons expert. There ain't a weapon invented I don't know how to make go bang. You should see me with a seventy-nine, a grenade launcher. I could win the U.S. Open with one of them suckers. Take it on the fuckin' golf course, score a hole in one every time. I got a certificate for it. For the rifle and the machine gun, too. I don't have no time for handguns, though. Dumb fuckin' things."

Marcus asked a question the answer to which he already knew.

"What's your best weapon?"

"One that don't fire bullets." Boyle leaned forward and seemed to get pleasure out of his reply. "The knife. Got it all over a side arm. Specially in a situation like, you know, two guys drinkin' at a table, say. A knife can do beautiful things under a table. One second a guy's reachin' for his drink, the next second he's reachin' for his dick on the floor."

Very deliberately Marcus picked up his glass. He was drinking left-handed now. His right hand had left the tabletop long ago.

"Wrong. A gun'll beat a knife any day of the week."

"You think so?" An evil little smile jerked at one corner of Boyle's mouth. "You don't know much, do you, dad? Take a look under the table. You got a blade six inches from your gonads."

Marcus finished his beer.

"I know that."

"Hey, fella. Hit me but don't shit me, okay?"

"Listen, Boyle. You probably know how to soldier, but you could take a few lessons in how to survive. You don't believe that, take a look under the table yourself."

Boyle's grin, which had faded somewhat, faded completely, replaced by a look of puzzlement. He moved back his chair, watched Marcus for a moment, then ducked his head and checked under the table.

The muzzle of Marcus's Airweight stared at him with its one unblinking eye.

Boyle straightened, moved his chair in again, brought

[51]

up a knife with a skeletonized steel handle, and dug carefully at some dirt under a thumbnail.

Marcus looked elsewhere. Gunmen got rid of their weapons after they'd used them, but knifers, never. So the blade picking at Boyle's grubby nails was the same piece of steel that had been inside him. Razor-sharp edge, mean, cruel arrow point, stabbing through flesh, slicing through muscle and tissue, piercing, cutting.

"You know something?" Boyle asked, concentrating on his manicure. "I'm really looking forward to it. Thailand or wherever the fuck we're goin'. I mean, the mercs they got hired, and you and me taking the stuff through the jungle. You leading the way, wastin' tigers and cobras with your popgun, me right behind you, safe and protected, like, bein' shown how to survive." Boyle moved his hand so that the light from the wall lamp flared on the blade.

Marcus, still refusing to look at it, kept his eyes on Boyle's plump and smirking face.

"Yeah," the man said, putting away the knife and pushing himself up from the table, "I wouldn't miss this trip for all the twat in Texas." He scooped up his jacket, walked toward the door, kept going.

Marcus went into the washroom, turned on the faucet, and splashed water onto his face, holding a couple of handfuls against his skin, his sleeves and his shoes getting wet.

He leaned on the basin, regarded his dripping reflection in the scoured mirror.

Terrific, Marcus. Way to go, kid.

You'd been going after Hinkler and Boyle.

Now you had them both coming after you.

5

BEHIND THE COUNTER of the Pan Am desk his old American Tourister rode the baggage belt for a few feet, then toppled over on its side. Watching it disappear Marcus wasn't worried; he knew that airports sometimes ran an X-ray check on hold baggage, but if they chose his, all they'd see was a holster, and it wasn't against the law to pack a holster as long as it was empty. It *was* against the law to carry the two live hand loads that were tucked away behind his belt buckle, but he wasn't worried about those, either.

What did bother him was something he'd discovered when he'd got back to his hotel room last night: the passport he'd had made up in the name of Boyd Dubin had been stolen, lifted along with three hundred dollars' worth of traveler's checks. Nobody was safe anymore; even Robbery cops got robbed. The loss of the passport was annoying but not overly serious, Marcus figured; it would only be a problem if Boyle somehow got a look at his real passport — Marks or Markum, Boyle had said; that was pretty close. Apart from that he figured he was in good shape: there'd been no hassle getting away from Decatur Street since he had a lot of vacation time built up. Before he'd left he'd bought himself, for two hundred dollars, a Georgia driver's license which showed an old photograph of him next to his new name, so that at least was something.

At the security check, going through the arch of the metal detector, the machine beeped, as he knew it would.

"My belt buckle," Marcus said. "Does it every time."

A security man looked at Marcus's belt, and the large oval-shaped clasp that said Rogers Leather, ran a hand bleeper over him, then waved him into the departure lounge.

Marcus spotted Boyle right away in what must have been his favorite bowling jacket. Boyle saw him, too, but apart from a blank, fat-faced stare, he made no acknowledgment.

The lawyer, Miss Tanner — Marcus had been speculating on her first name: something a little old-fashioned maybe, like Gwen or Margaret — was seated over near the windows reading a book. When she looked up and saw him coming she closed the book and slipped it into her handbag.

"Hi, Miss Tanner."

"Hello, Mr. Dubin."

A small smile; pleasant, but not much sunshine in it. She was wearing a clingy knit that gave her a nice full line below the neck, as Marcus's grandmother had always described the area. The dress was a light tan color. She wasn't about to exploit her yellow hair by wearing black or white, Marcus figured. Nothing too dramatic for Miss Tanner; a very understated lady.

"I've been wondering about your first name," he said.

In point of fact Marcus had been wondering about more than that. Ever since he'd first met her two weeks back he'd been thinking about her quite a bit. She was certainly a lot different from the kind of women he usually came into contact with — women who liked to hang around cop bars, girls at parties, girls some of his married fellow officers invited him home to dinner to meet. Marcus had had several pleasant relationships but nothing that had ever amounted to much. It always seemed to him that he wanted more than the woman did, more than just his dinner ready on time and enthusiasm in bed. So he clearly hadn't been dating the kind of women he wanted to, yet they were around; he knew that for sure.

"It's Claire," Miss Tanner answered.

"I was close."

She looked as if she were going to ask him what he'd thought it was but held off at the last moment. But the interest was there, Marcus saw.

"Was that a guidebook you were reading?"

"No. *Pride and Prejudice* for the third time."

"Never read her," Marcus said.

"You should."

"The kind of books I read all have legs on the cover." He sat down next to her. Her perfume — she wore just a hint — had a sharp, spicy smell; expensive. Her makeup was sparse, too: a touch of eye pencil, the palest of lip rouge, a ghost of eye brush. "So tell me about Thailand."

"I told you, I've never been," she said.

"But you've been reading up on it, haven't you?"

She took a moment before she said, a little surprisingly, "I get the feeling you're typing me, Mr. Dubin. The career woman devoted to her work. Stays home nights with a good book. Interested in music, travel, and history of dance."

"If you're staying home nights, Miss Tanner, it's because you want to. Men don't let girls who look as good as you do shut themselves away if they can help it."

She seemed ready to come back with something sharp, then appeared to change her mind.

"We'll be going up into the hills. Three or four thousand feet. There are some pretty unique tribes in that area, apparently. We'll be on the edge of the Golden Triangle. Opium country."

"Sounds exciting," Marcus said, wondering if she were probing. But there was no watchfulness behind her eyes, no overcasual attitude. There was no reason for her to be suspicious anyway; Marcus had done some checking himself, and going into Burma for rubies and sapphires was an established practice in that part of the world. He asked her how tight her schedule was, whether she'd have a chance to see something of the country. She told him she was taking advantage of being there by tacking her vacation onto the trip.

"I'd like to go into Burma as well. It's a part of the world not too many people get to go to, and that kind of thing appeals to me."

It was a second before he caught on.

"You're not, um . . . Miss Tanner, we're taking armed men for a very good reason. There are people up there who might try to mug us."

"I know that. But with an armed guard along I think I'd be safe."

"That wasn't part of the deal. The way Bendroit explained it to me, you get off at Chiang Rai."

Marcus knew the names of the towns now from studying the instructions he'd picked up from Bendroit the day after he'd first gone to see him. There'd been fifty thousand dollars ready for him, too. Marcus had sent it to George Chaska's widow.

And that helped a bit.

"One more in the party couldn't hurt. I'd appreciate it very much, Mr. Dubin, if you'd let me come."

The adventurous type, Marcus saw; not the easiest type to dissuade once they'd made up their minds. He took a quick and easy way out.

"It's not up to me. It's up to Bendroit's man in Thailand, Agosta. He's the trail boss. If he says okay, okay."

She didn't pursue it any further, and a few minutes later their flight was called.

Settling in beside her on the aircraft Marcus noticed a change. She fussed and fidgeted with her seat belt, squirmed around, couldn't get comfortable. When the plane began to move she sat dead still, waiting. Amazing — Claire Tanner, who was willing to go into the jungle and face river bandits, was afraid of flying. As the plane sped down the runway she shut her eyes, moistened her lips.

"It's okay," he said. "The faster we go, the safer it is."

A moment after the plane broke contact with the ground she clutched his arm at a sudden grinding noise. He told her it was just the wheels coming up, and nothing to worry about. He talked to her softly as the plane bucked through cloudy turbulence, gentling her, capping her hand with his own.

She was okay when the plane leveled out and flew through clear noonday sunshine.

They had a drink, chatted, ate the lunch that was served, then chatted some more, swapping backgrounds. Marcus could've got close just guessing about hers: she was a Westchester girl — Hartsdale — had gone to Sarah Lawrence, then NYU Law, had clerked for a federal judge after graduation, been hired by an uptown law firm, and had recently gone into partnership and established her own law firm. Bendroit was their bread-and-butter client; her partner had been his lawyer at another firm, and had brought Bendroit with him.

In return Marcus warped his history somewhat. He told her about his first job as equipment boy in a health club in New York, described the time spent on the road heading south, got as far as enrolling in the North Central Police Academy in Marietta, then lied from then on. He told her he'd flunked out of there, run around with some questionable acquaintances, got into trouble, spent some time as a guest of the government, then come out and gone into the bodyguard business. It seemed to be about what Claire Tanner had expected.

They watched the movie together, forty-one thousand feet up, and getting closer to the West Coast, then talked movies for a while, which fitted the image Marcus was trying to project: he'd yet to meet anybody who'd been inside who hadn't come out a movie fan.

They listened to music on their headphones, were served

dinner somewhere over the Pacific, talked together again and then, around midnight New York time, landed in Tokyo.

After that the plane made a stop in Taipei, then left on the last leg for Bangkok. During the takeoff each time he helped her through her phobia, found the right words to ease her nervousness.

They'd been traveling for over twenty hours when she began to fall asleep, her head on one side, then another, finally settling on his shoulder. When a stewardess went by Marcus caught her eye, asked in a whisper for a blanket.

The stewardess spread it over both of them.

Marcus dozed off himself, happy with the arrangement: the fresh sunshine smell of her hair, the spicy perfume that rose from the nape of her neck, the good, soft feel of a woman next to him.

They both woke at the same time when the jet was beginning its approach into Bangkok. They looked at each other for a moment, something passing between them, very fleeting but definitely there.

"I'm sorry," Claire said, straightening up, discovering the blanket that enveloped them both. "You should have woken me."

"No way," Marcus said. "For the last two weeks I've been wondering what it would be like to sleep with you." He gave it a half-moment while he watched her reaction. "It was great."

She picked her half of the blanket off her lap, handed it to him.

"Thanks," she said.

For the blanket or the compliment, Marcus wondered.

It was ten-thirty when they landed, and Marcus came up against his first test. A surly-looking Thai behind the immigration desk flicked through Marcus's passport as if he were looking for a missing page. Marcus could practically hear the question coming, could almost predict the man was going to say, "Are you here for business or for pleasure,

Mr. Marcus?" With Claire standing right beside him, it would have been all over there and then.

Marcus forestalled him.

"I'm here as a tourist, in case you're wondering."

The Thai grunted, stamped the passport, handed it back. Moving toward the baggage claim, Claire smiled and said, "I was beginning to think he was holding out for a bribe."

"He should have. I had a buck and a half all ready for him," Marcus said, much relieved that the problem had been so lightly disposed of. They got out of the soggy heat and into the airport hotel. Whatever downtown Bangkok was like Marcus wasn't going to find out that night; like Claire he went straight up to his room, took a long shower, hit the sack, and slept like a baby. They met for breakfast, then cabbed it back to the airport. They'd already flown over twelve thousand miles since leaving New York, and there were still another four hundred to go.

They made it in two hops: Thai Airways to Chiang Mai, the capital of the north, then boarded an Avro 748 and flew a hundred miles farther to Chiang Rai, the air fresh and cool and squeaky clean after the damp blanket of Bangkok.

There was a map inside the small terminal building, a kind of Southeast Asian You Are Here. Marcus and Claire checked it while they waited for their baggage. The town they'd landed at was just below the 20th parallel. Forty miles to the east was the Mekong River and the beginning of Laos. Three hundred miles farther east was the border of northern Vietnam. On the western side of Chiang Rai, just twenty-five miles from where they stood, was the Burmese border. And a little over a hundred miles north was the southernmost tip of China.

"We are definitely camping out," was Marcus's comment.

Boyle went by him then; he'd retrieved a big canvas holdall from a pile of luggage and was carting it toward the exit. He'd been on the same two flights from Bangkok and had acted on both of them, once again, as if he and Marcus had never met.

Passing Boyle, coming in to the terminal, was a dark-haired, heavyset man wearing jeans and a floral shirt that stretched over his nail-keg chest; a hard, tough-looking type. He walked up to Marcus and Claire.

"Dubin? Miss Tanner? If you ain't you sure fit the description."

"That's us," Marcus said.

"I'm Dom Agosta."

Marcus shook a hand like a bear's paw. Bendroit had told him a little about this man: Dom Agosta ran things for Bendroit in Thailand. He was a former Saigon hustler who'd moved to Bangkok when the hostilities had finished in Vietnam, and was now cashing in on his connections. According to Bendroit, his knowledge of the local villains made him indispensable to the project.

"Welcome to Chiang Rai," Agosta said. "A great little town as long as you're not dying for an egg cream. These yours?"

He picked up both their suitcases as if they were tote bags, then nodded to Claire to precede him. Walking toward the exit he said to Marcus, "That one's a lawyer? Shit, I could've almost forgiven the one I had if he'd looked like that."

Marcus laughed, surprised to find that Bendroit employed somebody with a sense of humor.

Outside, parked at the curb in bright sunlight, was a pickup truck with two Thai flags flying from a tall radio antenna. Grouped around the truck in a loose circle were five men, Boyle one of them.

"How about that?" Agosta said. "They all turned up."

"Who?"

"The mercs. I had a pal hire them in London but I didn't know till now if they were all gonna get here."

Marcus recognized the men with Boyle; they'd been on

the two flights from Bangkok that morning. He'd somehow thought mercenaries would be hard guys with steely eyes and stubble on their jaws, but none of these men looked anything like that.

Agosta led the way to the group.

"Find the place okay?" he asked everybody. "My name's Agosta. That's Harn Suk." He indicated a young Thai who leaped forward to take the suitcases.

A big, lanky man said, in a plodding Australian accent, "Well, I may as well start it off. My name's Turkenton."

Boyle had his hands rammed into the back pockets of his trousers.

"Turkenton?" he said. "What do we call you, Turkey?"

"If you like," the Australian said amiably. He was about forty-five years old with a face that looked like rough weathered boards hammered together. "Although they usually call me Shacka."

"Why?"

The big man, in rumpled pants and an old-fashioned two-tone cardigan, shrugged his broad shoulders.

"Dunno. I've been Shacka Turkenton so long I've forgotten why."

"I'm Woods."

It was the man next to Turkenton, a pleasant-faced thirty-year-old whose hair was tousled and untidy like a little boy's. The Australian held out his hand.

"Pleased to meetcha, mate."

The man next to Woods had a dark-skinned, Oriental face, short black hair carefully brushed. His whole appearance was careful; a gray suit worn with a green tie, everything neat and pressed, shoes shined to a high gloss. He was the only one of them who looked at all military.

"I am Limbu," he said.

"G'day," Turkenton greeted him. Then added in his friendly, ingenuous way, "You a Gurkha?"

Limbu nodded.

"Thought so. I seen some of you blokes before." Turkenton turned to Woods. "Bloody good soldiers they are, too."

"My name's Dubin," Marcus said.

"Mr. Dubin," Agosta told the men, "represents the management, so when he tells you something, listen up, okay?"

Boyle sniggered at that and looked bored.

Marcus introduced Claire to the group, and Boyle's interest perked up.

"Hey," he said grinning. "She coming with us?" He pointed to his T-shirt on the way to scratching his shoulder. "I hope she can read," he said to the others. The shirt was printed with a crude drawing of a winged skeleton clothed in jungle fatigues and carrying a machine gun. The words beneath it said "Yer Ass Is Mine."

"And what is your name?" Claire asked pleasantly.

"Boyle." He kept the grin on his face and blinked insolently at her.

"Well, Mr. Boyle, in answer to your question, yes, I can read." Claire pointed to his T-shirt. "And I'll just bet you handled the spelling."

Turkenton laughed. So did Agosta.

"Score one for the lady," he said.

Boyle's fat face had gone red. Like small dark beads moving, his eyes flicked to Agosta.

"Listen, scumbag, you wanna say something, wait'll I rattle your chain."

"What did you call me?"

Agosta, his mouth gone tight, started to move but Marcus stepped in front of him, blocking his way. He turned to Boyle.

"You trying to get me fired, sonny? I was hired to see that things go smoothly, and we got a long way to go. So settle down. Please."

Boyle made a blurty sound in his mouth, moved away, and sulkily fiddled with his gear.

Turkenton, trying to cool the moment, looked to his right, to the only member of the group who hadn't yet said anything.

"Didn't catch your name, mate."

"Burroughs."

"Put it there."

"Captain Burroughs," the man said. His tone wasn't cold, merely formal, his accent upper-class English but without affectation.

"Oh." Turkenton pulled back the hand he'd offered.

"Captain Burroughs," Agosta said, still scowling at Boyle, "is your CO. He's combat boss."

Burroughs pointed a finger in turn at each of the men.

"Boyle, Woods, Turkenton, Limbu. Correct?"

"Right," two of them said.

"Very good." Burroughs gave a quick nod as if he'd dismissed them from parade. Marcus remembered Bendroit telling him that the man had led tour groups through northern Thailand, and that he'd been a British Army officer before that. That last fact was obvious now; he looked like a British Army officer: he had good height with no excess to him, his gray hair cut short and parted just so. His face, like his body, was slightly elongated; small mouth, a small, fine nose that further sharpened his correct, precise appearance. He wore a uniform of sorts, too, a faded safari suit, desert boots, and a green cotton bush hat.

Burroughs looked at Marcus, who was the only man who hadn't reacted in some way when he'd announced his rank. Even Boyle had shown, by a slight straightening of his paunchy body, that he was in the presence of authority. It seemed clear to Burroughs that Marcus wasn't a military man.

"How do you do," he said, including Claire in his greeting.

"Let's move it," Agosta said, and got into the pickup's passenger seat. The young Thai boy, finished loading the baggage, hopped in behind the wheel. Everybody else climbed into the back, and sat bunched together opposite each other on two side benches. The truck, a Toyota, had a canvas top that rolled up and tied just above head level, so there was a pleasant breeze when they got going.

It was a silent ride into town, most of them just watching the scenery and letting the truck jog them into drowsiness. Boyle was the big exception; he was looking down at his hands, tight and resentful, still brooding over the put-down at the terminal.

Marcus saw his first problem: how to keep Boyle and Agosta apart. He'd seen a lot of guys like Agosta, cheery street thugs: big, strong muscle guys with bright, sunny personalities who could turn murderous in an instant. They were always very good, these people, quick, efficient killers. If Boyle was foolish enough to go up against Agosta, Agosta would peel him like a banana. And if that were to happen, Agosta would be doing a job that was rightfully his, Marcus's.

He'd thought it through in the small hours of many mornings. If Boyle hadn't stabbed him, he would have got off a second shot at Hinkler and probably got him. If he had, George Chaska wouldn't be dead, because it was Hinkler's second shot that had done the damage. Eventually Marcus could have forgotten about Boyle if all Boyle had done was stick him. But the man had played a large role in the death of his partner, and Marcus would never be able to forget that.

The Toyota cleared the surrounds of the airport and hit the main road, green mountains in the distance, farmlands all around, a bank of clouds like ocean breakers gathering in the west. The air rushing into the open sides of the truck was cool and refreshing, a crispness to it, and a sweet scent as if the truck were crushing flowers beneath its wheels. Tall sugar palms shaped like dandelions marched down the sides of the road, the edges of which were full of pedestrian traffic, mainly women carrying huge baskets suspended from a staff across their shoulders. The wheeled traffic ranged from dusty blue-and-white buses, mopeds, and fast Datsuns to very slow carts pulled by fat black oxen.

A saffron-robed priest walking toward town turned heads in the Toyota, and a wooden temple off by itself in a grove of trees drew another long look, its fancy gables carved in flame shapes, making its roof appear to be on fire.

On the outskirts of the town they passed an ancient *wat* like a giant hand bell made of white stone and covered in verdigris. It had a ringed stupa pointing at the sky like a rocket ship, and was fronted by guardian figures and Buddha images garlanded with flowers. Apart from the robed and shaven-headed priest, it was the first thing Marcus had seen so far that was anything like he'd expected.

The town itself, Chiang Rai, with its wide streets and new buildings, reminded him of one of those farm towns in the American Midwest that were going through a resurgence. The numerous tractor dealers enhanced this impression; there were two John Deere billboards for every one for Datsun.

The downtown section appeared to consist of four or five main streets divided into a dozen blocks with shops and stores, a post office, airline offices, a bus station, and a splendid covered market, plus seven or eight ancient *wats* which the town had grown up around. The hotel the truck pulled up outside was called the Ruangnakorn, a not overly pretty three-storied block of aluminum windows and dripping air conditioners. But the foyer was pleasant and airy, with pretty young girls behind the reception desk who spoke English in a charming high singsong.

Agosta told the group that there was a room reserved for anybody who wanted to crash for a few hours, and that they'd be leaving at six in the evening, driving up to the border, and staying there overnight. Everybody but Boyle opted for a room.

"I don't wanna lie down by myself," he said. "I'm going out to get me some company." He flicked his eyes at Claire. " 'Less I can get me some here."

"Hey, Boyle," Marcus began, but Agosta was already speaking.

"If you go out, take money," he said. "One look at you and they'll charge double."

Turkenton laughed. He didn't see any harm in the remark, didn't recognize an explosive situation.

Boyle shot him a baleful glance, then turned his attention to Agosta, his expression changing. His mouth was extended in a little grin, but the upper part of his face was frozen solid.

He said, "I want a word with you later, woppo."

"Why wait till —"

"Agosta." Marcus didn't say it loud but he said it hard. "We have to help Miss Tanner run an errand." He was referring to Bendroit's three hundred thousand dollars that Claire had to pick up from a local bank, the money for the "precious stones." He looked at Boyle. "You want to go out, go out. But be ready to leave by six."

Boyle muttered something, walked by Agosta with a lot of eye contact, and continued toward the entrance.

Claire told Marcus she'd check in, freshen up, then meet them outside. The four soldiers moved toward the reception desk but Marcus and Agosta went back out to the pickup truck.

"Who the fuck hired that fat yo-yo?" Agosta asked, getting into the cab. "What is he, somebody's brother-in-law or something?"

"You know Bendroit's guy, Hinkler?"

"Talked with him on the phone, is all."

"Boyle is Hinkler's buddy."

"He's gonna be his ex-buddy he don't stop bad-mouthin' me."

The veins in the back of Agosta's hands popped into relief

as he squeezed the steering wheel. The hair on his muscular forearms was thick enough to be parted with a brush and comb.

"I know how you feel. The guy's an asshole. But you're gonna have to stay away from him. You zip him and we've lost twenty percent of our hired guns."

Agosta grunted at that, angrily unconcerned.

Marcus pressed him.

"Okay?"

"Anything to oblige an old pal," Agosta said.

It was a facetious remark; the only previous contact they'd had was a ten-minute long-distance phone conversation.

"Did you remember my birthday?" Marcus asked.

Agosta opened the glove compartment, took out a paper bag, proud of what he'd been able to get.

"I got you a modified Clark Bowling Pin. Five-inch National Match barrel, polished ejector, lowered port, beavertail grip safety, low mount Bo-Mar sights, Wilson Rogers Shok-Buff and recoil spring, a two and a half pull, okay?"

Marcus turned the .45 in his hands. He could have done without the squared-off front trigger guard and the stippling because of the way he held a gun, but that was just splitting hairs; it was a first-rate piece of smithing. Not as good as Teddy Hepplewhite would have done but surprising quality for this neck of the woods.

"Nice job. Ammo?"

Agosta handed him a box of fifty rounds.

"Two-hundred-grain Speers. Okay?"

"Fine." Marcus put everything away in the bag. "Any trouble getting guns for the mercs?"

"You kidding? It's like Bedford Sty here, man. You want weapons you just flash your money. They got a town up there in Laos, Nam Tha it's called, I tell you, it's like the shoe department at Macy's. All brands, all sizes. Just put in your order."

Marcus checked the sidewalk and the hotel entrance; Claire would be a minute or two yet.

"So how do things look? Any problems?"

"We're all set. We get rolling on time, we should make the border at Mae Sai in two hours, say. We check into the hotel, well, they call it a hotel, then go out and pay the gem dealer for the shit."

"We're covered on that, are we?" Marcus asked. "The lady lawyer is a touch on the bright side. It's got to look like we really are buying stones."

"Yeah, I figured she's more'n just a pair of tits. No, we're okay there. This guy really is a gem dealer. He also just happens to be a king."

"A king?"

"Opium king. You new to the biz?"

"I don't know a goddamn thing about the industry. Bendroit hired me as a nursemaid for the mercs, dispatcher in Hong Kong, and super salesman in New York. I'd appreciate a rundown. I'm not crazy about being responsible for something I don't know how it works."

"I don't blame you," Agosta said. He swiveled the rearview mirror toward him, and began to run a comb through his thick, oily hair. "The kings are the middlemen. They used to warehouse the opium down in Chiang Mai till they had one too many street killings. Mai's a big tourist center so the government kicked 'em up north where there ain't so many Rotarians from Ohio."

Agosta's fingers and knuckles, Marcus was unhappy to note, were marked with some very fine white scars. The same kind of scars that Boyle had on his hands.

"The business has changed a hell of a lot. They used to have the opium processed into Nine Ninety-Nine and send it down to Bangkok. It'd be shipped to Hong Kong and turned into Red Chicken or White."

"White?"

"China White. It's what some people call heroin. Anyway, it got too tough to run a factory in Kong so now they process locally. There's no more Pui now, the kings deal in Number Four."

"You want to run that by me again?" Marcus asked. "You're talking to the new kid, remember?"

Agosta put away the comb and yawned in the warm sunshine streaming through the windshield. When he stretched he took up a lot of room.

"What didn't you understand?"

"All of it. Okay, I know what China White is, but what's Nine Ninety-Nine?"

"Morphine blocks. They look like a square house brick, only a different color. They call 'em Brick or Pui, but mostly Nine Ninety-Nine because they used to stamp three nines on 'em, like they do on gold bullion."

"Is that why they call it the Golden Triangle?"

Agosta gave him a negative.

"What happened was a lot of the opium used to come into the country from Laos up near Chiang Saen, about thirty-five miles northeast of where we're sitting having this terrific conversation. The three countries meet there on the edge of the Mekong. Burma, Laos, and Thailand. So they called it the Triangle. And because the early traders didn't trust the Thai baht, the local money, and didn't want to be paid in nothing but gold, it became known as you-know-what."

"What's Red Chicken, and Number Four?"

"Number Four's boy, scag, tragic magic, China White. Whatever you want to call it, it's the real shit. Pure heroin. Red Chicken's Number Three heroin, smoking heroin. Been diluted with barbital and dyed with tea. Red Rock, Pearl, Rock Heroin, Hong Kong Rock, Brown Sugar, they're all Number Three, mainly for the Asiatic market."

"Who are we buying it from?"

"Hold it," Agosta warned.

Claire was coming toward them.

Marcus got out.

"You okay?" he asked.

"Fine." She held up a small suitcase. "All ready to go to work."

"Could I ask you to ride in the back for a while? Agosta's taking me through some business."

"Sure." Claire smiled at the young Thai boy who took the bag from her. "Harn Suk can show me the sights."

Agosta stuck his head out of the cab and asked where she wanted to go.

"Do you know the Siam Commercial Bank?"

"You got it."

Claire and Harn Suk got into the truck, and Marcus slid in beside Agosta, who drove off into the traffic.

"A piece of crap named Wei Chun," Agosta said, continuing where they'd left off. "Used to live up the road in Ban Hin Taek, but they booted his ass over the Burmese border and he's up there in the Shan State now. Jesus, that guy. He's right outa an Alan Ladd movie. His father was a fuckin' KMT warlord, for crissakes."

"KMT?"

"Kuomintang. Chiang Kai-shek's old party. His father was one of Chiang's generals, and Wei Chun's still playing the part. Got his own little army, the Shan United Army, he calls it. Claims he's fighting a separatist war against the Burmese government in Rangoon. The bastard's even trying to get the UN to recognize him. He's jerkin' himself off. The DEA, that's the only organization's gonna recognize him. He's the world's biggest dope pusher, bar none. Numero Uno."

Somebody had stuck a supermarket price tag on the dash in front of Marcus. He picked at it slowly, pulling it away in the same steady manner he was pulling information out of Agosta.

"He must be the richest guy in Burma, then."

"If he could get the shit to market," Agosta said, driving around a car in front of them, "he'd be the richest sonofabitch in the world. He's got caravans leaving for the north regular as the Trailways Bus Company. They roam through the hills collecting opium from the tribes. By the time a caravan gets back it's three hundred horses long, sometimes. Fifty support ponies, two hundred fifty pack ponies, each one carrying thirty keys of opium. That's seven thousand five hundred keys. Okay, opium to heroin's a ten-to-one process, so that's seven-fifty keys of pure from that one trip alone. Which means that caravan, walking through central Burma, the last fuckin' place on earth, has a U.S. dollar street value of something like a billion two. Weird, ain't it?"

"Christ! How much of that will he get to keep? Let's say of the five hundred kilos he's already sold to Bendroit?"

"Three grand a key is what Wei Chun sells it for. That's heroin base, about sixty percent pure. He's gotta pay the king in Mae Sai six percent of that, plus a hundred grand for squeeze and expenses."

Agosta stopped at a red light, swung the rearview mirror toward him again and examined his large white teeth as if there were secret messages on them.

"I'd heard the numbers were big," Marcus said, "but that's gigantic. Maybe I should ask Bendroit for a raise. If he's paying three grand a key for six hundred keys, that's an outlay of a million eight, right?"

"Plus expenses, yeah. The five hundred keys that's already in, that's all been paid for. The Triads paid for that direct. They're bankrolling Bendroit. But this last hundred keys, that we got to pick up ourselves. That's cash on the barrel, three hundred grand."

"What will Bendroit sell the junk for?"

"Hard to say." Agosta finished with his teeth, turned the mirror back, got the truck going again. "The market goes up and down like a flag at a summer camp. But he's gotta get eighty-five, ninety a key, easy. Say fifty million for the lot. And the bastard'll get to keep forty of it."

"Who gets the other ten?"

"The Triads. That's their fee for transporting and watching over the five hundred keys in Hong Kong."

"The Triads are a major part of this, then."

"Oh, sure. That's how I got into the deal. Bendroit didn't know a soul in Bangkok, not on our side of the street, so he went to Hong Kong because he's big in shipping, and shipping's big in HK. He made a deal with the Triads. They gave him some names, he came over here and hired me. Money went down and wheels started to turn. I made a deal with this king in Mae Sai, and he made a deal with Wei Chun and some traders in Burma, and we been pulling shit outa there ever since, hauling it down-country, and floating it over to Hong Kong. The Triads been taking delivery and keeping it safe."

"Bendroit told me things had changed over here," Marcus said. "Something about the Thai Army. What happened?"

"Pressure, that's what happened," Agosta said, pulling the truck into the curb. They'd come to a busy part of the town, bustling shops and stores, people thronging the streets. The bank Claire had asked Agosta about was just two doors down the block. Claire came around to the driver's side and told them she wouldn't be long. Harn Suk joined her, flashed a smile at Agosta.

"I guard," he said, and went with her.

"Good kid, that one," Agosta said. "The Thais are beautiful people. You win one, you win one for life. And the women —" he pointed at a lovely girl crossing in front of them. She wore an ankle-length skirt made from some glossy pink material, a plain blue blouse low over her hips, and a wide-brimmed bamboo hat that sat on her lustrous black hair like an inverted bowl. It gave her a cheeky look, and she smiled good-naturedly when Agosta honked the horn at her. "Clean," Agosta said. "You could eat 'em off the floor. You want a little of that stuff, go to the Honey Honey tonight. It's a parlor in Mae Sai. Although, uh," he shot

Marcus a quick glance, a fast grin, "maybe you're all fixed up in that department."

"Miss Tanner? I'd have to argue her into it. What kind of pressure?"

"What? Oh. From the States. The government in Bangkok's spreadin' its legs for Drug Enforcement in Washington. They got the border cops and the fuckin' Thai Rangers riding herd on the regular trails, the ones we been using. So this time we're coming down the Kok River. The border bulls and the Rangers don't bother with it. They figure you'd have to be crazy to travel on it on account of the bandits."

"Are they right?" Marcus asked.

"Not if those mercs are any good. And we won't know that till they come under fire."

"How about the bandits? Are they talented?"

Agosta put one of his heavy hands on the back of his neck, massaged the muscles while he considered an answer.

"You wouldn't call 'em a fighting force, but they're not a bunch of drunken bums, either. They're mainly renegade KMTs and Shans turned nasty. They used to be strictly amateur night, stop a tourist boat, steal watches and a bracelet or two, send it on its way. But they've gone big-time now. There's a lot of 'em, and they all got automatic rifles, and they figure that if it's on the river, it's dinner."

"There's something I haven't told you," Marcus said.

"You haven't told me a fuckin' thing. I been tellin' you everything."

"She wants to come with us. Miss Tanner."

That brought Agosta's head around.

"What, you mean on the trail? What the hell for?"

"I don't know. Wants to measure skulls, or something."

"Don't she know about the bandits?"

"She's the obstinate type. Very independent."

"Easiest way is to leave her behind. Do a flit. She wakes up, we're gone. What can she do?"

The conversation stopped then and, a few minutes later, Claire and Harn Suk walked out of the bank, Claire carrying the suitcase fastened to her wrist, Marcus noted. Understandable if there was three hundred thousand dollars inside.

Agosta followed a different route back to the hotel, took the truck through a much older section of town: peeling wood-frame houses, telegraph poles bowed down by spaghetti strands of wire crisscrossing overhead. It was the original town here, the one which had sprung up on the edge of the river. The water popped suddenly into view as they turned a corner — Chiang Rai still wasn't big enough to have spread across its river; the far bank was just a scattering of dwellings backed by high palms and the thick foliage of broad leafy trees.

"That's it,"Agosta said. "The Kok. The river we're gonna be comin' down. Take a good look, you're seeing it at its best."

The river was swollen by rain but still turgid and lazy, flowing toward the east as if it had to be dragged there. Little eddies and swirls stirred its brown/green surface dotted here and there by boats full of fruit and vegetables, and one or two carrying pigs and chickens in cages. Driftwood floated in it, broken tree branches waterlogged and partly submerged. To Marcus it looked overweight, bland, and uneventful, hardly the type of river that played host to a band of marauders.

When they pulled up at the hotel Claire went straight inside to put the bag in the hotel safe, and Agosta had a last word for Marcus.

"Six o'clock on deck. And don't pack your passport. Keep it on you so you don't forget it tomorrow."

"Okay," Marcus said casually, but he was thinking hard. His passport? It was the one thing he wanted to keep buried. "I thought we were planning to sneak over the border."

"It ain't for the border, it's for Wei Chun. He likes to

put on a little act. If you're American, and he's never seen your face before, you gotta be working for the DEA. They're all over the Triangle like a madwoman's shit. Few years back they put a price on his head, them and the Thai government. Offered forty grand for him, dead or alive, so Wei Chun turned around and offered two grand to anybody greasin' a DEA man."

"He get any takers?"

"Yeah, in a way. Somebody shot a DEA guy's wife. I dunno, maybe Wei Chun paid half on that one." Agosta chunked the truck into gear. "See you at six."

6

THE TRIP UP TO THE BORDER, to Mae Sai, two
hours away, was not a happy one. They were jammed into
the back of the pickup again and, because the clouds that
had been building in the west had finally opened up, the
canvas sides of the truck were lowered, which exacerbated
the heat and congestion. The road was flat and fairly straight,
the countryside, glimpsed out of the back of the truck, was
obscured by the rain, which fell in a solid slant on tobacco
plantations and vegetable fields, the fading light sucking
the color from everything.

There was little else to see on the road; the largest town
they passed through, Mae Chan, was smaller than the one
they'd just left, and the other towns were just small clumps
of houses gathered around a few ramshackle stores. One of
the towns had a name, Pong Tong, that drew a laugh from
Boyle and a tasteless comment, which he made while grinning at Claire. He'd remained silent for a good part of the
trip, perhaps inhibited by the fact that Burroughs was sitting opposite him. Hating officers, he was uncomfortable
in their presence, and kept shifting on his haunches and
telling Turkenton, sitting next to him, to give him some
room. Turkenton moved a little each time, but not because

he was afraid of Boyle. It seemed to Marcus that the Australian didn't know that Boyle was picking on him; he was too big and amiable to see any threat in anybody. Turkenton tried to liven things up with a couple of corny jokes, and Woods, who was from Tennessee, told an anecdote in his soft Southern accent about a hunting trip he'd gone on once in the kind of weather they were traveling through. Marcus and Claire laughed politely but Burroughs remained as silent as Limbu sitting at the end of the bench. Boyle muttered something about a "dumb cracker," and the atmosphere remained leaden.

About twenty minutes from the end of their trip, the rain thumping down on top of the truck, and the bump and jostle of the ride, proved too much for Boyle.

"Some fun, huh?" he asked the canvas roof. "Drivin' around in the rain in a fuckin' tent."

"Shouldn't be long now," Turkenton said. "Where are we going again?"

"Mae something," Woods answered. "Last stop for gas before Burma, so they say."

"I don't care where the fuck it is," Boyle said. "Just so long as the beer's cold and the twat's hot."

Even in the gloomy light in the back of the truck Marcus had no trouble making out the leer on Boyle's face. He knew what Boyle was trying to do: in his bragging, ignorant way he was trying to show off in front of Claire, thinking himself witty and provocative. He was certainly provocative: Marcus wanted to punch his teeth in.

"Boyle." Marcus bit down on the name. "You'd oblige me if you'd mind your mouth. There's a lady present."

"Oh yeah?" Boyle said. He turned toward Turkenton. "You know what a lady is? A lay with an extra D."

"Hey, go easy," Turkenton said. He sounded embarrassed.

"Knock it off, Boyle," Marcus said.

Claire put a hand on his arm.

[77]

"It's all right," she said, in Boyle's direction. "When Mr. Boyle speaks, I don't listen."

"There, you see?" There was a smirk in Boyle's voice. "She ain't listenin', so what're you bitchin' about?"

"Because *I'm* listening, and I don't want to hear any more of your deep comments."

"I got lotsa comments I ain't even said yet, scummo."

Burroughs spoke up at last. Marcus had been wondering when he'd say something; he clearly didn't like being in intimate contact with his subordinates after having had his rank recognized, and he certainly hadn't been employed to settle barrack-room squabbles, but Boyle had to be getting to him, too.

He said crisply, "I think this has gone quite far enough. If I were you, Boyle, I'd save my energies for the trek ahead, which may well prove extremely arduous."

Boyle was silenced by the voice of command and the use of polysyllables, and lapsed into a sullen quiet for the remainder of the ride.

When the border town finally appeared, it was without any big announcement: the road broadened slightly, and there it was. Burroughs had been to Mae Sai before, and Agosta and Harn Suk had visited many times, but for the rest of the party the town was even smaller than they'd expected. It was really only one main street with shops either side ending in a wooden bridge over the river where, according to Agosta, Burmese and Thai traders met for a little international exchange. No tourists were allowed across into Burma and, apart from the traders and some members of the hill tribes, very few people got to cross the bridge going north.

The hotel entrance was sandwiched between a shoe shop and a grocery cum general store, its lobby up a dark flight of stairs with the ten-room accommodation fanning out on either side. After Marcus and Claire had dumped their bags in their rooms, Agosta told them that the easiest way of safeguarding the money Claire had in the little suitcase would be to make the payment immediately, and took them straight out again.

Harn Suk drove the truck a little way out of town and down a muddy track to where the Mae Sai River, much narrower than the Kok in Chiang Rai, separated the identical green banks of Thailand and Burma. He stopped the truck near a wharf in front of a high brick building with the proportions of a breadstick. Walking into the place, Marcus was assaulted by a smell so thick and pungent he felt he had to lean his body forward in order to move. Way above his head, drooping from long poles laid across rafters, a hundred thousand tobacco leaves hung like bats in a cave. Large and green and floppy, they covered every inch of the ceiling like an upside-down meadow, and sent their biting aroma spiraling toward the ground, reflected off the tin that lined the eaves of the roof.

"Are we buying rubies or cigars?" Claire asked, looking a little unsettled.

"From this guy you can buy both," Agosta told her. "Up here in the north you got real strong family ties. If a guy's wife has family in the cheroot business then he's automatically in the cheroot business, too. This country takes a little getting used to."

The curing barn led into a broad wooden warehouse filled with bales of tobacco stacked wall to wall. Steps at the far end of the building climbed to a glassed-in balcony, the temperature higher up here, the smell stronger. Behind the glass was an office, three men inside, one writing at a paper-strewn desk, one playing some kind of dice game, the third just sitting there.

All three looked up as their visitors walked in.

"*Sawaddee krab,*" Agosta said.

The man at the desk acknowledged the greeting while he checked out Marcus and Claire.

He said, in Thai, "What do we have here?"

"*Pem lah nugn*," Agosta replied. "Friends and money."

Agosta's Thai sounded nothing like the other man's. It was a tough language for a foreigner, being sung, like Chinese, in tones.

"Both are welcome," the man said. He was elderly with a fuzz of white hair on his scalp, his thin, almost emaciated frame barely supporting a sleeveless cotton undershirt. The cuffs of an old pair of pants peeked out from beneath the desk, his stubby toes divided by the thongs of rubber sandals.

Agosta motioned to Claire.

"Okay, Miss Tanner. Pay him and he'll write you out a receipt."

Claire didn't look too happy about the arrangements but she was smart enough to cover herself legally.

"My instructions are to make the payment to whoever you designate, Mr. Agosta."

"I designate him," Agosta said, waving a finger at the old man.

"I'm sorry to be stuffy, Mr. Agosta, but may I ask you, at this time, for some identification, please."

"No problem."

Digging into his back pocket, Agosta said to Marcus, "Bendroit hired a careful one here." He handed over his wallet. Claire glanced quickly at his ID, gave the wallet back, unlocked the handcuff around her wrist, unlocked the suitcase, and began putting bundles of money on the man's desk.

As the man laboriously began to count the first bundle, Marcus watched the other two men. It was clear who the opium king was: the one playing the dice game, thumping down a bamboo cup and moving counters on a colored board, had the only electric fan in the room, and was getting 100 percent of its breeze. He had a warrior's face, his nose the shape of a thick arrow, the eyes, under a high straight ridge of bone, like sharply elongated triangles. He could have been fifty, or ten years older than that, his coffee-colored skin like a piece of old leather.

The third man was totally different from the other two: something terrible had happened to his face; it was layered in patches of different skin that fitted together like an uneven jigsaw puzzle. His hair resembled a helmet settled carefully on his head; a barber had trimmed it in a rounded arch high over his ears, then given him long, knife-shaped sideburns ending in sharp points at his jawline. Heavy-chested and muscular, he sat cross-legged in a chair eyeballing Marcus and Agosta with the blank stare of a lizard.

The old man at the desk finished with the first bundle, boxed all the bundles into several lines, laid a long wooden ruler across each line, and checked that the ruler was the same height at each end.

"*Tuk yang to tong,*" he said. "An honest count."

He wrote out a receipt, stamped it, handed it to Agosta, who passed it to Claire.

Marcus got a look at it over her shoulder. It was printed in English and Thai. The English letterhead said "The Kreng Shup Trading Company." The stamp said "Paid. Received by," then the man's florid signature. He'd written in the blank space "$300,000."

"Don't you get a receipt?" Claire asked Agosta.

"Sure. A different kind."

The old man had risen and crossed to a heavy antique safe. From it he took out an envelope which he handed to Agosta. Agosta shook out half a playing card, a ten of clubs. It had been cut with scissors in a precise and jagged pattern.

"Up there in the jungle," Agosta explained, tucking the card into his wallet, "they don't read so good."

"The gem supplier has the other half, I take it," Claire said.

"You got it. When they match up, he gives me the rocks. It's simple and foolproof. Okay, we're all through here."

The old man went back to his paperwork. The opium

king rattled dice in his cup, slammed it down, and read the result without much joy. The man with the ruined face watched Marcus and Agosta all the way to the door.

Walking back through the curing shed Marcus said, "Three hundred grand for half a ten of clubs. You sure don't get much for the money."

"Listen," Agosta said. "In the diamond business, in London and New York, you don't even get that. All you get's a handshake."

It was a good line because it was true, and Claire, Marcus saw, stopped looking so uneasy.

The restaurant, a cheery, boisterous, Formica-and-aluminum place, lit by a blaze of strip lights, echoed to the sounds of five-year-old American hits belting out from a ten-year-old jukebox.

The English translations on the menu were almost as incomprehensible as the Thai script they were supposed to explain, but eventually Marcus and Claire found they'd okayed a fish-and-coconut curry and crispy fried prawns, both dishes alive with green chilies. It was a delicious meal, and certainly exotic: there was a sauce on the side whose main ingredient, they learned, was crushed water bugs from the rice fields.

They traded impressions on what they'd seen of the country so far, and discussed the strange transaction in the tobacco factory, although it didn't seem to Marcus that Claire had any suspicions. It had been so weird and different it had its own curious veracity.

They settled into a reflective mood, relaxed by the good food and the icy beer they drank with it, but Marcus thought that Claire had something on her mind which she was keeping back. Several times she'd leveled those dark eyes on him and he'd got the impression she'd been saying one thing but thinking another. When she finally came out with it, Marcus had to wonder whether she was particularly perceptive or whether he was simply a rotten actor.

"Shall I tell you something?" she asked. "There's something about this excursion that doesn't jell."

"What's that?"

"You."

"Oh?"

She speared some tiny shrimp on the tines of her fork, ate them watching him watching her back. She'd pulled her yellow hair into a ponytail behind her head, which put more of her face on show, revealing its fine planes, and the smooth whiteness of her neck. She'd changed into a simple striped blouse, and jeans that hugged her body, something that Marcus found he very much wanted to do himself. She was getting to him, this girl; the more he was with her, the better the peek he got behind the buttoned-up veneer she presented to the world.

"I told you when we first met," she said, "that I don't have crooks for clients. I have to qualify that. I don't have any that I know of. There are some rumors about Bendroit and some shipping frauds, none of them proven. Now this little jaunt he's got us doing isn't illegal but it's not officially condoned, so I'm not really surprised to find Bendroit involved in it. I can't stand the man, and if it wasn't for the fact that a fledgling law firm can't afford to turn down a big client, I wouldn't have anything to do with him. As I said, none of the stories about him has been substantiated. However, if he turned out to be cheating on his income tax, I wouldn't be at all surprised. So Bendroit fits the pattern of a quasi-legal precious stone importer."

"I go along with that," Marcus said, wondering about the point she was building to. "He struck me as a guy who likes to get an edge."

"Agosta fits the pattern, too," Claire went on. "He's muscle, that's very obvious. Okay, maybe you need a man like that so the gem dealers won't be tempted to rip you off. So I don't have to wonder why he should be here with us. But you . . . you're the odd man out."

There was a small condiment bowl on the table containing

[83]

pepper segments floating in vinegar. Claire picked up a spoon and pensively nudged one of the pepper bits. When it moved sluggishly through the clear liquid, bumped into another piece and sank, Marcus wondered if his cover was about to get the same treatment.

"Bendroit said he'd hired you to see that everything went smoothly. In other words, you're the troubleshooter. If any of those men step out of line, like Boyle's trying to do, your job is to push them back in again. And I assume that includes Agosta."

Marcus made a face.

"I wouldn't like to try pushing Agosta anywhere he didn't want to go."

"Nevertheless, that's your job. So that means you're a gunman."

"How do you know I'm not a karate expert?"

"Because all those men you're in charge of are going to have weapons. And you don't put a karate expert up against armed men."

"They do in Japan."

"You don't fit the personality pattern," Claire said, ignoring his comment. "I've never defended a gunman but I've met quite a few through my work. They're all mean-spirited and uncaring. To kill somebody is to deprive them of what they value most. It's the ultimate heartless act, and I don't think you'd do that."

"You can be a gunman without being a killer," Marcus said.

"You mean-you can be one without having killed somebody. True. But to be a gunman, and be any good, you have to be *willing* to kill somebody."

Marcus didn't reply to that; she was right. He said, instead, "Maybe you're just a rotten judge of people. You ever thought of that?"

She shook her head, her eyes steady on his face.

"On the trip over, all those takeoffs and landings, you

were very kind to me. Warm. Considerate. Then on the ride up here today, when Boyle started trying to be cute with me, you told him to pipe down."

"I don't like Boyle. I didn't want to miss the chance to tell him to shut up."

As if he hadn't spoken, Claire said, "At the airport, at Kennedy, you asked me if I'd been reading a guidebook, and when I told you it was *Pride and Prejudice*, your exact words were, 'I never read her.' You knew it had been written by a woman, yet you claimed to read only girlie books. So you don't jell, Mr. Dubin. But you fooled Bendroit, and you seem to have fooled Agosta, too."

"But not you, huh? Claire, I'll bet you're a very good lawyer."

"Fair to middling."

Marcus gave her a piece of victory on the theory that a flat denial would only confirm her views. He looked down at his plate, trying to appear a little embarrassed.

"I heard about the job. It wasn't for a man of my talents but I needed the bread. So I flexed my muscles and made myself out to be Wild Bill Hickok."

"Just what are your talents?"

"I'm a thief. But, like you, only fair to middling."

"You mean you were caught? Convicted?"

"Yes, ma'am."

"Where did you serve your time?"

"Reedsville, Georgia."

"Reedsville? When was this?"

"Eighty to eighty-four."

Claire picked up her glass, sipped at her beer, dabbed her mouth with a paper napkin.

"I know Reedsville. I was down there for a few days the summer of eighty-three. I was on the national committee of a concerned citizens' group. Prison reform. I remember the warden there, an awful person. Hated the inmates. Simms? Simmons?"

"Simpson. Ralph J. Simpson. The Prisoner's Friend, we used to call him." Marcus hadn't the vaguest idea who had been warden at the prison in '83, but he'd had to say something. No con ever forgot the warden's name. It was a dangerous area she'd taken him into, so to get out of it he went on the offensive.

"Okay, you've told me something, now I'll tell you something. I'm not the only one at this table who's posing."

The remark sat Claire up a little straighter.

"What do you mean?"

"The image you try to project. At Kennedy you asked me if I was typing you, the career woman devoted to her work, stays home nights with a good book. Those were *your* exact words, Claire. Maybe you chose them because that's how you see yourself. But it's not you."

"This isn't the first time I've been offered a ten-cent analysis," Claire said sharply. "And I've never found it worth the money."

"You were married, weren't you?"

"I'm thirty-two. A lot of women have been married by the time they're thirty-two."

"When it broke up, you broke up. From now on, you said to yourself, it's nose to the grindstone and you'll settle for reading about romance. Much safer. That's when you switched to corporate law, am I close? You wanted protection so you hid behind the *Wall Street Journal,* and got your kicks from mergers and takeovers."

Claire clanked down her fork onto her plate, her mouth compressed into a firm line.

"Shall we talk about something else?"

"Sure. Let's talk about your idea of coming with us in the morning. I spoke to Agosta about it. He's gonna give you an argument."

"I've been trained at arguing."

"It's not just the bandits, Claire. There are several small armies roaming around over the border. If you don't believe

[86]

me, talk to Burroughs. He knows the country. Used to lead tour groups into the hills. He'll probably tell you that any of those armies would regard a good-looking blond as long-overdue provisions."

"I'll wear a hat," Claire said, reaching for her handbag, getting ready to leave.

"I have a better idea. Agosta tells me we finish up in Chiang Mai. Wasn't that where you planned to go anyway?"

"So?"

"So why not go there tomorrow? It's supposed to be a lovely town. We'll be there in a couple of days, and you can show me around. How about it?"

Claire pushed back her chair, stood up abruptly.

"I think we should settle this now. I'm going to find Agosta."

The girls in the window of the Honey Honey, the massage parlor Agosta had recommended to Marcus, wore numbers around their necks. A two-digit number meant that an invigorating and healthful massage was the only service offered, which was the only service that many Thai men and women required. The girls who wore three-digit numbers were willing to extend their services beyond the invigorating and healthy into the realms of the erotic. The number system was used not only as a quick and fast advertisement, but because the Thais considered pointing rude, so a particular girl was requested by writing down her number and holding it up.

The Honey Honey sported a bar inside the door, a bamboo roof, and swing doors like a Western saloon set in partitions that sectioned off the place into a series of rooms. Woods had chosen a petite young girl of around nineteen who, unlike her sometimes shrill and often vulgar counterpart in the Patpong Road in Bangkok, did not wear a black bikini but a graceful silk sarong and a plain white blouse, the sleeves of which she'd pushed back.

Naturally, she was a three-digit girl.

She daintily removed his clothes, led him to a hot tub, and proceeded to modestly scrub his back, although the proximity of an inflated rubber mattress on the soap-shiny board floor held out the promise of more exciting things to come.

She worked her soapy hands over his shoulders, down his flanks, over his tummy, tickled him quickly under his crotch.

"Darlin', I can take plenty of that," Woods said, grasping her hand and trying to put it back where it had been. The young girl giggled and began soaping his neck again.

"You're not gonna turn out to be one of them heart-breakers, are you, sweetie?" Woods asked in his molasses drawl. He reached for her but the girl evaded him easily, and went to a tray which held some very curious bars of soap. They all had holes in their centers of varying diameters.

The girl took a critical look at Woods's engorged penis.

"Need right size," she said, smiling.

"Right now I think I'm a triple E large."

The girl chose some soap, slipped it over his swollen member, and began to move it slowly back and forth.

"Oh, my stars," said Woods.

The girl took the soap away.

"You clean now."

Woods protested that he was still filthy dirty but the young girl, smilingly and firmly, helped him out of the tub and, with surprising strength, began to towel him harshly all over. When she dropped the towel Woods sighed with relief and accepted her invitation to climb up on the massage table.

She spent five minutes on a straight massage, her expert hands alternately caressing, kneading, and pummeling his lean frame.

"This get out kinks," the girl said.

"I got some kinks in my dick need gettin' out, too."

"You want special massage?"

"I think I could go for that. Sure."

She slipped out of her sarong, revealing a honey-colored body, small-breasted and with a lot of curve at the hips, and a wild black thatch of hair. She led Woods to the inflated rubber mattress and motioned for him to lie down on his back. She took a wooden dipper of warm sudsy water from the hot tub, poured some down her front, and the rest over Woods, freshly washed, dried, and massaged. Then she began to massage him again, not with her hands, but with herself.

It was an incredible performance; she moved her breasts, her tummy, and her pudenda all over him in up-and-down circular motions, sliding on him, oozing over him in a contact bump and grind, sloshing and slithering on his body. There was no copulation; she expertly avoided Woods's attempts to enter her. With his penis pressed flat against his stomach she humped him faster and faster, bouncing, skidding on him, increasing her speed as he dug his fingers into the ripeness of her bottom.

When he began to moan she clung wetly to him, moving only her hips in a fast, suds-lathered hula, quickening it till he shouted out and came, kept it up till he'd exhausted himself.

She washed him again in a tub of clean water, dried him, helped him dress, and shyly accepted the tip he gave her.

Going out into the bar he ran into Turkenton emerging from another door, his long face pink and scrubbed, his hair still wet. Woods grinned at him.

"Hey there, Shacka. That set you free any?"

The big Australian moved stiffly, limping slightly.

"I reckon my girlie must've worked in a car wash. How was yours?"

"Little bit of heaven. She soaped me up, watered me down, dove onto me, and set a new record for the two-yard crawl."

They went together into the little wooden bar and sat on

rickety chairs. They were working on their third bottle of Amarit when Boyle arrived and sat down one chair away from them. It was his unsubtle way of letting them know that neither of them was his idea of a good drinking buddy. He'd already been with one of the girls and, deep in the grip of postcoital blues, began moodily knocking back shots of Mekong whiskey.

Woods and Turkenton had swapped backgrounds and were now down to their boyhoods.

"There was nothin' ol' Jesse was sceered of," Woods said, dragging out the words. "Fear? Shee-it, that hound didn't know the meaning of the word. Saw her go for a brownie once. I mean a whole entire bear, and she just flew at the thing like it was a tabby cat standing there. Stopped it colder 'n a bottle of beer at a whore's picnic. Got a ripped-up belly for her trouble, though. Took three hours to die, just lyin' there smilin' and thumpin' her tail. Not even a whimper."

Woods swigged at his beer, Turkenton keeping him company. They ordered another round.

"I had a dog once," Turkenton said. "I called him Blue on account of he *was* blue. Black spots but blue underneath 'em."

"Once you show 'em any sign of affection, pat 'em or stroke 'em, or let 'em in the house even, a huntin' dog's finished." Woods's mop of hair bobbed as he affirmed his own statement. "Yep. Good grits or good hounds, you got to go south."

"Hell, I'm from further south than you," Turkenton said. "I can out-country anyone I ever met. I spent most of me time in Sydney, but I grew up out in the mulga. Place called Minmi. How about that for a name? Minmi. I think it's aborigine for Many Yawns. No water unless it rained, no electricity. When the generator went on the blink we used kerosene lamps, which came in handy when you were crook."

Woods didn't understand the word.

"Crook. Sick," Turkenton explained. "For constipation you got a spoonful of kerosene. If you had the trots you got two spoonfuls of kerosene. The roof of the house was corrugated iron. When it was a hundred and one outside, it was a hundred and ten inside. The dunny was out the back. There was a stream running through the back yard but instead of grass there was mint growing wild. Going out to take a dump was like walking through the Wrigley's factory."

"Hey!" Boyle thumped his fleshy fist down onto the bar top. "Nobody's interested in your bird dogs or your goddamn boomerangs. Knock it off, for crissakes."

Turkenton, looking puzzled, moved his head to the right.

"What's eating you, mate?"

Boyle rolled his eyes. He was in a foul mood, the whiskey depressing him, dragging him down.

"Sheese! A dumb-ass cracker and a fuckin' Aussie sittin' next to me, and he wants to know what's eatin' me."

"That's not very polite," Turkenton said, sounding hurt. "There are some people who might take that the wrong way."

Boyle gave up. Turkenton was uninsultable, and Woods was feeling too mellow to want to fight. He knocked back his drink, banged the glass down, called to the Thai barman.

"Hey, Charlie Chan. Hit me again."

"If he don't, I'll be glad to oblige."

Boyle spun on his chair.

Agosta was standing there.

"Ain't they got no standards?" Boyle said, turning back and snorting in disgust. "They let anybody in here."

Agosta, remembering his promise to Marcus to stay away from Boyle, didn't reply but instead sat down next to Woods.

"So," Agosta said. "What do you think of the Honey Honey? You two guys get relaxed?"

"Oh, my word, yes. Right now I am one relaxed dumb-ass cracker."

"And I am one relaxed fuckin' Aussie."

Boyle, knowing he was being got at, but unable to prove it, hissed an obscenity.

"You say something, fat man?" Agosta asked. He was trying to behave but the guy just stuck in his craw.

Boyle turned slowly.

"Who you callin' fat man?"

With exaggerated movements Agosta checked Woods, checked Turkenton, then looked to his left, where there was nobody. He said to Boyle, "Well, I don't see nobody else looks like a tub of lard."

The light from the ceiling lamps bounced off Boyle's oversized head, sheening his pasty scalp. His mouth slid to one side, and his eyes got small and glinty.

"Ho, ho, ho," he said, running the palms of his hands down the sides of his pants. "Things are pickin' up after all." He was wearing a long-sleeved shirt over one of his regular T-shirts and, not so surreptitiously, he undid the button of his left-hand cuff.

They were interrupted by somebody coming into the room, one of the girls coming through the door. She was a two-digit girl who specialized in straight massage, young and lithesome; pretty. Agosta greeted her in Thai, began to chat with her when he noticed the swelling on one side of her face.

He asked what happened, and the girl flicked a glance at Boyle, looked away again.

"Nothing," she said, and hurried off.

Agosta pulled his bulk out of a chair and moved around the bar.

"Have you met that young lady?" he asked Boyle.

"A pig. A stiff. All she wanted to gimme was a fuckin' rubdown, for crissakes."

"That's what she does. That's why she wears two numbers. Didn't nobody tell you?"

"A whore's a whore. She wouldn't smoke the old white owl, so I bopped her one."

"How did you hit her?" Agosta was speaking very quietly.
Boyle, turned on his chair to face him, frowned.

"What d'you mean, how did I hit her? I hit her. I pay
her money, she just stands there. Nobody takes me for a
ride."

"I'm interested," Agosta said, his face like a slab. "Did
you hit her like this?"

Boyle went back on his chair, his glass flying from his
hand as Agosta, with insolent slowness, slapped his open
hand against Boyle's cheek.

"Or like this?" he asked, lazily backhanding him from
the other side. The second slap was heavy enough to turn
Boyle's head. He stayed where he was for a moment, shocked
and blinking, looking at Agosta, who stood in front of him
as if he were actually expecting a considered answer to his
question.

"Maybe you'd care to show me exactly how outside," he
invited.

Boyle barked at the man behind the bar, "Gimme a
towel!"

When his order wasn't understood he snatched up a bar
towel, and dabbed quite delicately at his mouth, tonguing
the cut on the inside.

"Sure," he said to Agosta. "Matter of fact, I was planning
to show you something outside anyway."

He tucked the towel into his belt, got off the chair, and
went toward the door, Agosta following, Woods and Turkenton right behind them.

A dark alley divided the massage parlor from a neighboring structure. It led to an area at the rear of the buildings
which backed onto a drainage ditch, the broken macadam
of the alley giving way to hard-baked dirt, soggy now from
the rain.

The light from a street lamp struggled fitfully into the
space, blocked in part by the bamboo roof of the parlor and
the leafy overhang of dripping trees. It partially illuminated

[93]

four overstuffed garbage cans, and the rat that sprang from one of them and fled into the night.

Agosta moved to the center of the dirt area, turned, and stood with his hands hanging loosely.

Boyle stopped several feet away from him, used the towel on his mouth again, almost like a woman putting on lipstick, then tucked it neatly back into his belt.

Agosta beckoned to him with his left hand.

"C'mon, shithead."

His other hand held a knife he'd taken from a hip pocket with about the same movement he might have used to reach for a handkerchief. He knew Boyle was a knifer; he'd spotted the scars on his hands when he'd first seen him at the airport in Chiang Rai. And Boyle had noticed Agosta's hands, so there was no surprise on either side. On the contrary, when Boyle saw Agosta's knife he looked like a kid given a present.

"O-*kay!*" he said, joyously.

Standing to the side, an audience of two, neither Woods nor Turkenton could believe the speed of the exchange that began the fight. They'd expected these big heavy men to ponderously slug fists into each other's faces, and they weren't prepared for the knives, nor for the balletic quickness and the astonishing skill with which they were used. The two of them said later that the fight had lasted a couple of minutes, but it only seemed that way because neither had ever witnessed anything like it. They'd both seen bayonets come out in army camp arguments, but it never got past the posturing stage, and Woods had once seen a man get cut in a parking lot after a football game in Chattanooga, but that had been two men and one knife, and a single clumsy stab in the shoulder. Neither had ever watched a fight between two expert knifers.

In actual fact, the contest lasted less than fifteen seconds. There was none of the amateur "West Side Story" stuff — no crouching low, or bending forward, or circling; no flashy knife-hand switching, no exaggerated feints, no knives held out, menacingly stirring the air where a pro could slice off fingers; no blades held flat to slide more easily between ribs, because the pros seldom went for the heart. Boyle waved his right hand in front of his left wrist and lunged at Agosta, and both onlookers thought that Boyle had thrown a right jab, and that Agosta had blocked a fist until they saw the thin gleam of blood across his knuckles, and the knife in Boyle's fingers.

They hadn't seen him draw it; it seemed to have popped into his hand like a piece of cartoon animation.

After that first lunge, the traditional opening of a real fight, almost a form exercise by one opponent to see if he could catch the other napping, Boyle and Agosta parted to check each other's weapon and grip. Agosta's knife was a single-edge type held in the saber forehand grip. Boyle's blade was about half an inch shorter but double-edged. He used the quarter-saber grip, thumb extended past the fingers. Both held their knives so that the blades were straight up and down.

The checkout took just a piece of a second, and they closed again in a lightning series of thrust and counter-thrust, their knives scything out from the guard position and darting back again in a strobing blur.

Only slow motion would have revealed the technique of Agosta drawing second blood as he caught Boyle with a snap cut. Cocking his wrist, Agosta raised the point of his knife forty-five degrees, his knife hand shooting out and stopping three inches above Boyle's hand. His wrist un-cocked, his arm snapped back in the same movement, and his blade sliced into the meaty part of Boyle's thumb as Boyle whipped his knife away a fraction too late.

From the guard position Boyle replied with a power slash, bringing his knife up, out, and down like a man painting a swift and violent half-circle on a wall. He wristed in a draw motion so that his blade would also cut on the return but Agosta wasn't there anymore, and the blade only sliced his shirt.

Agosta answered with the same tactic but doubled it up, slashing, reversing his blade, and slashing overarm again. Boyle dodged the first attempt and, suspecting the double, pinked Agosta's knuckle with a snap thrust.

Both were too experienced to try for a lethal blow this early; the idea in the opening stages of a knifers' fight was to cripple the other man's knife hand, or sever a large artery in the forearm. Real knife fights, as fast and as short as they almost always were, were still wars of attrition.

Agosta altered his angle and distance, thought about a snap cut, had to cancel it when Boyle, with a lot of elbow, wrist, and shoulder, produced two diagonal movements the knifers called a Figure Eight. His blade cut into Agosta's blocking hand, but he paid for the privilege as Agosta caught him with his heel in a sudden side-thrust kick. Had the blow landed where it was aimed, on the knee instead of the thigh, that would have been the fight, and Boyle knew it.

Mad at himself, and hurting from the kick, he got smarter.

"Fuckin' guinea!" he yelled, and leaped forward, punching a power slash at Agosta's torso.

The tactic worked.

Agosta thought Boyle had lost his temper at being so ignobly booted. He faked a block, stepped off his left foot and, with consummate judgment, let the knife graze his ribs, jumping forward as he did so and clamping his free arm down, pinning Boyle's knife under his arm and against his side.

It was exactly what Boyle had hoped Agosta might do, and he blocked a gut thrust with his free arm while, behind Agosta's back, he spun his knife in his trapped hand in a forehand shift. A fast pinch grip and palm pivot, and his blade was no longer pointing straight ahead; now it was pointing downward, the handle held for an overhand stab.

He had only to move his trapped wrist an inch in a quick hook thrust and Agosta got the tip of the blade in his kidney.

Even as he took the piercing jolt of agony, Agosta was realizing his mistake, knocking away Boyle's knife hand, and slashing up with his own at Boyle's throat. But it was a fast-moving target he was trying for, and his blade hit a couple of inches to the side, neatly passing through the lower part of Boyle's right ear like a razor through a piece of paper.

Both men knew the score now: Agosta had to end it, go for a fast kill before the kidney shot slowed him too much. It meant he had to press and take chances he normally wouldn't, which put him at a great disadvantage, because with his tactics dictated by his condition, he was an open book. So when he shaped for a beat at Boyle's knife arm, Boyle knew it had to be a fake in front of an all-out lethal attempt, like the counterclockwise spiral that came aimed at his stomach. Boyle batted away the blow with his free hand, and employed a move which had been popular since men had first used swords: he cleavered at the leg Agosta had awkwardly lurched forward on, catching him behind the knee and severing his hamstring.

It sagged Agosta instantly on his right-hand side, his knife side, and his arm sank below the guard position, too low to do anything about the power slash Boyle came up with.

Watching openmouthed a few feet away, Woods and Turkenton both thought the knife had missed, but then Agosta's throat suddenly gapped, and his carotid artery went off like a liquid red whistle.

With tremendous courage Agosta slapped his left hand over the spraying fountain and, forgetting about his ruined leg, tried to jump at Boyle. His leg folded under his weight, and he went down onto his knees. He said something which came out as a wet gurgle, and died there, kneeling like a penitent, toppling forward into a puddle of rainwater, staining it a browny red color.

Boyle reached for the bar towel in his belt, mopped his sweating face, cut and tore the towel in half, and put one piece on his bleeding ear and the other around his thumb, which had been opened to the bone.

"Fuck with me," he growled down at the body in the dirt. He was breathing hard, his plump shoulders heaving. He bent and took a wallet from the dead man's hip pocket.

Turkenton found his voice. Like Woods, he'd been shocked at the naked violence and its inevitable conclusion.

"What are you doing?"

"Gettin' his ID, what d'you think?" Boyle snarled, although it was the money he checked before he put the wallet into his own pocket. "You two, get 'im outa here. Toss him in that ditch."

"The ditch?" Woods repeated, mindlessly.

"You wanna leave him here for the cops to find? They'll come after all of us and there goes the job. I don't know about you guys but I need the bread."

Woods looked at Turkenton, who shrugged.

"The poor bugger's dead anyway," he said.

They took Agosta's shoulders and feet, struggled with the heavy body up and over a grassy bank, and tossed it into a drainage canal.

"Get this shit cleaned up."

With his boot Boyle pointed at the puddled blood and the red-soaked earth around it. They used straw and newspapers from the garbage cans, mopped up and kicked dirt and stones over the area, then followed Boyle back down the alley to the street.

Agosta's pickup truck was parked there, Harn Suk standing by it.

"There's that gook kid," Boyle said. He went up to him. "There a hospital or a sawbones around here?"

The young boy looked uneasily at the two pieces of stained towel the American held to him.

"A doctor, you know?" Boyle said.

"What happen?"

"Cut myself on a can of beans."

Harn Suk pointed at Boyle's ear.

"Cut there, too?"

"A cat scratched me, okay?"

With frightened doubt in his eyes, the boy looked past the three men in the direction of the alley he'd seen them walk out of.

"Where Mr. Agosta?"

"The fuck should I know? Inside havin' a beer. Look, I'm bleedin' to death here. Let's go, all right?"

Very reluctantly Harn Suk got into the pickup, Boyle alongside him, the other two climbing into the back. The truck made a U-turn, and sped away into the hot darkness.

Bugs bumped off open light shades on the telegraph poles, buzzed and zoomed back, trying again for incineration.

Marcus and Claire walked under the weak illumination toward the hotel entrance, both silent, both thinking about their dinner conversation, disturbed by it.

Especially Marcus.

If Claire was becoming suspicious of him, he was wondering how long it would take Boyle to feel the same way. Cops had to do a certain amount of acting, but some were better at it than others.

He was rolling it around his mind when he saw Agosta's truck pull up outside the hotel, and Woods and Turkenton get out of the back a little unsteadily. Then he saw Boyle get out, his hand bandaged, his ear taped over, and Harn Suk with tears streaming down his face. He strode over and confronted them, the anger building in him, asked them what had happened, although nobody had to tell him — Boyle with a hand bandaged, the young Thai boy in a state, Woods and Turkenton looking sheepish — a neon light in the sky couldn't have been any clearer.

Harn Suk burst into fresh tears; Boyle had bragged to him on the way back from the hospital.

"Mr. Agosta dead."

Marcus took an age to turn toward Boyle.

"Your handiwork, sonny boy?"

"He fucked with me," Boyle said, defiant. "Nobody fucks with me. He found that out."

"Boyle, you son of a bitch."

The words came out squeezed and flattened. Marcus was gun naked, the .45 was up in his room, and Boyle had to have his knife on him, but he didn't care. He was furious. Agosta had been nothing more than a dime-a-dozen street bopper, but he'd been worth two of a piece of garbage like Boyle.

"You goddamn *moron*."

Boyle set his jaw.

"You watch your mouth, buddy." He jerked his bandaged thumb at Harn Suk crying over his loss. "Plenty more where that came from."

Marcus looked over at Claire. Little white patches of shock were blotching her face. She held Marcus's gaze for a moment, looked at Harn Suk, then walked into the hotel and went up the stairs.

Patting at the tape on his ear, Boyle swaggered his oversized buttocks across the sidewalk and sat down on the bottom step of the hotel entrance.

Marcus turned to Turkenton. Woods was closer but Turkenton was ten years his senior, and should have been the more responsible of the two.

"Did you see it?"

"Yeah."

"Why the hell didn't you stop it? Do something?"

The tall Australian looked down at his boots.

"I would've needed a tank. You should've seen 'em. They went at it hammer and tongs."

Woods backed him up.

"Weren't nothin' we could do about it, coupla bear cats like that."

"I thought one of 'em was just going to go home with a sore head," Turkenton said. "But they pulled knives. If I'd stepped between 'em, I would've got me water cut off."

Marcus took a breath, forced himself down.

"What did you do with his body?"

"Dumped it in a ditch. A canal. Nobody'll find it for a while. And Boyle took his ID."

"But no money, huh?"

Turkenton licked his lips, embarrassed.

"Well, he took his wallet. I dunno if there was money in it."

"Get to bed. You too, Woods. On deck at five. And you'd better come down those stairs smarter than you're going up them." Marcus watched the two men shuffle into the hotel, then marched over to Boyle, who scrambled to his feet when he saw Marcus coming. There was still a lot of fight in him; he hadn't yet come down off his victory high.

"I want the wallet, Boyle."

"Bull-*shit!* Spoils of war."

Marcus was wearing a T-shirt and an open denim shirt hanging outside his belt. He put his left hand out, put his right one underneath his shirt at belt level, about where a holster would be.

"If I have to take it away from you, Boyle, you'll be lying down when I do it."

Marcus knew what would be going through the other man's head: he'd be remembering the time in the bar in New York when he hadn't believed there was a gun under the table. Now he'd be wondering if there was a gun in a belt holster.

He'd struck out once; Boyle would play the odds.

"I'm savin' it all up, cunt," Boyle said, flinging the wallet at Marcus. Marcus peeked inside it, made sure the scissored playing card was there, then walked over and handed the wallet to Harn Suk.

"Gonna split it, huh? You and the slope?"

"Okay, this is what you do," Marcus said to Boyle, holding himself back, trying mightily to not go upstairs, grab the Clark, come back down, and riddle Boyle where he stood. "You go up to your room. You come back down here at five ready to soldier. And if I ever hear you mention Agosta's name again, just once, I'll shoot both your eyes out. Now beat it. Get outa here."

"Sure, go ahead." Boyle raised his upper lip on one side. "You're runnin' no risk seein' I got this on my hand."

"You'll mend. Get out of my sight. Now!"

"Up your ass," Boyle said, turned, and took his time going into the hotel.

Marcus talked to Harn Suk, tried a few words of comfort, gave him a minute, then asked him about the arrangements for the next day, and whether or not he could do Agosta's job. Then he went up to Burroughs's room and told him what had happened. The Englishman received the news in silent disgust, went down to the street, got into the truck with Harn Suk, went over some maps with him, and established what he needed to know now that Agosta was not going to be around to tell him.

Lying down on his bed, the lights off, looking up at the dark, Marcus listened to the silence. The hotel was quiet; he heard Burroughs clumping up the stairs and going back to his room, then the sound of the truck driving off, its fading engine noise zipping up the night, leaving behind a hushed and empty street that led to a river and a jungle at the end of the world.

For the next several hours Marcus inhabited the room like a mummy, stretched out on his back staring at a ceiling he couldn't see. He thought about the argument, the perennial one about putting killers in jail and letting them out again after a while. The true killers did their time, came out, and killed somebody else. They killed people as a way of keeping score of their rotten, miserable, unhappy lives.

He'd have to kill Boyle soon, Marcus knew.

And Hinkler at the first opportunity. Because both men were riding a streak now.

Boyle.

Marcus was surprised.

He had to be pretty damn good if he'd got the better of a guy like Agosta.

At four-thirty he rose, washed, changed into heavy boots and jeans. He took the Rogers rig from his suitcase and slotted it on. Then he picked up the Clark, slapped in a clip filled with eight factory loads, pumped one up and set the safety, and dropped the pistol into the holster. He killed the light and was reaching for the door when somebody knocked on it.

"Yeah?"

"It's me."

Claire's voice.

Marcus had forgotten about the chore he had to perform; with Agosta dead, it would be up to him to tell her she wasn't coming.

She was standing there in the half-light when he opened the door, a kimono not quite covering her pajamas. Sleepless hours had left her looking drawn, her skin very pale.

"That outfit won't last two minutes in the jungle," Marcus said.

For a moment Claire let her eyes travel over him: the dark hair layered short and flat and unbrushed, the beenaround face, stubble enforcing the squared-off chin, the athlete's hard, solid shoulders.

"I've been thinking about it. If you do run into these bandits, and there's a gunfight, I'd be useless. And I don't like being useless."

"I know how you feel. Where will you go? Chiang Mai?"

"Yes."

"Where are you staying?"

"The Poy something. Poy Luang, I think."

"If I swing on by in a couple of days, can I buy you a drink?"

In the dim light of the forty-watt ceiling bulb in the corridor, Marcus got the impression she was looking at him in a way he hadn't seen before; not from Claire Tanner. He knew she was lying about the bandits; they weren't the reason she'd changed her mind. It was Boyle. She knew if she came, Boyle wouldn't have been able to keep his mouth off her. She could have ignored it but she had to know that he, Marcus, wouldn't have been able to. And she'd had ample evidence several hours back of what Boyle was capable of doing.

"You can buy me two drinks," Claire said, her eyes on his face.

"Okay then. Take care."

Marcus opened the door wider, close to her, her hair bunched and untidy, her warm woman smell coming to him, the slight chill in the dawn air tweaking her nipples, outlining them against the silk of her pajama top.

"You take care," she murmured.

He almost reached for her then, almost gathered her in, scooped her up. He was close to doing it, close to just grabbing her and taking her in onto the bed and forgetting about the trail and Boyle and Hinkler and Bendroit, and the whole goddamn thing.

He put a hand on her hair, lifted a tumbled wave back off her face, then forced himself to move past her, kept on moving down the dim corridor, and down the stairs to the street and the pickup truck that was coming fast around the corner.

7

THE RAIN HAD BEGUN AGAIN in the small hours and fell now out of a black sky in a steady and drearily constant downpour.

The dispirited weather reflected the mood in the pickup waiting in the darkness two hundred yards below the bridge border post, hidden from it by a bend in the river. Harn Suk, hollow-eyed and sleepless, sat behind the wheel peering through the windshield. The wiper blades had hardened long ago and smeared the water instead of clearing it. Burroughs sat next to him. He'd taken Marcus aside in the hotel entrance and explained that it was bad form for an officer to ride in the back of the truck with the men now that they were about to hit the trail — as CO, a certain amount of status had to be maintained. Marcus saw his point, and relegated himself to the rear again.

It was not a pleasant place to be.

Boyle had come downstairs with the bandage off his thumb and just a strip of plaster over his stitches; his knife hand looked sore, but in perfectly workable condition. His ear had evidently started bleeding in the night; the tape that clung to it was stained a dark red. He hadn't shaved and was still half asleep, his mouth opening on yawn after yawn, exhaling breath past teeth which hadn't known a toothbrush for a long time.

Woods and Turkenton looked beat and hung over; neither had yet got over the sight of seeing a man killed in a muddy alley.

Limbu was the only one who looked as if he'd slept; he was smartly turned out in pressed olive greens and freshly polished boots. He carried a fierce-looking kukri knife, the traditional Gurkha chopping sword, in a twelve-inch scabbard at the back of his belt. The other three were dressed for work, too: Boyle in leaf-pattern camouflage fatigues and jump boots, Woods and Turkenton in olive greens.

Nobody carried anything except Harn Suk, who had a small canvas bag with him. There were rain capes and bush hats supplied for everybody; the rest of their clothes had been left at the hotel and would be collected and taken to Chiang Mai.

The truck stayed parked, the rain slapping against its canvas top, not a shred of light anywhere to reflect off the black puddles pooling around its sides. For twenty minutes its occupants stayed immobile until, from somewhere near the river, a flashlight beam bored a brief hole through the night.

Burroughs appeared at the back of the truck.

"All right. Let's have you out."

He had the ability to keep his voice down and still imbue it with a tone of command, and the pickup emptied quickly.

The group hurried forward, seven men in rain capes and floppy hats, bunched together, wasting no time. Behind them one of Harn Suk's local associates materialized and drove the truck away.

The river appeared, a sluggish extension of the road, the hiss of rain-pelted water undercut by the mutter of an engine nearby. Marcus made out a jetty, then the outline of a flat-bottomed boat. They stepped into it and crouched amid a smell of fruit and vegetables, the boatman, wrapped in plastic sheeting, easing his craft out into the current.

The river could have been twenty yards wide or two hundred; there was no opposite bank to be seen. The boat slid forward, the put-putting engine straining against the heavy flow, the slow-roiling surface machine-gunned by the rain.

Fifteen minutes passed in this way before the boat slid alongside something, a different sound in their ears now as the rain hammered unresisting leaves.

One by one each member of the group uncoiled and stepped out of the boat into Burma.

Harn Suk led them up a track into a tangle of foliage that ate them up like a meal it had been expecting. Whatever ambient light had filtered through the downpour was blocked out as the trees closed overhead and the track, slippery and rugged, climbed a slope that didn't want to level out.

The first hour on the trail — which was wide enough only for two men abreast — was a sobering introduction to what they were in for. Burroughs and Harn Suk knew, having been there before, but the others were surprised at the steady climb, and unprepared for the uncertain footing which was the product of a previous month's rain. Boyle made by far the heaviest weather of it, puffing and blowing and complaining loudly about the terrain. When Burroughs called a rest halt after a couple of hours, as daylight was beginning to seep through the overhead cover, Boyle sagged onto a stump and said loudly, "About fuckin' time, too."

Burroughs did something then that Marcus had thought he might do: took an early opportunity to lay down the law to the only member of the group likely to give him trouble. He waited till the rest halt was almost over before he marched back to the rear of the line and confronted Boyle. Even dressed the same as everybody else, in the cape and the bush hat, Burroughs still exuded a military manner that set him apart. He wasn't the kind of officer who needed stripes or braid on show. Whatever his background was, he seemed to be in his element here, doing what he'd clearly been trained to do: run soldiers.

"Look here, Boyle. In the next three or four days we have some rough territory to cover, possibly an army of insurgents to get past, and a river we may have to shoot our way down. It won't be easy, but without discipline it will be impossible. We're going to move on now, and that's an order. If you choose to obey it, you will obey *all* future orders without question or comment. If you choose not to obey it, the trail will lead you back to Mae Sai."

Burroughs stalked back to the head of the group and kept walking, the rest falling in behind him. Boyle got off the stump, hawked heavily and spat, then ambled after the others spewing forth a torrent of obscenities, but not so loudly that he could be heard at the front of the line.

Their direction still lay north, the track continuing to rise as it curled through a forest murky with early morning gloom. Five thousand feet above them it had stopped raining, but it made little difference beneath their green cover; rainwater ten minutes old zigzagged down from leaf to leaf, and dripped and splotched onto the trail in unpredictable patterns.

They trudged uphill in a silent line for two more hours until the jungle wall, impenetrable so far, began to thin out and fall away. They could see a clearing up ahead as they emerged from the trees. It wasn't a natural clearing; perhaps twenty-five acres had been carved out of the jungle, the trees felled and the underbrush burned off. At the entrance to the clearing was a curious structure: three upright tree trunks, like roughly hewn telegraph poles, erected on one side of the trail where it widened to twenty feet. Three matching uprights stood opposite, two of them supporting wooden crosspieces raised high above the ground. Tied to the foremost one were rosettes of bamboo like small, many-bladed propellers.

Marcus peered up at the structure, and the figures beyond it, several male and female representations hacked out of tree trunks, the genitals grossly exaggerated.

"What do we have here?"

"An Akha sacred gate," Burroughs answered. "Most of the hill tribes are animists. They believe that spirits inhabit trees, streams, rocks, etcetera. Although as far as the Akhas are concerned, the thing they most believe in is opium."

They moved through the gate, the trail widening into a packed dirt road. The village itself was not an enthralling sight: an assortment of big and little bamboo huts standing on stilts six feet above the ground, the thatched roofs flopping over the huts like opened umbrellas.

The rain, which had eased to a stop now, had left behind a sea of mud on which goats and chickens, litters of squalling black pigs, grubby puppy dogs, and several brown-and-white cows wandered freely as if just released from an animal show. The men of the village sat on the verandahs of the huts and watched the women work. The women either pounded rice with flat, heavy poles, or prepared breakfast in blackened woks at an open stone fireplace. Their costumes verged on the fabulous; they looked as if barrels of streamers had fallen on them, as if they'd been pelted by gifts at a rich wedding. Their headdresses began with hundreds, thousands of fine green and yellow beads that hung all the way down to their waists in thick bright curtains. Twenty or thirty huge silver coins formed a solid layer on each side of a scalp piece made of beaten silver pearls. Festooned over the coins were silver baubles like plump bunches of grapes, and beneath these lay flat pieces of silver pounded into stirrup shapes fringed with delicate silver chains.

Marcus stared at the outfits, as astonished as anyone seeing an Akha woman for the first time.

"Have they just come from a parade?" he asked.

"That's their everyday costume," Burroughs said. "They

even sleep in those headdresses. The only time they take them off is when they wash their hair."

Harn Suk was talking with a woman near the cooking fire, and when he'd made a bargain with her, young girls began to bring bowls of food to everybody.

Boyle accepted his from a girl, smiling crookedly at her, blatantly checking her over. When he looked at what she'd given him, his expression changed.

"This is breakfast? This is what we eat?"

"You don't like Chinese tucker?" Turkenton asked him. "Try it. It's bloody good."

"I can't eat this shit."

Boyle dumped out his bowl onto the ground, narrowly missing the young woman's bare foot.

Burroughs was watching but said nothing; it was a soldier's prerogative to gripe about rations. He could have told Boyle that the hill tribes ate only what they grew; there wouldn't be anything else but rice and vegetables from now on.

The women also served the men of the tribe, most of whom ate quickly, then lay down on the verandahs of their huts. The women brought them embers from the fire which the men placed in the bowls of curvy hardwood pipes. From jacket pockets came dark brown cakes of dried opium; tiny corners were pinched off and dropped into the burning pipe bowls.

The men began to smoke slowly, their eyes glazing over, a vacant, faraway look creeping over their faces, the white smoke issuing thick and heavy from their slack mouths, clouding around their heads, and hanging in the air of the breezeless morning.

Apart from Burroughs and Harn Suk, none of the party had ever seen opium smoked before. It was a sad and depressing sight.

"The women don't smoke?" Marcus asked Burroughs.

"Only the older women. The younger ones don't have time. They do all the work."

"What do the men do?"

Burroughs nodded his head toward the hut opposite them and the smokers stretched out on the verandah.

"You're seeing what they do. The Akha men are addicted. Of all the tribes they're the heaviest smokers, them and the Meos. They're the poorest of the tribes, too, for exactly that reason."

Marcus watched the smokers, who lay on their sides blinking slowly, an eerie underwater quality about them, as if they'd been drowned, pronounced dead, then revived.

"They're no different from junkies anywhere," Burroughs said. "They'll do anything to get money. I was in an Akha village a few years ago and a man offered me his little girl, three months old, for the equivalent of twenty-five dollars."

"Charming," Marcus said.

Burroughs sipped a cup of tea and pointed up the slope to some huts at the back of the village.

"That's where the grandparents live. They've been opium smokers all their lives and now they're helpless as babies. Feebleminded, incontinent, wasting away. It's a degenerative drug, opium. Attacks the central nervous system." He put his cup down abruptly and said so everybody could hear, "We'll move on now."

They set off again, walking up through the village to its highest point. Behind them were the green hills they'd climbed through that morning with the river they'd crossed a brown streak in the distance, a rolling gray cloud bank hovering over it. Ahead thick curtains of rain mist were drawn across the forest, obscuring the far side and making ghosts of the trees a hundred yards up the track.

Low mountains sailed out of the mist as they climbed, three thousand feet above sea level now, a crispness in the air, their faces cool, their bodies hot from the heat trapped by their rain capes.

Above them narrow white waterfalls cascaded briefly over rocky outcrops like chalk marks drawn on cliffs. Small fields of soybeans and maize appeared, and tobacco, garlic, and upland rice ready for planting. Higher up, clinging precariously to steep hillsides, tea bushes grew next to severe rows of orange and *lamyai* trees.

A mile farther on Harn Suk stopped and motioned everybody off the trail. There was no urgency in his signals, so whatever he'd seen didn't bother him.

They stood in the trees and waited.

Down the trail came a man astride a heavy black bicycle which he rode, with amazing skill, in a kind of controlled skid down the muddy track. He was bare to the waist, and his entire upper body was covered in black tattoos. On his head sat a red cloth turban, and he sported a magnificent black mustache which seemed to have jumped his lip to his chin.

Marcus asked Burroughs about the tattooed cyclist, asked him what he was doing there.

"What we're supposed to be doing," the Englishman answered. "He's transporting precious stones. If you took that bicycle of his apart, you'd find a couple of blood rubies stuffed into the frame."

"Will we see anything of the mines?"

"We won't even get close. They're three hundred miles northwest of here. A mountain town called Mogok. It's one of the few places on earth where you can dig up fine rubies and sapphires."

"He's ridden that bike three hundred miles?" Marcus was impressed. "Where does he sleep? He wasn't carrying anything."

"In the Shan villages along the way. We've been in the Shan State since we crossed the border."

Marcus grabbed hold of a broad-leafed fern to help him up a steep section of the trail. The track alternatively flattened out, then rose, then flattened again, like steps built for a giant.

"And the tattoos?" he asked. "What's all that about?"

"Magic," Burroughs answered, hefting himself up an incline. "They're all magic designs against illness, baldness, impotency, poverty, or whatever they want to repulse. The Shans we'll meet on the river, the renegades, they'll have tattoos designed to repulse bullets. And tattoos to guide their own bullets as well," Burroughs added, glancing at Marcus.

The talk died as they settled down to a steady slog in and out of the jungle tunnels. The rain changed its mind continually, either coming at them in a fine, almost invisible spray, or breaking out of the sky in short violent bursts. Around noon Burroughs called a rest stop, during which they ate some cold rice cakes Harn Suk had bought at the Akha village, and drank rainwater caught in the mug-shaped leaves of a ficus tree.

Two hours later they were close to the village they'd been heading for.

The smell hit them long before the village came in sight; it was unmistakable, a stomach-turning stench.

When the trail opened up, and the village appeared, a flock of large-winged birds rose heavily at their approach and flapped off into the trees. It was three pigs and two cows that had held the birds' interest, and had evidently done so for a couple of days. They were the only things in the village alive or dead — there were no people, no dogs or chickens — the place was a deserted ruin. Most of the huts were tumbled in blackened heaps, thin wisps of smoke curling up from some in spite of the rain. The ground around the dwellings was deeply pockmarked, the earth gouged out in chunks. A stone grain mill lay in jagged pieces, and firewood, once so neatly stacked in the communal storage hut, had been blown all over the compound.

"Well," Turkenton said, surveying the wreckage, "they bashed up this place, didn't they." He kicked at one of the holes in the ground. "A gunship did that. This village has been strafed."

Burroughs confirmed it. It was a Shan village; the Burmese Army had staged one of their periodic attacks against suspected Shan insurgents. The village had also been shared by some KMT, as they found when they entered one of the huts which had been untouched by the raid.

The smell in here was different, worse in some ways than the smell of the dead animals outside.

It was a pungent chemical smell that tweaked their nostrils and smarted their eyes. The floor was a disgusting mess of tin and enamel dishes, mixing bowls, and plastic jerry cans of acetic anhydride. A piece of grubby cheesecloth hung from a nail above a chipped zinc tub containing traces of raw poppy resin, some old torn towels thrown over it, some half-full bags of sodium carbonate and lime next to it. Squat brown bottles that had once held chloroform and ammonium chloride overflowed from bamboo baskets, and lay around the floor like the aftermath of a drunken party.

In one corner a sheet of plastic partially covered by a brown paste of dried morphine, the extract from the poppy resin, was bunched up next to a broken box. Inside the box were the additives that went into Number Three heroin, the smoking heroin: caffeine, quinine, strychnine, scopolamine, ephedrine, novocaine, and paracetemol. None of the mess was the result of the raid; according to Burroughs, this was how a KMT heroin factory usually looked.

"They make heroin here?" Turkenton asked. "God, I've seen Chinese brothels neater than this."

Woods wrinkled his nose.

"Makes you want to rush out, buy a deck, and stick it in your arm, don't it?"

Even Boyle was turned off by the sight, and Limbu, who so far had given the impression of being impossible to unsettle, looked ill and went back outside.

Marcus found out later that Limbu hadn't properly understood what it was he was being hired to guard, and that when he'd discovered the truth he'd tried to get out of his contract, being totally antidrugs, but by then it had been too late. He'd given his word, so he'd honored it.

[114]

The village depressed everybody; it was a place to put behind them, but they were stuck there for a while; a rendezvous had been set up, and they were forced to wait around and suffer the charred and fetid smells.

Harn Suk found an iron pot and some bamboo cups in one of the huts, fetched water from the forest, and got a fire going. He and Burroughs drank a fast cup of tea and went off to reconnoiter a trail that came in from the east, the direction from which they were expecting the last member of the party. The rest of the group shucked their hot and sticky rain capes and sat on logs drinking tea, watched by the carrion birds waiting patiently in the trees for the intruders to leave.

Overhead the clouds were leaden and sluggish, and seemed to compress the atmosphere in the village. Boyle appeared particularly irritated by the surroundings, and constantly shifted around as if his boots were pinching him. Woods was showing Turkenton a photograph, talking to him about it, when Boyle leaned over and snatched it away.

"Not bad," he said, examining the shot. "Wouldn't mind dickin' that myself."

"Give it me back," Woods said.

"Gotta be nice up there, huh?" Boyle's mouth edged to one side and his thin eyebrows arched. "I'll bet it's downright dangerous when she gets a wide-on."

Turkenton spoke up.

"Hey, Boyle, take it easy. That's his girl."

Boyle's smile got a little dirtier.

"With big boobs like that it sure ain't his brother."

"Give it me back," Woods said again, harder this time.

"Bet you have to tie a two-by-four to your ass 'less you disappear up there, right, Reb?"

"Give it a breeze," Turkenton said. "It's getting boring."

"Butt out, Turkey. Me and this genelman from de Souwf are talkin' tail. How about it, Woods? She give good head?"

Woods got to his feet.

Marcus could see what was going through his mind: he

had to know that Boyle would have the knife on his arm, and Woods had already witnessed Boyle's dreadful skill with it. So he'd be looking for a weapon of his own.

If Marcus had been in Woods's shoes, his first thought would have been a stout piece of firewood; snatch up a piece and slam it into the side of Boyle's thick head like taking a cut at a baseball, getting his shoulders into it, breaking his wrists halfway through the swing. But the nearest piece of decent firewood was fifty feet away.

However, there were all kinds of weapons. Once, at a late-night coffee shop in the West End district, a couple of punks had tried to push Marcus around. He'd decked them both with a sugar dispenser.

"She ever sit on your teeth?" Boyle brought the photograph close to his nose and nuzzled it. "I'll bet that's a five-star main course."

Marcus knew what Woods would use: the water in the pot on the fire. It had long since stopped boiling, so it wouldn't scald Boyle but it would certainly distract him.

Moving easily, as if he'd decided to ignore the comments and just get some more tea, Woods picked up a rag, lifted the pot off its tripod stand, turned slowly, and hurled the hot water at Boyle's leering face.

It should have sloshed into his nose and mouth and cheeks, causing him to cry out and fling his hands up, exposing his beer gut to the hard right hand Woods was getting ready.

But it didn't.

Woods had made the same mistake that everybody did who got into a fight with Boyle: underestimated the man's astonishing speed and reflexes.

The hot water sailed over Boyle's shoulder, the knife jumping into his hand from his sleeve scabbard.

It was the second time Woods and Turkenton had witnessed that trick, and it was no less impressive for having seen it before.

It was the first time for Marcus. The guy was fast; a lot faster than he'd thought he'd be.

"Oh, you done it now," Boyle said to Woods, flapping his free hand as if he'd been badly burned. "You really done it now. I'm gonna have to seriously bleed you a little."

"Boyle."

Marcus said it quietly, but it carried in the still air.

"With you in a minute."

"Put it back on your arm, Boyle."

"Be glad to. Soon as I slice a few ounces off nutsy here."

Marcus took a half-step forward, just a brief little piece of movement, but it focused Boyle's attention.

"I got a job to do, Boyle. I got to get a hundred keys of crap down a river and across a border, and I need men with guns to do it."

"One less won't hurt."

"We're already one less because of you."

Boyle moved to his left away from Marcus. Woods turned with him. He'd slipped his belt out of his pants and was wrapping it around his left fist. It was all he knew to protect himself against a man with a knife.

"So we'll be two less," Boyle said. "It won't matter none. That wop wasn't no soldier. And as for this dummy, I never met a cracker yet could hit the side of a shithouse."

Marcus brushed back his shirt, revealing the Clark .45.

"Boyle, if I don't stop this, you'll kill Woods, won't you?"

"Fuckin' A. The sonofabitch tried to scald me."

"But to stop it I may have to kill you. So you're forcing me to choose," Marcus said. Then he added slowly, "Guess who I'll choose."

"Bullshit, Dubin. You're not gonna ace me. I get the grenade launcher, and when you get on the river you're gonna need one of them babies."

"You see those birds up in the trees, Boyle? Right now they're waiting on two cows and three pigs." Marcus drew the gun with slow deliberation. "If that blade isn't back on your arm by the time I've finished telling you to put it there, those birds'll be waiting on four pigs."

It was such a colossal insult, put the way it was, that

Boyle's jaw snapped shut in anger. But when he saw the gun come up, he had no hesitation in slipping the knife back into its sheath.

"Okay," he said, burning. "But you and me, we're gonna discuss this another time. I fuckin' promise you that."

Marcus wheeled around in Limbu's direction. Like Turkenton, the Gurkha had watched the drama with an immobile cup of tea held in front of him like a beggar's bowl.

"Limbu. Let's see that chopper of yours."

Limbu reached behind him for his kukri. It was a fearful-looking thing with a very wide, banana-shaped blade about a foot long and a quarter of an inch thick, and was more like a cleaver or a short sword than anything else. There was an Asiatic snake named after the kukri, because its large back teeth were curved in the same manner as the Gurkha weapon.

Both kukris were very dangerous.

Marcus pointed at Boyle.

"From now on your job is to watch this man. If he makes one wrong move, cut off his ear, then call me. You understand?"

Limbu nodded, held the kukri by his side, and fixed his dark, impassive eyes on Boyle.

"Fuckin' headhunter," Boyle said, and glowered at Limbu, his fight with Woods forgotten now that he had a new source of antagonism.

The group broke up and dispersed to various parts of the shattered village, keeping upwind of the dead animals.

Marcus went off by himself looking for something special.

A target.

The speed with which Boyle had got that knife into his hand was staying with him. It had shaken his confidence, and without confidence he didn't have a hope.

He entered the factory hut, picked up an empty plastic jerry can, walked into the jungle, and followed a track cut through shrubs and low bushes and stringy grass roots that grabbed for his boots. There was no insect noise, no bird song, no sound at all except for the chafing of some tall trees, their tops stirred by a breeze that made no impression on the stolid ground-level heat. The bush fell away into a natural clearing, a tree on the far side bent over at a crazy angle. Marcus hung the can on it, about chest-high, then paced off fifteen yards.

He settled the Clark in the holster, which was positioned just in front of his left hip.

It was beautifully designed and made, the holster; a holster built for a quick pull.

A crossdraw model.

It was fashioned from a single piece of firm, stiff cowhide three-elevenths of an inch thicker than was normal for a holster, and cut in a high, looping shape with a scooped outline like a violin. It had been lined with soft suede and turned in on itself, and the edges lockstitched with waxed linen thread, then caught two-thirds of the way down by a brass tension adjustor.

A channel had been molded down the center line so the sights of a gun wouldn't snag, and a metal shank had been inserted down the rib to angle a gun handle in the direction of the draw.

A holster for shootists.

Marcus assumed the stance Teddy Hepplewhite had taught him: left foot slightly advanced, body turned a fraction in the same direction. He stood still for a moment with his hands in the air, palms level with his head, as if he were surrendering.

Then he drew and fired.

The noises were too close together to separate: the roar of the heavy pistol, and the thunk of the jerry can being blown out of the tree. The kick was a heavy one, yet there'd been no flinch in Marcus's hands, no anticipation of the blast. Teddy Hepplewhite had taught him to be "surprised" when he fired a gun, as if he hadn't been expecting it to go off.

To somebody casually watching him, unprepared for

Marcus's move, it would have been over before they'd had a chance to see how he'd done it.

They might have thought they'd missed something somewhere, yet it had all been there.

The lower part of his right arm, pivoting down from the elbow, had dipped across his body, and his hand, as if bouncing on rubber, had come up with the Clark in it, his thumb knocking off the safety when the gun was six inches clear of the holster. Then his left hand had grabbed his gun hand in the Weaver grip, and pushed his arm straight out in front of him at eye level, and he'd fired.

It was as simple as that, yet it had been done so smoothly he'd achieved extraordinary speed.

His arms were the only part of his body he'd moved. There'd been no knee bending, no crouching. Teddy Hepplewhite always laughed at the walk down Main Street in the movies. Some of the cowboys would actually grab their crossdraw holsters with their weak hand, risking their own bullet through their wrist. And the cops on TV were even stupider, Teddy said. Crouching down when they drew as if they were ducking something. Crazy. How could you expect accuracy with your body going one way, and your gun going another?

Marcus returned the gun to the holster and pulled twenty-five more times without firing, then went over and examined the target.

The Clark had hit a touch higher than he'd aimed, but it wouldn't matter; the hand load he'd be using when he went up against Boyle was lighter than the factory round he'd just shot, so it would hit slightly lower anyway.

As short as it had been, Marcus was satisfied with the test. If he'd been back home in Atlanta, trying out a new piece, he would've put a hundred rounds through it out at the range, wearing his B&L Quiet-Ears, and his Kali-chrome safety glasses, and using loads like #68 Hensely and Gibbs sized a fraction larger than the slugged diameter of the barrel. But out here, in the moist heat of a rain-soaked jungle, in the border reaches of a remote Asian country, a one-round test would have to do.

He arrived back in the village in time to see Burroughs and Harn Suk coming in. Behind them walked a man leading four horses, a hill trader, a Meo tribesman who looked Chinese. His hair was worn short in something akin to a crew cut but with a plaited queue dangling down between his shoulder blades. Beneath a struggling mustache was a beard that looked like a dozen wispy strands of hair sewn to his chin. His clothes were the traditional uniform of the hills: indigo jacket and pants, nothing on his feet, and a fat, hollow silver necklace like a yoke around his neck.

His horses were tan-colored Tibetan ponies, short and thick through the shoulders; sleepy-looking docile beasts with close-cropped manes and long tails. All of them had packsaddles lashed to their backs, sturdy wooden panniers with a double pommel. These held a variety of bundles, two of which, wrapped in blue plastic, were immediately unloaded and unrolled on the ground.

Blue steel shone dully, and the faint, sweet aroma of gun oil rose into the still air.

The trader had carried the guns a hundred miles through the hills from Laos. They'd been bought to Agosta's order after Burroughs had specified the weapons he'd wanted. Burroughs had subsequently made sure that the men he'd hired were experts in the weapons he'd chosen. They tested them there and then, taking not much longer than Marcus had, repacked them in their blue bundles, lashed them to the horses, and gratefully left the village to the birds in the trees.

Harn Suk led them down a trail heading west, going cross-country now, moving toward the Kok, which lay hidden behind low hills. They made good time but they needed capes and hats again when they were ambushed by a wall of rain which sheeted down for the next half hour, leaving the track slick and treacherous. Giant stands of bamboo leaned over the party, plunging them into half-light, and banyan trees, their trunks strangled by snakey lianas, filtered forty-eight hours of rain squalls down onto their heads.

Sound came back into the world: the screech of birds, the howl of unseen monkeys, the snorting of the horses laboring for footing on some of the steeper parts of the track. The vegetation constantly changed; the bamboo groves would give way to stiff explosions of ferns, replaced in turn by broad teak saplings or shoulder-high grasses, or clumps of a delicate tree whose leaves crumbled at the merest touch. Sponge-like lichens clung moistly to exposed rocks around which jungle orchids sprouted, white or red or purple-spotted, colorful little surprises against the solid wall of green.

The light changed, too; the way ahead would be dark one moment as if night had come, then a hundred spears of sunlight would slash down, quiver and shake for a minute, then wink out.

Several miles farther on the forest stopped the way forests do in fairy tales, suddenly and without warning, and they sloshed into a rocky stream that gurgled through cropped grass as smooth and green as the surface of a golf course. It was a forerunner of the rivers that would have to be crossed, the first of which appeared a mile later like a trap beneath a clump of high reeds. A narrow stretch of gushing white water, it was a tiny offshoot of a branch of the Salween, which rose in the mountains of eastern Tibet to make the fifteen-hundred-mile trip to Burma, only knee-deep, but drenching all the same, and difficult to cross with horses. The trail opened and flattened out for a while, making the going easier, allowing them to walk with a regular stride.

"Can I ask you a question?" Marcus said, drawing level with Burroughs. "If this is opium country, where are all the magic poppy fields?"

"We've passed several today," Burroughs said. "Perhaps you didn't recognize them."

Marcus didn't get it; he knew what poppies looked like; pretty things on long green stalks.

An hour later, as they were rounding the side of a hill, Burroughs pointed ahead to a piece of land.

"You wanted to see a poppy field?"

Halfway up the hill the green cover gave way to a long wide spread of blackened earth topped by rain-sodden gray ash.

"They've just finished burning off," Burroughs said. "If we'd been here a couple of months ago all the hills would have been on fire. Smoke on the horizon in every direction. You have to come around Christmas to see the bloom; then the hills are just red-and-white carpets rolling on for miles all throughout the Triangle. A magnificent sight, botanically speaking."

Marcus peered up at the hill and its blackened side. A decrepit mess of scorched earth and broken stubs, it looked washed-out and barren, and about as productive as a sand pit. The track they were following eventually brought them to the edge of the field, where Burroughs stopped to pick up something from the ground. He showed it to Marcus: a dry green poppy bulb.

"*Papaver somniferum*," he said. "Scratch any other type of poppy in the world and all you'll get is a sticky sap. Scratch this one, and you've got opium."

Marcus took the bulb from him. It looked as if a three-tined fork had been raked down its sides, wounding it a dozen times all the way around the pod.

"Looks ordinary enough. Could you grow it in your garden?"

"If your garden was at least two thousand feet high and subject to months of torrential rain," Burroughs said. "But the soil would still determine the quality of the opium."

"It's like pot, huh?" Marcus said, tossing the pod away. "Stronger depending on where it's grown."

"Very much so. The poppies with the highest morphine content of any are grown in Tasmania, believe it or not."

Burroughs seemed happy to talk; he was the only one of the group who appeared to be enjoying himself. Give him a dog and a walking stick, Marcus thought, and he'd be the typical Englishman out for a healthy stroll in the woods.

They settled down to a steady rhythm, covering the country at a good clip when the rain held off and the going wasn't too hard. They lost most of their light before long when the sun dragged itself down behind the distant mountain range that sheltered the Irrawaddy River 350 miles away in the land of the original Burmans. Even though they'd been on their feet for fourteen hours, Burroughs kept up a fast pace, and it paid off when something swam out of the mist ahead, faded, then came back into focus: a dozen huts on a cleared hillside.

It was a Lahu village, the owners of the poppy fields they'd been seeing for some time now, and much like the Akha village where they'd breakfasted: the xenophobic dogs that rushed out to bark at them, the chickens, the cows, pigs, and kittens wandering around, and the children shouting at their games seemed interchangeable.

The women cooked dinner for everybody, the ubiquitous rice and vegetables again which, this time, Boyle did not turn down. Harn Suk was also able to buy a gourd of Lao, a sake-like rice liquor that was deceptively strong. Boyle had two large cupfuls, stretched out in the hut the foot soldiers were to share, and passed into oblivion, exhausted by the day's hike.

"Too bad," Turkenton remarked, looking at the snoring, inert form. "He was scheduled to be our after-dinner speaker."

Marcus and Burroughs were housed in a neighboring hut and ate their food watched by a group of men who sat on the verandah smoking opium. Burroughs talked about the day, sounding pleased with the way things had gone, although he was a little less sanguine about their prospects for the following day.

"There are two problems that could arise. The rivers are higher than I thought they'd be and getting the horses across could be difficult, but we won't know that till we see what we're up against. Wei Chun will be our main concern. I'm a bit worried about him. He doesn't enjoy a wonderful reputation." He looked up as Harn Suk came in with some tea. Marcus switched to it, not wanting to be ambushed by the rice liquor.

"Have you met him, Harn?" Burroughs asked. "Wei Chun?"

"One time. With Mr. Agosta." Harn Suk's face dropped when he said the name.

"What's he like?"

"One minute good. One minute bad."

"That's what I've heard," Burroughs said. "A very unpredictable chap."

Marcus drank some tea, needing all the restorative he could get; his shin muscles were on fire, and his feet ached badly.

"It sounds like we're gonna be outnumbered," he said. "Agosta told me he has an army."

Burroughs grunted; a derisive sound.

"A ragtag lot. He has a force of about three thousand men, and he runs them the way his warlord father ran his bandits in Szechwan. I understand that recaptured deserters are beaten to death in front of their old comrades as a lesson to all." Burroughs looked away for a moment, then glanced at Marcus, uncomfortable about something. "I've also been told he does the same thing whenever he catches a DEA man."

"And you figure he'll suspect me?"

"Well . . ." Burroughs gave his version of a shrug, a slight inclination of his head, "you're obviously not a military man. He's a soldier, he'll see that. So he could wonder who you are." The Englishman took a quick sip from his tea. "You brought your passport, did you?"

Marcus tapped his top pocket.

"Right here."

"Then he can hardly accuse you of being a spy, can he?"

"Hardly," Marcus said. "More tea, Captain?"

Burroughs had been right about the rivers. They met the first one several miles from the village, the world gradually swimming back into postdawn wakefulness, the rain, which had drummed on the roofs of the huts most of the night, dropping away like a falling gray blanket. The streams were fast-flowing and rocky-bottomed, the swirling water knee-high in most places, but with the riverbeds potholed and uneven, the men often sank up to their armpits and, once or twice, lost their footing altogether. It made a mockery of wearing their rain capes so they packed them on the horses and kept going, drenched to the skin.

White-water streams veined across their path all day but none was too deep to be waded; they locked arms and formed a safety chain, and held each other against the tug of the current, the stolid ponies, unafraid of the water, acting as welcome anchors. Only one of the rivers was bridged, a tree bridge which was another rendezvous point. A little way beyond it, emerging from a solitary bamboo hut, two teenagers appeared.

In their Kodak logo T-shirts, jeans, and multistriped track shoes, and with their fashionable full heads of hair, they looked as if they'd just arrived from the streets of Bangkok. The only thing that distinguished them from any big-city Asian youths was the Soviet AKM assault rifles they carried.

After Harn Suk had had a quick word with them, the young men shouldered light backpacks, and set off up the trail.

"They're KMT," Burroughs explained to Marcus. "Wei Chun's men. They'll guide us in."

The village came out of the distance some time later. The two KMT youths led them a tortuous snake dance to avoid the booby traps their general had planted, and as they got closer to the compound Marcus saw that the place was deserted.

The village was a stage stop for Wei Chun's caravans, as was demonstrated when his two young soldiers uncovered a piece of flooring in one of the larger huts, revealing a food store in a hole in the ground. The teenagers threw some sesame oil into two big woks on a wood fire and served up a makeshift meal of canned dace — a carp-like fish — water chestnuts, bean curd, and agar and turnip slivers. As a postprandial extra, some Thai cigars were produced, their tobacco aromatic with the scent of tamarind seeds. After that there was little to do but sit around and wait for the arrival of the man they'd traveled halfway around the world to meet.

It was an hour before anybody sighted anything.

"There," Limbu said, pointing.

Marcus, standing next to him, couldn't see a thing for a moment, then a green strip on the hill shimmied for a second before the shredding mists closed ranks, cutting off his view.

"How many?" Burroughs asked Limbu.

"Twenty-six. Three horses."

Like white cotton candy, clouds sailed through the valley blotting out most of the surroundings, and it was a good forty minutes before the first of the convoy appeared over the ridge about a hundred yards below them.

Harn Suk spoke to Burroughs.

"Wei Chun will make himself . . ." he searched for a word — "strong in front of his men. He pretend to be very big man. You must have . . ." The language defeated him and he pantomimed a bow.

"Respect," Burroughs finished for him.

"Respect. Yes."

Watching the band of men getting closer, Burroughs spoke for everybody's benefit.

"This chap that's coming is used to power. He's been brought up to it. His father had fifty thousand men under him, and even Chiang Kai-shek had to respect him. But this man gets no respect from anybody important, and that must rankle. So I think it would be wise if we pandered to him. Buttered him up. If he felt insulted I've got a good idea he'd call off the deal."

"What is he, a chink?" Boyle said to nobody in particular. "I'm not crawlin' to no goddamn chink. Fuck him."

Burroughs said nothing, and Marcus let it go, too. They both knew that Boyle wouldn't be quite so brave facing a large bunch of armed men.

The two young soldiers went out to meet the oncoming group, taking, Marcus noticed, as Burroughs surely had, their Russian assault rifles with them.

"We go here now," Harn Suk said, and led the way around to the back of one of the bigger huts. Apparently there was protocol to be observed.

Burroughs called Boyle, who ambled over, taking his time about it, and the group waited there out of sight listening to the stamp and whinny of the horses getting closer, and the tread and movement of a body of men.

Harn Suk gave it a moment, then went through the door into the house. They heard the sound of boots clumping onto the wooden floor, the scrape of a table being shifted, a man's voice, loud and guttural; then Harn Suk reappeared looking a little scared. He motioned to Burroughs.

"You come now. Everybody."

The party trooped inside.

The man who'd commandeered the hut's only table and chair looked them over, and was in turn studied by everybody else. He was about fifty, a plump-faced Chinese with extremely elongated eye folds. His eyebrows looked plucked, and there was a crease above his nose that could have been the result of a lifelong frown. The face was too fleshy to show cheekbones, the nose had broadened with the advance of years, and the mustache he wore was like a third eyebrow sprouting above his heavy lips. His chin was obscured by his hand, which held a fat cheroot to his mouth as if he'd glued it there and was waiting for it to stick.

He wore a field dress uniform: a battle jacket with numerous buttoned pockets, khaki trousers, American boots, and a soft cloth military cap that might have been old enough to be a legacy of the Sino-Japanese war.

Looking at him, Marcus wondered if the reason he kept his hand on the cheroot in his mouth was in order to show off the Rolex Oyster glittering on his wrist. Marcus had to smile about that — they were in a wood-and-bamboo hut in the middle of a Burmese jungle, and the world's biggest dope peddler was showing off his wristwatch as if he were sitting in the Polo Lounge in Los Angeles.

A dozen soldiers flanked Wei Chun, carbon copies of the two teenagers who'd guided them in from the tree bridge. They were all under twenty-one, all dressed in sneakers and jeans and talking T-shirts, some wearing baseball caps with Bell or Exxon or Ford logos on them. They carried a variety of automatic rifles: M16s and Soviet RPKs, Kalashnikovs, and the Czech copy, the M58, and a few had Chinese stick grenades dangling from their webbing belts like long brown truncheons. Most of the men had darker skins than Wei Chun, being the offspring of Chinese fathers and Shan mothers. Some had features that were pure Tibetan.

Showing off his lung power, Wei Chun sucked on the cheroot and blew out a globe of smoke the size of a basketball. His eyes roamed the men in front of him before he stabbed the fat cigarette at Burroughs, recognizing an officer in command.

"Who?" he grunted. He had a few words of English and was proud of it.

Burroughs brought his heels together and threw him a smart salute, the British kind in which the forearm hinges at the elbow and vibrates for a second.

"Captain Burroughs. Good afternoon, General."

The drug lord was pleased. He understood the word "general." He quarter-turned in his chair toward the men around him to make sure they'd noted the snappy salute he'd been given. He returned the salute with a puff of smoke.

"Brit-ish?" He knew an English accent when he heard one.

"Yes, General."

The rank again. Wei Chun decided he liked Burroughs. His gaze washed slowly over Burroughs's men, evaluating them thoughtfully. His examination stopped when he got to Limbu and, speaking Thai, he rumbled some words to Harn Suk, who translated for Burroughs.

"He ask what tribe Limbu."

Wei Chun had thought he was from the hills, and was wondering if he was a Kachin or a Naga.

"Gurkha," Burroughs told Wei Chun. "British Army."

The warlord was impressed; he'd heard of the Gurkhas, and looked at Limbu in a different light. The man he'd perceived to be a humble tribesman from the northwest of Burma was now revealed as a legendary fighter from the Himalayas.

"Gurkha," he said. "Brave," and again gave that quarter-turn toward his men, this time as if he were saying "Take a lesson." He lighted on Boyle next and made a comment that caused his men to laugh.

Boyle instantly bristled.

"What'd he say about me?"

Harn Suk was happy to tell him.

"He say that one eat well."

"Tell him to blow it out his chink ass."

"Steady," Burroughs said, making it sound like an order.

The soldiers were still laughing, and their leader had a smile on his mouth, too. Marcus suspected that this was just the calm before the storm, and the way Wei Chun kept glancing at him, and sliding his eyes away as if he weren't really interested, he figured he was going to be caught in the center of it when it broke.

The warlord pointed at Turkenton, who stood half a head above anyone else in the room.

"Brit-ish?"

"Australian."

That didn't impress Wei Chun; he'd seen a million Australian tourists when he'd owned a villa in Chiang Mai, and hadn't thought much of them.

"You?" He blew smoke in Woods's direction.

"I'm from Tennessee," Woods said cheerfully.

Burroughs was about to tell Wei Chun that that was a state in America, but Wei Chun looked interested and said, "Jonnah Karsh."

"What?" Woods said.

"Jonnah Karsh." The general made a motion like strumming a guitar.

"Johnny *Cash*," Woods said, understanding. "Sure. Nashville, Tennessee. I'm a Waylon Jennings man, m'self."

Wei Chun forgot about Woods, saving the best till last. The end of his cheroot glowed red as he clamped his mouth around the stem and stared at Marcus.

"Where Agosta?" he asked.

"Dead," Burroughs answered him.

"Real dead," Boyle said behind him.

Wei Chun didn't know the word.

"Tai," Harn Suk said, dropping his chin.

The news didn't please the general. He brooded about it for a minute, appearing to take it as a personal affront, glaring at Marcus as if he were the one responsible. He took one last drag at his cheroot, then suddenly flung it on the floor, grabbed clumsily for the holster hanging at his waist, jerked out a pistol, and fired two shots into the roof. The gun, a vintage Chinese Browning, made a colossal noise in the enclosed space, its muzzle waving wildly around before pointing at Marcus's chest.

"DEA!" Wei Chun yelled. "You DEA!"

[131]

The echo of the gunshots took a while to die in the silence. Wei Chun looked furious, and the smiles were off his men's faces. They shuffled and straightened and gripped their weapons tighter.

Marcus was pretty certain the man was just blustering, putting on a show in front of his troops, but it still took something to step forward toward the leveled gun.

"No." He pointed a finger at himself. "Not DEA. If the DEA find me . . ." He drew a finger across his throat.

Wei Chun searched Marcus's face, checked his unmilitary clothes, the blue work shirt and the chinos. He slammed the pistol onto the table and snapped his fingers impatiently.

"Pars-port."

Marcus handed it over without a qualm because he was sure that Wei Chun only pretended to read English.

He got a nasty shock.

"Marr-Kuss."

It seemed to Marcus that the air vibrated with his name as if a gong had been struck, or as if he'd been announced into a room full of waiting people.

"That's where I was born, Marcus, Iowa. My name's Dubin." He turned to Harn Suk. "Tell him."

The boy translated.

Marcus waited, not looking at Boyle, wondering if he knew that U.S. passports listed only the state the bearer was born in, not the town. He was also wondering if the name Marcus would twig his memory and, if it did, whether he'd start wondering if that was just too much of a coincidence.

Wei Chun's frown hardened as he struggled with the broken machine-printed type.

"Buff-a-lo," he read out under the words "Birthplace — Lieu de Naissance."

"That's where it was issued," Marcus said.

Thoroughly confused, Wei Chun did what he always did when something baffled him: got rid of it. He slapped the passport closed and flipped it away from him. It landed at Boyle's feet, where it lay ignored. Boyle was looking at Marcus but with an expression Marcus couldn't read.

"Let's cut all the crap," Marcus said. He nodded at Harn Suk. "Tell him we're here to buy heroin."

The warlord picked up on the word.

"Heroin," he said. "Heroin bad." Then he rumbled a laugh, checking behind him, and the soldiers joined in on cue. He clicked his fingers, one of his men responding by stepping forward and putting a small oilcloth bag on the table. His chief opened it, took out a stub of candle, a box of matches, and a piece of aluminum foil about the size of a cigarette paper. He opened the matchbox, pushed out the inner box, and emptied the matches. Wei Chun struck one of them on the matchbox, lit the candle, and let the wax slide down the side and drip onto the table, then squished the base of the candle into the melted wax. He dipped two fingers into the oilcloth bag and brought out some small pieces of a hard substance that looked like pink pebbles off a driveway.

Marcus was pretty sure that this was Red Chicken, the Number Three heroin that Agosta had told him about.

Wei Chun dropped a few pieces onto the foil and began to pass the foil over the candle flame. Almost immediately a pale halo of smoke rose from the heroin chips, a wispy, tobacco-like smoke that was practically odorless. Wei Chun picked up the matchbox cover, brought it down to the smoke, put his mouth around the box, and sucked up some fumes.

Talking about it later, Burroughs said the technique was known as playing the mouth organ, and that Wei Chun wasn't an addict but had been simply showing off in front of the foreigners.

The warlord quit his little demonstration after a few puffs, snuffed out the candle, and returned his works to the cloth bag.

"Heroin bad," he said again, sounding a little sleepy.

Harn Suk handed the cut playing card to Marcus, who held it up for Wei Chun's inspection. The general turned his head and shouted something in a slurred voice. A moment later hooves clattered on the verandah and three ponies were led into the room, not liking the board floor and tossing their heads in protest. Each horse was loaded with a bundle packed on either side of its saddle in the same manner as the trader's ponies: in blue plastic sheeting caught by ropes. The soldiers removed the bundles and dropped them to the floor. Marcus chose one at random, and this one was unwrapped and its contents spread out for examination.

It could have been an order for a cut-rate bakery.

Lumpy, gray, unsifted flour it looked like, packed in five-pound clear plastic bags, seven of them, folded at the top and closed by double elastic bands.

Marcus knew this was supposed to be heroin base and not the finished product, but he had no idea how to test its quality, or even if he was supposed to. He did know that anybody who put heroin on their tongue was crazy, so he settled for opening a bag, taking a pinch of the powder between thumb and forefinger, and letting it crumble back in again. He resealed it, and counted the bags when all the bundles had been unwrapped. There were forty-four bags in all, and with 5 pounds in each bag that would make the correct amount: 220 pounds — 100 kilos.

He put the playing card on the table.

Wei Chun produced his half of the card and slid the two sections together. They butted up in an exact fit.

Appearing now to be very happy with the world, the general pushed his bulk up out of the chair. He reminded Marcus of a department-store Santa Claus at the end of a full day.

"Guns," he said, waving the split playing card. "Many guns."

Marcus figured it. Over a year's period Wei Chun

had been paid, counting in this last payment, a total of $1,800,000, and if he had three thousand men, as Burroughs contended, that worked out to $600 a head. The Shan United Army should be a formidable force, but somehow Marcus doubted it.

The drug lord nodded his pleasure at Marcus and Burroughs, and wandered smilingly out of the door followed by his men and his horses.

The room relaxed, everybody trading glances, even Burroughs seeming relieved. Turkenton picked up Marcus's passport and handed it to him.

"You're lucky he didn't smoke it," he said. "Jesus Christ, what an actor that bloke is. He could give Laurence Olivier a run for his money."

They trooped outside in time to see Wei Chun's party disappearing over the ridge into the drizzle. He'd left ten of his soldiers behind as shipment guards — part of the bargain he'd made with Agosta — but with Agosta not around to check them, Wei Chun had cheated. It was obvious to everybody. The ten soldiers, all of whom had been inside the house, no longer carried a flashy array of automatic rifles; they'd been left with some rusty-looking eight-round Garands, and some Czech ZH 29s, which had been the Thai Army's rifle in the Second World War.

"Looks like we been flimflammed," Woods said.

Boyle was more vociferous.

"Will you look at what that bastard left us? There ain't a decent piece between the lot of 'em."

"I don't reckon he thinks much of our chances," Turkenton said.

Boyle spun on him.

"What?"

Woods chuckled, shaking his head as he watched the last of Wei Chun's force drop out of sight.

"He's a smart ol' boy, that one. He's not gonna risk losin' those Ruskie forty-sevens."

Boyle's mouth turned in on itself as he shouted at Harn Suk.

"Just how many of them bandits there gonna be, huh? I'd really like to know that. I really fuckin' would."

Surprisingly, it was Burroughs who replied; he had his own reasons for doing so.

"Hard to say. At least thirty or forty, I should imagine."

"Thirty or *forty?*" Boyle looked horrified. "I didn't sign on for no suicide mission. Nobody told me we was goin' up against an entire fuckin' squad. Look at us, for crissakes. We got five guys know how to soldier, and ten kids from Romper Room with rifles wouldn't stop a fox terrier. And we're goin' up against forty dope-crazed slopes? Outnumbered more'n two to one? Screw that!" He rounded on Marcus, anger puffing his face. "Dubin, you gotta be the moneybags now. Pay me, I'm out of it."

As if he were pondering a difficult question, Marcus said, "I don't get it. I mean, I'm going, and all I've got is a forty-five. You've got a weapon that can blow a dozen men away, and yet you're the one wants to drop out. How do you explain that?"

"You're outa your fuckin' gourd, that's how I explain that. All of you. I'm goin' back the way I came. In one piece."

"In one very large piece," Marcus said.

"You watch your mouth, dad. Gimme my bread. I was promised two grand. I'll settle for half."

Marcus didn't hesitate. He reached for the backpack Harn Suk was carrying.

"Okay. I'll pay you off. But I want a formal resignation."

"What?" Boyle screwed up his face as if a dreadful smell had invaded his nostrils. "You're kiddin'. You want it on *paper?* Here? Middle of a goddamn jungle?"

"An oral resignation will do. If you want your money you have to say, 'I'm quitting, Mr. Dubin, because I don't have enough guts to make a pair of yellow garters.' Go ahead, say it and I'll give you the thousand."

"Okay . . . all right . . ." The words hardly made it out of Boyle's mouth. "I'll stay . . . I got somethin' to stick around for now. Somethin' to look forward to."

"Mr. Boyle has decided to join us after all," Marcus announced.

Boyle leveled a pudgy finger at him.

"Better hope the chinks get you, Dubin, 'cause I'm gonna fuck you over so bad . . ."

Burroughs took control then. He called the trader, who repacked the heroin, and loaded it onto his horses; then the party set out, heading west again, their numbers swelled by the KMT contingent with their antique rifles.

Leading one of the pack ponies, Turkenton said to Woods, "Hey, Woodsie. What odds do your army advisers recommend for a combat sit?"

"Four-to-one your way."

"Same as the Aussie advisers."

"What would your guys say," Woods asked, "about two-to-one against?"

"They'd tell you to stay home in bed with your hat on."

Woods grinned.

"So would our guys," he said.

8

HEADING WEST AGAIN into new country, they walked in a steady descent under fat, gray clouds that gathered lugubriously overhead, trapping a murky sun. Toward evening they reached the village they'd been making for, a Shan village on the edge of the Kok River, the huts poking out over the water supported by stilts sunk into the riverbank. To Marcus the river here looked only distantly related to the glimpse he'd got of it back across the border in Thailand. It was narrower and darker, a racy-looking stream now, a canoeist's delight.

The party ate dinner on the verandah of the main house; they'd been accommodated in two huts again, Wei Chun's soldiers camping out under a piece of plastic sheeting. Mugs of Mekong whiskey were served with the meal, which went down very well. Limbu didn't drink but he seemed happy to watch Woods and Turkenton enjoy themselves. Boyle, who'd been in a smoldering sulk ever since his attempted resignation, removed himself outside, where he drank his whiskey glowering bitterly at the river, distrustful of it, and of the jungle on the opposite bank that rose straight up like a huge green butterfly taking wing.

Harn Suk enlisted the aid of the village headman, who

drew a map of the river from the village to the Thai border. He made a mark at two points where there were rapids, telling Burroughs, through Harn Suk, that they were dangerous with the river as fast as it was now, and would have to be portaged.

It wasn't good news; they'd be vulnerable at those two points, and the bandits would be sure to attack at one of them. That the bandits *would* attack was beyond question; their spies would have seen the group arriving in the village and would guess they were there for the sole purpose of coming downriver into Thailand, smuggling something in. Whatever it was, it would be worth stealing, so the bandits would definitely try an intercept.

Burroughs went over the map several times, and by the time he put it away the evening sky, cleared of cloud, had gone pink and violet like a swelling bruise, then darkened quickly into night.

Lanterns were lit in the huts but their flames didn't burn for long. The group had put two long, slogging days back to back, and the weariness clamped onto their muscles and sucked at their bones.

Marcus stretched out on a pallet on the verandah, felt the night air nibbling at him. Because the tribe had cleared the forest for their fields, the heat loss was sudden after dark, and a chill crept in, coming not from the river but rising up from the ground.

He shivered as he listened to the village going to sleep, the loudest noise the swirl and gush of the river running by a sandbank, and the life it supported: the *ree-reep* of frogs, the splash of a fish jumping for the moon, the anxious cry of a night bird fading over the water, a lonesome sound.

He thought about Claire.

How long ago had it been since he'd stood close to her in that brief, marvelous moment in the early morning darkness of the hotel corridor in Mae Sai? A little over forty hours? Impossible. It felt like a week.

The cold pressed up against the floor of the verandah as the day's warmth was wicked away. Marcus hugged his arms, imagining her enfolded in them, imagined kissing her mouth, the softness of her body, wondering about the look on her face as his hands moved on her. The strength of his need, the urgent sense of wanting her, surprised him by its intensity. He realized, again with surprise, how quickly his feeling for her had developed. That was something that hadn't happened for a very long time, meeting a woman and being dazzled by her. Although maybe dazzled wasn't the right word; "dazzled" was a shiny, skin-deep word, reflective, glittery. What he felt about her went a lot deeper than that.

A few feet away Burroughs coughed as he got comfortable.

"Captain?"

"Yes?"

"If everything goes okay tomorrow, what time do you think we'll make Chiang Mai?"

"It's about twenty miles to Tha Don on the border. If the bandits aren't too troublesome, and the portaging's not too difficult, we should make Tha Don in about two and a half hours. It's the best part of a day's hike from there to Fang, then an eighty-five mile drive . . . say about twenty-hundred hours in Chiang Mai."

"Eight o'clock," Marcus said. "Okay."

"Do you have an appointment?" Burroughs asked.

"Yeah."

"What time?"

"Eight o'clock."

"Better count on being late," Burroughs said, turning over and settling himself. "Just to be on the safe side."

The noise woke Marcus at the edge of daybreak: the racket of motors popping. There were four boats, the type they called longtails — skiffs weighed down at the stern with exposed outboards that looked and sounded like small airplane engines. Burroughs, briefed the night before by Harn Suk, had been expecting them, and explained to Marcus what he had in mind while they drank a fast cup of tea.

"The middle two boats will take the horses and the shipment. I'll be in the lead boat with Harn Suk and Boyle. I want that chap where I can keep an eye on him. You'll travel in the second boat with Woods and three soldiers. I want the trader, Limbu, and three soldiers in the third boat, and we'll put Turkenton and four soldiers in the last boat to guard our rear. There'll also be a helmsman in each boat, of course, so that will make four men in the first boat, and six in the others."

They went outside and got it arranged, and Burroughs gave some last-minute instructions to the assembled group, Harn Suk translating for Wei Chun's men.

"Right," Burroughs said, the introductory word a call to attention.

"Nobody pulls a trigger till I say so. But when I do say so I want a screen of intense and concentrated fire. We're not out to take scalps, all we want to do is make them keep their heads down till we've passed their position. Do I make myself clear?"

Nobody had any arguments, although Boyle might have said something if Burroughs hadn't looked directly at him.

"Very well," Burroughs said. "Full magazines, one up the spout, and on safe, please."

The heroin was loaded into the two middle boats, then the trader walked two of his horses into the river and lashed them to one of these boats, a horse on either side like outriggers. After he'd done the same with the other two horses — roping them each side of the third vessel — the men climbed in, engines were kicked over, and the boats steered into the flow of the river, picking up speed. The convoy could only travel as fast as the two center ones but, even with the horses slowing them down, they still managed about ten miles an hour.

The helmsmen were river people, short, brown, curly-headed men with proud mustaches. They stood in the rear of their boats, the handles of the long drive rods grasped behind their backs, and navigated with a simple ease around sandbanks, debris, and torn and floating tree branches. The state of the river was the reason why the trip couldn't be attempted at night; nobody went down the Kok in the dark in the rainy season.

With the village left behind, the river widened and bent to the left, green forest cramping the banks on both sides. The water was a chocolate color, flowing with a quiet full energy, rippling its muscles. Flocks of kingfishers shadowed the river, and some early morning swallows swooped and dived and patrolled the banks in flashes of speed. The sun, angling through a gap in the cloud layer, burned the tops of the trees on the western bank, but the sky overhead remained moody and indifferent.

Marcus shouted to Burroughs in the lead boat above the roar of the engine noise.

"When do you figure?"

He didn't have to tell him what he was talking about.

"The second rapids, I should think," Burroughs called back. He was loading a strange-looking weapon, a Heckler & Koch submachine gun. It looked like something from a thirties space serial, being extremely short and squat with protrusions everywhere, and a front handhold like one end of a rolling pin. "If nothing happens at the first one they'll be counting on us to think they're not around today."

"Maybe they ain't around today," Boyle said loudly. He was wearing a crossed bandolier over his shirt, the pouches bulging with shot shells, ferocious-looking rounds full of pellets big enough to use as sinkers on a fishing line. He also had several forty-millimeter grenades stuck into more pouches around his belt. The palm of his left hand ran up and down the smooth barrel of the weapon he cradled, which looked like a short, fat rifle.

"They're around," Burroughs called back. "You can depend on it."

All through the convoy, ammunition was being laid out and guns were being checked. Woods was setting down thirty-round magazines for his M16, and Limbu was doing the same. Limbu's weapon was similar to Woods's, a CAR 15 Colt Commando. It had a short ten-inch barrel with no flash hider, which was why Burroughs had wanted it in the party. In the last boat Turkenton crouched beside a heavy machine gun, a U.S. Army M60. It was normally operated by two men, but a big man like Turkenton could John Wayne it, as it was called, and work it by himself. The ammunition in the belt he was hooking onto the gun's feed tray had been ordered specially by Burroughs: every single round was a red-tipped tracer bullet.

The rain, which the massing clouds had so far kept to themselves, sprinkled down for a moment, dried up, then belted down in sheets, whipping the river's surface into a froth.

Marcus watched a boat pass them heading upstream, its engine straining to buck the current. The boat's pilot, an elderly Shan, wielded a paddle to help his laboring motor, and when he pulled it through the bustling water the blue tattoos covering his shoulders and arms rippled and moved as if living a life of their own. When the convoy negotiated another snakey bend, it was alone on the river again.

In the lead boat Burroughs checked the headman's map and the drawings of recognizable landmarks — a little village, a large rock, a broken and tumbled tree — and called to Marcus, telling him that their pace was good. Marcus could see that Burroughs was also happy about the horses, which had to have been one of his main worries; they appeared to be perfectly content roped to the two middle boats. There were no predators in the river to bother them and, with their heads held high, they seemed to enjoy their swim, grateful for the rest from their loads.

The river bent again, and a sound different from the drumming rain came up the new corridor as the first of the rapids announced itself. The helmsmen steered their craft into a cleared section of the bank, the horses were released, and the boats beached, then two of the longtails were lifted onto the shoulders of the KMT soldiers, who set off down a track hacked through the forest.

Woods and Limbu planted themselves at the river's edge, their guns trained on the opposite bank. Nothing moved over there except the jungle itself, bobbing and swaying under the watery onslaught, a billion leaves glistening slickly.

The trader roped his ponies together and led them off as the soldiers returned for the other two boats. The rear guard followed them into the jungle along the trail, which paralleled the river. Through a gap in the trees Marcus caught sight of the rapids, brown water belted into a roiling white froth as it charged down a shallow incline peppered with rocks and boulders.

A tough trip for a boat.

Similarly, when the trail ended a few yards past the rapids, Marcus saw that nothing could have moved any farther through the jungle, either. It was super dense, solid with trees and bamboo and lianas twisted into tangled cat's cradles.

Burroughs held the caravan in the shelter of the forest for a while but, apart from the darting river birds, and some waterfowl squawking in a clump of reeds, there was no sign of life on the other bank.

When they got moving again Boyle spat into the dirt, staring warily at the line of silent trees.

"If they'd hit us back there we would've got the shit kicked out of us."

Marcus had been thinking along the same lines, and Burroughs was well aware of their vulnerability.

"The horses are the problem," he said to Marcus, watching the trader retie them to the boats. "Too cumbersome if we have to stop." He borrowed a knife from the trader, handed it to Marcus, and gave him instructions to cut the horses loose if they ran into trouble. He told the same thing to Limbu, then got the convoy underway again.

The river followed a meandering course for the next forty minutes, swelling and thinning unpredictably, passing through a narrow chute, the riverbanks groping for them like a pair of smothering arms. The remains of an abandoned village slid into view as the waterway curved west. This was a landmark which, according to Burroughs's map, put the second rapids about a half-mile away.

They got off to a false start with the tip of a rock just breaking the surface, the water knifing on either side of it giving the rock the appearance of a speeding torpedo. The boats, just fifteen feet apart now, began to move faster as the swirl of the current built up momentum. Apart from the four helmsmen, everybody was peering through the rain at the riverbank up ahead, the massed trees keeping the jungle private and secret, like tight green shutters on a locked-up mansion.

The river ran on for fifty yards, swerved left, straightened, and at the end of this stretch appeared to fall away and continue at a lower level. A short distance in front of this drop, just visible through the rain, about forty Shans stood on the bank in attitudes of quiet patience, their weapons held lackadaisically over their shoulders, watching the convoy being sucked relentlessly toward them.

The majority wore nothing but turbans and a pair of pants, and seemed to be relying on their myriad tattoos to keep out the weather. Their look of boredom was, in a way, far scarier than if they'd been yelling and brandishing their rifles. They gave the impression that resistance would be futile, and the result an expensive failure.

"Jesus God!" Boyle yelled. He snapped open his weapon, pulled the shot shell he'd loaded, and slammed in a grenade.

"Boyle!" Burroughs's voice had claws in it. "I want that round on the sandbank, do you understand?" He knew what Boyle was about to do: lob a grenade right into the middle of those forty men, and Burroughs wasn't looking for a massacre.

"You kiddin'?" Boyle said, incredulous. "They're just standin' there."

"Do as I say, Boyle."

"Fuck that. It's my ass, too."

"Do it, Boyle." Burroughs had his submachine gun up and pointing. "Do it, or I'll do it for you."

Boyle rapped out an enraged obscenity, snapped the weapon to his shoulder, and shot it off into the sky. The missile looped high into the air, armed itself at the top of its arc, whistled down at the sandbank, and exploded in a blur of earth and water.

For the men on the bank of the river, the effect was startling. Like a school of frightened fish darting into a coral reef, they fled behind the first line of trees, and began a slow and inaccurate return fire.

Burroughs stood and called out to free the horses.

Marcus hacked at the ropes that held two of the ponies to his boat. In the boat behind him, Limbu freed the other horses with two fast swipes of his kukri sword.

Released into the drag of the current, the horses threw back their heads and kicked against the turbulence that tried to suck them under, whinnying in terror, fighting for buoyancy.

Another volley from the bank straddled the convoy, bullets whining through the trees or hitting short, spattering the water.

"Wait for it!" Burroughs yelled.

But wait was something that Boyle couldn't do. Screaming something at Burroughs he cut loose with his weapon and, rather than try to stop him, Burroughs released the others.

To the bandits, invisible behind their screen of jungle, it seemed like the river had caught fire and exploded. The noise was cataclysmic, and the result awesome. An entire section of their jungle cover was shredded and mashed, leaves and branches torn away and pulped as a massive wall of lead chewed at the forest like a lawn mower savaging grass.

For the handful of Shans brave enough to attempt some defense, the sight they saw was horrendous: a devil in the third boat — Limbu with his open-muzzle Colt — had a rifle that spat like a flamethrower, an enormous, torching tongue of fire that strained to reach them like a crazed dog on a leash. And, from the last boat — the big machine gun, pumping out a stream of tracer bullets — the flame did reach them, a never-ending bridge of white incandescence that leaped the water and brought leaves and vines and whole branches tumbling and smoking down onto their heads.

The bandits hugged the wet undergrowth and waited for relief, but it never came. In the boats on the river fifteen men, caught up in the frenzy of the continuous barrage, operated guns in an ear-shattering paroxysm of noise and smoke.

Marcus held his fire — his pistol would have been a negligible addition — but he was as caught up in the thundering fusillade as any of them.

Watching Boyle he was amazed; the man was terrific with the launcher. He'd fire, eject, scoop up a shot shell, load and fire again in a continuous action, and the effect of those shells was shattering. They tore gaping holes in the green cover, punching deep swathes through the foliage, blasting small trees in half and decimating everything within a fifteen-foot radius of wherever they hit.

Compared to the savage sledgehammer blows of Boyle's weapon, Woods's and Limbu's automatic rifles were like swift scalpels. They sliced quickly and deeply, wounding the jungle terribly, their slender, sharp-nosed bullets hitting fast and traveling far, boring right through trees rather than breaking them off, the high-velocity projectiles moaning through the boughs, slashing a thousand paper-thin rips.

But it was Turkenton's weapon that was the great destroyer. If the jungle had been made of cement the result would not have been much different. Exploding out of the barrel, the tracers ignited after thirty feet and turned into white-hot, copper-clad fists searing a path through the rain, smashing against the green wall, knocking it down in clumps, and devastating the bandits' cover.

Even so, one or two of the Shans didn't know enough to understand what they were flirting with, and succeeded in getting off a few shots of their own. They came at the worst time for the convoy, right when it was dead opposite the bandits' position, and one of the KMT soldiers in Turkenton's boat pitched forward into the river as if he'd stood up and dived for a coin.

The river seized the first boat and propelled it forward, shooting it through the channel formed by the sandbank. The helmsman gunned the motor, took the boat surging toward the center of the rapids, where the river crashed down a short staircase of submerged rocks. The boat bucked and tossed and slammed from side to side, but Boyle didn't miss a beat with the launcher; he braced himself, and sent shell after shell slamming into the trees, sending up fountains of dirt and twigs and shredded leaves. The boat bounced on an angle, straightened, then swooped down the drop, belted into the pool at the bottom of the fall, shook itself, lunged forward, and was swept safely out of the lower part of the chute.

The second boat followed, Woods's gun still hammering away, spent shells spewing all over the seats. When the boat plunged, Woods would have gone over the side if Marcus hadn't grabbed him, and they rode the fall locked together like kids on a carnival ride. The two screeching horses were swept over behind them, flipped over the fall, and dashed down into the pool.

Limbu's boat made it with surprising ease when it was lifted by a sudden change in the flow, shot off the top of the fall like a ski boat taking a jump, and smacked down onto the pool on a dead-even keel. The ponies which Limbu had released were just a tumble of heads and hooves. They disappeared, were thrown up, and vanished again.

The last boat, with Turkenton in it, still raking the forest with a blistering fire, looked to be having the same good luck as Limbu's till a quick surge lifted its stern at precisely the wrong time. It fell at too steep an angle and nose-dived into the pool, catapulting everybody over the bow — Turkenton, the helmsman, and the three soldiers. The river snatched hold of them and pushed them through the water like ducks going over a weir.

Burroughs hadn't seen the accident; the torrent had whipped his boat around a bend that lay at the immediate end of the rapids. Sweeping around the curve, they surprised three bandits who were about to launch a canoe, evidently detailed to pick up and search any corpses that might have been washed over the rapids as a result of their compatriots' fire. The three Shans stared in dumb wonder at the boat on the river and the two men in it who carried guns. Like frightened deer they stood still for the briefest part of a second, then turned and bolted up a clearing.

In the boat Boyle had slapped a grenade into the launcher.

"Hold your fire," Burroughs snapped.

"Why?" The weapon was already tucked against Boyle's shoulder. "Coupla slants for the table."

Burroughs shouted at him as the weapon banged, the grenade arcing through the sky and exploding several feet in front of the running men.

Almost gracefully the three Shans leaped into the air, then flopped onto their faces in a jumble of arms and legs.

Burroughs's face had gone white. He took two strides down the boat and wrenched the launcher out of Boyle's grasp.

"I've had a lot of men serve under me, Boyle, but none as rotten as you."

Boyle gave one of his snorting laughs.

"Up yours, Captain," he said, and lay back in the boat as if he were on a Sunday cruise.

The second and third boats came into sight, then the men from the fourth boat, swimming with the horses in the river, the torrent bringing them around the curve.

As nationalities and backgrounds went, all the occupants of that boat were excellent choices to be tossed into white water. The three soldiers, like the Shan helmsman, had grown up on the Burmese rivers, had washed and swum and played in them since they'd been toddlers. And Turkenton had spent a large part of his youth surfing at the beaches of Sydney.

"Flamin' hell," Turkenton said as the boats fished the dripping men out of the river, "I haven't cracked a wave that good since Bondi."

The boats scurried about gathering the horses in an aquatic roundup. Three of them had made it over the fall; the fourth one floated by on its side. There was no sign of the soldier who'd been shot.

The convoy put a mile between itself and the rapids, and pulled in to the bank to regroup.

Burroughs checked the shipment, which was untouched.

"One man, a boat, and a pony," he said. "We were lucky." He removed his bush hat, rolled it up, and squeezed out the rain. "If they'd had any decent kind of leadership, we'd have been facedown in the river by now."

"There gonna be any more of them?" Marcus asked.

"No more. It's only ten miles to Tha Don. It'll be plain sailing now."

Marcus thought that Burroughs sounded wrung out, as if part of the man had been in the hat he'd just squeezed. Watching him, Marcus recognized somebody whose job was over and would now have very little to contribute. Worse, he wouldn't be asked to contribute — Harn Suk would be the key man from here on in — so Burroughs was about to be relegated to the role of unnecessary specialist.

With the bandits removed as a threat, the KMT soldiers were no longer needed, and would wait on the bank until the boats returned to take them back up the river. Burroughs said there'd be no danger going back past the bandits; soldiers traveling north never had anything worth stealing except their guns, and in this case the bandits wouldn't want the KMTs' ancient rifles.

Harn Suk handed Marcus the canvas backpack he'd been carrying.

"Mr. Agosta pay bonus," Harn Suk said, indicating the men. "One hundred dollar."

Marcus pulled out Agosta's expense money and gave each soldier a hundred-dollar bill. They snapped the bills and crinkled them at their ears, trading smiles with each other. Marcus held up a tenth bill.

"For the guy who didn't make it. Share it."

They understood but they all shook their head.

"For his family then . . ."

Harn Suk spoke to the men, then told Marcus that the boy had had nobody.

"Then he can take it with him." Marcus tossed the bill into the river.

Boyle made a grab for it but it was wafted away on the current.

"Hey," he said. "You want to throw bread around, throw some over here."

Nobody answered him; nobody even looked at him.

The flotilla shoved off again, leaving the nine soldiers on the bank, and made the village of Mong Hsim in under an hour, the last Burmese village before the border. All the weapons and ammunition were dropped into the river here; from now on money would be their only weapon.

Fifteen minutes later the town of Tha Don came up. There was no checkpoint, no international bridge, nothing much at all to mark the division between the two countries. They unloaded the heroin a little way short of the town on a backwater creek of the river. Marcus gave each of the helmsmen the same bonus he'd given the soldiers, tripling it for the man who'd lost his vessel, and then the boatmen took off upstream to pick up the soldiers.

With the heroin bundles back on the ponies, the caravan got going, skirted the town, and followed a trail that had been cut by smugglers when the Kok had been a main artery into Thailand. It was becoming overgrown now but was still passable, and they settled down to slog the distance to the town of Fang, arriving at its outskirts in the early evening.

Harn Suk led them to a ruined farmhouse on a rise overlooking the settlement, where they found the Toyota truck, which had been driven there from Mae Sai. While the shipment was loaded into it Marcus had a word with Harn Suk about the financial arrangements Agosta had made with the men. Then he drew Burroughs aside.

"I'm gonna pay off everybody here," he said, and put five thousand dollars into Burroughs's hand.

"You've given me too much," the Englishman said.

"You did a hell of a job," Marcus explained.

"Very decent of you," Burroughs said, looking a little embarrassed.

Marcus paid the trader for his services, compensating him for the loss of his horse. The man went happily off with his three remaining ponies to buy goods in the town below. Then Burroughs made an announcement to the others.

"We'll split up here. We can't have too many in the truck, we've got checkpoints to get through. Woods, Turkenton, and Limbu, you take the bus from Fang to Chiang Mai. Check into the Hotel Poy Luang, that's where your gear is. There'll be airline tickets for you at the desk."

"Enjoy the bus ride, suckers," Boyle crowed. "Don't let the chickens crap on you."

Marcus opened the backpack and gave two thousand dollars to each of them, their agreed-upon fee.

"You got a bonus coming, too," he said. He gave Woods, Turkenton, and Limbu another thousand, then closed the backpack.

Boyle couldn't believe it.

"Hey. How about *my* bonus?"

"We didn't vote you one," Marcus told him.

"Who didn't vote me one?"

"The bonus committee."

"What bonus committee? Who's on the fuckin' thing?"

"Just me," Marcus answered.

Very slowly Boyle reared back. His eyes got bright, and his jaw widened as his mouth stretched.

"I earned that bonus, Dubin. I did more'n any of these dummies. I saved your asses with that seventy-nine."

"You were good with the weapon, I'll grant you that. Even when you didn't have to be. But you fell down in other areas."

"What other areas?" Boyle was shouting.

"Personal hygiene."

"Personal —" Boyle broke off. "What the fuck do you mean?"

"I've been with you for three days now, Boyle. And in all that time I never saw you use deodorant once."

Boyle stayed very still for a moment, then began to nod as if a problem he'd been struggling with had become a lot clearer.

"I been watchin' you for three days too, putzo. You been struttin' around with that handgun of yours like you was Clint Eastwood. You're a worse actor'n he is, you know that? I don't think you can use that thing."

"I can use it," Marcus answered quietly.

Boyle squared his stance, his right hand unbuttoning his left sleeve. "You're gonna have to show me."

The five men watching found themselves in a loose circle

around Marcus and Boyle. The circle broke as everybody stepped back.

"First I have to load it," Marcus said.

"It's loaded. You didn't fire one goddamn shot back there. Think I didn't see that?"

With a lazy, almost delicate movement Marcus pushed back his shirt, and lifted the Clark from its holster with two fingers of his left hand.

"It's not loaded the way I like it."

He dropped the clip into his hand, ejected the round in the chamber, reached in behind his big oval belt buckle, and took out one of the hand loads he'd secreted there.

Frowning at it, Boyle lifted his chin up and down in a fast question.

"What you got there?"

"Little something I made up," Marcus said, loading it into the pistol.

He cocked the weapon, placed it back into the Rogers holster, and moved away several feet to a piece of flat ground.

"Okay, fat man. Lunch is on the table."

Boyle cranked out a short laugh.

"Good. I'm gonna carve."

He came down to Marcus and stopped about twelve inches farther than an arm's length away. Marcus had his hands at his sides, Boyle held his at belt level. Both men stood rock-steady.

Marcus had his eyes stitched to Boyle, ready for the slightest twitch, but it was another man he was thinking about: Teddy Hepplewhite. "This guy standing in front of you," Teddy would have said had he been there, "he's not the guy put you in a hospital bed, nearly killed you. Don't see him like that. Just see him as a miserable sonofabitch who's lived too long."

A gust of rain glided in but it affected nothing, neither the two antagonists nor their audience, which wasn't about to interfere.

Burroughs was as motionless as Limbu, both of them watching something they'd been expecting to see for some time now. Woods and Turkenton had been here before when it had been Agosta facing Boyle, so they not only knew what to expect, they also had a comparison for this confrontation. They were both certain, after watching Marcus and Boyle stand frozen for several seconds, that it had been Boyle who'd moved first, and that his draw had been much faster than it had been against Agosta. His hand shot up and didn't appear to go into his shirt sleeve for the knife — he just seemed to suddenly have it in his grasp as if he'd been holding it all along.

And there was no second movement; he didn't draw the knife sideways, then stab it forward; it was all done in one action.

Somebody told Turkenton later that this was called Iaijutsu, a technique belonging to classical Japanese swordsmanship where the drawing of the blade and the killing stroke are done in the same movement. But Turkenton had doubted that Boyle was the type who'd study a fancy Oriental discipline; he was just a natural knife fighter who'd learned a few tricks.

His stroke was the same one he'd used to vanquish Agosta, a power slash with most of the movement coming from the forearm, his elbow stiff, his weight shifting, his arm arcing outward with phenomenal speed. His small, quick feet moved a minisecond after he'd got his weapon into his hand, taking his knife arm eighteen inches closer to Marcus.

The razor-edged steel slit the air with a fine, thin hiss — an amazing sight to behold: fat, slobby Boyle moving as fast as a rattler, so surprisingly light on his toes, so swift and deadly in his darting lunge forward.

The blade was less than a foot away from Marcus's neck when Marcus's hand load smashed through Boyle's chest.

The onlookers had seen two pieces of magic: Marcus's crossdraw had conjured his pistol into his hand, drawing and firing in the same seamless movement that Boyle had employed.

But a little faster.

The force of the bullet punched Boyle back and killed him while he was still staggering.

As the echo of the shot faded into the hills, Burroughs was the first to say anything. He issued his last order of the trip.

"Woods, Turkenton . . ." He looked down at the body stretched out on the ground. "Find something to dig a hole with and bury this man."

9

 T HERE WERE ONLY TWO CHECKPOINTS on the road before they reached Chiang Mai, both of which they sailed through courtesy of a prearrangement.

When they made the Hotel Poy Luang there were no big good-byes; Burroughs thanked Harn Suk for his help, shook hands with Marcus, and went inside. Marcus had a word with Harn Suk about the delivery down south, and waved as the boy drove off into the night.

As he registered at the desk, Marcus checked to make sure Claire was staying there, and was moving to a house phone to call her when he caught sight of himself in a mirror. A three-day stubble shadowed his face, his clothes were a stiff-dried mess, and his boots were gray with mud.

He went straight up to his room, called Room Service for a couple of bottles of beer, went into the bedroom and found his suitcase there, brought by one of Harn Suk's helpers from Mae Sai. He tore off his clothes, and spent fifteen minutes under a hot shower shampooing the rain-water out of his hair, and shaving twice.

He'd just reached for a towel when the door bell rang.

Soaking wet, his hair plastered down, he wrapped the towel around his waist and got the door, thinking it was his Room Service order.

"I was at dinner," Claire said. "They told me you were here as I left the dining room, so I came on up."

"I'm glad you did," Marcus said. "I would've embarrassed you if I'd come down and grabbed you in the middle of dessert."

"What?" Claire asked, with not much volume to her voice. In a sky-blue dress, and with her yellow hair around her shoulders, and her pale, perfect skin, she looked like some kind of vision standing there. She took in the water on Marcus's body, the big drops running down off the breadth of his shoulders, collecting in the scoops above his collarbones, dripping into the matted hair on his hard, flat stomach.

"You'd better dry yourself before you catch cold."

"You're right," he said, closing the door, then stepped into her, soaking her dress.

It began with little movements, lips pressed briefly to cheek and mouth as if they weren't sure where to start. They kept breaking off to hug tighter, their arms seeking better purchase, kissing with their eyes open, looking at each other. Claire treated her clothes as barriers that had to come down quickly, even the thinness of the wet dress too much distance to have between them now.

It took a long time for them to reach the bedroom, unwilling to simply break apart and walk in there.

For both of them it was a process of discovery, of finding out how close to the mark they'd been when they'd imagined what it would be like with each other.

Below him Claire became a boat rocking him through storm and calm, carrying him on a warm sea which he let engulf him, submerging to its moist, silky depths. Above him she was a pale silver bird swooping on him again and again to carry him off to new heights.

They absorbed, blended, merged, passed through each other, drifted into myth: two heads on a single body.

Once he slid her halfway off the bed, laid her back, and

entered her standing, thrashing and hammering against the wild bucking movement of her hips, flesh and bone colliding with sounds like slaps.

They dozed, woke, melded, exhausted themselves, found new strengths. Since they'd swapped those few awkward words of greeting they'd said nothing to each other. There was only one thing that needed to be said anyway, something they both knew was hanging like a transparent division between them and, sometime in the small hours, with shards of light creeping across the ceiling, and the air in the mountain city cool enough for them to tuck and nestle together, Marcus came out with it.

He put his palm on the side of her face and moved his hand down her neck, stroked the skin of her shoulder, pressed his teeth gently into its smooth firmness, then said, with his mouth now close to her ear, "So what was his name?"

She only had to tilt her head a little bit to be looking into his eyes.

"Whose name?" Although he could see she knew what he was talking about.

"The warden at Reedsville in eighty-three. You called the States and checked, am I right?"

"Robert C. Brewer," Claire said, with no particular tone in her voice.

"You trapped me nicely, Counselor. What tipped you off? My lousy acting?"

"You're not a bad actor. The part was just wrong for you, that's all."

When Marcus remained silent, Claire said, "You certainly look the part." Her fingers traced his face with gentle pressures. "This split eyebrow of yours, and your build. But you just didn't come off as an outlaw. At least, not to me."

"I've been a detective for too long, huh?"

"Is that what you are? I thought maybe Government."

"Why would I be Government?"

"Only if there was something wrong with this deal I helped go through. If, for example, my client Bendroit wasn't bringing back precious stones from Burma, but something even more valuable."

Marcus changed position, rolled over so that they were joined together at the hip, kissed her between her breasts, left his chin there, looking up at her in shadow.

"When did you figure it out?"

"When I was sure you were faking it. I wasn't even suspicious about that tobacco factory till then. The whole thing was just weird enough, and exotic enough, to ring true."

Claire cupped his face in her hands, spread her fingers and moved them slowly around to the back of his neck.

"You should let your hair grow out a little."

"Then I'd have to buy a comb."

"Ralph Jones," Claire said.

"What?"

"Well, I assume your name isn't Boyd Dubin."

"No, it isn't."

"Arnold Weiss?"

"Do I look like an Arnold Weiss?"

"Monty Stringfellow."

"God, no. William Marcus."

"William Marcus. That's a lot better than Monty String-fellow."

Marcus explored the circumference of a nipple, compared its dimensions with the oval shape of her navel.

"Seeing you know anyway, I suppose I'd better tell you. We trekked to a deserted village and bought a hundred kilos of heroin base from the son of a Chinese warlord. It's on its way to Bangkok. Then it goes to Hong Kong. I'm supposed to go there and help a guy named Hinkler put it on a ship for New York. Hinkler works for Bendroit. You ever meet him? Hinkler?"

"No. Have you?"

"For about ten minutes. We didn't get on."

"Then what?"

"Then I go back to New York, wait for the ship to arrive, and flog the junk to a guy named Morici, who I'm pretty sure is a biggie in the Mob. Morici then sends the money to Bendroit in London. And that's how it's done."

Claire moved her hand down his flanks and across his back, felt the cicatrix of the knife wound, knew it was some kind of past damage, marveled at the fact that she was in bed with a man whose line of work brought him into severe contact with knife blades and bullets, and boots and fists.

"Are you going to do all that?"

"It's the only way I can get to Bendroit."

"Who do you work for, New York Narcotics?"

"Atlanta Robbery. It's a long story, but I'm free-lancing on this one."

Marcus fashioned her hipbone with his fingers; a roller-coaster ride.

"Will you let me help you?" Claire asked.

"Why? I mean, why do you want to help?"

"Because I think you're going to need it."

"I'm gonna need all I can get. But again, why you?"

Claire lifted one shoulder, trying unsuccessfully for a careless shrug.

"I don't know. Maybe I care about your future."

"Are you going to be in it?"

"Your future?" Claire allowed her answer to dangle for a moment. "If I'm invited."

Marcus hauled himself up, closed in on her. "You're invited," he said.

They moved together, then, sealing whatever kind of agreement had been made. Then, after a while, Claire asked another question.

"How are you planning to fix Bendroit?"

"Well, my first thought was to get some cooperation from New York Drug Enforcement."

"A deal? With the DEA?" Claire's hair tickled his chest

[161]

when she shook her head. "I don't think so. They have a reputation for playing things their way."

"That was my second thought."

They let some time dissolve; a tiny piece of the early morning slid by while they lay there loosely draped against each other, hands moving with slow curiosity over hollow and mound, recess and extension.

"So what's the bottom line?" Claire asked.

Marcus kissed her mouth, her eyelids, the throb at the side of her neck.

"We'll just have to make a deal with somebody else," he said.

10

CHARLES BENDROIT delayed his return to London for twenty-four hours in order to fit in with the schedule of an extremely attractive airline stewardess. Not, as might have been expected, because of the woman's talent in the bedroom of Bendroit's New York town house — she'd never been invited to his house — but because of her in-flight expertise on a British Airways Concorde.

Whenever he crossed the Atlantic he would find out when she was flying, and make his travel arrangements accordingly, as he had this time.

She was looking after passengers several rows behind him, and didn't get to speak with him until coffee and liqueurs were being served.

Although the excellent meal had been nowhere near Bendroit's idea of haute cuisine — the *boeuf en croute* had been a touch overdone, and the Château Siran a trifle aggressive on the back of the throat — he'd nevertheless found it not entirely unpalatable, and was feeling replete and at peace with the world. He was extremely confident of success, now that he'd found this Dubin chap to run things, and the thought of what that success would bring brought a glow to his whole being, the like of which even the fine champagne cognac couldn't begin to match.

Charles Bendroit knew what he wanted out of life.

Recognition.

It wasn't possible in shipping unless you were an Onassis, an Olsen, a C. Y. Tung, somebody who was worth a couple of hundred million. But fame could be had for far less than that, and in a far more sociably accepted milieu, and one he desperately wanted to be a part of: bloodstock breeding. As the owner of a successful racing stable his would become a household name, and in the best of households. But it would take a lot of money to start: thirty million. At least that much. To compete at the sales at Goff's and Tattersalls and Keeneland with men like Sangster and Niarchos, Sheik Mohammed, Prince Abdullah, to pay two or three million for a horse knowing full well it might never start a race, let alone win one, that took real money.

That was the reason why he'd thought up the idea of an outrageous amount of heroin bought at source and shipped to America in one huge consignment for one huge payment. He was doing it not for the respect money commands, but for the fame it can bring.

Not the power, but the glory.

The jet banked, marginally correcting course, and a piece of sunlight stabbed through the window and flared on Bendroit's bald scalp, visited his thin mouth, and fled as if it didn't like the neighborhood.

"Mr. Bendroit . . ."

Leaning in from the aisle the stewardess brought her presence closer, a tall, dark-haired girl with a sexy way of parting her lips, a warm, deep voice.

"Another cognac?"

"Thank you, no."

When she leaned fractionally lower, her blouse front jutted, and Bendroit dropped his eyes to an exciting shadow of cleavage.

"I believe there's one free now," she said, as if she'd been asked a question. She began to walk back down the aisle.

Bendroit got up and followed.

She stopped at the bank of toilets.

"This one is free, sir."

She smiled and vanished into the galley.

Bendroit went into the toilet, closed and locked the door, and stood there with a fine trembling running through him.

A soft tap at the door.

When he opened it the girl stepped inside, locking the door behind her.

"Hello," she said, already unbuttoning her blouse.

They were within inches of each other in the tiny washroom, so when she reached back to unsnap her bra, her breasts lunged forward and rested on the London-shrunk, Australian merino wool of Bendroit's suit jacket.

Fruit-salad tits, Bendroit called them in his mind: smooth round grapefruits with cherries on top.

"Come along, Mr. Bendroit," the girl said, a smile in her voice — she was unfastening his belt — "let's get these beautifully cut pants off so we can screw."

Bendroit never responded; he liked to pretend it was the first time anything like this had happened to him.

"While I'm doing this," the stewardess said, unzipping his fly, "you can play Customs if you like."

"Customs?"

She nodded her chin at her breasts.

"You can check these to see if I'm trying to smuggle anything."

Bendroit accepted her invitation, his hands moving, not in a caressing action, but patting and squeezing, almost as if he were indeed checking for hidden contraband.

"Think you can take over now?" She left him in charge of lowering his pants while she went up under her skirt and slipped her panties down two very shapely legs. She reached behind him, lifted the toilet seat cover, and pressed him backward so that he was forced to sit down, then hiked her skirt up to waist level, revealing a triangle of pubic hair as neat as a Prince Edward beard.

She straddled him and did something that never failed to turn him on: moved her hips and thrust her mound at him in a mime of copulation, three, four, five fast movements that were so erotic they always got him instantly hard.

She expertly popped him inside her, and with quick forward and downward pressure, sat in his lap.

Her hips seemed independent of the rest of her as they swiveled back and forward, up and down, her vagina like a warm, wet hand over him, subjecting his anatomy to a fast, moist flogging.

Her right shoulder bent back as she dipped her right arm down underneath her bottom into the top of the toilet bowl, reached further and strummed her fingers on his balls.

There were sounds all around him: the thrum of the jet's engines, the hiss of the fresh-air valve in the bulkhead, the squish and suck of the woman's talented crotch, then his own involuntary cry as he came like a rocket.

He wasn't completely finished before she reached out and zipped tissues from the dispenser, then raised herself and covered his still pumping member. She attended to herself, stepped back into her panties, layered them with two paper towels, pulled them up into place.

Trying to get his breath back, Bendroit had started to think about his dignity sitting there on the toilet seat holding Kleenex on his cock. It was the only drawback to the whole thing. He dressed hastily, got his wallet out of his jacket, paid the girl three hundred dollars.

"Thank you," she said, smiling. Her quick fingers had buttoned her blouse and were straightening her skirt. "And thank you for fucking British Airways."

She reached for the door handle and was gone, leaving Bendroit to compose himself. He spent a few minutes recovering, then returned to his seat.

An hour later, relaxed, well fed, confident, and sexually content, he landed on time in London.

* * *

Not long after the Concorde touched down at London's Heathrow Airport, Cathay Pacific's Flight #201 from Hong Kong landed at Gatwick, thirty miles south of the capital.

The Immigration people quickly processed the flight, none of the passengers being thought anything to worry about. However, had they known a little more about one of the visitors, he would have been held under armed guard and put on the next flight out. His passport said he was a citizen of Hong Kong, which was correct, and that his name was Yong See, also correct. And that his profession was in the clerical area.

Which was anything but correct.

Yong See, known to his friends and enemies alike as Jay Jay, was a fighter, an enforcer, with the rank of Sei Gai Tsai, a Forty-nine boy; but in no way did his appearance reflect his violent trade. He was a slim thirty-year-old with an old-fashioned back-and-sides haircut and a fine-skinned Oriental face unmarked by any aggressive instrument. He wore a brown windbreaker over a plain white shirt, blue suit pants and black, lace-up dress shoes. To the Immigration man who cleared him he looked a lot like the man behind the counter at the Kowloon Gardens, his local Chinese take-out.

Jay Jay took his bag toward the Customs exit without fear of being stopped. There was nothing incriminating in his suitcase — he never carried a weapon; his favorite was a simple household item that he could easily find in almost any part of the world.

However, had he aroused suspicion for some reason, and been strip-searched, the tattoos on his chest — a lurid red-and-green dragon on the right side, a red-and-blue phoenix on the left — would certainly have got him kicked out of the country. The Asian experts attached to Her Majesty's Customs would have known that this was a man who had had his pricked thumbs bled into a bowl of rice wine and chicken blood, had drunk from that bowl, and then been initiated into Hong Kong's largest Triad society, the Sap Sei K. The Fourteen K, as it was called in English.

Jay Jay took the shuttle train to Victoria Station, then the Underground to Leicester Square, and went to an apartment the Society owned on Lisle Street. He slept for eight hours, had a breakfast of scallops in black bean sauce at the restaurant downstairs, then made a phone call.

"The Bendroit residence," a voice answered.

"Mr. Bendroit, please."

"Mr. Bendroit is at business." The voice had precise, round tones.

"Who are you?"

"I am Mathews, sir. Mr. Bendroit's man. If you wish his number, I will be glad to furnish it."

"He is not there?" Jay Jay asked. In his accented English his confusion sounded genuine.

"No, sir."

"What time there?"

"Mr. Bendroit usually arrives home about five-thirty, sir. May I ask who is calling?"

"Please?"

Mathews took a guess; anybody with a foreign accent who phoned the house usually turned out to be a squash pro. His employer fired them as fast as he hired them.

"Are you, by chance, the new squash professional?"

Jay Jay seized his opportunity and said yes.

"Mr. Bendroit will expect you here tomorrow morning at seven-thirty, if that is suitable. Do you have the address?"

"Yes. Thank you, I come."

Jay Jay cut the connection.

Bendroit took squash lessons at his house? That meant he had a private court, but then the rich had anything they wanted. Anyway, that was the problem of access solved.

Jay Jay went back to bed to drain his jet lag, then, around four, strolled down to Lillywhite's and bought the things he'd need: a squash racket, a sports bag, a pair of sneakers, and a warm-up suit. He changed into the clothes in the store, put what he'd been wearing in the sports bag, checked Bendroit's address in a street atlas, and caught a tube train west.

Green Park, Hyde Park Corner, Knightsbridge. He got out at the next stop, South Kensington.

Cathcart Road wasn't far, a row of terraced town houses built in a solid block, twelve of them, elegant and expensive, with Number Thirty-four making up the last three. Three houses in one: a millionaire's accommodation.

A man in a butler's apron opened the door.

"I am the new squash professional," Jay Jay told him. Mathews examined him: the warm-up suit, the racket in the sports bag were normal enough, but a Chinese face? The master's squash teachers were invariably dark-skinned inhabitants of the subcontinent.

Jay Jay saw the doubt.

"I'm from Singapore." Squash was very big in Singapore.

"I said tomorrow morning. Seven-thirty tomorrow morning. You must have misunderstood."

"No, I phoned Mr. Bendroit at his office. He said to come now. He wants a lesson this evening."

"I see."

Mathews didn't notice that the new squash pro's English had improved considerably since the morning. Jay Jay had been exposed to the English language early in his life when a farseeing uncle had bribed the caddy master at the Hong Kong Football Club, a man responsible for the hiring of menials at that erstwhile establishment. Jay Jay had become a ball boy on the club's tennis courts and got a solid grounding in the language while chasing tennis balls and running errands for the pro. Later on he'd become a busboy in the club's dining room, then a waiter, all the time polishing his English and learning to stop singing the words and put breaks between them. In all he'd spent ten years at the club, before being snapped up by the Triads, and now spoke the language extremely well.

The butler stepped back and admitted him into a beautiful foyer. The layout was magnificent; it was obvious how Bendroit's architect had made three dwellings into one: wide openings had been punched in the party walls that had once separated the three houses, and the openings had been buttressed with wide-flanged I beams which were now disguised by scoops and whirls of molded plaster. The entry halls and staircases of the two side houses had been removed, long French windows had been added, and large, grand rooms created.

"Such a big house," Jay Jay remarked.

"Yes, sir. Very large."

"You are by yourself in this big house?"

"At the moment, sir. Yes. Mr. Bendroit should be here in about fifteen minutes. I'll show you the court."

Having said this, Mathews turned and began leading the way.

Jay Jay didn't want to hurt him. He slipped the squash racket out of the sports bag, placed the bag down without breaking his stride, wrapped his fingers around the narrow throat of the racket and, in a fast stabbing motion, jabbed the end of the handle into a pressure point between the butler's shoulder blades.

He caught the man as he folded, laid him down, found a closet full of cleaning equipment, and dragged Mathews in there. He trussed him up with the cord of a vacuum cleaner, stuffed a cloth duster in his mouth, making sure he could breathe.

Jay Jay was quite gentle with him; he always was with innocent people. He read with revulsion newspaper accounts of people who murdered for personal gain. The men he'd dispatched had all tried to cheat the Society in some way. They were therefore enemies of the Society and, like any good soldier, he had no compunction about killing the enemy.

Jay Jay never used a gun; they were too impractical. In Hong Kong the gun laws were ferocious, handguns being totally banned from the colony, so to own one was asking for trouble. There was always a melon knife, like some of the other Forty-nine boys used, but if you were stopped and found with one of those up your sleeve you could be arrested. So when he was on a job Jay Jay carried something that appeared to be completely innocuous, carried it in full view over his arm: a freshly dry-cleaned sport jacket in a clear plastic wrapper.

The jacket was on a thin wire coat hanger, and it was this item, the wire coat hanger, that Jay Jay used to dispose of the Society's enemies. He'd bend the hanger out of shape, slip it over the enemy's head from behind, put a knee in his back, and pull the hanger's thin edge tight against the man's throat. Afterward he'd bend the hanger back into its original triangle, rehang the jacket, pull on the plastic wrapper, and stroll away, just a man who'd picked up his dry cleaning.

Jay Jay shut the closet door on Mathews, and began to explore. The rooms were beautiful: oil paintings, ornaments, fine rugs everywhere.

He took the small elevator to the second floor and wandered in and out of more splendor: a two-thousand-volume library, a billiard room with not only a billiard table but a full-sized snooker table as well, a music room containing back-to-back harpsichords, several plush guest bedrooms, and an office cum den that Jay Jay guessed would alone be worth a fortune. Had he known anything about antiques he would have been able to identify a Victorian Gothic chimneypiece by John Francis Bentley, a Louis XIV Boulle work commode with splayed bombé sides, and a stunning eighteenth-century kingwood and tulipwood parquetry desk signed by Pierre Roussel.

The top floor was clearly Bendroit's personal preserve. Apart from the expertly laid-out squash court, and the changing room with its floor of sanded wood-end blocks, there was a superb little salon which overlooked the garden at the rear. Judging by the hot plate and dishes on the sideboard, Jay Jay figured it for a breakfast room. Had Mathews been with him, instead of being tied up in a closet downstairs, he would have been able to confirm this: this was indeed where the master breakfasted every morning. The sideboard was a seventeenth-century Spanish refectory table that Bendroit had had sawn in half to fit. The bowl near the food warmer was made of Vienna porcelain and had been decorated in 1730 by Ignez Preissler. Bendroit used it for his morning muesli and bran mixture, which Fortnum's made up for him as a special order. The glass next to it, a Jacobite Amen goblet engraved in diamond point, was for the passion-fruit juice that Bendroit had flown in from Kenya each week.

But as rich as the breakfast salon was, it was the master bedroom that most interested Jay Jay, and the dressing room off it. The double closet held enough suits and shoes to outfit a small men's store, although what caught Jay Jay's attention were the lounging clothes arranged on a valet stand in a corner. It looked as if the Englishman was in the habit of changing when he got home in the evenings. In which case he'd be coming upstairs.

Convenient.

Jay Jay went into the bathroom and saw just how an indulgent millionaire pampered himself. The glassed-in shower section, a good-sized room in itself, contained a white plastic divan big enough for two, and had been designed for fun and games beneath the warm water that would tumble down from the five separate shower heads. The soap on the marble basin was from Woods of Windsor, the hand towels from Descamps in Sloane Street. The Crombie's shaving mirror was a full twenty-four inches across, and the razor, in its little ceramic rack, had been fashioned by Asprey's in sterling silver. Culpepper had supplied the shaving cream, and the gallon bottle of pink toilet water was a personal blend from Penhagligon's. As for gadgets and appliances, there seemed to be two of everything. Jay Jay looked them over and chose a professional hair dryer, one made of stainless steel, and with a rubber grip on the handle.

A pair of nail scissors supplied him with all the tools he needed. He picked up the dryer and snipped carefully at one side of the white plastic cord, making an incision just deep enough to expose the copper wire inside. With a blade of the scissors he worked the wire strands out into a little loop, checked a cabinet, and reached for a roll of adhesive tape and two gauze pads. He took everything into the bedroom, plugged the dryer into a wall socket near the bed, and put down next to it the belt from a dressing gown he found.

Then he waited in a room on the front of the house until he heard the mutter of a taxi's diesel engine idling at the curb.

Peeping through the curtains, Jay Jay saw a man get out of the cab and start up the steps toward the front door; very well dressed, pink and barbered, and impressive-looking — he fitted the description exactly. Very faintly Jay Jay heard the front door open and close. He moved out of the room into the elegant corridor with its Allan Dodd trompe l'oeil wall paintings, and its seventy-foot-long Khorasan herati pattern runner, and looked around for a weapon. On an alabaster plinth, spotlighted from above, was a handsome piece of primitive art, a male figurine with two small cowrie shells inserted into the eye sockets. Holding it by its legs, Jay Jay went into the bedroom and on through to the dressing room.

The whine of the elevator came to him, the sound of its gate sliding back, then footsteps muffled by the Turkish carpet in the corridor. He waited with quiet patience, his slim body as immobile as the door he stood behind.

The footsteps changed from a measured tread to a soft

scuffing as shoes came off the carpet onto heavy broadloom. The well-dressed, big-bodied man walked into the room. When Jay Jay stepped out and hit him with the wood carving, its cowrie-shell eyes popped out of its head, fell to the floor, and lay there as if a wave had tossed them up onto the beach-white broadloom.

Bendroit collapsed on the bed, rolled off, and thumped onto the floor facedown and barely conscious. It was perfect positioning for Jay Jay; he'd felled him like a lumberjack placing a tree. With brisk efficiency he fished a wallet out of Bendroit's jacket, checked his identity, then rolled him over, placed a gauze pad over each of his eyes, and stuck the pads down with pieces of adhesive tape. He did this not because he didn't want Bendroit to get a look at him, but because he knew that an unsighted person feels far more vulnerable than one who can see.

Bendroit, at that moment, could only make out a blur anyway, his vision stunned out of focus by the blow to his head. He felt his arms being lifted and something soft and silky being slipped around his wrists — Jay Jay was wrapping the dressing-gown cord around them and securing the cord to a leg of the bed. To immobilize his victim's legs he hefted a brocaded winged armchair, walked it over the broadloom, and lowered it so that its considerable weight rested on Bendroit's ankles.

He unbuckled Bendroit's belt, lowered his pants, lowered his shorts, then went into the bathroom and came back with a glass of water which he dashed into Bendroit's face.

Bendroit grunted, fluttered back to full awareness, his head turning, alarmed at his sightlessness.

"Mr. Bendroit."

Bendroit's head stayed still. He tried to reach for the weight on his feet and found his arms were tied above him, tied to something. "What . . . ? What . . . ?"

"Mr. Bendroit, can you hear me?"

Bendroit flicked his head from side to side trying to get rid of the sticky pressure over his eyes.

"I've come to talk to you about money, Mr. Bendroit."

"What?" Bendroit's voice trembled as understanding of what was happening to him seeped into his clearing brain. He'd been attacked by a thief who'd somehow got into the house, got past that fool of a butler. Bendroit was very afraid, but he made a stab at taking control.

"I don't keep money in the house. Take some silverware. Take anything. Just get out of my house."

Jay Jay went on speaking as if there'd been no response.

"I am from the Sap Sei K." He saw the reaction: a tightening of the body; Bendroit's guard going up. "The Sai Bat Yat is worried, Mr. Bendroit."

"Who?"

"The Four Eight One."

Again Bendroit reacted. The Four Eight One was the head of the Society, the man with whom Bendroit had made his deal. Bendroit wouldn't know his name — even Jay Jay himself didn't know his name — but he would know him by his title.

"He is confused, Mr. Bendroit. There is something he doesn't understand. The agreement was that we would handle the transportation of your goods from Bangkok, protect them for twelve months in Hong Kong, then see that they were put on a vessel of your choosing. In return we would be paid ten million dollars, twenty percent of your gross. Is that not correct so far, Mr. Bendroit?"

Bendroit kept silent. His throat felt desiccated; he had a horrible suspicion they'd found out about the *Maloya Dan*.

"The fifty million," Jay Jay continued, "was to be shipped from New York, on a freighter of your choice, to a port in this country, and the ten million to be picked up by a representative of the Society. Four weeks ago you informed the Sai Bat Yat that cargo space had been booked on board a ship called the *Aztec Flyer*, leaving New York August twenty-eighth, arriving Dover September fifth. Through the Society's excellent shipping connections, Mr. Bendroit, we were able to get hold of a copy of the ship's manifest for that date. There is no cargo booked by Bendigo Shipping, your legitimate company, nor for any of your brass-plate companies. And again, due to our excellent shipping contacts, we know the names of those companies."

"I used another one," Bendroit said too quickly. "A new one."

"What is its name?"

Bendroit raced his brain. A name, quick! Winchester, his old school.

"Winchester Trading."

He heard a sickening noise: the rustle of a piece of paper being unfolded.

"I have brought a copy of the manifest with me . . ." Ten seconds of sweaty silence . . . "There is no cargo booked by Winchester Trading."

Jay Jay clicked on the hair dryer. The heavy motor whirred loudly in the stillness of the room. He spoke over it in his slow, correct English.

"Do you know what that sound is, Mr. Bendroit?"

No answer.

"It is the sound of discomfort."

He was standing above Bendroit. He bent and placed the metal nozzle of the dryer in Bendroit's crotch. It didn't burn Bendroit — the switch was on low — but it made him realize, for the first time, that he was half naked. It was an alarming feeling to be exposed as well as blind, and he squirmed and tried to turn over, but the heavy armchair kept him pinned.

"I think you have tried to cheat us, Mr. Bendroit."

"No. There's been a mistake, that's all. A mistake."

Jay Jay moved the nozzle of the hair dryer so that it just touched Bendroit's genitals. It was still on warm, pleasurable rather than painful.

"Tell me the name of the ship the money is coming on."

"The *Aztec Flyer*. Some idiot clerk has obviously —"

Jay Jay took the hair dryer's white plastic cord, bent it very carefully and, for the briefest instant, touched the part he'd cut open, the exposed copper wiring, to the metal base of the appliance. Bendroit screamed, tried to jackknife his body, thrashed on the floor like a worm on a hook, whipped his head around, and vomited on the broadloom. He coughed and choked, tried to curl himself into a ball, couldn't. His face had gone as white as the gauze pads over his eyes, his breath coming in heavy chunks, little moans on the end of each exhalation.

Jay Jay waited until the sounds had become whimpers, then clicked off the hair dryer but left the nozzle where it was.

"I repeat. What ship is the money coming on?"

He switched on the dryer so that Bendroit could again hear the sound of discomfort.

It was enough.

"The *Maloya Dan*."

The words were produced in an exhausted sob.

"Sailing when?"

"The twenty-seventh of August."

"Arriving . . . ?"

"September fourth."

"At . . . ?"

"Dover."

Jay Jay switched off the machine, brought his flat, tight face closer, his garlicky breath settling on Bendroit like an aromatic cloth.

"You are to be let off with a warning this time so that arrangements can be satisfactorily concluded. However, I am instructed to tell you that the penalty for late payment is very severe." He loosened the knots of the dressing-gown cord, rose, crossed the room, turned for a final word. "I am also instructed to tell you that the penalty for non-payment is even more so. Good-bye, Mr. Bendroit."

Jay Jay flew back to Hong Kong that evening and, the next day, reported to his superior, a ranking White Paper Fan.

His superior checked on the *Maloya Dan* and, sure enough, on August twenty-seventh, sailing from New York, cargo space had been booked for Merriweather Imports of Camberley, Surrey, which was one of Charles Bendroit's brass-plate companies. The White Paper Fan asked his chief Forty-nine boy what he'd used to extract the information.

"A hair dryer," Jay Jay answered, a made-up word in Cantonese.

The older man chuckled and said, "I'll bet he's sorry now he didn't buy a towel instead."

11

WHEN BENDROIT had come up with the idea of hoarding heroin and shipping it to New York on a massive scale, the first thing he'd had to do was find a buyer.

There could only be one organization with the ready cash to handle such a consignment, and Bendroit knew very little about it, so he'd engaged a former member of the organization to fill him in, and to help him with the negotiations.

And that was when he'd first heard the name Marco Morici.

"They call him Moreech," the man had told Bendroit. "He's the guy we're gonna see first up. We lay out the deal for him, and if he likes what he hears he talks to his boss, Roccobonno. If Roccobonno likes what he hears, he gets to hear it from us."

"Can't we just talk to this Rocco person? I don't want to waste time with assistants."

The man had cringed at Bendroit's usage. Rocco person. Jesus! Bendroit had done some cringing of his own; he found it abhorrent to be associated with low criminal types like Hinkler and this ex-Mafia man, but it was, unfortunately, unavoidable.

"Look," the man said. "I got to explain a few things. First of all Morici ain't exactly an assistant. We're going in pretty high. He's in line for the top slot, so this is not a clerk with an eyeshade and sleeve garters. Besides, you always want to deal with the number-two man if you can, because in an hour's time he might be the number-one man. Specially in the outfit we're gonna be seeing."

"What do you mean?"

"I mean where we're going, Palermo, they're all a little wacko. It's like a coral reef down there. You get one fish swimming a little woozy, and the barracudas move in."

"Internal disagreements. Is that what you're saying?"

"Yeah, you might call it that. The cops go after a family, make a few collars, wound 'em a little, somebody else in the family jumps in and finishes the job."

"I'd always understood," Bendroit had said, "that the Mafia had a reputation for loyalty."

"That's bullshit. Men of honor, men of respect, the *padrinos* that preached courage and dignity, that kinda crap's all gone now. There's too much money to be made to worry about dignity anymore. Instead you got guys like Morici and Roccobonno trying to think up ways to off each other."

"Do you know anything about their backgrounds?"

"Sure. Roccobonno's from Gela on the south coast. One of them Greek writers, Ecolips or something —"

"Aeschylus?"

"Yeah, that guy. He was killed in Gela. Got hit by a tortoise shell dropped by a passing eagle. That's how bright they are in Gela. Rocco's one of the *quarantennis*."

"That's his family?"

"No, he's boss of his own family. *Quarantennis* means forty-year-olds. They're the new boys. Rocco's got the smallest slice of the drug biz so he's the hungriest. He's still futzing around with the yo-yos in Marseilles and Beirut that supply Germany and Spain. But he'd sell his balls to go into the big market. So of all the families, he's gonna be happiest to see us."

"It all sounds rather amateurish," Bendroit had said with a disapproving frown.

"Mister, that's the word. The Sicilian Maf's got this great big reputation, supposed to be smarter than the FBI or something. Believe me, they're just a bunch of killer farmers, shitkickers, hayseeds who came down for a day on the steam cars and stuck around. In the States the families are all organized. They got their act together. But the Sicilians, well I mean, they already got a strike against them because they stayed in Sicily. Too dumb to know to get out. They chose to hang around an island in the Mediterranean where if you want real status you buy a washing machine. And you know what the families do with all that dough they make? Build apartment houses in Palermo. They only got forty or fifty already, but they're like kids with blocks. What money they got left over, which is like, maybe, seventy percent, they stick in the banks. Not the Swiss banks, the banks in Trapani, a dopey little town where for a big day out you go down to the *porto* and watch the gulls fightin' over fish heads. You know how many banks they got in Trapani now? This is a fact. More than they got in Milan, one of the great financial centers of Europe."

Bendroit had been disturbed by what he'd been hearing; he'd always found it unsound business practice to deal with fools.

"What about the other man? Morici?"

"Yeah, Morici." The man had curled his lower lip over his bottom teeth and rubbed at his cleft chin. "Morici's a different kettle of *pesce*. He is one smart eyetalian. They used to send him to Milan to make deals with the Turks, and only the bright boys get to do that. You don't have to worry about Roccobonno, he ain't got enough brains to shuck almonds. But Morici, you get to dealing with him, you gonna have to watch out he don't eat you with a spoon."

Marco Morici.

When he'd finally got to meet the man, Bendroit had

agreed with his new associate's summation: Morici was smooth and slick. An operator. A trifle smarmy, of course, as a lot of Continentals tended to be with their showy manners and easy command of language. The man was entirely too unctuous, his manner altogether too winning. He even looked like a gigolo with his almost feminine Latin features, and his absurd idea of never wearing a tie with a suit. Bendroit didn't like him but had to admit the man was smart. Was glad to admit it, in fact: it was always better to deal with an intelligent person — the stupid ones were usually too greedy to make any concessions.

For his own part, Marco Morici had thought Charles Bendroit a perfect example of what the English called an upper-class twit, although he had to admit that anyone who could be a start-up man, buyer at source, Hong Kong shipper, and U.S. wholesaler for over half a ton of heroin had a certain amount of style, too.

Morici had met with Bendroit on several occasions to discuss details of the arrangement both in London and New York.

On one of these trips to New York Morici had met with somebody else, too.

A member of the New York City Police Department.

He'd found the man with the help of the New York family he was dealing with. They knew a great deal about the local police, and when Morici had described the kind of man he was looking for, the family said they had just the guy for him. He was perfect. All he'd ever taken home was his salary.

He was one of those.

They explained to Morici how it was with cops in big-city America; it wasn't much different from how it worked in Sicily. Or anywhere else in the world. Policemen made a decision to either take now and then, or take not at all. The now-and-then takers tended to become full-time takers as they got older. And the non-takers began to think about taking as *they* got older.

The older takers all had their Florida money stashed away in triple-A-rated securities; they never flashed it — no Cadillacs, no foreign vacations. They ate sirloin steaks and drank Wild Turkey in the privacy of their homes, but there was never anything on show, so there was never anything for Internal to get nervous about. Or for the non-takers to get envious about.

Except at retirement time.

The cops with Florida money stashed away retired to the Gold Coast or Tampa Bay, and if the houses they bought and the boats they acquired and the golf clubs they joined seemed a little too fleecy to be paid for out of the savings from a policeman's salary, Internal didn't worry; the takers were out of the Department, and so couldn't besmirch its good name.

Fat retirements bothered the non-takers; it reminded them of what schmucks they'd been. After a lot of years of being dumped on by criminals and solid citizens alike, and going to work every day with the prospect of being brought home bleeding, what kind of rewards were they looking forward to? A framed letter from the commissioner to hang on the wall, and maybe a sideways shift into a security company, if they were lucky.

The man the family gave to Morici was due for retirement, and had no favors to call in. And, being a non-taker, there would be no condo in Pompano or St. Pete to move to. So he'd discreetly let it be known that he was ready to win a raffle, because he was damned if he wasn't going to have something to show for all those years.

Morici arranged a late-night meeting, and got to his offer in a roundabout way, easing into it, showing the policeman a photograph on the theory that one picture was worth a thousand words.

It was a color shot of a house in Fort Lauderdale taken from the rear so as to include the twenty-foot Chris-Craft tied to the dock in the waterway. The house had a riot of hibiscus and small palms in the garden, a screened pool attached, and stood under a sky that was like spilled blue poster paint.

The policeman considered the deal: Six hundred kilos was an insane amount, so he asked for a Chrysler Cordoba, too, plus a hundred grand pocket money.

"If I say yes, will you say yes?" Morici asked.

"Bet your ass," the policeman said.

He would have said yes for the Chris-Craft alone.

For their final meeting before the shipment changed hands, Morici came to London.

Bendroit suggested they meet for tea at the Connaught Hotel.

"The Connaught," the Italian said. "What an excellent idea. I haven't been there for years."

"It's not as stuffy as it once was," Bendroit told him. "They've relaxed their rule about ties in the summer months. Quite sensibly, too, I think. Will four o'clock suit?"

Bendroit had been lying, of course; the hotel never relaxed its rules about neckwear. But he had in mind Morici's penchant for wearing tieless shirts with his sporty Roman suits, and he knew what would happen: Morici would arrive at the Connaught, the hotel's policy would be politely pointed out to him, the maître d' would supply a tie, and the meeting would begin with a little edge in favor of the home team.

Bendroit was good at small maneuvers like that; he prided himself on his ability to gain the upper hand from the outset. It all went with being dynamic, a man of instant response and assuredness, although it was true his confidence had received a bit of a knock when the Chinese thug had broken in. It was something he was still having difficulty coming to terms with. To be tortured in one's own bedroom was not only degrading, it was ultimately incredibly insulting. As much as he hated to admit it, he'd badly underestimated the Triads. How in the world had they found out

the names of his brass-plates? They had to have an intelligence service better than those of most governments. Still,
cheating them would have made it awkward for next year's
shipment; and now, at least, he wouldn't have all the bother
of making new arrangements. He'd pay the heathens their
ten million, and try not to think about the seven or eight
Thoroughbreds the money would have bought.

Bendroit arrived at the hotel's unremarkable entrance
on Carlos Place at four-fifteen, allowing time for Morici to
have got there before him. The Italian was seated in the
lounge, a black tie knotted clumsily around the pale yellow
shirt he wore under a white jacket.

Bendroit smiled to himself, knowing very well there was
nothing clumsy about his own tie, handmade by Hilditch
and Key and knotted in a creaseless half Windsor.

"So sorry I'm late," he apologized.

"Not at all. I just arrived myself," Morici said in his soft,
pleasant accent.

Bendroit allowed his glance to fall on the poorly knotted
tie.

"Oh, dear. I fear my information was wrong. I'm so sorry."

Morici tried to make light of it with a tolerant smile.

"It is of no consequence. When I walked into the hotel
apparently I was not a gentleman." He flicked a disdainful
finger at the tie, flouncing it out. "Now, apparently, I am."

"We could leave if you like. There are plenty of other —"

"No, no. I shall suffer the curious customs of the natives."
Morici settled back, a small-boned, slender man in his mid-
forties. He said amiably, "So, I trust you have been well?"

They spent several minutes discussing the weather, the
London theater, the recitals, the galleries, the best places
to dine — the usual summation of what was desirable, fashionable, or interesting when a well-heeled traveler arrives
in a world capital. They were sitting at the rear of the
lounge, which was a quiet, comfortable area like somebody's immaculate living room, small tables spread with

pink cloths placed between chintz-covered winged armchairs and velvet settees. Two young waiters in black tuxedos served them expertly, then politely retired.

"Such a civilized institution," Morici allowed, taking a small bite from a sandwich. Actually he thought it absurd to have picnic fare an hour and a half after lunch; he'd never understood the attraction. Also, he hated tea. "And tell me. Is everything proceeding well?"

"We are on schedule. I heard from Bangkok only yesterday."

Bendroit was lying; the arrangement was that Hinkler would call him from Hong Kong when the last one hundred kilos arrived.

"Excellent," Morici said. "I had no doubts, I assure you."

He lifted his cup, then put it down again, fingering the tie around his neck in what he hoped would look like discomfort — he was well aware of Bendroit's little trick, and had decided to give him his paltry little victory.

"I have a request, Mr. Bendroit. I have a favor to ask of you."

"I'd be only to happy to oblige."

Morici's handsome face expressed his thanks. He could speak freely; they were relatively isolated. An overweight stockbroker type was fiddling with some pills at a far table and, at another, a couple of plump young men, mildly stupefied from lunch, were recovering with some tea while they perused the dinner menu.

"It concerns Mr. Roccobonno," Morici began, "who, incidentally, sends you his kindest regards."

Bendroit could just imagine the brooding, cigar-smoking, ex-village bully boy sending his good wishes.

"Thank you. And please return mine."

"Before Mr. Roccobonno achieved the exalted position he enjoys today," Morici said, using, for Bendroit, his most flowery English, "he was involved in the transport of cigarettes."

[186]

Bendroit blandly cocked an eyebrow.

"Really?"

"Yes, you see there's a government monopoly in Italy. The cigarettes are inexpensive but of rather poor quality. You can buy American cigarettes but they cost more than twice as much, so we take pity on the poor Italian smoker. We bring in American cigarettes from Switzerland which are made under license there. We contract with a wholesaler in Lugano and arrange for delivery in Milan. It's a clandestine operation, naturally."

"I'm surprised," Bendroit said. "I would have thought that cigarettes would be too much time and trouble, too small a return these days."

"Profits are good but not stunning. Forty billion cigarettes are moved every year, so money can be made. However, in Sicily the business is regarded as foreign since its main operation takes place on the Continent, and Mr. Roccobonno would prefer a more homegrown industry, and a more lucrative one. That is, of course, the reason why we are sitting here."

"Just so," Bendroit agreed. "But you were mentioning cigarettes . . ."

"Ah, yes." Morici took a small bite from a cucumber sandwich. There was no dressing on it, it was just plain cucumber. The English were crazy.

"As you have explained, Mr. Bendroit, the shipment will be packed in fifty-five-gallon oil drums. I trust those arrangements have undergone no change?"

"None whatsoever."

"Good, good," Morici said, and took another bite from his sandwich. Bendroit could tell he disliked the food as much as he disliked the tea, so it was clear to him that the Italian was stalling, putting off whatever it was he had to say because he was embarrassed by it. Bendroit recognized a man with a request he would have preferred not to have to make.

"Good," Morici said for the third time. "Because according to our measurements you'll be able to fit one hundred and nineteen kilo bags into each drum if you lay them flat, or one hundred and thirty-two if you stand them upright. So it's to be assumed you'll go for the more efficient figure which, at six hundred bags, will fill four and a half drums."

"I cannot comment on the number of drums, that is all being handled in Hong Kong. But I've no doubt you are correct."

"Then you will need some kind of filling for the half-empty drum."

Morici dropped his eyes as he said this, and Bendroit saw that he was right about him being embarrassed. "Mr. Roccobonno wonders if you'd be so kind as to include some cigarettes as a filler."

"Oh? How extraordinary."

"It's a kind of joke, you see. One of the buyers in New York used to be with Mr. Roccobonno. In cigarettes. Mr. Roccobonno thinks it might be —" Morici searched his vocabulary for a word that would appeal to Bendroit's private-school background — "a good jape. It's harmless enough, and it would be doing my employer a favor," Morici concluded with a weak little grin.

Bendroit made a gesture of avuncular tolerance, as if he were agreeing to the amusing request of a child.

"I don't see why not. Is there any special brand of cigarettes you'd like?"

"Good heavens, we certainly don't expect you to supply them. They'll be counterfeit American cigarettes made right there in Hong Kong. They're very popular in the Asian market."

"Then consider it done."

"How kind of you. Personally" — Morici moved his head in a way that suggested mild annoyance — "I think it a trifle frivolous, but . . ." Leaving the rest of the thought unexpressed he brought out an envelope, which he handed over. "All the details are inside. Including the way Mr. Roccobonno would like the drum marked for easy identification."

"I'll get it off to my man immediately."

They both rose. Bendroit tried to pick up the check but Morici wouldn't hear of it.

"A delightful idea," he said. "Tea at the Connaught."

At a doorway of the lounge Morici unknotted the black tie and handed it to the maître d'.

"Thank you," Morici said. "I enjoyed wearing it."

The maître d' accorded him a faint bow.

"Not at all, sir."

Bendroit insisted Morici take the first cab, and watched him leave.

Roccobonno.

He was going to make a fortune on the deal but he still couldn't resist making an extra few thousand dollars on cigarettes. A greedy oaf.

Bendroit shut the Sicilian out of his mind; he felt too good to bother with ciphers. Hinkler and Dubin should be meeting in Hong Kong in about a week's time and putting the shipment on the tanker. A safe, slow voyage to New York, a quick sale, then the money on a freighter bound for Dover. The whole thing, the culmination of so much work and planning, was so close now that perhaps a little celebration would not be out of order.

Bendroit set out in the fine, soft evening heading for Andre Simon's splendid wine shop on Davies Street. Possibly they might still be able to find some of that '47 Cheval Blanc. It was expensive, in dollar terms well over four thousand a case, but what was that to a man about to be worth fifty million?

Well, forty million.

Damn Triads.

12

ONE WEEK.

Seven days before Marcus had to be in Hong Kong.

He and Claire grabbed their chance and hugged it to them in the same way in which they enclosed and surrounded each other. Being together was a lot sweeter and deeper than it had been in Chiang Mai; they realized now that their relationship could have been something else entirely if they hadn't been alert enough to recognize it for what it was. For Marcus it could have been nothing more than a pleasant little dalliance with an attractive business associate. For Claire, had she responded for the same reason — and she knew she well might have — it could have been written off at the end of the trip like a shipboard romance, something that's quickly begun and just as quickly ended. So both felt that what they had between them was like a beautiful and rare vase that had almost been fumbled above a concrete floor, and was now that much more precious for having been saved.

They spent most of their seven days in Phuket, the resort island south of Bangkok. They lazed on the white sand of the long, perfect beaches, rented a sailboat and skimmed over the clear depths of the Andaman Sea, watched the sun fall toward a blue ocean and sink into a red one. They took trips to Phangnga Bay, and rode an outboard through the mangroves and in and out of the extraordinary limestone islands that were taller than they were wide. They wangled a Land Rover and made the bumpy excursion to a deserted inlet near Kata and made love with the water lapping over them and the sun on their skins.

And they made plans. In a roundabout way.

Claire brought up the subject on their last night when they were sitting at a little beach restaurant, clumps of bright stars beginning to pop out above the rattan roof, their white light mimicked by the flutter of hurricane lamps set up on the rough wood tables.

The knowledge was there between them, unvoiced so far, that there could be little future with one of them in Atlanta and the other in New York. Claire had been giving it a lot of thought and saw that the easiest way out of it would be for her to make a decision. It was either that or lose Marcus, so the decision was an easy one to make.

"I've been thinking about something," she said.

"Tell me."

"It's just that if we nail Bendroit, my struggling little law firm will have its biggest client in jail."

"Offer to defend him for a large fee," Marcus said, then stopped smiling and put his hand over hers. "That thought occurred to me, too. I'm afraid that, professionally, this is all going to be a little counterproductive for you."

"So I was thinking," Claire went on, making a design on the tabletop with the bottom of her wineglass, "that instead of trying to get going again in New York, I thought maybe I'd try another town. Atlanta, maybe. It'd mean qualifying for the Georgia bar but — "

"Atlanta? That's too bad. I was hoping we'd be seeing something of each other."

Claire's head came up quickly.

"Won't we?"

"Not if you're in Atlanta. I'm planning a move to New York. Been working on it for some time."

Claire didn't tell him he was a consummate liar; instead she said, "But you've been with the police department for twelve years. You can't just toss that away."

"What am I tossing away? Twelve years of taking orders. I'd like to try being the boss for a change. Go into corporate security, maybe. Spend a year with a firm, learn the ropes, then go out on my own, something like that. Security consultant to corporations. So it makes sense to go where the most corporations are."

"I see," Claire said, then got up from her chair and came around and kissed him hard. "Billy, you're sure?" The flame in the center of the table bounced off the moisture in her eyes.

Marcus, trying to keep it light, said, "You betchum, Red Ryder."

He'd been giving it a lot of thought, too. He knew very well that what he was proposing to do would mean twelve years of his life down the tubes, and that there was no guarantee that, once back in the States, Claire would feel the same thing for him that she felt right then; but the way he saw it, even if it meant as little as six weeks with Claire, it would still be worth the twelve years.

He told her later that night about the trek into Burma, a subject they'd both previously stayed away from. Marcus told her that he'd shot Boyle; told her about Hinkler and that he was going to kill him, too. Told her why.

She didn't agree.

"I'm sorry about your partner, Billy. But I don't think one death justifies another."

"My God, I'm in love with a bleeding-heart liberal." When Claire's face stayed serious, Marcus said, "What if you knew, beyond any doubt, that a person who'd killed somebody was going to kill somebody else? Would you — what's the word? — sanction that person's killing in a case like that?"

"You're talking about an infallible crystal ball. Is that right?"

"Right. Absolutely infallible."

"If I knew for sure that I'd be saving a life, then yes, I'd sanction a killing. That's the whole principle of self-defense."

"Okay, then."

"Okay then, what?"

"I know for sure that Hinkler is going to try to kill somebody."

"Who?" Claire asked. Then, with fear in her heart, knew immediately the answer to that question when Marcus slowly smiled at her.

He put Claire on a flight to New York, took a plane in the opposite direction, arrived in Hong Kong around nine at night, and plunged straight into the whole clamoring, sign-infested, shop-jammed, people-teeming city.

He knew nobody in the colony to buy him a gun so he'd taken a risk and packed the Clark in his suitcase.

He was glad he had when, less than thirty minutes after he'd reached his hotel, Hinkler called up from the lobby: they were all ready and waiting for him. Marcus strapped on the Rogers rig, dropped the pistol in, hid everything under his shirttails.

Downstairs there was a cab at the curb, Hinkler sitting in it with a tall Chinese who, forty years behind the times, sported a snappy blue suit, two-tone shoes, and a mouth full of gold teeth. If this was a Triad member, as Marcus felt he surely was, the man was doing nothing not to draw attention to himself.

"It get here okay?" Marcus asked, getting into the taxi.

"If it hadn't you would've been in very deep shit," Hinkler answered, setting the tone of the reunion.

Nothing more was said while they drove through traffic-choked streets to what a sign said was the Middle Island marina. They walked past a fleet of cabin cruisers and boarded a sixty-foot Cheoy Lee trawler yacht which got underway immediately. It eased out into a harbor that seemed almost as crowded and hectic as the cacophonous streets they'd left behind; tankers and freighters, tugs and scows and junks and sampans, smoke, rust, garbage, floating ordure. The yacht picked up speed as it cruised toward the Lei Yue Mun channel, the wind beginning to shift the thick, heavy air.

Marcus leaned on the rail and watched a jet float through the night toward the airport runways built out into the harbor. When he brought his eyes down, Hinkler was standing there ostensibly captured by the pyrotechnics of the Mercedes and Seiko signs atop the Wanchai high rises. Marcus could sense the tension as the man balanced his boxer's body against the roll of the yacht, his big hands gripping the rail in a stranglehold. He was pretty sure Hinkler wouldn't make his move until after the transaction in New York, which was fine except for one thing: Marcus didn't want to wait that long.

He spoke up over the beat of the yacht's engines.

"You didn't ask me about the trail. It was pretty exciting."

Hinkler hawked and spat into the black water.

"Who gives a fuck?"

"Boyle had himself a real time. He killed Agosta."

"The guinea? Best thing for him."

That stopped the conversation for a while, both men settling for the sight of peaks rising into the night sky like Christmas trees. The wind came at them from a different quarter as the yacht began its turn into the channel. The engines deepened their sound, and the bow began to dip and carve through the chop. Tung Lung Island, the original Chinese settlement, floated by on their left, and then they were sailing into darkness.

Marcus made a claw of his hand, ran his fingers through his close-cropped hair, turned toward Hinkler, who was still gazing over the side.

"He killed a couple of Shans, too," he said, picking up

where he'd left off. "They were unarmed. I heard they were running away at the time."

"Anybody gets that guy mad," Hinkler said, "they'd be smart to run away."

"You're right. Hell of a temper, your boyfriend."

Hinkler snapped his head around.

"What do you mean, boyfriend?"

"Okay. Hell of a temper, your friend."

"Better remember that and stay away from him."

"I recall you telling me that once before. However, it wasn't possible."

"What do you mean?"

The blue-suited Chinese came out on deck, his hands mired in his pockets, a cigarette stuck at a crazy angle in his mouth, hanging down like a saber tooth. He sucked at it, exhaled smoke with a lot of lip power, took a fast look at the intemperate water, and went back inside.

"What do you mean?" Hinkler asked again.

Marcus turned away.

"I'll tell you later."

"You'll fuckin' tell me now."

"I'll fuckin' tell you when I want to."

Hinkler's hands had left the rail, and there was a moment when his right one might have darted inside his jacket. Marcus had his arms folded on the rail, hands very close to his belt. Hinkler had noticed that belt — Marcus had caught him looking at it in the taxi — the big oval buckle that said Rogers Leather. A guy like Hinkler would have to know what that could mean.

The big man swung around abruptly, crossed the deck, and went below, leaving Marcus to watch the progress of the yacht. They were passing little islets now, round chunks of scrubby rock, little more than navigational hazards. A flight of pelicans swished overhead mast-high. They flew fast, in a hurry, as if they knew that water so black and forbidding couldn't possibly hold anything appetizing.

Ten minutes later the engines changed their sound once

more, dropping down half an octave. The breeze slowed with the yacht's speed and the heat, a soggy overcoat, flopped onto Marcus's shoulders again. Ahead he could just make out a dim light slowly growing in intensity. Behind it, barely discernible, an outline darker than the night took shape and became, after a while, rocks and a wisp of beach.

"Po Toi."

The Triad with the gold teeth had come up next to him.

"Pardon?"

The man pointed, an Inca treasure flashing in his smile. "Po Toi Island."

It lay low in the water and down on one side like a torpedoed ship. The listing effect was heightened by a line of scraggy trees that had grown tired of fighting the monsoons and stood slumped over in a humbled group. A nervous wooden jetty tongued out from the tiny beach and swayed in the waves of the boat's wake as the yacht maneuvered alongside it. The structure leaned and moaned and creaked arthritically; a flashlight beam pounced on them, a hand caught a thrown rope.

Two men Marcus hadn't seen before emerged from the cabin carrying large cardboard boxes. They stepped onto the dock, the Triad man following, Marcus bringing up the rear, Hinkler staying on board. They picked their way over the broken slats of the jetty onto a shingle beach littered with broken baskets and redolent with the smell of seaweed and rotted fish. The shingles yielded to a rocky track, then Marcus felt grass squishing under his shoes as a silhouette of big-leafed trees pushed against the darkness. The group followed the man with the flashlight for maybe five minutes, then walked into a sea monster's breath as the track curved and a cave opened in front of them.

The Triads had picked a good one; the entrance narrowed quickly, bent into an antechamber, then widened and became a cavern of considerable dimensions, the artificial illumination, three kerosene pressure lamps, invisible from the outside. The air was cool here, almost cold, and from somewhere at the shadowed rear came the pulse and movement of the sea.

There were six men present, four of them fighters: trim, athletic types in jeans and baseball jackets. From the rear of the cave the fighters carried out five Sunkist orange crates, each one containing twenty one-kilo bags of a snowy white powder with the fine consistency of laundry detergent. The last time Marcus had seen this substance it had been a lumpy gray color, and he wondered out loud what had happened to it in the meantime.

The Triad, bragging about his organization, was happy to fill him in. He told him that Agosta's assistant — which had to be Harn Suk — had unloaded the original five-pound bags onto a rice barge at a town called Nakhon Sawan, about 150 miles north of Bangkok. The barge had plodded down the Chao Phraya River into the *klong* system of the capital, where the shipment had been repacked into waterproof bags, transferred to a Thai trawler, and ferried to Hong Kong under a catch of snapper and gilt tail. A local junk had fished up the bags from the drop-off point, and taken them on a moonlit sail to a carp farm up near the New Territories. The bags had been off-loaded into a van and driven over the hairpin bends of the Twisk Road into the concrete jungle of Mong Kok in Kowloon.

There the finishing factories had been set up in five different apartments, nothing in them except what was needed: a Calor gas ring, a large enamel tub, some lime trays, a Buchner flask, a vacuum pump, ice, an electric fan, freezer bags, a heat-sealing machine, and the necessary chemicals: ethyl alcohol, hydrochloric acid, ether, plus a bag of activated charcoal.

What had gone in as 60 percent pure diacetylmorphine — heroin base — emerged a day later as 90 percent pure diacetylmorphine hydrochloride — the real stuff. With his question answered proudly, and at some length, Marcus watched the fighters pile up the orange crates, grab the end of a large tarpaulin, and peel it back.

Five black oil drums sucked up the light from the gas lamps. Four were sealed, the last had had its top cut out leaving a short flange around the inside of the rim.

The men packed the heroin bags neatly into the drum, then opened the cardboard boxes which had been carried from the yacht. When they began to take out cartons of cigarettes, Marcus turned to the Triad official.

"Buyer used to be in smoke business," the man explained, sounding amused. "Still want to be in smoke business."

The cigarette cartons, faked to look absolutely genuine, were packed into the drum on top of the heroin bags until it was brim-full. Then a man with an arc welder, and a small Honda generator, braised the top onto the drum. When he finished he took a hammer and chisel and began to make marks in the rim to distinguish it from the other drums.

The fighters had already begun to move them out of the cave. They rolled them slowly along the grassy track to the creaking jetty and, two to a drum, lifted them onto the yacht. Everybody boarded the boat, which immediately headed out to sea toward its rendezvous, sailing south through a hot and sluggish tide.

Twenty miles behind the stern pole the reflected joys of Hong Kong daubed the sky with a faint pink glow that slowly began to fade: pink to red, red to blue, blue to black.

The tanker came out of the night like a high, dark hill.

Ponderous and huge, rumbling along at less than five knots, it exchanged a quick visual signal with the yacht, which curled around and ran parallel to the ship, drawing up beneath the lowered gangway.

The Triad went up first, Hinkler followed, then Marcus. Behind him came men who'd been in the cabin out of sight, two young Chinese wearing swimsuits. They had diving tanks buckled to their backs, and scuba masks on their foreheads.

There was nobody to greet them on deck; a single light had been rigged at the rail but, beyond that, darkness ruled. Marcus had never been on a tanker before; it was like walking along the side of a building that had collapsed intact. The deck stretched ahead forever, a raised catwalk dividing it into two immensely long halves. He went by a slanting breakwater, stepped around several tank hatches and the loading/discharge pipes that spanned the deck at right angles. The accommodation stack at the stern looked like an apartment building, yellow lights behind square windows. It seemed calm and undisturbed.

They stopped and waited while the Triad went off to find somebody, the lifts of his two-tone shoes ringing out sharply on the steel deck. When the sound died away the only noises were the whomp of the ship's engines and the eerie moan of the breeze blowing through the catwalk.

The Chinese returned eventually with four men in tow, a big, dyspeptic-looking man with striped epaulets on his shirt, and three Filipino seamen wearing boilersuits. The officer, who had a gauze patch over his eye from some injury, led the way forward and stopped in front of a hatch which the seamen proceeded to open, undoing the ratchet locks, and hinging back the metal cover.

Marcus couldn't see inside it but he could smell salt water. He knew little about tankers, but the ship couldn't have been carrying any oil riding so high out of the water as it was; it would have to be in ballast, so this would be a saltwater ballast tank the men had opened.

A heavy whirring sound came from the direction of the bow and, looking up, Marcus saw the white bulk of an oil-hose crane turning on its axis. There was somebody underneath it with a flashlight. The crane swung out over the rail and lowered its grappling cable over the side. Guided by the flashlight the yacht below pulled ahead and positioned itself directly beneath the crane. A brief silence was sliced apart by the crane's engine as the cable came up dangling a black drum, snap hooks biting in securely around its rims. It was swung in over the rail and lowered to the deck. After a minute, two seamen came out of the darkness rolling the drum in front of them. They stopped at the hatch and began to encase the drum in a webbing sling while the two divers got ready. The first of them, stepping up onto the hatch, turned and felt with his foot for the top rung of the ladder that descended in three stages to the bottom of the tank. He snapped his air hose into position over his face, lowered his mask, and was swallowed whole as he began the long climb down through a couple of million gallons of black salt water.

The underwater lamp he carried around his neck was no use to him because he needed both his hands; he just had to feel his way, pushing himself down the ladder against the natural buoyancy of the tank's contents.

At a depth of twenty feet he came to the second stage of the ladder and paused. It was blacker than black around him, far darker than a sea diver ever gets to experience. The tank was like a liquid hole in the earth, claustrophobic for all its immense volume, the water seeming thick and suffocating.

The second stage now, hand over hand down another twenty feet, the pressure increasing in his ears.

The final stage took him sixty-five feet below the deck, way below the water line, the engines vibrating the bottom girders beneath his bare feet. He reached for his flashlight, and lit up his partner coming down to the top of the third stage.

Up on deck the five seamen hefted the drum, now swathed in a cargo sling with a long nylon rope attached to it, up onto the lip of the hatch. They snaked another rope through the webbing, this one about twelve feet long with clamps on either end. The officer peered into the midnight color of the tank and saw the watery blink of the diver's lamp, three short flashes. When he murmured something to the men, the drum was rolled off and dumped into the tank, sending up a shower of water as it kerchunked in and sank beneath the surface. Its rope snapped taut, and the seamen, leaning their weight against it, began to pay it out.

From the bottom of the tank the divers looked up into reflected light, the beam of the diving lamp bouncing back at them from the water over their heads. It was a few minutes before they caught the gleam of the drum. It appeared above them sinking with an evil slowness, the way a depth charge languidly glides down before blowing a hole in the sea.

They let it come all the way and bump almost soundlessly on the bottom girders. They untied the lowering rope, jerked a signal on it, and made sure it was retracted. Then they pushed the water-supported drum to a corner of the tank and clamped it to a web-frame girder.

Watching it happen, watching the drums being lowered into the dark water, the diver's lamp a shimmering glow almost twenty fathoms down, Marcus could see that Bendroit had picked a very smart hiding place. It made sense: the guy was in shipping, he'd know the business back to front. The huge ship laboriously moved the sea aside for another mile, then the divers came up dripping.

"All finish," the Triad said in the dark. "We go now."

Hinkler, who hadn't liked any part of his time on board the ghostly vessel, was first to the rail, first down the gangway and back onto the yacht. The two divers, as wet as seals, were the last to drop onto the boat; then it swung away in a wide looping turn, and left the tanker to dwindle in the night, the choppy sea ironed flat by its enormous bulk as it continued west.

Hinkler waited until the yacht was back at the marina before he came near Marcus again. No sailor, he wanted dry land beneath his feet if he was going to get into something.

He attended to business first, going into the marina's office and calling Bendroit's shipping firm. He left an innocent-sounding message to the effect that the cargo had been dispatched on schedule, then came out and rejoined Marcus.

The Chinese with the gold teeth bid them both a cheery good-bye, got into a taxi, and left them together. They walked silently, side by side, through the neon wash of a parking lot.

Hinkler was as transparent as a sheet of glass.

His mouth got tighter as his step got slower, letting Marcus get half a step ahead of him.

Marcus stopped and turned.

"You got a question, Hinkler?"

"Yeah. What about you and Boyle?"

"We had an argument."

"What about?"

"Speed."

"Bullshit. He don't touch that crap."

"Oh, I don't mean funny-colored pills. I mean the other kind of speed. He thought he was faster than me." Marcus shrugged. "Maybe he just had an off day."

Realization threw a net over Hinkler's face, and his expression flattened. He said, "Maybe he did," and turned away as if he were giving it some deep thought.

Marcus had seen that move before. In front of Atlanta's Fox Theater he'd seen Hinkler make the same action: turning away, then coming right back again with a gun in his hand.

This time the man only got halfway through the move before hearing the unmistakable sound of a gun clearing a holster.

"Put your right hand on your jacket," Marcus ordered. "Open it . . . now take out that piece with two fingers of your left hand."

Hinkler hated to do it; he had to grip the gun awkwardly, lift it in reverse from the Alessi shoulder rig, let Marcus take it from him for the second time in his life.

"Let's walk a ways," Marcus invited.

Hinkler preceded him through the parked automobiles, his sloping shoulders rigid, his long neck stiff with anger.

They kept going past the edge of the lot, the smell of tar and rope and salt water superseded by the aromas of broiling charcoal and hot cooking oil coming from the truck restaurants at the other end of the parking area.

Across the street, edged in one after the other, their interior shelves clogged with goods, shops formed a solid line, their sidewalk bins pyramids of merchandise: food, tools, clothes, car wax, shoes, candles, radios, anything that could be wrapped up or squeezed into a shopping bag. They walked by them, surrounded by people, jammed in.

Looking for some privacy, Marcus directed Hinkler into an alley cut like a firebreak through the blue smoke of traffic, but it was just as bright and raucous as the street they'd left.

They moved along it, walked beneath shirttail water splotching down from balcony clotheslines, hugged the alley walls to dodge tricycles zipping through on deliveries, the crowds rolling back after each noisy intrusion. There were no strollers; everybody bustled, everybody's arms were full — boxes, bags, baskets — nobody noticed a Westerner carrying a pistol near his leg.

"In here," Marcus said.

It was just a doorway, but it was open, and the interior seemed calm and deserted.

They went through the door.

Fish looked at them from behind glass. Mouths made small O's.

The place was a tropical-fish warehouse, row upon row of aquariums on tables, the tank lights casting a pale blue glow over the swimming inhabitants.

Marcus closed the door, shutting out much of the traffic

noise. The hum and bubble of heaters took over, the soft thump of a generator sifting in from the rear.

"Hinkler . . ."

Hinkler turned.

"How many men have you killed?"

"Not enough."

"That's not a bad answer."

Hinkler spoke as if the words were painful in his mouth. "I should've taken you out long ago, Dubin. I made a big mistake."

"Your big mistake was believing my name is Dubin. It's Marcus. That ring any bells?"

Hinkler stared at him; the name meant nothing.

"How about George Chaska? That mean anything?" When Hinkler just stood there Marcus said angrily, "Jesus Christ. You kill a man, and you don't even remember his name?"

Hinkler was frowning, uncertain of what Marcus was talking about.

"I killed this guy? Chasga?"

"Chaska. In Atlanta. Four o'clock of a Thursday morning about four months back. You and Boyle were down there on a little drug business for Bendroit. George thought you were lost, driving around and around the way you were, so he came over to help. You gave him two in the chest for his trouble."

"That was you? The other guy?" Hinkler was peering at Marcus as if there were a grubby window between them. "The guy Boyle stuck?"

"That was me."

"You're a cop." It came out a damning accusation.

"Yeah."

"I should've greased you instead."

"Wouldn't have made any difference. It'd be Chaska who was shooting you instead of me."

With nothing to lose Hinkler set himself to charge.

Marcus slanted the .45 so that it pointed at the man's right eye.

"Hold up, buddy. You'll spoil the surprise I got for you."

Marcus took Hinkler's revolver from his belt, stepped back a good ten feet, and put his own gun, the Clark, down onto a table. He hit the cylinder release on Hinkler's gun, poked out four rounds, leaving the fifth bullet in, and snapped the cylinder closed.

Hinkler, suspicion etching lines into his forehead, watched him pick up the Clark, drop the clip, eject the bullet in the chamber, and feed in a round he took from behind his oval belt buckle. Holding the Clark on Hinkler, Marcus walked closer, put the man's revolver within his reach.

"We have one round apiece. Pick up your gun and we'll play hide-and-go-seek."

"Fuckin' con artist," Hinkler said.

"Go ahead, check your weapon, you think I shortchanged you."

With steady, careful movements Hinkler picked up the revolver and popped the cylinder. Then his head began to shake slowly, looking at Marcus as if he'd just committed some unpardonable sin.

"You're crazy, mister. Either that or bone stupid. You don't give a guy like me a chance."

"Hinkler, you have a chance," Marcus said, with a lot of slow emphasis. "But what you don't have is a hope."

Hinkler said something that Marcus didn't catch, then spun around, hurried up the aisle, and disappeared in the dark among the glass tanks at the far end of the room. He moved around for a moment, then there was silence.

Marcus stayed still, let twenty seconds tick by, then got going.

The room was arranged on a grid pattern, six or eight aisles running north and south, a similar number east and west. The blue lights over the tanks were the room's only illumination, low-powered strip lights that threw no shadow.

Marcus started down the same aisle Hinkler had taken because he was certain Hinkler would expect him to come up one of the others. He stopped, crouched down, moved some more, stopped again.

A Siamese fighting fish, with a tail like a skyrocket, mouthed at the limits of its world, eyed Marcus and wondered about him, watched him move into a cross-aisle.

There was still no sound from the far end of the room. For the moment, Hinkler was staying put.

Marcus went back the way he'd come, turned a corner, turned another, moving like a knight on a chessboard: a few feet down a cross-aisle, then twice that distance down any one that joined it.

He stopped.

Froze.

Listened.

Water burbled through tubing. Heaters hummed.

Fins fluttered. Scales glittered. Gills filtered oxygen.

The glass tanks shone with their bright jewels, the silent, glistening swimmers. Near a tank in front of him he spied a box of fish food.

It arced through the blue fluorescence when Marcus tossed it, landed with a loud *gall-opp!* thirty feet away.

Water slopped and splashed, dripped for a second, dried up.

It brought a shuffling noise from a far corner.

One more aisle up and in, then Marcus waited.

Hinkler wouldn't like the sudden silence; he'd be no good at waiting, a man like that, all action, short on patience. Hinkler was a guy who dived into that shoulder holster and got off a couple before he thought about it.

Twenty seconds. Thirty. Forty. A minute.

The shuffle again. Hinkler was too big to move quietly.

Another sound.

Different.

Sure. Hinkler taking off his shoes.

Crouching on his haunches, Marcus waited.

A few inches from his right cheekbone a red-and-green gourami bullied a smaller one, chased it like a dog herding sheep, cutting it off, cornering it, furious.

Another of the tank's inhabitants, a black-banded damselfish, investigated a water thermometer and took no notice of the squabble.

A minute's silence became two. Stretched into three. Then a noise.

Slight but sharp.

A cricking noise, the way knees sound when somebody straightens up.

Hinkler was coming.

A thin furrow appeared in the sand in the bottom of the tank, and a red coolie loach emerged and began to busily vacuum a layer of pebbles. Marcus watched it, wondering what made it such a frantic housekeeper. Like skaters in tandem the gouramis, their spat temporarily forgotten, whirled around behind the glass in sudden acceleration, then leaned against the water and glided to an elegant stop. The loach, burrowing back into the sand, disappeared; the damselfish turned and froze in profile, and all movement in the tank ceased.

But there was movement elsewhere.

Very, very faintly, hard to hear over the mutter and bubble of the pumps, came the tiny elastic snap of fiber catching on a rough wooden floor.

Marcus watched the marine life, suspended in their element like a gleaming mobile, listened to the scuffing of stockinged feet.

The sound ceased, and a hush followed; tingling, electric.

Hinkler was listening for him.

Marcus moved only his eyes. There was a clipboard on the table near the tank, a sheet of ruled paper uppermost displaying spidery Chinese ideograms, some with a penciled tick against them. It was probably just an inventory,

Marcus thought, yet the formed characters, written with a felt tip, made the document pretty enough to frame.

Three aisles up and one aisle in; that was where he figured Hinkler was. Moving again now, coming slowly.

With small, contained movements Marcus slid the buttons of his shirtfront through the buttonholes, undid his sleeve cuffs, eased out of the shirt, held it loosely in his left hand.

Hinkler had reached the corner now, the corner of the cross-aisle which Marcus was on. He'd be about forty feet away. Marcus let him get maybe ten feet closer, then did two things simultaneously: belted the table with the barrel of the pistol, and hurled his shirt up into the air and out into the aisle.

A bullet tore through it instantly, the bang of Hinkler's revolver melding into the splintering of glass as the slug traveled the length of the room, smashing the tops of a dozen aquarium tanks.

Marcus stood up. He said, "You lose, Hinkler," and took the man's gun on the eyebrow as it came flying out of the blue-tinged darkness.

It shocked Marcus, rocked him. He hadn't expected a reaction that fast in a guy of Hinkler's size. Blood fell into his eye, and a black dizziness leeched onto his brain and sucked at it, and had Hinkler kept coming it would have been close, but the man was running for the far end of the warehouse where a three-sided sliver of light outlined a door.

Marcus snatched up his bullet-holed shirt, tried to staunch the blood, found he couldn't, and got a better idea. He grabbed the clipboard he'd been admiring, pulled the bulldog off the top, pinched the gashed flesh over his eye, and clamped it closed with the steel lips of the clip. It hurt like hell, but that was one of the very few advantages of having a knife blade slipped into your back: from then on any other kind of pain was minimal in comparison.

The door Hinkler had fled through led into an alley that paralleled the one on the other side. He was carving out a path through the crowds, plunging through them like a fullback hitting a line.

Marcus ran after him, ran through a wake of staggering people, trays of spilt oranges, a woman knocked off a bicycle, a bamboo cage full of squawking chickens tumbled on its side.

Hinkler was heading for the marina, maybe for the yacht; there had to be weapons on board that. But he'd got his direction wrong, Marcus saw. Instead of turning right when he reached the parking lot he kept going straight, toward another section of the lot where the truck restaurants were parked. The trucks, flatbed types without sides, hauled freight during the day and rented out as open-air eateries in the evenings. They were parked in rows, long trestled tables set up on their flatbeds, ropes of colored fairy lights strung above the diners, who sat on folding chairs on each side of the makeshift tables. At the rear of the trucks, near portable wooden steps that led up to the flatbeds, aproned cooks stirred bubbling woks and turned skewers over charcoal braziers, blue-white gas lanterns singing above their heads.

Hinkler stopped running as he realized his mistake, glanced back, and seemed mesmerized by what he saw: Marcus, a steel bulldog clip protruding from his eyebrow, blood painting one half of his face, a still-loaded .45 in his hand, pounding toward him.

The big man shook himself out of his daze, whirled around, and took off again, going nowhere now, just running from the gun.

He made another thirty yards, halted at the wooden steps of a truck restaurant, and looked wildly around as he realized his aimless flight.

He took two fast strides, snatched up a knife from a chopping block, jumped up the wooden steps, and dashed down the flatbed past a row of astounded diners. A young woman near the end of the table saw him coming and, with wide eyes and a choked yell, seemed to know her destiny.

Hinkler almost knocked her over pulling her to her feet, hugged her to him as if she were a loved one he hadn't seen for years.

Marcus pulled up at the bottom of the steps, and the two men stood very still, both breathing hard.

Hinkler gulped air.

"Back off or she goes," he said.

The Clark came up, dead steady in the double-handed Weaver grip. The muzzle of the gun pointed directly at Hinkler's head, but the man's sweating brow was just a blur to Marcus. There was nothing wrong with his master eye, his shooting eye — the bulldog clip was squinching the other one — he was just taking aim as Teddy Hepplewhite had taught him: the only thing in focus was the pistol's front sight.

"It's up to you, cop."

Hinkler held the girl crushed to him with his left arm, the knife in his right hand, the long, thin blade angled in under her jaw. She was tall for a local Chinese, her lustrous black hair reaching to Hinkler's throat.

The diners at the interrupted meal sat very still, eyes fixed on their bowls. It happened now and then in Hong Kong, the sudden appearance of weapons, the quick violence. The people on the flatbed truck lived in a city where every single Chinese male over the age of sixteen was involved, in some way or other, with one of the societies that ran the colony. Public disagreements were common, and had to be quietly waited out like the lashing rain squalls of March and April.

"Boyle told me you were shit-hot with a gun, Hinkler. You ever done any handloading?"

Hinkler said nothing, looking at him.

"I do it all the time," Marcus told him. "I got a hand

load ready to go right now, as a matter of fact, in back of this five-inch National Match barrel that's pointing at your head. I even made the slug. I got a bucket of wheel weights from a gas station, and melted them down over a barbecue with a bit of solder wire thrown in. The tin in the solder hardens the alloy, and the slug'll feed better in an auto. But a gunman like you, you'd know that, right?"

Hinkler was confused; he didn't know why the cop was prattling on like this; didn't realize he was being psyched into making a move. Marcus figured he had a 99 percent chance of hitting Hinkler and missing the girl, and a 1 percent chance of it happening the other way around. One bullet, one girl, one killer with a vegetable knife. A 1 percent failure risk was a little too high.

"I poured off the alloy into a double-pin mold, and cast a bullet with a hollow base to shift the center of mass forward, and recessed the nose so it'd expand when it hit a meat-and-bone target. Although there ain't much meat in the head, is there, Hinkler? It's mainly bone."

Hinkler blinked, and a drop of sweat landed on the ribbon of white scalp, the parting in the girl's hair.

Around the trestled table food began to congeal, and cups of sweet P'o Lei tea grew cold.

Hinkler had his eyes riveted to one tiny point in the parking lot: the half-inch circle of the pistol's muzzle, trapped by its unwavering gaze. The bullet he was hearing about waited in the dark at the end of that short black tunnel, ready for its phenomenal acceleration to begin.

The terrified girl, crushed to his chest in a fierce embrace, felt him swallow, heard from his throat the dry difficulty of the action.

"For the cartridge," Marcus said, a gout of blood seeping out from beneath the clip over his eye, "I took a once-fired case and tumble-cleaned it in a rotating barrel full of crushed fruit pips. It's a damn good abrasive. I punched out the old primer, and got rid of any factory mouth sealer with a little salt and vinegar. Then I reseated a new primer, and measured in four and a half grains of Hercules Bullseye chopped into wafers."

Hinkler was getting close. He was looking around now, looking for an out. He hated being where he was, felt exposed, vulnerable, as if the truck's cab behind his back was a firing-squad wall.

"But you know what I seated on top of the charge? A steel ball bearing. Then I cut the slug to fit, sat it in front of the ball, and crimped in the neck of the case real tight. So that's what's gonna be coming at you, Hinkler. And you know what'll happen when it hits?"

Hinkler's grip on the girl had loosened; the knife had absently wandered away from her neck, and was now next to her collarbone. He licked his lips.

"The slug will flatten against your skull but the ball will be right behind it, and it'll keep on going and push the slug on through. You'll end up wearing your face on the back of your head."

Hinkler went then; shoved the girl aside and jumped off the side of the truck, jumped into the air going for the asphalt of the parking lot, both arms going up to aid his leap.

Marcus shot him at the top of it.

He'd been telling the truth about the round in the pistol; he'd made it exactly as he'd described. The hollow-nosed slug slammed into Hinkler's left side and blossomed as it broke off a piece of rib. The ball bearing pushed the flattened lead, and the bone fragment, right on through Hinkler's chest cavity, carrying everything in its path before it. The bullet, once so carefully shaped and molded, emerged from under Hinkler's right armpit as a jagged piece of bloodied and gristled shrapnel.

The big man jarred in the air like a shot bird, and crash-landed onto a glowing brazier. The cook, released from his frozen trance, jumped aside as the brazier toppled over, splattering Hinkler with sizzling patches of cooking oil, and steaming green leaves of bok choy.

A single charcoal briquet, red turning white, landed on Hinkler's jacket, and began to burn into the fabric. The cook knocked away the briquet, sloshed water out of a can, and the miniature fire died a few seconds after the jacket's owner did.

13

THE MOB had been known to cut off a guy's thumbs for skimming a hundred bucks off the numbers take. What would they do to somebody who tried to take half a ton of heroin away from them?

And could it be done, anyway?

Questions Marcus battled with.

But to say he'd been able to think of nothing else would not have been true.

Claire filled his mind.

Since Marcus rejoined her in New York twenty-four hours after chasing Hinkler through a parking lot in Hong Kong, they'd been together constantly for a week. Claire showed him her private city, took him to the places that were her own special favorites, like the Roerich Museum, the Jumel Mansion, the Tibetan Museum on Staten Island. They redid the old New York, the one Marcus had known during his college years — the Thalia, the Eighth Street Bookstore, the Nom Wah Tea Parlor, the White Horse, the Five Spot — and took a fresh look at the new one: the clubs and galleries and bistros in TriBeCa, and the revamped uptown West Side.

To celebrate their second week together they had dinner in the florid pink-and-white dining room of one of the city's establishment hotels. A flying corps of waiters worked the tables in a discreet and gracious panic, while two white-tuxedoed maître d's oversaw both triumph and tragedy with smiling, angelic composure. It was a good example of a successful, expensive New York restaurant, exciting, even brilliant in patches, the pace, like the noise, impossible to keep down. The diners — for the most part rich citizens of the town — had come as much for each other as for the nationally acclaimed kitchen, each table watching another, each new arrival rated according to private scoring systems of the highest standard.

Heads swiveled when Marcus and Claire were guided through. The men chewed the exquisite cuisine thoughtfully as they took in Claire's fresh loveliness, the hippy glide of her walk, the mass of yellow hair.

The women, their egos smudged, checked her out with vague hostility, then shifted their attention to her escort, a big man with hard good looks and an easy way of wearing a navy blue blazer. Their companions, on the other hand, wore expensive suits and shoes made from the skins of reptiles, and had an investment-quality watch ticking at the end of their silk shirt cuffs. They themselves were squeezed into boutique dresses with clumps of fiery stones on their fingers and at their ears, a far cry from Claire's simple cream silk dress and pearls. Yet Marcus and Claire owned that restaurant; they were the stars. The way they felt about each other showed in the glow that sparked between them, something that was almost palpable, and obvious to everybody in the room.

They led a late kind of life: got to bed late, made love late into the small hours, slept late in the mornings, went out into a new kind of city, came back and made love in the late afternoon. It was a time-out period for both of them, a wind-down, a mini-vacation from what had been and what was coming up.

Marcus went back to Atlanta and his duties on the Robbery squad. He told his commander, and his partner, and whoever else asked, that he'd spent his vacation in New York, and explained away his newly scarred eyebrow — the one Hinkler's revolver had split open — by saying he'd run into a couple of Mets fans who'd disparaged the Braves. Everybody had bought it except his good friend Danny Mead, the 230-pound pathologist, who knew that Marcus could have cared less which team won the pennant.

On weekends Marcus flew back to New York to be with Claire.

It was as good together, as warm, as surprisingly right as it had ever been for either of them with anybody, but the calendar gradually began to assert itself. According to the information sheet Bendroit had given Marcus, the tanker — its name was the *Adrono* — was due in New York on the twenty-fifth of the month, a date he confirmed by checking with the local office of Lloyd's. He flew into New York on the twenty-third, took Claire to dinner, took her home to her apartment and into the bedroom, and made love to her with a patient and slow urgency. They'd long passed the point where they held any of themselves back; they knew each other through and through now, yet there were still discoveries to be made, tiny surprises.

They dozed, slept, woke in the early morning, went out to the kitchen, made some herb tea, climbed back into bed.

The color of the robe Claire wore put Marcus in mind of melted butter. He often thought of her in edible terms; it was a very oral thing a man felt for a woman. He wanted his mouth on hers, and on the lips between her legs, tongue fluttering in there, deep-kissing. And his teeth sham-biting her shoulder, and the juicy little muscle that runs above the collarbone. Breasts licked, navel tongued, eating her up in gentle savagery.

He lay across the bottom of the bed on his stomach, his head propped on an elbow. Claire put her cup of tea on a side table, and waited to hear what he'd brought back from Atlanta.

"I asked a few discreet questions, and my buddy in Narcotics agrees with us. If we're talking deal, don't expect to get much from any federal agency."

"Then that only leaves the New York PD," Claire said, "who are not the most trustworthy bunch in the world."

"That's the magic word. I know people I'd trust with my life, but not with six hundred keys of heroin."

"So what does he suggest?"

"He's given me the name of somebody. A narc cop. His name's Hightower. He doesn't know him personally, but he says he's got a good rep." Marcus shifted, viewing Claire from a different angle, the cane headboard behind her a rococo frame for the fine planes of her face and the dubious expression that showed there. "There are no completely honest cops," Marcus said. "We all lie to different people. The difference is, some do the job for the salary and benefits, as crazy as that sounds, and some expect a little more than that."

"There are policemen in this town," Claire told him, "who'll kill people on contract for two or three thousand dollars."

"It's a big force here. The bigger the force, the bigger the difference in the heads on the uniforms."

The air conditioner, boxed into the bedroom window, changed its song as the compressor took over, filling in some of the silence that followed.

"Did you check on him? Hightower?"

"Yep. As clean a sheet as you'll get."

"A clean sheet always bothers me."

"You'd trust me, wouldn't you?" There was the merest hint of a smile on Marcus's face.

"What's your sheet like?"

"Spotty."

"Then you'd probably be a good bet," Claire said.

Marcus remembered something.

"How about that pal of yours, the British law guy? You talk with him?"

Claire nodded her head, saying, "If Bendroit is grabbed

[217]

receiving the money, he could be charged with conspiracy to traffic."

"What's it carry?"

"Maybe ten years."

"Hell, that's pretty light for a guy who's had people killed."

"At least it's better," Claire said, "than having him walking around free with a fortune to spend."

After a moment Marcus said, "You really think I'd be a good bet?"

"Reasonable," Claire said, extending a hand toward him.

Her forward movement molded her breasts in soft scoops against the fabric of her robe. Marcus had often slipped his hand inside that robe, and touched the dark hardness of her nipples which, like an On button, would start the sweet machine of their lovemaking.

He came up the bed to her, spread the robe, brought his mouth down.

"When are you going to see him?" Claire asked, her hand on the back of his head.

"Who?"

"Hightower."

"Not within the next hour," Marcus said.

He had no trouble picking out the man; Ralph X. Hightower was trying to appear casual but there was a touch of belligerence in his stance, as if he were the only person in the building who had a right to be there. As a cop he was a dead giveaway with his look of timeless boredom, automatically checking out people, flicking through a mental file of mug shots. He was not aptly named, being bulky, and on the short side. His cheeks were puffed out like a horn blower, and the booze spider had spun fine red webs under his eyes. He looked to Marcus as though he'd lived a life and a half, most of it in the suit he was wearing.

"Hightower?"

"Yeah."

"I'm the guy who called you."

"You didn't tell me your name."

"Brown."

"Try again."

"Green. Choose your own color. The point is, I'm a fellow officer from out of town, and I'm gonna John Doe on this one. Safer all 'round."

Hightower took in the build, and the fresh scar near an old one over the left eye.

"Well, you're either a cop or a criminal."

"So I've been told."

Hightower sucked at his teeth and let out a breath, a weary sound, a legacy of a lot of years spent fencing with people. The fatigue seemed to come naturally; he looked to be about fifty-five, and his skin was not a good color.

"So what you got for me, doctor? It better be for real. I get all the fairy tales I need from the regular civilians."

Marcus pointed to a table. They were in an immense brick atrium of a newish building on Madison whose architect had been dreaming of the granite glories of French Romanesque. At least, Marcus thought, it made a change from everybody else's steel and glass.

A waitress brought them coffee. Hightower didn't even wait for her to leave.

"So let's have it."

"There's a shipment coming in."

"You told me that on the phone." Hightower looked around impatiently. He had a wave of white hair glistening with Vitalis, and his turned head revealed acne pits on his neck.

"It's still true," Marcus said.

"What is it?"

"China White."

"When and where's it coming in?"

"We'll get to that in a minute."

Hightower snorted.

"There's no money in it for you. Forget it. They cut back on budgets."

"I don't want money. I want a deal."

"What, you got caught dippin' into something here? You want to trade favors, that it? We cut back on those, too."

"I want the guy who's shipping the stuff."

"Where's he?"

"London."

"I can't help you."

Marcus watched Hightower start to push back his chair. "It's six hundred kilos."

The man stayed seated, a look of tired disgust appearing on his face.

"Jesus," he said. "It's a hundred and forty degrees out there, I come all the way from downtown in a cruiser somebody must've forgotten to put the air-conditioning in, and what do I get? A guy claims he's outatown Law who's only got a lousy six hundred keys. Six hundred keys? You talking about drugs or wheat?"

"I've seen it. Well, a hundred keys of it, anyway."

"Oh, sure."

"I watched it being loaded in Hong Kong."

"It's from the Triangle, huh?"

"That's right."

Hightower was looking at Marcus as if he were some form of lower life.

"You don't know much about the business, do you, buddy? Six hundred keys would be about half a year's supply from the Triangle. Nobody brings in that much in one go. You're a goddamn jerkoff, and you wasted my fuckin' time."

"I was on the caravan that collected the last part of it. Up there in the Shan State."

Hightower paused; Marcus had a pretty good idea that very few of the policeman's informants would ever have heard of the Shan State.

"We bought it from a gentleman named Wei Chun."

"Wei Chun." Hightower was taking his time now. "You met this guy?"

"Yep."

[220]

"What's he look like?"

"Like somebody's Chinese uncle. Plump, a little psychotic. Smokes Red Chicken through a matchbox. Doesn't care for the DEA."

Hightower regarded Marcus for a long moment, then said, "He sold you a hundred keys of pure?"

"Base. It was finished in Hong Kong. When I saw it there it was in heat-sealed kilo bags."

"But you didn't see the other five hundred?"

"It was already sealed up in drums. We took them out to a tanker and they were loaded in one of the tanks."

"They dropped them in the oil?"

"It wasn't carrying oil. It was in ballast, so that's where they put the drums, in a ballast tank of salt water. They had two scuba divers take them down."

That seemed to do it, Marcus saw; the mention of something as outlandish as the divers, plus his description of Wei Chun, appeared to have swayed the guy.

"Six hundred," Hightower said. He sounded awed.

"You want it?"

"You kidding? I make a collar like that they'll make me mayor of this town. Who's this guy in London?"

"A man waiting for his money. It's going to be shipped to him there. To grab him, the payment has to go through."

"I do not like the sound of that," Hightower said, frowning. "We bust 'em, we get the shit *and* the bread. The case is that much stronger."

"How much stronger does it have to be if you score over half a ton of White?"

"I'll think about it," Hightower said. "Give me the name of the ship."

"No."

Hightower moved his lumpy shoulders as if something heavy had landed on them. He picked at his teeth with a finger like a sausage; his nails were either bitten down or in need of clipping.

"Mister, do you know what you're doing? You have information about an illicit narcotics shipment and you're withholding it. That's impeding the cause of justice and, cop or no cop, you can fall as fast as anybody else."

Marcus let him have half of a slow smile.

"You're gonna lock me up and miss out on six months' supply of pure?"

Hightower rubbed a hand over his mouth for a while, then seemed to get fed up with the conversation, fed up with the coffee he was drinking, and the people around him.

"Okay, what do you want?"

"I told you. I want the payment to go through. If you don't say yes to that, I'm not saying another damn word."

Marcus drained his cup as if he were getting ready to leave. Hightower glanced up at the dizzy heights of the atrium, then down at the pattern on the floor. When his gaze returned to head level he had the look of a man who was settling for something.

"Okay."

It was a very quiet utterance.

Marcus indulged in a little amateur dramatics. He pointed a finger at the man's glistening hair, and put some steel into his voice.

"You cross me, Hightower, and the roof is gonna fall in on all that greasy kid stuff."

"Hey!" Hightower sounded angry. "Take the dagger out, okay? I been a narc for a lot of years now and done all right. You think I woulda done all right I didn't know how to keep a deal?"

Marcus gave it a beat, making sure of his man. Hightower's truculent attitude had changed; he'd stopped dishing out, now he was taking.

"The ship's name is the *Adrono*. It's due in tomorrow."

"The *Adrono*. A super tanker?"

"I don't think so. But it's big."

"What kind of cargo?"

"Fuel oil."

"It'll probably discharge up the river then. That where they gonna transfer the shit?"

"No. Brooklyn. Pier Six repair dock. Eleven the next night."

Hightower watched Marcus while he scratched at his stubbly jaw. He hadn't stood very close to the razor that morning; all in all, not the most together of men. He said, "They're getting smarter, these people. You go in for repairs, you only need a skeleton crew. Less people to pay off." He considered something for a moment, then said, "What's your angle? You fall out with the boys or something? They cut you in, then cut you out?"

"Something like that."

"You gonna be at the payoff?"

Marcus got to his feet.

"Got to be. I'm the man."

With new respect in his voice Hightower said, "You're in deep," and rose as well. "Call me tomorrow and we'll do the nitty-gritty. Details, stuff like that." He put something akin to a pleased look on his face as if he were realizing for the first time the ramifications of what had just transpired. "Six hundred keys. I'm grateful to you, champ. I got retirement coming up in a few months. This'll be a lulu to go out on."

"Retirement, huh?" Marcus said, just making conversation as they reached the sidewalk. "Where are you going? The Sunbelt?"

"Florida," Hightower said, squinting into the hot sunshine. "Fort Lauderdale. I been saving for something I always wanted."

"What's that?"

"A twenty-foot Chris-Craft," Hightower answered.

14

WAITING.

Some were better at it than others.

Marco Morici had no problem with it at all. Before flying to New York, he'd spent most of the time taking care of regular business in Palermo, and commuting back and forth to Roccobonno's villa in Cefalù. He'd assured his boss that things were going according to plan, spelling it out so the dummy could understand: the tanker had proceeded from Hong Kong to Sumatra, where it had picked up a cargo of Minas crude. From there it had traversed the Indian Ocean and the Red Sea, passed through the Suez Canal, sailed through the Mediterranean into the Atlantic, and was on schedule for New York. Furthermore, just to be on the safe side, he, Morici, had bought a senior New York City narcotics detective to guarantee the shipment an untroubled dockside delivery.

He'd taken Roccobonno through it twice, spelling everything out in detail.

Everything, that is, except for the part about the cigarettes. He hadn't told Roccobonno anything about the cigarettes.

That was a little secret Morici was keeping to himself.

* * *

Jay Jay also handled the time well.

He'd spent most of it back in Hong Kong counteracting the constant sniping of some of the other societies. They were never ever at peace but bickered like children wanting a bigger slice of each other's pie. Jay Jay's main achievement had been teaching the Hong Moon not to be so presumptuous when, one night, they tried to muscle in on the Fan Tan, Pai Kau, and Dai Sai games the Fourteen K ran in the back of a fruit warehouse.

Jay Jay's team of six fighters, armed with lengths of water pipe, sent home the Hong Moon gang holding their heads and wishing they'd never been born.

Another of the societies, the Wo Sing Wo, who were the Fourteen K's main rival, had also been troublesome. Jay Jay's fighters had caught two of their men trying to steal a drug delivery from its drop-off point near Heung Lung Island. Not being full members of the Wo Sing Wo, and thus untattooed, they had been simple to dispose of: they'd been stripped and drowned, and left for the harbor police to find in the water. With no identification, the bodies were assumed to be freedom swimmers, a couple of men who'd tried to bypass the border by swimming into the colony from the mainland.

Two weeks before the freighter, the *Maloya Dan*, was due to tie up at Dover, Jay Jay returned to London, took care of some other business, then settled back to await the arrival of the ship. He passed the first few days at one of England's green and pleasant racetracks indulging his native love of gambling. And a very smart gambler he was, too: he picked five money horses, one of which went off at huge odds and won going away.

Bendroit, on the other hand, was very bad at waiting.

Hinkler's cheering message from Hong Kong, that the cargo had been successfully loaded, had been followed the next day by disturbing news: Dubin had called personally to tell him that Hinkler had got himself killed. Dubin had given no details but Hinkler had no doubt died in some vile back alley, probably in an argument over some almond-eyed temptress. The man had always been far too belligerent for his own good. It meant Dubin would be handling the sale by himself now but, as he'd proved most capable, Bendroit didn't feel that that would present a problem.

Every day he would buy a copy of Lloyd's List and check on the progress of the *Adrono,* and try not to think about all the tankers that had run aground and broken up, or the unexploded World War II mines which were said to be still drifting in the oceans.

He was much better in the evenings.

For a rich, eligible bachelor there were always dinner and party invitations and lovely young ladies. He'd recently got rid of his latest live-in convenience and was casting for a successor. It meant a lot of mindless trial fucking but at least it kept him from thinking about unexploded mines or freak summer icebergs.

He was well aware that his life had been bumped out of the smooth groove to which it was accustomed but was equally aware that it would revert to order once the fifty million dollars arrived from New York. There was nothing like an infusion of money to calm the ripples on life's little pond.

That didn't bother him.

What did bother him were the dreams he kept having, weird dreams about a horse race in which the winning post kept moving.

Stress, probably.

But he defeated them, because a man of intelligence and breeding could defeat anything: he bribed a doctor to prescribe him some amylobarbitone, which dropped him into a layer of sleep too deep for dreams to reach; so deep that if it hadn't been for the steady rise and fall of his lungs an observer stationed by his bedside might have been excused for thinking that it was sleep's elder brother that came nightly for Charles Bendroit.

15

THREE MILES off the misty coastline, within sight of the scimitar shape of the famous sand spit, the *Adrono* crossed into U.S. intercoastal waters.

Two boats came out of the morning mist to meet her, two boats that met every tanker arriving in New York: the Sandy Hook pilot boat, and a sleek Coast Guard cutter whose red-and-white-striped paint job put a lot of people in mind of a cigarette pack or a candy bar. It didn't bother the captain or the first officer of the *Adrono* that the Coast Guard was on board; since the ship was carrying a cargo of oil the ballast tanks were empty, and the Coast Guard wasn't concerned with empty tanks.

When they'd checked all the certification, and made sure none of the cargo was leaking into the bay, they passed the ship for entry, and took their cutter back to Fort Jay.

The Sandy Hook pilot took over then and guided the ship through the Narrows and under the gravity-defying leap of the Verrazano Bridge. Entering the Upper Bay two red-and-black Moran tugs accompanied the tanker while the Sandy Hook pilot was dropped and the berthing pilot taken on board. The *Adrono* was now half a mile west of Governors Island with two other islands on its port side, both of an incredibly small acreage when measured against their fame: Liberty and Ellis. Ahead the towers of Wall Street appeared to be a group of giants peering over one another's shoulders for a better look at the new arrival.

When her bow came around a few degrees to starboard, the *Adrono* began the approach to the East River. In the next half-mile her keel moved over four subway tunnels and one road tunnel before the top of her signal mast slid under the Brooklyn Bridge, missing it by just twenty-five feet. The *Adrono* owned the river by virtue of its size, although there was little to get in its way: a couple of white cabin cruisers coming down from City Island, a tug pushing a low-gunwaled oil barge, a sailboat moving on its diesel.

Off to the left the city appeared to be burning down. The sun slanted onto a million sheets of window glass and fired up a range of hot colors as it simmered on the bumper-to-bumper metal on the FDR Drive. Locked into rush-hour traffic, the drivers watched the ship's stately progress, envying it its cool, uncluttered waterway.

Three more bridges, then the tanker split the west channel opposite the narrow ribbon of Roosevelt Island, made the turn into Hell's Gate, steamed along the western edge of Astoria, and allowed the tugs to nudge it into its berth at the Waldorf facility.

The Immigration people were the first on board.

They checked documents, crew lists, issued landing passes, then turned the ship over to U.S. Customs, who collected the usual declarations.

The next step would have been to search the ship.

But they didn't.

It took forever to go through a tanker, bring in a rummage squad and crawl through the ship's innards, so that was usually only done when they'd received a tip. But they'd heard nothing interesting about the *Adrono* so, like their counterparts in Immigration, they finished their business quickly and left.

There was only one other official to get past, the terminal representative whose job it was to measure the amount of oil in each tank, and to take a sample. He'd be the only person to come anywhere near the drums but, even so, nobody on board was worried.

When he'd finished with his steel tape and weighted flasks, he moved on to the ballast tanks to make sure they weren't carrying any illicit oil. He opened the hatch covers and shone a beam gun down.

Straight down, in a vertical line.

Nothing showed but iron ladders and bottom girders. The five drums, over on a far wall in the starboard ballast tank, could only have been seen if the terminal rep had actually climbed down into the tank.

And that was something terminal reps never ever did.

With the ship cleared, and all the paperwork signed, hoses were craned up from the wharf, connected to the manifold, and discharge was begun.

It took eighteen hours to drain the tanker.

At nine the next morning, seventy thousand tons lighter, and sixteen feet higher in the water, the *Adrono* was tugged out of its berth in Queens and guided back down the river to Brooklyn to have a fuel pump rewound. In actual fact, the pump was running smoothly.

Just as everything else was.

Claire parked their rented Camaro on a side road off Furman Street directly opposite Pier Six. The *Adrono* was perhaps three hundred feet away alongside the pier, a piece of it illuminated by work lamps, the rest in shadow.

The dock was open to the world.

There was no security, not even a constructed one; the long cyclone fence was crushed and flattened as if a ceaseless iron rain had thundered down on it. What had once been the gate house was a peeling, broken-windowed ruin guarding nothing more than abandoned cars, uncollected dumpsters, and rusting light stanchions long since climbed and denuded of their bulbs. A victim of the shipping recession, the docks just south of the Brooklyn Bridge rotted with neglect.

The buildings in back of the docks were in a similar state: dark, broken-down tenements, most of them with their windows boarded up, standing there steeped in hopelessness like old dogs waiting to be shot.

Beyond the tanker it was a completely different story: the black water was dappled by a shimmering wash of brilliant whites and glowing yellows, gilded by the spectacular display from the towers of light in Lower Manhattan.

Claire felt intimidated by the view, outnumbered. She and Marcus were about to take on a large piece of the wickedness of the city, and as she gazed at its bright, soaring heights the nervousness she'd kept at bay for so long began to jangle through her.

Sitting in the passenger seat, Marcus was watching the dark shape of the tanker unmindful of its brilliant backdrop, and wondering if there was a contingency he hadn't allowed for. He knew the man he'd be dealing with was called Morici — that had all been explained in Bendroit's fact sheet — but there'd been no mention of the name of the freighter that would transport the money to England because that wasn't part of the job he'd been hired to do. But finding out the freighter's identity seemed straightforward enough: Morici's man would almost certainly take the money to a dock warehouse, and once they knew which warehouse, getting the name of the ship wouldn't be much trouble. Then they'd simply put in a call to the British police.

For the second time that day Marcus said, "They won't be expecting a tail, but if you think they've spotted you, forget the money and get out of there."

"Don't worry," Claire said. "I'm not anxious to get myself killed."

It didn't fool Marcus; he knew she'd take it all the way

to the wire, and maybe a bit beyond if necessary. It was the weakest and, for him, by far the most worrying part of the whole thing.

Claire felt differently: it was Marcus who'd be the most exposed. She said, after a moment, "If they spot me I can simply make a turn and lose them. But you'll be right in the middle of them, Billy. How do you get out if you have to?"

"I'm not gonna have to. Bendroit's promised them another shot next year. Another six hundred kilos. They won't get cute. Next time, maybe, but not this run."

When Claire told him she still didn't like it, Marcus said, "Look, I don't know how many there'll be, but let's say a carful. Morici will have a truck and driver for the drums, and probably a van for the money. When we trade he'll follow the truck, you can bet on that. Hightower will pick his spot and move on the truck and Morici's car. The van won't be touched, and neither will I. I'll be out of there."

"Where will you be?"

"Back at the apartment. If I can't find a cab I'll get the subway."

It sounded pretty thin to Marcus as he said it. What the hell was he going to do at the apartment, sit down with a beer and wonder if Claire was okay? He knew what he should have done: hired a pro to follow the money to the freighter, but Claire wouldn't hear of it. She claimed it would reduce her role to that of a chauffeur, and she wanted to be more deeply involved than that. There was another reason, too, one she kept to herself: while she was well aware that her presence in any kind of emergency might not be of any great value, she nevertheless wanted to share the risk with him, feeling that it would bring them closer still, hitch them up yet another notch into a new area of affinity, although it was true she was worried about the arrangements, and beginning to feel a distinct lack of preparation. Faced with implementing it, they saw their plan now as more than a little flimsy, with no backup in case things took a wrong turn.

She said, looking at the lights of Manhattan sheening the water, "I think we have to face something, Billy. I'm sure this man Hightower doesn't give a damn about some guy in London who sent the shipment. He may grab the money as well to make the arrest that much stronger."

"I've thought about that. But if it's medals he's after, I'm betting he'll let the payment go through. Bendroit gets pinched picking it up, and Hightower becomes the man who broke the English connection, or whatever the press would call it."

"There's that to it," Claire admitted, although her tone was equivocal.

Marcus checked the clock on the dash.

"I'd better move." He slid over the seat, opened the door, and got out.

"Billy . . ."

Marcus said, "I'll see you later," and kept going. To linger would have meant trading meaningless directives about being careful, and at this stage it was either go through with it or forget it.

He crossed the street, moving toward the ruined fence. There was no sign of any police presence but he knew that Hightower would have to be around somewhere: a couple of blocks away maybe, his men spread out, the squad cars hidden.

Marcus went through the leaning gate and traversed an area of broken asphalt as large as a ballpark. It was strewn with the detritus of the shipping business: bits of rusted machinery, lengths of rope lying like dead and colorless pythons, old tires that had once kept fresh painted hulls scratch-free. Halfway down the pier, like a five-story building, the *Adrono*'s accommodation stack rose beside the river. Six hours after it had begun discharging its oil, water had been pumped into its ballast tanks. It had sailed back down the river in ballast, and when the tugs had pushed it into the repair dock it had pumped out the water and was now completely empty.

One of the Filipino seamen was sitting on the bottom of the gangway putting a match to a long brown cigarette. He waved as Marcus went by him. Up on deck the first officer watched Marcus climb toward him, recognizing him from the night of the loading.

"Everything okay?" Marcus asked.

The officer ponderously moved his head up and down. He'd lost the gauze pad from over his eye, and some minor surgery had left the orb bloodshot.

"Good. All good." His accent was as thick and heavy as the rest of him. "We start now?"

"If it's safe."

The officer swept a hand around to indicate the deserted dock.

"Is nobody," he said, then signaled to somebody further along the deck. The drums had already been raised from the ballast tank and were lined up near the open hatch. The starboard crane groaned and, one by one, the drums were picked up, swung over the side, and lowered down to the Filipino seaman, who released them. The lights on the deck were too feeble for anybody to view the operation clearly from the road, and as there were no vessels at the piers on either side of the *Adrono*, there was no chance of anybody becoming curious.

Fifteen minutes after the last drum had been set down on the pier, the buyers arrived.

They came in a weird-looking convoy: a red late-model Buick, a U-Haul van too beat up not to be privately owned, and a white garbage truck with the legend "Atardi Brothers Refuse Co." painted gaudily on the sides. The vehicles made a big circle, and pulled up facing the way they'd come.

Marcus descended the gangway, and waited beside the

drums as four men got out of the Buick, two from the truck, and one from the van; seven men in all. There was nothing special about six of them. Marcus hadn't had much to do with the Mob, and although he hadn't expected busted noses and cauliflower ears, he had thought that the buyers of half a ton of heroin would look a little more sinister. But these men looked like the kind of guys you'd see in any neighborhood Italian restaurant, eating up big and keeping the waiters hopping.

However, the seventh man was totally different.

While the others looked Italian, they dressed American in T-shirts and jeans, but this man, in a suit of dashing Continental cut, and a high-collared, open-necked shirt, could have just stepped off an Alitalia flight.

"Mr. Morici?" Marcus asked. It was an easy guess: Bendroit had included a not very flattering description of the man in his fact sheet.

"Mr. Dubin." Morici held out his hand, a smile on his handsome face. "A pleasure to meet you. Mr. Bendroit speaks very highly of you."

"Well, he should know."

Morici chuckled, then said, "Please don't think me rude, but I think it would be prudent if we got to our business straightaway."

"Whenever you're ready."

Morici spoke to somebody behind him, starting some activity. Four of the men carried two wooden boxes from the back of the van, and set them down near the drums. Each box was large enough to contain a big TV set.

"Surprising, isn't it?" Morici said. "Fifty million dollars doesn't take up very much room, but its weight is considerable. Nine hundred and forty-six pounds, to be exact."

Marcus nodded at the drums.

"Six hundred kilos, to be exact. I'm not sure what that is in pounds."

"One thousand, three hundred, twenty-two and three-quarters," Morici said. "And I'm sure every one of them is there. However, for the sake of good form, shall we check each other's wares?"

Marcus invited him to pick a drum. Morici inspected them, noting the one with the indentations in the rim.

"The cigarettes?" he asked, pointing to it.

"Right."

The Italian indicated a drum next to it.

"Let's try this one."

Since the pouring spouts had all been soldered closed on the drums, it was necessary to get in some other way, and Morici had taken this into account. One of his men stepped forward with a tool which looked like an ordinary hand drill except the chuck gripped a circular hacksaw blade. It took him less than three minutes to cut a hole in the top of the drum, a hole about the size of a drink coaster.

With the help of a flashlight Morici peered at what the cut revealed: a few inches of a clear plastic bag full of a gritty white powder.

Another of Morici's men stepped up then. He was bigger than any of the others, with an old-fashioned hair cut and rimless glasses like priests used to wear. He put Marcus in mind of a ball player he'd known who'd gone to Fordham, a Catholic scholar who'd also been very good at flattening plunging halfbacks.

The man snapped the catches of the briefcase he carried, and took out three things: a white tile with shallow scoops in its face — like something a painter might use to mix colors in — a small brown medicine bottle closed by a rubber eyedropper, and a roll of Scotch tape. He placed these items on top of the drum, took a pin from his jacket lapel and, very, very carefully, pricked a hole in the plastic bag.

From his shirt pocket he brought out an ordinary kitchen match, snapped off the head, wet the splintered end on his tongue, and worked it with great care into the tiny hole he'd made. He withdrew the match and tapped it onto the white tile, scraping a single grain of the heroin into one of the recesses.

A buzzing noise sounded from somewhere, the phone going in the Buick, but nobody seemed anxious to answer it; they were all far more interested in the test they were watching.

Using the Scotch tape the man repaired the puncture he'd made in the kilo bag, picked up the brown medicine bottle, and shook it hard. Inside the bottle was a colorless fluid called a Marquis reagent, a few drops of formaldehyde in 10 cubic centimeters of concentrated sulfuric acid. The man unscrewed the lid, squeezed the bulb, sucked up some of the fluid, and expertly squeezed a drop of the reagent onto the white grain in the tile.

When the fluid instantly turned a deep purple the man whistled, impressed. The faster the liquid changed color, and the deeper the color it changed to, illustrated the heroin's quality and purity.

"Okay?" Morici asked.

"Like mother used to make," the man replied. "Eighty-five, ninety percent pure."

Morici smiled at Marcus.

"As advertised," he said. "Excellent, Mr. Dubin. I will, of course, take your word that there are six hundred bags in these drums."

"Why not?" Marcus tapped his toe against one of the wooden boxes. "I'm gonna have to take your word for an honest count."

"Mutual trust," Morici said smoothly. "Always the most civilized way to do business."

The man with the cutting tool brought out something from his pocket: a square piece of black aluminum with a waxed-paper backing. He tore off the paper, revealing a heavy layer of Black Magic adhesive, then pressed the aluminum piece over the hole he'd cut, sealing the drum good as new.

When this had been completed Morici invited Marcus to pick a box.

Marcus chose the first one; its lid was unscrewed and lifted off, and a heavy smell of tar paper escaped.

The paper was slit with a Stanley knife, allowing Marcus to reach in and slip out a bound bundle: 250 crisp, new hundred-dollar bills. Marcus cursorily flicked through them, then gave the bundle back to be repacked.

"Fifty million. That's what I've got here?"

"Exactly that," Morici said. "Verified twice."

"Then we're trading fair."

Nothing more was said for a while, everybody watching two of the men work on the boxes. One of them mended the razored tar paper with a wide strip of insulating tape, then both resealed the lid with security screws, using special tools for the job. The other box was also closed in the same way.

At a word from Morici, the first of the drums was rolled toward the garbage truck, and Marcus took the opportunity to follow it, looking as if he were just making sure the transportation arrangements were adequate.

They were not only adequate, they were pretty smart: the trash compactor had been removed from the truck, leaving a very large and smelly open hopper; perfect for something like five big oil drums.

Marcus strolled over to the U-Haul van and, out of sight of everybody, identified it for Claire. He took a New York Mets sticker from his pocket — a circular sticker got up to look like a baseball — peeled off its back cover, and stuck it on the van's right side headlight.

He heard the buzz of the Buick's phone again, and this time it was answered as he saw when he ambled back to the group. Morici was leaning into the automobile with the handset to his ear. The men had finished loading the boxes into the van and were hefting a third drum into the garbage truck, one of them standing in the hopper, using a tire iron to help ease it in.

"Mr. Dubin."

Morici had come back to the truck and was looking at the drums as if he'd seen something that bothered him.

Marcus walked over.

There was no warning. He had no idea he was in trouble until after he'd been hit.

The man in the truck's hopper leaned out as he went by and whacked him with the tire iron, catching him at the join of shoulder and neck. Marcus staggered and dropped as if he'd stepped into a hole. He was quite conscious, but his body seemed to have temporarily fused.

Above him Morici's face, like an image switched off an old TV screen, reduced to the size of an egg, then popped back to normal again. The pain expanding his head pumped bile into his chest, making him cough and gag, his heart hammering his rib cage. His focus returned, and his brain resumed control, sensation creeping back into his limbs.

Morici was bending to him, his eyes hard and flat, his mouth thinned into a censorious line.

"I've heard them say, in this city, that you can never find a cop when you want one. The reverse would also seem to be true."

Rough hands frisked Marcus, found the Airweight on his hip.

"Fuckin' narc," a man muttered, then walked away leaving Marcus wondering at his own stupidity. Everybody had his price, so he'd been told. Had he seriously expected fifty million to be too low for Hightower? Hell, the guy had even told him he was retiring, and that this haul would make a lulu to go out on. He hadn't been kidding.

Still slumped on the ground, Marcus got back to his immediate and lousy situation. Morici had left only the one man on him, but it was the guy with the tire iron, and he was hefting it in his hands like a golfer considering a choice of clubs.

Marcus put his back against the truck, and shakily pushed himself to his knees. He heard the noise and felt the vibration as the last drum was bundled in.

One of the men came around, looked with some disgust at him, hopped up into the cab, and started the engine.

"Hey, Joey!" somebody called.

The driver got out and went back to check something.

Car doors opened and clunked shut. The Buick started up, and the U-Haul van drove off.

Marcus tested his body. His neck felt as if a steel rod had been inserted inside it but his vision was clear, and the numbness had gone from his shoulder.

He made a big production of struggling all the way to his feet, blinking heavily and swaying a little. To the man guarding him he looked completely defenseless.

"Got to go now, honey," the man said, getting a new grip on the tire iron. "Nothin' personal but I gotta break a leg or two so you'll stick around for a while. I tell you what, though," he added reasonably, "I'll give you a little antisetic, little tap on the head like. That way you won't feel nothin' when the legs go."

He stepped forward, bringing the tire iron up and off his shoulder in a lazy swing.

The man was so confident, his action so slow, that Marcus didn't have to try to block the blow — he kicked off the side of the truck and made a piston of his forearm, ripping his right fist into the man's gut just above his groin.

Air left the man's mouth as if he were blowing up a balloon, the tire iron dropped to the asphalt, and with a look of amazement he slowly, almost devoutly, went to his knees.

Marcus leaped behind the wheel, mashed the truck into gear, tried to take it away. It bucked and bounded and stalled on him. He wrenched the ignition key over, tromped the gas pedal, bringing the engine to life, and tried another gear. The truck rumbled forward this time but he'd lost the surprise, and somebody came at him, rushing for the cab. The man jumped for the running board but was batted off as Marcus, with a quick, violent movement, shoved the door open, belting him away.

Shots sounded but they could have been blanks for all the effect they had. Marcus took the truck roaring up the dock, pulling at switches and buttons to find the headlights. They sprang on as he bore down on the ruined gate, braked going through it, took a wild right-hand turn into the flow of light traffic.

Immediately the first of the sirens whined in the night.

He knew they'd be there; Morici would simply have called Hightower from the Buick. Hightower was coming in a hurry, and in force. Two squad cars now, a third behind that one, all siren noise and exploding blue lights. Marcus fought for some speed but it wasn't built into a truck designed to haul garbage. He drove badly, floundering through the unfamiliar gears, over-revving the engine. He hadn't the faintest idea of where he was going but wherever it was, it had to be someplace where Hightower couldn't get his hands on the drums, which he could hear bouncing around in the hopper, belting off the sides and crashing together. The colossal mistake he'd made hit him a second time. He'd been worried about Hightower going after the money but entirely confident that he'd grab the shipment . . . and the bastard had been waiting not to intercept it, but to escort it.

He moaned at his stupidity, the sound blending into siren howl as the first of the cruisers zoomed up on his left, the cop in the passenger seat bringing up a pump gun. Marcus jerked the wheel over, the truck slammed into the cruiser and sent it into the path of the oncoming traffic, swerving and braking its way through shrieking horns.

The truck's windshield sharded outward as something warped the air by his ear. They'd worked a pincer movement on him — a cruiser had sneaked up on the inside and tried to take his head off with a riot gun.

The police car paid for such sloppy work.

Marcus swerved left, cut back in sharply, and bounced the cruiser into the cyclone fence like a hockey puck slapped into a net. It caromed off, its driver losing control, hit the side of the truck again, rebounded into the fence, caught its front bumper on a support, and spun through 360 degrees on smoking, popping tires.

It couldn't last; he'd been lucky but he couldn't drive the truck well enough, and it was just too slow and cumbersome. A reek of hot oil filled the cab, and the engine heat flowed through his cotton pants as if he were crouching over a burning stove.

Where?

His mind raced with the engine. Where could you put five fifty-five gallon oil drums so they couldn't be got at?

A squad car flashed by him, then another, zipping past to set up something ahead — a roadblock, or some kind of diversion to channel him down a side street where they could slow him up, bottle him up, get at him, get into the hopper.

Think!

Where was he?

On the edge of Brooklyn heading south. He could go only one of two ways: turn off left, or keep going straight, because a right turn would take him into the river.

The river.

The idea expanded like a paper flower in liquid. Run the truck off the end of a dock, bury the thing in thirty or forty feet of water. Just drive it off and jump clear: a dark river at night, even darker underneath the piers; Hightower wouldn't have a hope of finding him.

Marcus trod the brake, skidded, clashed gears changing

up, swerved the truck toward the dock entrance coming up on his right.

It wasn't quite as ruined as the tanker dock; half the gate was still standing.

The truck smashed the remaining part off its rusted hinges, rode up and over it, bulldozing it out of the way, but the impact shattered the headlights, leaving Marcus with no illumination.

He didn't care, he could just make out the end of the pier, the glimmering, light-slicked water beyond it. He was going to make it! The realization sang through his bones and sinews. Five, ten minutes back he'd been wondering if they were going to put his own gun into his mouth, send a slug ploughing into his brain. The brain couldn't register sensation; he would have just felt the bullet crunching a molar, and a burning in the roof of his mouth. Then nothing. But it wasn't going to happen that way; he was going to survive, and more than half a ton of a killer drug was going to end up in the mud where it belonged. He'd been reprieved like a character in a comic opera, and he yelled, laughed, pounded the horn, gripped by a surging release even as he saw what could have been another truck coming at him.

He stood on the brake pedal, compressed air locking every wheel, rubber screaming, dying, peeling away.

Just ten feet was the difference. Had he had another three yards he would have stopped short of the dumpster somebody had left near the edge of the dock.

The truck banged into it at the end of its tearing skid, not a smash but hard enough for the engine to stall and die. Marcus knew as he listened to the labored whir of the starter that the motor was too overheated to catch.

And there was a car making a turn into the dock, spanging up and over the busted gate.

He floored the accelerator trying to pump life into the engine. He needed just five seconds to back up, twenty more to go around the dumpster and let the truck's momentum bounce it over the safety step at the end of the pier.

But he wasn't going to get them.

He jumped out of the cab, risked a glance behind him as he began to run for the river.

What he saw halted him dead.

There were no white stripes on the car racing toward him, and no frantic roof lights. The car was a dark, solid color.

A Camaro.

Claire.

He knew instantly what had happened: she'd heard the shots and seen the truck coming hard through the gate, maybe even caught a glimpse of him behind the wheel, so she'd forgotten about the van and followed him. But it wasn't going to do either of them any good because, howling through the gate, in an expertly controlled skid, was a car that did have white stripes and roof lights.

The Camaro slammed to a stop, then Claire was out and running toward him, her mouth shocked into a circle as a handgun banged repeatedly and bullets clapped through the night. The cruiser, two hundred feet away, was coming at them as if it meant to run them down.

Marcus lunged, grabbed Claire's wrist, kept her running, racing for the end of the pier. He felt the reluctance in her body, a holding-back as she understood — Claire was a poor swimmer, and the river was black, and there was a solid mile of it between them and the beckoning lights of Manhattan.

The gun was all the inducement she needed. It cracked out again above the siren scream, slugs howling around a pair of fleeing felons.

They went into the river like kids jumping into a summer lake, holding hands and leaping high. It was hard to judge distance in the dark, and the river surprised them, buckling their legs as they splashed into it in a clumsy tangle. They came up together, kicked and struggled back to the safety of the pier, the river viscous and dirty in their mouths when they swam into the blackness between the concrete stanchions.

Above them cars wheeled in, brakes squealing, sirens dying, doors banging open, the sound of boots. Claire reached for a girder, lacerated her hand on some barnacles, and cried out.

"They're underneath," a voice called.

A figure appeared at a ladder behind an inquisitive flashlight beam that darted around the pilings, caught the movement of water.

"I got 'em! Two guys in the water here."

No voice corrected him, nobody said, "What about the woman? There was a woman driving the Chevy." Nobody said anything, and that told Marcus a lot. The man on the ladder wasn't Hightower, so it meant that Hightower had brought at least one other cop in on the deal.

A couple more squad cars arrived; that made five as far as Marcus could tell.

"What do we do with 'em?" the man on the ladder called up.

Hightower's voice answered him.

"They're in the harbor, ain't they? We'll let the harbor boys handle it. Manchee, get 'em on the horn."

Marcus heard it, an order to call the Harbor Precinct. He knew it wouldn't be carried out.

"Farquar." It was Hightower's voice again. "Tell 'em how it is."

The man on the ladder called to them, his words booming in the enclosed space under the dock.

"Hey, you two. Listen up. We want you should stay put. There are men with guns up here. You try to swim outa there, you're gonna find that out. The harbor guys'll be around to fish you out in ten or fifteen. Meantime, remember, it's an offense to pee in the river."

Somebody laughed at that, then the flashlight went out as the man climbed back up the ladder.

Marcus had been correct with the squad-car count; there were five of them parked on the pier, ten men in all, three in plainclothes, counting Hightower, the rest in uniform.

"All righty," Hightower said. "Let's take a look at what he got."

Flashlight beams played on the oil drums in the back of the garbage truck.

"We got a nice one here," somebody said.

"Gotta be hash," somebody else said.

"It's boy," Manchee said.

"What?"

"Jesus H. Christ!"

"Let's get one down," Hightower said. "That one."

The drum with the indentations in its rim had been loaded last so it seemed natural for him to choose it, it being the closest. As it was rolled out and lifted to the ground somebody said, "It can't be boy. Not five drums. Probably morphine brick."

"Could be," a voice replied. "They busted a lab in Virginia coupla weeks back."

From the trunk of a squad car a patrolman brought out a hammer and a cold chisel. The drum was stood up on its bottom, and the man went to work on its lid.

"You know what you done, don't you?" Manchee said to Hightower. "No way the Department's gonna let you leave now."

Farquar, grinning, held out his hand.

"Congratulations, Captain."

Hightower shook hands briefly, enough to acknowledge the gesture but not long enough to appear to be bragging. Farquar and Manchee were from the same mold as Hightower, old-time cops with tree-trunk bodies. They watched the chisel slicing into the drum, punching through the metal in a wide circle.

Marcus could imagine the scene above him: the patrol-

[245]

men gathered around, intent on their prize, nobody watching the river. Now would be a good time to try for the next pier about 150 feet away, but he held back, treading water and clinging to a pylon, one arm around Claire. Too many men up there. If he waited, maybe the odds would get a little better.

They listened to the bang of a steel drum being cut open.

The man with the chisel had completed a wide semicircle. He shoved the chisel into the cut he'd made and prized up a piece of the lid. Eager hands grabbed it and peeled it back a few inches.

Flashlight beams speared into the drum.

"What?" Hightower said.

There was stony silence as he reached in and lifted out a cigarette carton.

"Aw, c'mon," he said, and savagely pulled open the carton, spilling out cigarette packs. He ripped open a pack, tore it apart like an animal, broke a cigarette in half, sniffed at the tobacco. He dived his hands into the drum opening and pulled out five, six more cartons, tossed them aside, pulled out several more, then hurled them to the ground.

"Fucking *bastards!*" he yelled. "Five drums of fuckin' *cigarettes!*"

"Shit!" somebody said.

Some of the men groaned.

Farquar picked up a pack off the asphalt and examined it.

"Hong Kong Marlboros." He flicked it away in disgust. "Beautiful."

Hightower had walked off by himself, his back to his men, facing the river. They looked at their captain, nobody saying anything now, embarrassed for him. He turned and came back, shaking his head and snorting through his nose.

"Jesus. My mother gets better tips at Aqueduct. That cocksucker *swore* it was high-quality smack. Said he'd seen it being packed. Said he was right there when they did it."

"Dreamers," Farquar said. "I tell you, if I shat into a

jelly jar in Hong Kong and tried to smuggle it in, somebody would call up and say it was chocolate."

"Okay." Hightower took a breath and let it out in angry little pieces. "There are a million stories in this town, this has been one of them. Let's get it to the warehouse. Maybe the American Cancer Society will give us a citation."

"What about the water rats?" Farquar asked, pointing down at the pier. In his disappointment Hightower appeared to have forgotten about them.

"Oh yeah, the big-time weed smugglers. I'll baby-sit them till the harbor guys get here. I can use the air right now."

"I'll stick around, too," Manchee said.

"Want me to drive the truck?" one of the patrolmen asked.

"Nah, I'll do it," Manchee said. He made little shooing motions with his hands, inclining his head in his boss's direction. "It's a wrap, okay?"

The men picked up the cigarette cartons strewn over the dock, shoved them back into the drum, and hefted the drum into the truck with the others.

"Tough one, Captain," one of them murmured. They got into their cars and drove off in a line toward the ruined entrance.

A few minutes later the red Buick arrived.

"The shipment," Morici said to Hightower, sticking his head out of the window. Anxiety had widened his eyes and taken some color from his face.

"No sweat. We got it all."

Morici sank back against the plush of the rear seat.

"You should have told me about that man before."

"Didn't want to worry you."

"He fooled me. I thought he was half unconscious, but he was just acting. You get him? Where is he?"

"Taking a bath," Hightower said, pointing down at the pier.

Morici leaned forward, anxious for the right answer.

[247]

"How did the rest of it go?"

"Bing, bang, like that. Opened the drum, the squad saw the ciggies, and I put on an act would've won me an Emmy."

"Excellent," Morici said, relaxing. "I shall talk to you later."

"You bet," Hightower said, walking away.

Morici told his driver to take him back to his hotel; he had a call to make, one he'd been dreaming about for a long time. It would be five in the morning in Cefalù, the little blue and white town on the edge of the Tyrrhenian Sea. Roccobonno, in sweater and pants over his striped pajamas, which would be buttoned all the way to his fat neck, would be driven to a little stone house with a safe phone, would take the call in the front parlor with the wedding photographs on the polished, doily-strewn sideboard.

"Don Roccobonno . . . I have disastrous news . . ." Morici knew the voice he'd use: passionate, ragged, shot through with emotion.

"The shipment . . . we were given away. It was stolen."

Rocco's face would blanch, then blood would rush into it, pumped in two massive strokes from his thick peasant's body.

"Stolen?"

"The police. The New York City Police. They were tipped off. They were waiting for us. It was the Triads in Hong Kong."

"No!" Roccobonno would yell, his throat swollen with rage.

"They put cigarettes in one of the drums. The police opened that one. It must have been marked . . ." A sob there, choking out the words now: "That's what they confiscated officially, cigarettes."

"Cigarettes . . ."

"They stole everything . . . a disaster, Don Roccobonno."

[248]

A disaster, yes, because when it got through to his farmer's brain Rocco would know that there was no comeback, not against the Triads in their harbor enclave on the other side of the globe, with their unfathomable language and their Martian faces. The fat peasant would be able to do nothing except pick up the phone and smash it against the wall, killing the bringer of bad news.

"You know something?" Morici said to the man sitting next to him as the Buick turned north. "There's really no difference between stealing a hundred dollars or a billion dollars. All you need is the right arrangement."

16

On THE PIER Hightower was holding a little meeting with his two lieutenants.

"We got to get going pretty soon, but we can't leave 'em healthy. They get to a phone booth, we could be found before we're ready."

"Off 'em, then," Farquar suggested. "I got a factory Smith in the cruiser. The tide'll take 'em downriver, and we can dump the Camaro in Bensonhurst."

Hightower grimaced as he ran his fingers over a puffy cheek; a smart thinker but not a man given to snap decisions.

"We don't want anything official. Arrested they could hurt us, dead they could hurt us. Delayed is what we want 'em."

"Maybe I could wing 'em a little," Farquar said. "Slow 'em down that way."

"That Smith clean?" Hightower asked.

"Ain't even been test-fired."

Farquar, like Manchee, was part of the small percentage of New York City detectives who'd bobbed like corks over the cleansing waves of the Knapp Report, and had survived the storm that had followed. As narcotics cops they were diligent in their jobs except when it was worth their time to be sloppy. When things were slow they supplemented their incomes by doing a nice line in stolen handguns.

"Better get it," Hightower said. Then he walked over to the edge of the pier and called down. "Hey, John Doe . . . I got a deal for you. Come up outa there, you and your girlfriend. Be our guests for half an hour till we get done what we gotta do, a little business in town. Then you walk away, no hard feelings. That way I get done what the man's paying me for, and you go home to Nebraska, or wherever the fuck you're from, knowing you gave it a good shot, and lucky to be in one piece. How about it? Did you hear me, John?"

In the water, Marcus's arm was getting numb supporting Claire, the muscles in his other arm aching as he hugged the slippery concrete of the stanchion. As warm as the river had been when they'd first splashed into it, they were growing cold now, their upper bodies immersed and immobile, generating no heat.

"I hear you," Marcus said.

"So how about it?" Hightower's heavy voice reverberated off the surface, seeming to come from three directions at once.

Marcus felt Claire shake her head. It was his answer, too; Hightower had fooled him once and was probably getting to like it.

"I'll think it over," Marcus called.

Up on the dock Farquar climbed into the cruiser, took the stolen gun from the glove compartment, got out silently, tiptoed along the far side of the pier.

Manchee went down the ladder.

"Hey, fella," he called. "You're not using your noggin. You want to come out of this a little ahead, okay, there's enough to go around. But if we hang around here much longer nobody's gonna make bean one."

By moving his head a little and peeking around the stanchion, Marcus could see the detective's tubular shape outlined faintly on the ladder.

"I'm still thinking about it," he called.

He was, too. All of it. He'd heard them discovering the cigarettes, and listened to the performance Hightowerhad put on in front of his men. Marcus knew what was going to happen: they were going to switch trucks, that much was obvious. Somewhere they had an identical garbage truck, and in that truck would be five black oil drums — one of them chiseled open — containing nothing but cartons of Hong Kong Marlboros. They'd have to take a sledgehammer to that truck now, belt in the headlights and smash it up a bit to get an exact look-alike. That would be the truck they'd drive to the Police Clerk's Property Office to be impounded. And the one up on the dock with the heroin would be delivered to Morici. Just why they were doing it this way was anybody's guess, but something was going on.

"Hey, Ace. Be reasonable." Manchee, on the ladder, was shining his flashlight on the stanchion like a man trying to tempt fish toward a light. "I mean, what're you afraid of? You got a woman down there. Now maybe we ain't altar boys, the captain and me and my buddy, but I honestly can't remember the last time I did a broad."

Marcus put his face close to Claire's ear.

"I'm going to try to get him off that ladder, then we'll go the other way. Can you hold on for thirty seconds?"

She moved her head in a nod, staying silent, clamping down on her panic.

As he reluctantly relaxed his grip, Claire grabbed the cold slipperiness of the stanchion and fought the river, kicked at the horrors down there, held them off with her feet and her mind.

Marcus took a fix on the ladder, exhaled, sucked in air, and duck-dived. He swam through a deeper, colder layer of what could have been liquid pitch; it was so dark. With his eyes open or closed it made no difference; the thin ambient light that was faintly present under the pier was much too frail to penetrate the surface.

He pulled himself through the cold blackness, expelling air in small bursts, breaststroking and feeling for the ladder. He thought he'd gone by it, or got the direction wrong, but he kept going, just kicking his legs now, stretching his arms in front of him.

The upright of the ladder brushed his left hand. Marcus curled himself, got a grip on the upright, broke the surface, charged up the ladder, grabbed the back of Manchee's jacket, and pulled.

The detective got an awful fright. He'd heard the splash of water, felt the ladder shake, caught a quick glimpse of something coming up at him, his mind turning the form into some creature from a black lagoon.

He yelled out as he was wrenched away, and plunged heavily into the water with his feet up in the air.

Marcus swam, kicking out in a strong crawl, back underneath the pier. He didn't see Farquar coming down the ladder on the other side, but he saw the flashlight beam and dived immediately. The water muted the boom of the gun, robbed the slug of its pace. Marcus felt a hard tap against his shoulder and knew he'd done something unique: he'd stopped a bullet without bleeding. When he made it to the concrete stanchion Claire grabbed at him, half to help him, half to help herself, needing his buoyancy.

Voices shouted, folding into each other.

"Sonofa*bitch!* The bastard pulled me in. I'll *kill* the mother!"

"Farquar, you get him?"

"Arm shot, I think."

"You *think?*"

"Gimme a break, Captain. It's like a Hundred and Twenny-fifth Street down here."

Manchee was struggling in the water, gargling curses as he scrambled to haul his sodden bulk up the ladder. Marcus pulled Claire closer to him; that was the direction to go in now, away from the man with the gun.

"Breathe out and take a deep breath. Let it out underwater bit by bit. When you're bursting, squeeze my arm and we'll come up and get under again fast. You ready?"

The last thing she wanted to do was put her head under that oily, liquid night, give the black water a chance to rush into her mouth and throttle her, but she said yes, and gulped some air.

Marcus pulled her under.

Three or four feet and he knew it was impossible. With one arm around her he just couldn't get the drive to pull them through the water. And Claire was digging her nails into his arm, the breath she'd bottled up already strangling her.

They broke the surface in a rush of expelled air. The flashlight beam probed and yellowed them for a moment before they dived, gunshots echoing absurdly loud in the enclosed space. Bullets ripped into the water, decelerating at a tremendous rate as they met heavy gallons of resistance, becoming lumps of spent lead sinking in a crooked line, drifting softly to join the garbage lining the riverbed.

Manchee yelled at his partner.

"Watchit, will ya! You tryin' for me or them, for crissake?"

Farquar heard the sound of his targets surfacing behind the stanchion and knew he'd missed. He'd been aiming for an arm or a shoulder.

"This time?" Hightower's voice called down to him.

"No. Shit, how'm I supposed to hit something with the lights out? Gimme a break, huh?"

"Come up outa there. You too, Manchee. Pair of clowns, the both of you."

Hightower had seen something that had given him an idea. In the back of the garbage truck were the hammer and the cold chisel which had been used to open the cigarette drum. Hightower fetched them and moved toward the end of the pier and the thing that had caught his eye outlined against the reflected lights of the river.

A gasoline pump.

He broke the lock with the hammer, uncoiled the hose, and handed the nozzle to Manchee, who was dripping water beside him.

"Here," Hightower said. "You want to fill 'em up?"

"I'd like to shove it up his ass," his lieutenant growled.

Farquar arrived dangling the revolver. When he saw what was happening — the gasoline pumping out fast, splashing down onto the water in a steady stream — he nodded positively, impressed with his boss's thinking.

"Should do it," he said.

An oil barge had passed in the direction of the Upper Bay five minutes before, and the waves of its wake, expanding toward both sides of the river, came lapping in, moving water against the pier. The gasoline rode on top of it, floating in past the rotting wooden piles, curling around the stanchions, seeping up against Marcus and Claire, sluggishly clinging.

The fumes sneaked up their nostrils and grabbed at their brains, attacked the backs of their throats, the smell of the gasoline identifying it instantly.

Marcus let go of Claire, struggled out of his jacket, grabbed her again. She didn't have to be told that this time they had to go and keep on going.

They heard the crank of a metal handle, and the ponderous sound of the gasoline flow lessen and dry up. As they snatched breaths and curled into the water, a single match flew briefly through the dark, then went down in flames into the river.

The air shuddered, concussed by the *whoommfff!* of instant ignition. The pier, a jet-black finger a millisecond ago, now looked like an aircraft carrier whose lower deck had exploded. Its flat, wide top was in darkness, unaffected, but down at the water line it twisted and squirmed in an agony of heat and flame.

Beneath the surface, kicking out hard, Marcus stared up at the blue/white canopy stretching over them. It lit them like fish in a pond, showed him Claire floundering beside him, her hair clumped around her face, layered on her shoulders, her cheeks bulging, her eyes jammed shut as if expecting a stinging blow. They made very little progress before she squeezed her hand into his arm, the balloon in her lungs about to burst. Her eyes had shot open, and when she saw the sheet of light above her she felt like a tiny Alice figure that had fallen into a birthday cake aflame with a thousand candles.

As Marcus jerked her up toward the surface she had another crazy impression: she thought that he was trying to drown her, trying to smother her.

They burst up into the liquid fire, the jacket Marcus was holding over Claire's hair a crown of flames on her head. She gulped at burnt oxygen through the soaked denim of the jacket, the fire biting her struggling arms, white-hot tongues licking at her shoulders, tasting her.

He forced her under again, but now the jacket which had protected her face began to attack it, flattening against her mouth and her nose like some cloying river growth trying to find a way into her throat. She panicked as an animal panics tied into a sack and dumped in the sea. She fought Marcus, kicked and clawed her way to the surface, the balloon back in her chest, expanding, stretching membrane-thin.

Surging up into the stench and taste of petroleum Marcus tried to belt the flames away, clear a space around them, but it wasn't water that splashed through his hands, it was fire, and the fire didn't part as they came up into it, it rode with them and went on burning on top of them.

Down again into the drowning underside of the river, a few feet made through the water, then up again to be raked by the searing liquid. Three more times they dived, pulled themselves a little way beneath the surface, came up into the boiling caldron, plunged down again away from the trembling, crackling, blue-centered heat.

Beneath the jacket Marcus refused to take from her head, Claire saw choking blackness one moment, blistering incandescence the next, which, during the brief, agonizing exposures, was not much less than Marcus was able to see as the flames reached for his eyes.

Then they were through it, through the worst of it.

The fire had thinned at the deep end of the dock, burning fitfully in small, scummy pools. It still raged at the other end where the gas had bulked against the retaining wall, but here at the outer section of the dock, the fire waved tiny blue flags, heatless and without energy, until these too flickered out and the darkness returned to salve the wounded surface. They grabbed hold of the ladder and hung there, taking in great chunks of the night air, hanging like weights neck-deep in the dark folds of a river that separated Brooklyn, New York, from the plains and forests and farms of the rest of America.

"Up," Marcus said.

Claire began to climb the ladder, Marcus following, bringing with him out of the water the smell of burnt hair, scorched fabric, toasted skin. They flopped onto the dock, pooling water, their soaked clothes dragging on them.

At the far end of the pier the three detectives, coughing and shouting at each other over the roar and crackle of the flames, were checking the sides of the dock, thinking that their quarry had tried to swim not the length of the fire, as they'd done, but its width. The squad car was parked ten feet from where Marcus and Claire were lying, the garbage truck a little farther away.

Marcus told her to get to the truck and hunch down on the floor, cut off questions about his condition, made her do what he'd said.

He pushed himself up, snatching his breath as the skin on his shoulders and arms stretched into acid lines, ran in a crouch to the car.

The keys were gone, but there was something better on the front seat: a twelve-gauge Ithaca riot gun. The glove compartment held a single pack of double-aught buck shells.

Marcus took them, took the matchbook sitting on top of a pack of Camels, and got out of the car. The gas-pump hose was lying on the pier a few feet away. He grabbed it, thrust the nozzle through the open car door, pumped gas over the radio and the wiring under the dash, tossed the pump aside. He pulled two matches from the matchbook, closed the cover, stuck one of the matches in, struck the other one, lit the protruding match, lobbed the matchbook into the car, and started his dash.

The squad car rocked as the gas ignited, a concussive shock of sound overriding the noise of the fire in the water. Marcus swung up the riot gun as Hightower and the other two whipped around, sent a blast over their heads that dropped them flat. They got off several shots but Marcus had made the cover of the truck and was jumping for the cab, Claire reaching to help him in. The engine, cooled from its earlier exertions, kicked over the first time.

Marcus pushed Claire down onto the floor, reversed the truck in a wide, roaring sweep, shoved the shotgun out of the window one-handed, and answered the salvo that peppered the door.

There was nothing the three policemen could do but watch the truck drive forward and roll away as smoke billowed from their crippled squad car. They heard the bang of the riot gun again, and saw the left front tire of the Camaro blown into shredded rubber.

Marcus might have laughed if it wouldn't have stretched the skin over his blistered mouth. He said, superfluously, "This is the second time I've stolen this truck tonight."

Claire came up off the floor.

"Billy. Your face. We've got to get to a hospital."

"You're right." Marcus took the truck through the busted gate, wheeled right, going with the traffic. "Soon as we get rid of the junk. How you doing?"

He shot a glance at her: there were some ugly patches on the backs of her hands, and her hair was singed and plastered to her head in burnt pieces, but her face had escaped damage.

"You got all my burns," Claire said, looking anxiously at his bubbled skin.

Marcus checked the side mirror, and the rearview, belted the truck along.

"It'll take Hightower about five minutes to find a phone. So we've got maybe ten minutes to get off the road. You got any ideas?"

When Claire shook her head she added a little more water to her sopping blouse.

"I don't know Brooklyn very well."

The truck rumbled over a small bridge, the dark waters of a canal moving beneath it. Marcus took a second look at a sign pointing to Prospect Park. Could you hide a garbage truck in a park? Stick it behind some trees? Unlikely.

He swung onto a residential avenue, nodded to his right at an elevated highway, raised his voice over the noise of the straining engine.

"Where's that go?"

"I think that's the Queens Expressway. Coney Island. Sheepshead Bay."

The truck swept by the turnoff to Greenwood Cemetery. Five open graves and they could bury the drums.

Marcus checked the rearview mirror again, listened for sirens; with something as heavy and slow and visible as a refuse truck they weren't going to get very far.

And this time, if Hightower caught them, he'd kill them.

The drums clashed together as the truck juddered over

railroad tracks, railroad yards off to their left and right: no solution there. Marcus swerved into a cross-street, went three blocks west to the river, ran a red light, searched for a higher gear that wasn't there.

"Goddamn it!" He tried to swallow and couldn't; some of the liquid fire had got inside his mouth, raising blisters on his gums and his tongue. "This thing moves like an elephant. And where the hell do you hide an elephant?"

"Behind another elephant," Claire said.

He thought she was trying to keep it light until he saw what she'd spotted. A hundred feet ahead of them, coming out of someplace near a huge gas tank, was another garbage truck.

Marcus slowed, followed a high chain-link fence, made a turn and pulled up outside a closed double gate.

A man with an open newspaper at his side came out of a gate house.

"Boy, you only just made it." He moved nearer the truck, peering up at the occupants over a pair of half-frame reading glasses. "You brought the missus, huh? I used to do that now and then when I was cartin'."

He looked closer at Marcus. "I ain't seen you before."

"I'm new on the job."

The man took off his glasses, squinted in the weak light spilling from the gate house.

"What did you do to your face?"

"Cigarette lighter. Damn thing exploded."

"The old ones'll do that," the man said. "So they threw a bucket of water over you, eh?"

"Yeah."

The man chuckled and said, "The missus shouldn't have stood so close."

"Right." Marcus put the truck into gear. "Straight ahead, is it?"

"Into the shed and dump it on the barge. Better hurry. Tug's just hookin' up."

"The tug?" Marcus put the truck back into neutral. "Where does it take the barge?"

"Fresh Kills. Didn't they tell you anything?"

"What's Fresh Kills?"

"The landfill on Staten. Boy, are you from Missouri. It's the biggest dump in the world, which ain't surprising when you're dumpin' twenty-eight thousand tons of garbage every day." The man moved to the gate, swung it wide. "In fifteen years' time," he said, louder, "they say it'll be the highest point on the Eastern Seaboard."

Marcus got all the power he could out of the truck, driving it hard across an open space toward a long rising ramp which disappeared under a huge roof.

"They could trace them, Billy," Claire said. "Sooner or later Hightower will check this place and find out we were here. He'll just pick up the drums from the dump."

"They're not going to the dump," Marcus said. "They're going into the harbor."

The truck hit the bottom of the ramp, roared up it and out onto a pier lit by high ceiling lights. Several bays were cut into the structure, and slotted into one of them was an open iron barge piled high with garbage. Behind the barge a tug was edging into position.

The pier trembled as the truck barreled along it, braked quickly, and reversed up to the safety curb. Marcus jumped down, unlatched the hooks at the rear of the truck. The tailgate flipped up, and the drums tumbled out, banged together, and smacked down on top of the garbage, stirring up a fetid smell that hung like an invisible fog in the shed.

A deckhand on the tug called something to him, something about cutting it a little fine. Marcus ignored him, talking fast to Claire.

"Go back to the gate house and call a cab. Tell the gate man the truck quit on us and you're going back to the office for a part. Can you change a tire?"

"Billy —"

"Yes or no, can you change a tire?"

"Sure, but — "

"Take the cab back to the dock, put the spare on the Camaro, and get out of there."

"Billy, that dump has to be way around the back of Staten Island. It'll take hours to even get close, and you need a doctor this minute."

"What I need is a little cooperation."

"At least let me come with you. Help you with the drums."

"C'mon, you're not thinking. Hightower would've been too busy back there to take the number of the car, but when it occurs to him he'll send somebody for it, and your name's on the rental agreement. And there's no way either of us is gonna come out of this if Morici finds out who we are."

"Let him. We'll get protection. The main thing — "

Marcus snapped. The gasoline fire had burned its signature into his whole upper body, and was reminding him of his mistake every other second.

He yelled at her: "For crissakes, Claire. I fucked up. I trusted the wrong cop, and that bastard Bendroit's gonna make a fortune and not do ten minutes of time. I lost on that one but I'm not gonna lose on this one. Those drums are going into the drink, and if Hightower tries to stop me, a lawyer's not gonna be much goddamn use." He slapped money into her hand. "Now get outa here! Go on!"

Instead of being stung Claire took a half-step toward him and said quietly, "Billy, if you don't come back to me, I'll never forgive you."

Marcus cooled instantly, his pain and his anger doused by her beautiful threat. It hurt his flesh to hug her to him, but he didn't care.

"Believe me, there's no way I'm gonna miss out on you, lady. Whatever happens, I'll be back." He spun her, pushed her gently, made sure she kept going. Then he grabbed a shovel from a rack on the side of the truck, pulled the riot gun from the cab, and checked the tug in back of the barge.

The captain, partially lit by a soft glow in the wheelhouse, was watching behind him, the water there roiling and tumbling as the powerful screws reversed.

Marcus launched himself, made a semisoft landing onto a pile of black plastic bags, bursting some of them open. The concertina effect on his raging skin, plus the heavy stench of what he was surrounded by, produced a heaving surge of nausea, and he lay on his back, the shovel in one hand, the shotgun in the other, breathing through his mouth, and staring up at the stars that popped into view as the tug pulled the barge out from under the roof of the shed.

A quick salt breeze, unblocked now by the pier, swept in from the bay, danced over the barge, taking much of the smell with it, and he slowly recovered. After a few minutes the backward movement ceased. Lines were cast off, and the tug moved past the barge and made fast to the bollards at the front of the craft, then began its tow.

When the tug's deckhands had disappeared, Marcus got to his feet and stepped over the barge's high iron gunwale, and walked on the flat outside edge, about six feet above the choppy waves, down to the rear of the scow. The geography had changed considerably since the last time he'd been near the river; there were no blazing skyscrapers ahead of him now. Manhattan was way to the north, its bright white windows flying high over the bulge of South Brooklyn, and the stumpy battlements of Governors Island. To the south headlights flashed and faded as the Shore Parkway rounded the curve of Bay Ridge. In front of him, in front of the barge and the stern light of the tug, the bay stretched dark for three miles to St. George on Staten Island. Twenty minutes, Marcus figured. About that, anyway. New York harbor had to have a channel to handle ships the size of the *Adrono* — a very deep channel because four-fifths of a fully laden tanker sailed beneath the surface; wide too, that channel, too wide and too deep to be trawled successfully. Unfindable, unrecoverable, the drums would rot down there in the blackness, rust to pieces in the salt and the slime and the mud.

If he could get them rolling so they'd drop over the side.

Marcus climbed back inboard. He loaded the shotgun, put it where he could reach it, picked up the shovel, and with the first icy pangs of shock spinning in his body began to shift garbage against the inside of the gunwale, building the base of a ramp.

Marcus was right on the button in the first of his time estimations; it took Hightower only five minutes to get to a phone, and not long after that he was standing beside a squad car, a map unfolded over its hood.

"Okay," the police captain said, quiet, low-key. "He tried to destroy the shit the first time, he'll try it a second time."

"I'll kick his fuckin' face in," Manchee said. His heavy fist left a damp patch on the cruiser's top when he thumped it.

Farquar, like his boss keeping his anger out of the way of his thinking, poked a stubby finger into the flashlight beam, and traced a line over the map.

"He took a right leaving the dock, we saw that. He would've kept going for sure. Maybe crossed the Gowanus here, then gone down Second or Third looking for another dock to drive off of."

Hightower read out the marked piers.

"Twenty-third, Thirty-fifth, Thirty-ninth Street. The Marine Terminal we can forget. Too much security to — " He broke off, shouted at them. "Get in! Get in, quick!"

His lieutenants didn't question the order; they jumped into the car, and the driver took it howling away. Hightower yelled at the man behind the wheel.

"The Battery! Get down to the Battery!"

"The Battery?" Manchee said. "Why would he go there?"

Hightower gabbled into the radio to one of his squad cars, then thrust the map at Manchee, stabbing his finger down as if he were trying to puncture it.

"Read that. Right there. What's it say?"

" 'Sanitation Department. Fifty-second Street MTS.' The hell's an MTS?"

"Marine transfer station. It's where the garbage trucks go. Look at it. Less than two miles from where he was. And what's he driving? A garbage truck. If you wanted to hide a garbage truck, wouldn't you go there?"

"Christ, yes," Farquar said from the front seat. "Specially if I wanted to ace what I was haulin'."

Manchee, grumpily negative, said, "Maybe. Maybe not. The bum coulda gone someplace else."

"Bullshit!" Hightower said. "That's where he went. The Fifty-second Street transfer station."

"How do you know?"

"Because I'm a fucking good cop, you dummy."

With careful anger, tired of the disparagement, Manchee said, "Then if you know he went there for sure, Captain, why are we going to the goddamn Battery?"

"Because," Hightower answered, bracing himself as the driver zoomed through a red light, "it's the closest place that's got a fast boat ready to go."

With the siren screaming, and the roof lights radiating blue emergency, the squad car Hightower had talked to burned to a stop at the westernmost extremity of Fifty-second Street, Brooklyn.

A detective jumped out and barked a question at the man standing in front of a double gate.

"A guy and a broad soaking wet in a white truck. You see 'em?"

"The girl just left." The gate man pointed. "Got into a taxi a few minutes back."

"Fuck the girl, where's the guy?"

"On the pier. His truck quit on him right after he dumped."

"He unloaded? Into a scow?"

"Into a barge, yeah. The tug just left."

"Going out to the Kills?"

"Yeah. What's up?"

The detective ducked back into the cruiser, grabbing for the radio.

In the squad car wailing down the southern tip of the FDR Drive, Hightower replaced the radio's handset.

"Jesus, Cap," Farquar said. "How do you do it?"

"I read the *New York Times.*" Hightower checked his watch, then snarled at the patrolman behind the wheel. "You afraid of getting a ticket or something? Move it, for God's sake."

The car rocketed down off the Drive, ran the reds, shot by the pulled-over traffic, made it to the only all-wooden structure in Lower Manhatten: Company #1 of the Marine Division of the New York City Fire Department, a hexagonal clapboard building standing in the water looking as if it had been transported whole from Nantucket.

Two minutes after Hightower and his two assistants charged in waving badges and shouting orders, the duty crew was running with them to the fireboat moored below.

Twenty-four hours of every day in the year a fireboat was ready to go; this one gunned away as if racing a competitor.

"So where's the fire?" the boat commander asked, a young lieutenant who liked to have his little joke.

Behind him Hightower held on against the quick surge of speed. The boat was a brand-new one on trial, a thirty-footer whose hydraulic jets could sit the craft up and blow it through the water at better than thirty-five knots.

"Some nut stole some oil drums. Dropped them onto a scow at the Fifty-second Street MTS. We got to stop him, the price of oil being what it is."

The young lieutenant grinned at the only other member of the crew, a firefighter a couple of years younger than himself who was stationed behind the wheel.

"I thought all the crazies had moved to Los Angeles. That barge going out to the Kills?"

"Yeah."

Spray whipped over the water cannon mounted on the bow, splattered against the cabin windshield as the boat sliced into the chop.

"Why us?" the lieutenant asked. "The Precinct boat got a puncture?"

"This trip's unofficial," Hightower told him offhandedly.

The grin on the firefighter's face shrank half an inch.

"What do you mean, unofficial?"

"He means," Farquar said, "that whatever happens out on the bay, it was a false alarm. That's what you report, a false alarm. You get 'em all the time, right?"

The boat commander took a longer look at the three policemen, uncertain now.

"I don't think I can do that."

Manchee, in his puddling suit, was gripping a handrail, feet planted against the buck of the deck.

"Sure you can do it," he said. "If you don't do it, you'll go over the fuckin' side. Understand?"

Hightower glanced at the helmsman, said to the lieutenant, "You and your buddy can split a couple of grand. I wouldn't ask professionals to donate their time for free."

"Hear that, fire man?" Manchee asked. "You're getting paid. Now get this thing up on its ass."

The boat commander swallowed, nodded at the helmsman, who nervously pushed at the throttle and sent the boat shooting straight down the middle of New York Harbor.

Wood, metal, rubble, cardboard, paper, wet and sticky kitchen refuse from busted plastic sacks — the shovel bit into small mountains of the stuff, shifted its mass, raked it down into the trough along the inside of the gunwale.

Marcus swore through his bubbled lips at the heat in his flesh, leaned on the shovel and took a look at his position. About two miles ahead the dark mouth of Kill Van Kull split Staten Island from New Jersey, the beginning of Bayonne just visible. Behind him the Sunset Park section of Brooklyn, where he'd begun his voyage, had receded into the western edge of the borough, the bright pinpoints of the Verrazano Bridge strung across the sky to the south.

He figured the barge was about halfway across the bay.

Marcus climbed up the garbage pile and went to work on the first of the drums.

He shoved and hefted one end around, maneuvering it so that it ended up parallel to the ramp he'd built. He retrieved the shovel, stuffed the blade under the drum, put his weight against the shovel handle, and levered the drum into movement.

It rolled forward an inch, then another, got going and bumped clumsily down the garbage slope, hit the top of the gunwale with a whack, crashed into the water, and sank out of sight.

What were they worth, these drums he was pushing into the bay? He was thinking about that as he battled with a second one. About 132 kilos per drum, each kilo with a street value of over two million . . . when this one went he would have gone through over half a billion dollars in about ten minutes. How many people had ever done that before?

The drum shifted grudgingly, took an age to get going, began to move. Marcus watched its thumping plunge, saw the waves embrace it, wash over it, swallow it up. Two million a kilo. And yet Marcus recalled Burroughs telling him that to get a kilo of heroin, a Burmese family had to produce ten kilos of opium, for which they'd be paid maybe three hundred bucks apiece.

The third drum fought him; didn't want to move. He had to manhandle it at both ends, risk breaking the shovel to budge it at all. It went finally, bumping heavily onto the gunwale and hanging there for a heart-stopping moment before it toppled over onto the iron surround, and plopped into the bay.

Marcus had to rest then, on his knees in the garbage, keeping his eyes and his mouth wide, fighting dizziness. When he got going again, part of the ramp had to be rebuilt, a frustrating, backbreaking chore, the loose trash constantly shifting and potholing beneath him.

He was working on the drum with the cigarettes, almost had it in position, when the fireboat came roaring out of the night on a bow wave the size of an ocean breaker. It burst in on Marcus as if it had crashed through a wall, its searchlight beam snapping on, picking him out, nailing him to the dark. The gunshot that accompanied it sent a bullet ploughing into a tin can in the garbage next to his knee, almost as if the shooter were merely getting in some practice.

Diving backward, spinning and flinging himself headfirst into the trough against the gunwale, Marcus didn't waste time wondering how he'd been found — Hightower was either smart or lucky or both — he was thinking hard about the riot gun he'd left on the other side of the barge.

Without that weapon he was dead.

He figured it: to get the gun he could crawl along the trough and go around the perimeter of the gunwale, but if Hightower came right up alongside he'd spot him when he turned the corner of the garbage hill. All the guy would have to do then was lean in over the gunwale and waste him. So he couldn't go around the garbage.

And if he tried to go over the top that searchlight would explode all over him, and he'd never make it down the other side.

So if he couldn't go around the garbage, and he couldn't go over it, there was only one way he could go.

Through it.

* * *

The interception course couldn't have been much simpler: they'd powered down the center of the Upper Bay until they'd seen in front of them, moving with turtle slowness, the running lights of the tug, the stern light of the barge, creeping across their path, practically side-on.

A nudge of the throttle, the whoosh of acceleration, then the high roar of the engine dropping to a solid low beat as the bow plunged, the vessel slowing as if its keel had scraped a sandbank.

The boat's searchlight, like a bolt of frozen lightning, revealed the scow and its mountain of garbage, and the ramp built with that garbage. Then came Manchee's hurried shot, and the figure vanishing on the far side of the mountain, and Farquar's stunned voice.

"Christ almighty! Two drums. I only see two drums."

Hightower hissed something under his breath, then rounded on the boat commander so quickly the young man flinched.

"How deep is it here? Is it deep?"

"What?"

Hightower's heavy neck puffed as he shouted, "The fucker's tossed three drums over the side. We gotta get 'em back."

The helmsman worked wheel and throttle, held the boat steady while his superior explained something, reluctant to bring the news.

"Where do you start to look? It's two miles over to Brooklyn. He could've started dumping them right away maybe, in the Bay Ridge Channel. If he dumped them later, they could be on the bottom of the Anchorage Channel, the one we're over now."

"But we can trawl for 'em, can't we? Drag for 'em?"

"Good luck on that one. Both those channels are over half a mile wide, and they're dredging them all the time. Something like an oil drum would just get buried in a mud hole."

When Hightower looked as if he might slug the young

lieutenant, Farquar said quickly, "There's still two left, Cap. We better concentrate on saving those, so let's get that guy."

"I think I got him," Manchee said, playing the searchlight over the barge.

"You didn't get shit, you fuckhead." Again Hightower rounded on the firefighter. "How many men on board that tug?"

"Five. Wait, they got a cook. Six."

"A cook on a tug?"

"It stays out for a week at a time, just hauling scows."

"Bring us alongside. Farquar, get on board that thing. A grand apiece, double for the master or they all start swimming. Manchee, get ready to hop onto that barge."

"No way. The sonofabitch's got a pump gun, remember?"

With a sneer in his voice Hightower said, "I thought you said you got him."

"What am I, the Pope? I could be wrong, couldn't I?"

The fireboat spurted ahead and kissed against the bunched rope of the tug's bulwarks. Farquar dropped down onto the wide rear deck, a shotgun in his hand taken from the squad car that had picked them up.

"He's in there somewhere," Hightower called to him. "When he comes up for air, take his fucking head off."

The garbage was alive.

While he'd been standing on top of it, the salt breeze in his face, and the comforting chug of the tug's engines in his ears, it had been simply a loosely packed hill of smelly trash. But in it, *in* it, buried in its foul midst, burrowing through the filth like a blind mole, the garbage lived.

There were things all around him.

Moving.

Insects and roaches probably.

Rats definitely.

There had to be rats; there was no way these barges

[271]

could ever have been emptied completely — the garbage wouldn't be tipped out, Marcus was sure of that, it would be dug out by cranes in big spilling bucketfuls, snatched at by huge scoopers that would never be able to get to the bottom layer. That layer would have been there for months, years maybe. And the things that lived in that layer, traveling back and forth across the bay — like rats, the traditional sea voyagers — would just have gotten bigger and fatter.

Marcus dug with his hands, tunneled out a passage for himself, heard a rustle and scamper that wasn't caused by the detritus shifting ahead of him, heard squeaking that didn't come from discarded metal.

The black plastic bags he'd trodden through on top of the garbage had been mainly whole, intact, but here, several feet under, they'd ruptured beneath the weight of the upper layers and spilled their reeking contents.

Marcus crawled through unnameable things, moist, slimy things that squished against his face, his closed eyes, his bit-tight mouth. He burrowed forward on his belly, pulling himself through the stinking blackness, his fingers rasping one moment on jagged masonry and broken glass, the next moment plunging into oozing softness that stuck and clung to his hands like a greasy gel.

Something crossed his leg; didn't fall on it or scrape against it, but ran across it. His trouser legs had gotten hiked up, and he felt the scurry of membrane paws on his bare calf. He yelled out, not in fear of the rodents, resentful of the uninvited guest at the feast, but at the noxious offal that encased him in its black and stifling grasp.

He tunneled like a wild thing, wriggled and kicked and swam through the cloying miasma, the tips of his clawing fingers finally touching clear, clean, open space. Fighting the stuff, widening the hole with his arms and elbows, he squirmed through, pulled his head and shoulders out the other side of the garbage hill, lay there panting, drawing the sea breeze into his lungs, feeling like a worm halfway out of a rotten apple.

The fireboat was standing off, just ticking over, keeping pace with the tug. The tug had a searchlight, too, mounted on top of its wheelhouse, and it was probing the mound of trash in the forward part of the barge. Of the two targets, the two searchlights, the one on the tug would be the easier shot.

Marcus wriggled out, slid down the hill on his belly, grabbed the riot gun lying where he'd left it, then came up fast, pumped, sighted, and fired in one movement.

The light snuffed out behind the shattering of glass; somebody yelled an oath, and guns banged repeatedly — a handgun from the boat, a shotgun from the tug — slugs and shot belting into the trash, bouncing off steel and aluminum, smashing bottles, tearing into ripe and soggy bags.

Marcus got off two quick ones at the fireboat which, with a quick surge of its engines, powered away and scooted around the bow of the slow-moving tug. Not good, Marcus thought; with the pump gun in front of him on the tug, and the fireboat able to zoom around the barge at will, sooner or later they'd apex him and pick him off. He'd have to hurry.

He scuttled through the garbage in the trough, only ankledeep here but treacherous underfoot, worked his way around the back of the scow and up the other side.

The fireboat was coming slowly, switching its searchlight on and off in bright fast stabs, not wanting to offer a target. Climbing the garbage, scrambling over fat plastic sacks and tumbled cardboard boxes, Marcus raked his shin on a rusted bed frame, lost his footing, went in up to his knees when a patch of wetness sagged under him, fought his way up again. He got his hands on the shovel, levered the blade beneath the fourth drum, put his weight behind it, leaning into it.

The fireboat's searchlight burst over him, seemed to knock

him flat. He snatched at the riot gun, and spun and twisted down the other side of the heap, bullets winging in from the fireboat, shot charges from the tug blowing divots out of the hill above him. Rolling into the trough against the gunwale, coming up on one knee, he fired, pumped, fired again, trying to silence the shotgun on the tug, heard the lead smack into the funnel, heard somebody yelling, but not in pain; the cop was calling to his captain on the fireboat.

"It's going!"

He was talking about the drum.

Some trash shifting beneath it had completed what Marcus had started, and when the drum dropped a few inches it kept rolling down the ramp, caromed off the top of the gunwale, flopped into the bay.

The event brought a furious burst of fire from both directions as they tried to riddle him in revenge. He waited it out, then jumped for the only place that was safe anymore: back into his hole in the garbage. Feet first he slithered into the tunnel he'd made, hauling himself in backward, raked stuff over the entrance like an animal disguising its burrow.

It was a stinking, demeaning, ridiculous place to be, but it was the best thing he could do now; they couldn't get to the drum without boarding the barge, and if they did that they'd first have to try to weasel him out, dig for him, and he could just pop up and blast them. In effect, what he was doing, hiding in the middle of that foul junk, was booby-trapping the scow. Hightower would realize that, just as he'd realize that they couldn't stay out here much longer without attracting attention, even in the immensity of the Upper Bay. In fact, when Marcus had got off the shots at the cop on the tug, he'd caught a glimpse of some kind of vessel coming out of Staten Island. Hightower would have to give up on the remaining drum soon, or make his move now and risk getting blown away.

Confined in the rank and itchy darkness Marcus winkled

some shot shells out of his pocket, reloaded the riot gun, and began to breathe through his mouth.

And wait.

In the brief stab of light that had bathed the scow Hightower had seen the fourth drum go, helpless to do anything but curse and grip the rail, and watch it plunge into the waves.

He shouted over at Farquar; on the upper deck of the tug he was the one with the best view.

"You see him?"

"He's squirreled in there somewhere," Farquar yelled back. "Buried in all that shit."

Manchee, at the rail of the fireboat, mindlessly fired his revolver at the garbage hill until his superior shouted at him to stop.

"One left," Hightower said with sweat under his arms. "We got to save it."

Manchee waved his gun at the barge.

"Get Farquar to go in with that pump gun. I'll cover him."

"Big of you," Hightower said. He wasn't looking at his deputy, he was looking at something on the deck in front of him. He went quickly back into the cabin, started talking urgently to the lieutenant.

"That water cannon. How accurate is it?"

"Depends what distance."

"From here to the scow."

"Hell, that close it could take the cherry off a sundae."

Hightower turned toward the slow progress of the barge and said, "We got to get that drum down from there. Think you could cut into the pile of trash, cut away the slope without you put the drum in the bay?"

The lieutenant smiled; the challenge appealed to him.

"Piece of cake," he said, and gave orders to his helmsman.

The boat surged into a wide, swishing turn and came up in back of the barge, the searchlight settling its white fire on it. The lieutenant hurried out onto the forward deck and readied the cannon, which was really just a giant nozzle that directed water pumped up under enormous pressure. He grasped it by its twin handholds, lined it up to hit to the right of the barge, pushed at a lever.

There was a deep rumble, then a hissing roar as a stream of water, as thick as his arm, shot out in a perfectly contained, dead-straight trajectory for a hundred feet before it fell off and hammered flat the waves of the bay.

With great care, and a large degree of confidence, the firefighter began to swing the cannon onto his target.

In the harsh brightness of the spotlight the thundering jet of water looked like a thick white pole coming slowly around to swat the barge. When it touched the right-hand edge of the ramp Marcus had so laboriously built, it carved through it with a neat and irresistible precision, driving a forty-foot segment of trash into the night as if the garbage had been dynamited in a controlled explosion.

Hightower, back out on the deck, shouted, "Watch the drum! Watch the drum!" but the boat commander was expert with the cannon. He bit the stream deeper into the ramp, blowing garbage the length of the barge, smashing it against the tug's superstructure, plastering it with wood and rubble and shredded paper, and the slops of a dozen ruptured plastic bags. The stream of water — rock-hard at sixty miles per hour — took another explosive chunk out of the trash hill, and the ramp began to fold. Gravity sniffed at the drum and, with its support crumbling, it rolled harmlessly down the collapsing ramp, and clunked safely into the trough beneath the high gunwale.

At the boat's rail Manchee thumped the air.

"All-*right!*"

Hightower was at the boat commander's elbow, yelling to him over the noise of the pounding water jet.

"Take the rest of that junk apart! Get him outa there!"

Looking worried and a little scared, the young man cut the pressure and shook his head.

"I wouldn't want to hit a guy with this baby. Be nothing left of him."

"For crissakes, he's a killer. You seen that pump gun of his. He gets outa there, gets on to that tug, he could do the whole crew. You want that on your conscience?"

"He killed somebody?"

"Back at the transfer station. Two cops."

The young man understood it all then; even cop killers walked sometimes, so these guys didn't want to take him alive. Cop killers. They were as bad as the bastards who phoned in alarms, then shot a firefighter.

Calling orders, signaling the helmsman, the lieutenant had the boat brought around parallel with the barge's left-side flank, then lined up the cannon for a final salvo.

For a moment Marcus didn't get it.

The sound came to him cocooned inside the hill muffled, indistinct: a whooshing noise he couldn't identify. When he felt the juddering impact he wondered if the tug had stopped and the barge had drifted into it. But when the water reached him, dripping down as if a violent thunderstorm had come up the bay and burst overhead, he realized what had happened: Hightower had found himself the perfect weapon.

It had to be sheer luck, but there it was.

Marcus was moving, getting out of there and doing okay until what might have been an express train smashed in on his left.

When it hit again he was instantly drenched, and the wash of the searchlight was angling in through a gaping hole in his cover. He heard the drum go then, heard it slide down the soaking debris and clang into the bottom of the barge, and knew it wouldn't be joining the others. He couldn't lift a three-hundred-pound oil drum up and over a gunwale four feet high; not now or the best day he ever saw. But he could still keep them from getting their hands on it. Get the searchlight, drive the man away from the water gun, and dig in.

That was the plan.

And it probably would have worked if the world hadn't exploded just then; if he hadn't suddenly found himself falling through the air. The water jet scythed in like an artillery shell, cut a swathe through a piece of the hill, and a whole section of the jumbled rubble that had formed one wall of his shelter was blown clear out of the barge, whipped away into the night to strafe the bay a hundred feet ahead.

Like the drum which had just rolled down the slope, Marcus bounced and tumbled, and thumped down hard into the bottom of the scow.

He heard a shout: "There he is!" and the crash of the shotgun, felt a slashing burn across his arm as he came up shooting: two quick ones in the tug's direction, a fast swing and a hip shot to keep the handguns quiet, then a snap potshot at the boat's searchlight — a miss. He ran clumsily through the amorphous trash going for the only piece of the mound still standing, fast-firing, laying down his own cover. He threw himself behind the sagging hill, went up it on his belly, feet and knees and elbows digging for purchase.

The engines of the fireboat whined under a brief burst of power, and Marcus knew what Hightower was doing: trying to outflank him, keeping his man on the tug stationary but moving his own firepower around.

On the other side of the garbage hill the searchlight shut off. Another smart move. Not only had Hightower taken away a target but he could hide his position, especially if he had the boat's running lights switched off, too.

Marcus began to load the last of the shells. One good shot was what it came down to; one hit on that searchlight and they'd have to grope for him in the dark. And that would take time. And time would run out on them.

Lights blazed for a half-second, caught him feeding the shotgun, unprepared.

A quick and tremendous jolt rocked the mound beneath him, and then he was traveling on it, riding the collapsing garbage in the middle of a hissing roar, shooting down the hill like a man caught in surf, slamming up against the gunwale in a flood of water.

It had been a random shot from the cannon — he realized that when there was no follow-up searchlight, no gunfire — so they couldn't know they'd knocked him off his perch.

The fireboat's engines sounded once more, a sustained burst this time. Hightower changing direction? Probably going up and around the front of the tug to surprise him on the other side.

Thoroughly soaked again, the skin on his face and hands like starched fabric, Marcus crawled along the gutter beneath the gunwale, feeling his way through a soft/hard melange of flotsam awash in swirling water. It wasn't difficult to know what to do; he only had the one option: keep Hightower from catching him in an exposed position.

As much as he hated the idea, there was still only one spot for him: back on top of what was left of the garbage pile; dig in behind its protective bulk and take out that searchlight the moment they flashed it.

He moved in a stumbling crouch, squelching ankle-deep in a tangled mire of scrap, began the climb up the side of the trash heap, which was now cloven sharply down one edge like the steep incline of a quarry.

There were no stars now, no moon to see or be seen by, no sound except the low pulse of the tug's diesels, and the steady drip and slosh of water in the barge, objects bumping and slapping together like the remains of a wreck washing onto a beach.

Climbing, pulling himself up over split and reeking bags of kitchen waste, Marcus got the sequence together in his head: try to fix the fireboat's shape against the dark, get a rough idea of where the searchlight was on top of the cabin, take a bead on it and, when they threw the switch, straddle the light with three fast shots. That would leave him with four rounds; enough to keep them from boarding the scow.

With quick, positive movements he came up in a crouch, dug hard for the top of the slope, reached it, flopped onto his belly, the riot gun rammed into his shoulder, pointing.

There was nothing on the other side of the barge.

Nothing showed but the salty blackness backed by the faint lights of Jersey City miles down the bay.

The fireboat had gone.

Marcus suffered a moment of dumb noncomprehension, then in a painful flash of understanding knew where the boat was, and what Hightower had done: he hadn't gone around the tug at all, he'd merely moved ahead of the tug, stayed on the same side, and let the tug overtake it. The boat had to be in the same position it had been in before.

Behind him.

Marcus came up, whirling around.

With its engine shut down, in total silence, total blackout, so close he could almost touch it, the thing bulked against the darkness, a piece of the night.

A ray of dazzling light flattened against him, and loud voices collided.

"There! There!"

"*Get* 'im!"

Hightower had surprise on his side, and it shaved a moment from Marcus's reaction. It gave Manchee time to swing up his gun, snap it into line, but the boat commander was quicker.

Marcus blasted away at the searchlight, sharding the lens, blowing up the bulb, the kick still in his arms when the jet of water sledgehammered into his ribs and belted him straight back through the air, pinning him to its colossal power, carrying him into the night a good thirty feet past the side of the barge before he fell away and skip-smacked into the bay.

Had it been dry ground instead of water, the impact of the landing would have killed him instead of just knocking him senseless. And the water saved him a second time when its cool touch revived him before he'd got a lungful. Even so Marcus thought he was going to die from the pain in his smashed ribs when he coughed up what he'd swallowed. With his arms moving feebly, his feet hardly pushing at the water, he felt like a broken bath toy somebody had tossed away. He floated on the edge of consciousness, the bay chop gently slapping against his neck, making him pay attention, and keeping him from passing out.

He wondered dimly if Hightower would come after him, try to find him without the searchlight, or would he figure that anybody belted into the middle of a midnight bay by a high-pressure water cannon was either already dead or about to be?

Well, he was half right about him being already dead, and probably 100 percent right if he figured he was going to be.

Marcus forgot about the police captain and his men, and let his mind drift like his wounded body, let it float along without direction as the rest of him was doing.

He spent fifteen minutes like that — or maybe five or fifty minutes, he couldn't be sure — when he became aware of lights some way off. In a gentle, mindless daze he thought they might be the same ones he'd seen earlier coming out from Staten Island. Either that or his vision had doubled, and it was the fireboat arriving to finish the job. Wave to them, Marcus; if it was Hightower you wouldn't want him to think you'd snubbed him, fellow police officers and all that.

He got an arm into the air — the pain didn't count any-more — and waved it back and forth, back and forth.

"Hey, Hightower . . ." His voice was just a croak, squeezed thin by his busted ribs. "Hightower. Fuck you, man."

A hundred feet away, for only the second time in sixteen years this far from Manhattan, the captain of the *Robert B. Jones* ordered the engines of his ferry into reverse.

Marcus perceived it as a yellow blur.

All those lights . . . the fireboat with its searchlight didn't have as many as that. What searchlight? He'd shot it out. Shot something out.

A big white object splashed down near him, floated to-ward him, bobbed in the water like a stick waiting for a dog to fetch it. So he'd fetch it. Bowwow. Good dog. Down, boy.

Not a stick, but a giant peppermint Lifesaver; somebody had thrown him some candy.

Hey, it was moving; he was being pulled through the water, dragged through the face-smacking waves toward that yellow blur. Being hauled up — Jesus God that hurt! — onto a punched metal deck. Laid out like a prize catch.

Marcus saw people above him, gathered around, eyes full of curiosity, mouths full of questions.

"You okay, buddy? You all right?"

"What?" Marcus looked groggily around him. "What is this . . . a ship?"

"The ferry. Staten Island Ferry."

"What were you doing in the water?" somebody asked.

Marcus stopped struggling against his flagging brain, let meaning float away, and sensation drain from his nerve ends as he answered the question.

"Trying to save the fare," he said, on his way to oblivion.

17

WHEN THE DRIVER of the battered U-Haul van had left the pier carrying the crates of money, he'd driven into Manhattan, taken the Holland Tunnel under the Hudson, skirted acres of railroad yards near the industrial morass of Jersey City, and headed back toward the river again through the drab streets of Hoboken.

Two stevedores standing outside a bar gave him directions to the freight-forwarding depot he was looking for. It was in a dock area not unlike the one he'd just come from in Brooklyn, except this one had a gate man and a strong security fence, and cranes servicing freighters alongside finger piers.

The warehouse was a corrugated iron affair with light pooling out of triple garage doors, a vast hangar of a place choked with crated cargo arranged in ordered blocks like a small town. A young warehouseman met the driver, busy and full of self-importance, working at a wad of gum in his mouth as if it were an enemy in the last stages of defeat.

"Cargo for the *Maloya Dan,*" the driver told him getting out.

"Not sailing," the man answered.

"Hey, c'mon."

"Waiting for an engine part. We got another ship taking its cargo, though. The *Eastern Pearl*. Going to the same place, so you got the same deal. Okay?"

"When's it get there?"

"The ninth. Gets to Dover on the ninth."

The warehouseman produced a bill of lading and a customs form. The driver described the contents of the boxes as novelty playing cards. Then a man with a forklift maneuvered the two crates out of the van and onto his machine, taped them together with steel ribbon, and drove them through the cargo rows to where a ship waited at the dock, a real workhorse whose white superstructure was stained with age. The forklift man stenciled a code onto the two boxes and fitted them snugly into a shiny new aluminum container that was just about full.

The van driver waited long enough to see the container winched up to the deck of the freighter, then drove back to Manhattan, where he sent a cable to Charles Bendroit in London. The cable read: "Cargo dispatched today on MV *Eastern Pearl* arriving Dover 9th Stop. *Maloya Dan* unavailable." It was signed with the initial M.

Bendroit received the cable at his office, about six hours after Marcus had been fished out of New York Bay. Bendroit had been about to go to lunch but immediately canceled his reservation at Rule's and surprised his luncheon guest, a marine insurance broker who was often good for inside information, by taking him to Le Poulbot for *tourte de saumon* and a bottle of Clos de Chene Marchand.

"Splendid lunch, Charles," the broker said. "Absolutely super." He sipped his port, a Dow's '46, and reckoned that the wine bill alone would be close to two hundred pounds. "You've clearly had some kind of success."

"As a matter of fact," Bendroit said offhandedly, "I've pulled off rather a coup."

It was the most he allowed himself in the way of a boast,

and the most he could ever tell anybody about it, but he could revel in it in his own mind. In twelve days' time he'd be driving down the coast to pick up all those millions of dollars. Fantastic! The thought thrilled him, kept him bubbling over all through the remainder of the lunch, put a spring in his step as he walked back to his office. Once inside the door he reread the cable, pleasuring in it again.

The *Eastern Pearl.*

He reached for that day's copy of the Shipping Index to find out who the owners were. It was merely a delicious little point of interest, although there was a more practical reason for knowing, too: if the owners had a reputation for running tight ships, and keeping their engines in good condition, it would mean the arrival date would be a firm one.

The *Eastern Pearl,* according to the entry, was owned by the D.A.C. Corporation, whoever they were, sailed under a Panamanian flag, was classified by the American Bureau of Shipping, had been built by Richardson, Westgarth in '62, and had a gross weight of 6,417 tons. Small, and old enough to have some character, Bendroit noted; a ship with personality, unlike your giant modern containerships that looked like floating office blocks.

With his five-star lunch digesting nicely he sat back in his chair, softly burped a fond memory of the excellent claret, and checked the front of the magazine under the Owners/Managers listing.

The D.A.C. Corporation was the Dobey, Atcheson Corporation of Panama, a firm he'd never heard of.

Curious about them, he called a man known to him as Eastie. Bendroit had used his services for years, and although he was uncomfortable with the relationship — Eastie was from the other end of the social spectrum — he had to admit that the man's knowledge of shipping affairs, both legal and clandestine, was unparalleled.

[285]

Eastie got back to him within half an hour.

" 'Ullo, squire," he said in his cheerful Cockney. "They treating you awright?"

"Fine, thank you. What do you have?" Bendroit asked, balancing on the edge of rudeness.

"Right ven," Eastie said. "To the vessel in questchun, the *Eastern Pearl*. Owned by the Dobey, Atcheson Corporation of Panama. Now" — Eastie paused to release a loud catarrhal sniff — "Dobey, Atcheson is two lawyers named Sanchez and Escabara in Panama City. There are only two nominee shareholders in the corporation and they're them, okay?"

"Continue."

"Dobey, Atcheson is just one of the Panamanian companies what's managed by the Narvis Company of Zug, Switzerland. And the Narvis Company is owned by, you'll never guess . . ."

"Pardon?"

"Yer ol' mate, Kazadoupolos."

"Kazadoupolos? What an extraordinary coincidence."

"Not really. 'E owns a piece of a lot of ships, y'know."

This was true, of course, but surprise was still Bendroit's first reaction. However, the knowledge brought with it a measure of satisfaction, too; his ex-partner, a cheat and a scoundrel, would have no idea that a ship of his was carrying two crates, listed on the manifest as containing novelty playing cards, that were actually worth twenty-five million dollars each, and was being paid just regular cargo rates for the privilege.

On the other end of the line Eastie was starting up a phlegmy chuckle.

"Anyway, squire, 'ow did you know about the *Eastern Pearl?*"

"What do you mean?"

"I mean, it's making an unskedjooled stop, i'n' it? Kazadoup's up to his old tricks again."

[286]

The walls of Bendroit's office seemed to advance on him, the oxygen drawn out of the air and ducted away.

"No . . . not possible." The words were just breath.

"You say sumpthing?"

"It must reach port. That ship must reach port."

"I can't 'ear. What say?"

Bendroit found his voice; shock had twisted it into a lank and shapeless knot.

"I have cargo on board that ship. Very precious cargo."

"Oh, dear. Vat's a right cock-up, vat is."

"He must be stopped," Bendroit gabbled. "*Now!*" He slammed down the phone, fumbled for his address book, tearing pages in his rush, dialed with a shaking finger. Thirteen digits to get out of the country and into Greece, to Piraeus, and a particular telephone in that ancient seaport city.

With his face the color of paper Bendroit stared at the phone on his desk, a mean, white plastic box full of wires and circuits and vibrating pieces of metal that was giving him nothing but spiteful little clicks and pauses. Then, at long last, a ringing noise, and the sound cut off by a voice answering with some unintelligible phrase.

"Mr. Kazadoupolos, please. I'm calling from London. It's extremely urgent," Bendroit said in something close to his normal manner. He'd got a firm grip on himself now. It was just another phone call to correct some errant shipping arrangements; he'd made hundreds of them in the past, dozens of them to Greece.

The connection was not a good one, and there followed twenty seconds of what sounded like bacon frying before Kazadoupolos came on.

"Yes? Who is this?"

"Perhaps you can tell from my voice."

"Indeed I can. Yours is the only voice that truly grates on my ears."

Bendroit, well aware that their dislike was mutual, let that go by.

"I am anxiously awaiting the arrival of a ship called the *Eastern Pearl*, which I believe you own. Would you be good enough to give me its latest position, please."

"The *Eastern Pearl*," Kazadoupolos said, as if trying to place the vessel. "You have cargo on board, I take it?"

Bendroit forced himself to speak slowly, to wait out these preliminaries.

"Garments. My client has a fashion opening or some such thing, and needs the shipment as soon as possible."

"I see. That is too bad. I understand there have been some mechanical problems with this ship. I am told they are likely to result in a very serious delay."

It didn't matter anymore, speaking in code, keeping his voice ordered and polite; it didn't matter if it was an open line. Bendroit exploded and yelled into the phone.

"That ship must get here, do you understand? It *must!* I don't care what you have to do. I want that ship in Dover!"

"I am sorry. But to change arrangements now would mean a large loss to me."

The math did itself quickly in Bendroit's head: the ship would be an old rust bucket worth perhaps $750,000. The Greek would have bribed a surveyor, got an inflated valuation, and insured the hull for twice that figure. Say $10,000 for the crew; that left him with a profit of around three-quarters of a million.

"I will underwrite your loss to the tune of half a million dollars."

"I could not possibly disturb my arrangements for less than two million."

"Two *million!* That's absurd! Ridiculous!"

"I doubt you'll have to pay it. It's probably too late, anyway."

That roused Bendroit to a chilling anger. The Greek was lying in his teeth, pretending it was too late so as to make a last-minute rescue seem all the more worth it. So transparent. So coarsely blatant.

"One million dollars," Bendroit said. "My last offer."

"Every second we spend arguing," Kazadoupolos said coldly, "makes the possibility of any action more remote. Two million and I will do my best, but I promise nothing."

"Very well. Two million." Bendroit hung up before he could deliver the stinging diatribe that was rising into his mouth. An easy touch, that's how the Greek regarded him; a fool soon parted from his money. Kazadoupolos was a bloodsucking leech; he'd found that out in the first few weeks of their short-lived and ill-starred partnership. The thieving beggar! Trying to make out that it could be too late . . . such a foreign, Greek thing to do. A Levantine churl, a piece of Piraeus garbage.

Bendroit gradually calmed down. The main thing was that a dreadful calamity had been averted; but it had been touch and go. Another few hours perhaps . . . he put the thought from his mind; it didn't do to dwell on such things. Fifty million dollars, a whole year's work, his entire racing stable and his future way of life in jeopardy . . .

He thought about something else instead; that phone call had pumped a lot of adrenaline into his system, a substance that had nowhere to go, no energy outlet. Unused, its sour residues could sink into his intestinal tract, build up trouble in later years.

He marched out of his office, got a taxi home, changed, went straight onto his squash court, and gave himself a vigorous and sweaty workout.

Wrong.

Bendroit had been wrong.

Once again, as with Morici and the cigarettes, his inability to read the signals, and know what was in a bargainer's mind, had been his downfall. Kazadoupolos wasn't lying; he really didn't know whether or not it was too late to

[289]

change the arrangements. But he did know the difference between two million dollars and the three-quarters of a million he could have realized on the insurance claim, so a radio message was immediately flashed from Piraeus to the *Eastern Pearl*.

It wasn't received.

And for the simplest of reasons: the radioman was not in the radio shack. He was sitting in a lifeboat with the other members of the crew, watching the effect on the *Eastern Pearl* as the Atlantic Ocean rushed through the open valves in the sea chest, flooding the double-bottom tanks, then rose through the open manhole covers into the cargo hold.

The elderly freighter died quietly and with great dignity, dipping its bow under the calm water as if to protect it from the growing heat of the early morning sun.

It tilted forward through a waterline axis, raised its propeller for a rare look at the world, then slid under carefully as if it regretted disturbing the flat perfection of the surface.

Watching it go, fascinated by its slow, elegant departure, the radioman received from the ship the last signal that would ever come from it: a fast dash, then three dots — the letter B, ironically enough — as the rising sun flared on a shiny new aluminum container sitting on the forward deck.

Since he'd arrived back in London, Jay Jay had made it a point to call Lloyd's every day and check on the status of the *Maloya Dan* to make sure there'd been no change in its departure date. This was how he'd found out that the *Eastern Pearl* was sailing in its place.

It was quite a surprise, on his third day in the city, to hear that the *Eastern Pearl* had indeed embarked on time, but had unfortunately foundered just seven hours later in a deep part of the Shelf. An engine-room explosion, apparently.

Suspecting Bendroit of a double cross, Jay Jay next tried

to ascertain whether or not the money had really been put on the ship. The Sap Sei K, which knew all about the principals in the deal, contacted Morici and got from him the name of the man who'd delivered the dollars to the freighter. This man was then exquisitely questioned by two Sap Sei K fighters in New York. The man swore he'd taken the money to the *Eastern Pearl* and seen it loaded.

So there it was.

A piece of bad luck.

The twenty-seventh had been an inauspicious date on which to begin a voyage: two and seven totaled nine, which was a number of evil portent belonging to the dog in the Ten Celestial Stems, and the Twelve Terrestrial Branches, a beast of uneven temperament and scavenger qualities.

Jay Jay decided to return to Hong Kong without delay and make his report. He booked a seat on the evening flight, bought a present for his girlfriend, and packed his bag, which left him only one thing to do: take the Underground to South Kensington, and have a word with Charles Bendroit.

Actually, there was one other thing he had to do.

On the way to the tube station, he stopped off and picked up his dry cleaning.

EPILOGUE

TOTALLY NAKED, and wearing masks over their faces, the women looked like players in an old-fashioned stag movie.

There were five of them sitting at a round table, the mirror top of which had been cut exactly to the table's generous dimensions. Only one other person was present, their boss, a bulky man in his fifties who was fully dressed.

The women chatted as they worked, and tapped their feet and swung their heads along to the pop rhythms that Z-93 Atlanta delivered via the radio on the floor. They wore the masks over their mouths and noses so that the heroin they were working on wouldn't get them high. And they were without clothes so there'd be no pockets to hide any of the stuff in for resale later. At the end of the day the women would line up and squat in front of the boss so he could make sure they hadn't put any in their natural pockets.

The heroin was part of the 132 kilos which had been in the drum Hightower had recovered from the barge. Marco Morici, when he'd at last got over the trauma of losing the other four drums, had taken it to a warehouse in New York, where he'd doubled the quantity by adding the same amount of manite, a baby laxative which, being water-soluble milk sugar, made an ideal cutting agent. This new amount had been broken up into twenty-five-kilo lots and sold to the families that ran the business in nine major eastern cities.

The family that bought twenty-five kilos in Atlanta did what all the other families did: used lactose to double the quantity again. The Atlanta mill owner for whom the masked ladies worked had bought an eighth, and it was this amount, four ounces of 22.5 percent pure, which the women were giving a four-cut with dextrose and a little quinine, mixing the ingredients on the mirror top with playing cards, and scooping the blend into glassine bags.

When the work was finished the boss had himself eight bundles, or forty bags, of 5.6 percent heroin. This he sold to the owner of another mill, who used inositol and lidocaine to cut it a shade further to 3.75 percent, a good, hot street load. He put his bundles in the trunk of his car, rode around Atlanta, and sold all of them within two days.

The pushers who bought from him were happy with their purchase. It was fine stuff they were peddling: top quality from the Triangle, so the word was, nicely handled along the line, and stepped on gently by caring people — in short, a fun batch; finger-lickin' good.

One of the pushers who bought a bundle ran a meals-on-wheels snack wagon, fried fruit pies and Pepsi, with a gram of White for dessert if you had the extra fifteen bucks. After making a call at a vacant lot on Simpson Street, and another outside a launderette on Chappell, the snack wagon turned east in time to make a green light, and continued on its regular route. One of the cars it passed, part of the southbound traffic waiting for the light to change, was a dark blue Celebrity belonging to Danny Mead.

Marcus was sitting beside the big man.

Neither of them had noticed the snack wagon, or knew anything about the unadvertised extras it sold. But even had Marcus known what the wagon carried, he wouldn't have done much about it; he was no longer interested in drugs, or the people who bought and sold them.

He shifted in his seat and watched the city slide by as Danny Mead took the car away. The white bandage that covered part of Marcus's face gave him a rakish look — Mead had told him he looked like a well-dressed pirate. Marcus had spent two days in Intensive Care in a New York hospital till he was out of danger, and was then removed to a burn ward, where he turned out to be what medics call a quick patient, the kind who are flat on their backs with tubes leading out of them one day, and sitting up and asking questions the next. The worst of his burns had been on his scalp: his shoulders, arms, and face got off a lot more lightly. His upper half had been swathed in gauze wrapped around silver sulfadiazine, the bandages stopping just below his hairline, with several more patches on his nose and cheeks. None of the burns had been deep enough to release anything toxic into his bloodstream, so there'd been no complications. As for his busted ribs, they'd healed slowly and painfully.

His official story for the hospital records, and the police injury report, was that he'd been getting some late-night air on one of the West Street docks when he'd interrupted three guys loading cardboard boxes into a powerboat. They'd grabbed him, beaten him up, then, for good measure, had some fun with a can of gasoline and a box of matches before dumping him in the bay. Weirder things had happened in the city, so the police had bought it.

He'd told the same story to his division commander, and his fellow officers at Decatur Street. Nobody had believed it, but they'd accepted it in silence, the same way his commander had accepted Marcus's resignation. He'd known it would be futile to try to talk Billy Marcus out of anything, but privately he'd cursed the loss of a good cop.

Danny Mead, the best of Marcus's pals, had been determined not to say anything either, but he was finding it hard not to bring up the subject now that they were on their way to the airport.

He hung a left, went down the hill, joined the flow of automobiles on Seventy-five, the highway that cuts through the eastern edge of the new downtown section like a metallic river.

"I'm still having a hard time with it," he said. "Moving to New York City." He shook his head, then remained silent right up until he swung off the highway and took the long, looping approach to the enormous airport with its parallel runways. He said, looking straight ahead, as if he were concentrating on his driving, "It was because of George Chaska, wasn't it? All this time up there. Limping back here wrapped up like Christmas. You went after somebody, didn't you?"

Marcus looked across at the pathologist. He liked Danny; he'd been a good friend. Maybe he owed him something better than the standard story he'd been dishing out, especially seeing that the guy had helped him with Boyd Dubin's fingerprints.

"A guy named Hinkler killed George. Hinkler and a buddy of his were down here on a drug deal, and George and I fell over it. They worked for a guy named Bendroit."

"Uh huh," Mead said, as if he'd been expecting to hear something like that. "So you tracked them down and then punched their ticket."

"Yeah. Although somebody beat me to Bendroit. Somebody strangled him."

Claire had told Marcus about it. She'd been buying the airmail edition of Lloyd's List for the shipping movements. The murder of a member of the shipping community had made page one.

"That's the way it goes in the drug biz," Mead offered. "You get rich or dead."

"As it happened," Marcus said, "Bendroit wouldn't have got rich anyway. He ran into a little bad luck."

Danny Mead glanced sideways at Marcus's face.

"You ran into a little bad luck yourself."

"Sure, but mine will get better," Marcus answered as Mead glided the car to the curb.

A sidewalk porter checked Marcus's suitcases through, then Marcus held out his hand to Mead.

"Danny, it's been a pleasure."

The big man grumpily shook hands, then called out as Marcus followed his baggage toward the doors.

"Let me know when you want some grits airmailed, goddamit."

The plane caught a favorable tail wind and zipped the miles to New York, landing at La Guardia way ahead of schedule.

Marcus waited in the pickup area for twenty minutes before a car pulled up and Claire got out.

"Sorry I'm late," she said quickly, a nervous smile skimming across her lovely face. "The traffic was fierce."

"No problem," Marcus said, and picked up his suitcases.

Claire hardly heard his answer; she was trying to get her mind around the fact that he was here, standing in front of her with his baggage. He was here, he was all right . . . Billy!

Claire shifted on her feet and coughed, needing to say something ordinary and everyday.

"How was the flight?"

·Marcus dropped the suitcases, stepped forward, and reached for her.

"Too damn slow," he said.